The
Unwilding

The Unwilding

Marina Kemp

4th ESTATE · *London*

4th Estate
An imprint of HarperCollins*Publishers*
1 London Bridge Street
London SE1 9GF

www.4thestate.co.uk

HarperCollins*Publishers*
Macken House, 39/40 Mayor Street Upper,
Dublin 1, D01 C9W8, Ireland

First published in Great Britain in 2024 by 4th Estate

1

Copyright © Marina Kemp 2024

A catalogue record for this book is
available from the British Library

ISBN 978-0-00-863785-9 (Hardback)
ISBN 978-0-00-863786-6 (Trade paperback)

Typeset in Goudy Oldstyle Std
Printed and bound in the UK using 100%
renewable electricity at CPI Group (UK) Ltd

For James

SICILY

'How easy life is, I thought, for women who are not afraid of a man.'

The Dry Heart, Natalia Ginzburg

N

My mother spent those long summers cooking.

The kitchen was a large room on the north side of the house, accessed from the garden by descending four or five steep steps. It was large and shadowed, even dark, and though it was always clean it was so cluttered, and all its kit so battered and outmoded, that it could never look as if it was. We were generally hot, we spent most of the day hot, and yet whenever you stepped down into the kitchen, shady as it was and with its tomb-cold stone floor, it was as if a cool breath rushed in around your face. Often I lay on that floor, its pumiced flagstones wonderfully smooth against my cheek, and watched as my mother rolled dumplings in her square hands, slapped pastry with flour, shelled peas with her little pocket knife and calloused thumbs.

The only times I saw her at rest were for snippets of ten, fifteen minutes, when she would remove her apron and hang it on a hook and take a book of crosswords and word searches into the dark games room. Out of the way of the rest of the house, the games room sat largely neglected. It smelled like a chalet or sauna, its wood panelling a throwback to the 1950s; and with its billiards table and jukebox and bar – complete with goatskin bar stools and shelves lined with sticky, defunct spirits and liqueurs – it had a sleazy air, louchely aspirational, that appealed hugely to us as children and young adults.

All of that was entirely at odds with my mother. When she sat on the low sofa there with her word puzzles and a biro, her expression immobile with its habitual half-smile, her feet up on a stool to ease the pressure that built up from whole days spent standing, she looked out of place to me. Immensely small, then, and sweet, so that I felt a sharp whistle of something painful that I could hardly bear.

We took the house in Sicily every year, from as early as I can remember up until my eleventh summer. We rented it, though my father spoke occasionally – and very vaguely – of buying it. They could have Magda work her magic on it, he'd say; it wouldn't take too much coaxing to make something quite striking out of the place. I thought of Magda's London home, which we'd visited many times – a thing of beauty overlooking the Thames, white columns and wide empty walls in extraordinary colours: powder blue, magenta, saffron. I wondered how that bold, cosmopolitan palette would work in this place, against its dry and dusty summers.

My father took a large, central top-floor room for his work. It had a high window overlooking the courtyard at the front of the house, and sometimes we saw the full length of him standing at that window, staring out. Then we became quieter, knowing only that a sacred and secret process was at work in his mind and that it was fragile, could be snapped like the gossamer strings of a web.

We had a constant flux of guests, spilling in and out of the bedrooms. My favourite was Poppy, a seventeen-year-old with shy, sheep-like eyes and dark cropped hair, who came to stay on her own when I was five or six. Without being asked, she undertook to become a nanny for the youngest of us. She sang lovely songs I'd never heard and could never recreate; she made costumes for us, bunny ears and tails from cotton wool and space helmets out of cardboard. She helped my mother in the kitchen, she entertained us tirelessly. We learned that she didn't have her own parents, which struck me as a wonderfully mysterious affliction.

There were other guests I loved, but not as many as those we took against. We disliked the academics, who claimed they were there to work and complained about our noise, only to spend idle afternoons at the large shady table with jugs of wine, long after lunch had finished. We dismissed many of the guests' children. We disliked nearly all the divorced and single women who stayed. But of them all, there was none we abhorred with more passion or devotion than Tuva Brøvig.

Tuva came for two weeks every year and when she was there she acted as if the house was hers. She told us to go to bed after supper, she arranged day trips and bustled us out of the house to give my father some quiet. She organised lunch parties, inviting anyone vaguely illustrious she'd heard was on the island, whether locals or other tourists. More than all the women who clucked around my father, I think she truly believed that her presence was both unique and essential; that hers alone was the indispensable work of ministering to his spiritual and intellectual and emotional needs. Every year she'd say 'I can always stay on longer' at least twice, sing-song, as if it were she who set the limits of her stay.

The one realm she didn't intrude upon was the kitchen, though even so she managed to absorb some credit for the endless platters and bowls that emerged twice daily onto the long, linen-covered table. 'They're so fresh, it's a crime to add much more than breadcrumbs,' she'd say if the anchovies were complimented, so that it was hard even for me to believe she hadn't chosen the recipe. She made a great deal of her one real contribution to the meals, which was choosing the wine. She implied effortlessly that it was the wine pairing that brought out the excellence of the food, not the cooking of it. 'What you're about to have is a funny local white,' she'd say; 'sweeter than you think you'd want at lunch, but you'll find it's the perfect counterpart to the intense saltiness of the cheese.'

She spoke often of how many countries she'd travelled to; she reminded us that she'd been a competitive speed-skater as a young woman, representing Sweden. She frequently let slip that she was the only female advanced sommelier in the UK, affecting that it was a fact to be regretted and not something of which she was extremely proud.

We wondered how my father, who claimed to dislike braggarts, could stand her. We whispered and schemed constantly about how to get her to leave, or put her off coming the following year. The youngest of us – Etta and I – made ourselves believe one summer that she was truly a witch; we snuck into her bedroom and searched her drawers for evidence of wicked charms: feathers, dolls, needles, dead animals. We watched her looking out over the courtyard from her bedroom window and tried to make out spells that she might be whispering through clenched lips.

Some years her husband came with her; some years he didn't. We put this down to how much he could tolerate her that particular summer. Annoyingly, we adored him; annoying because, if he was worthy of being adored and seemed to tolerate her well enough, it added a counterargument to her blatant fundamental evil. We had the impression, regressive as children can be, that she had chosen him for his money – he was a successful financier – and because, the good-looking child of quite a famous Indian film star, he lent her an exotic glamour. Without those things, and in spite of her speedskating past, we considered her to be utterly devoid of anything anyone could respect. She didn't even have children, which we deemed the very least a woman could do.

Krish didn't seem to resent my father for the singleminded fervour with which Tuva devoted herself to him and his needs. In fact they got on well, cutting an odd figure when they chatted together at the end of the table: one groomed and spry, the very picture of urbane modernity, the other a craggy monolith of thought and study and words. Krish didn't seem in thrall to my father. He even teased him a little, which was something we didn't often see. When he did, Tuva smiled nervously, eyes flicking from one to the other. We thought that she was jealous when my father's response was to laugh.

In this way, I suppose the adult guests loomed large for us. Certainly we were fascinated by many of them, perhaps more than as children we should have been. And yet my over-whelming memory of those burning summers is that of a teenage-run domain. It was ruled over by Malachy and Tree, my eldest siblings, whose influence was absolute – and as a domain it was, until they turned fifteen or sixteen and crossed over into a different world from Etta and me, entirely cohe-sive. It might have seemed feral and lawless from the outside – we heard many adults, not just Tuva, comment on our lack of discipline, on how we were allowed to run wild – but to us there were clear governing principles.

There were the people to whom we were loyal; there were those to whom as a unit we were opposed. There were things we must respect – our father's work, the need to help our mother on the rare occasions she asked, and little else – and values we must uphold, in particular a collective front when one of us came into blame. We could scrap and fight among ourselves as viciously as needed, but if one of us encountered opposition from an outsider, that outsider was automatically the enemy of us all.

Other children had a tricky time of it. They must have sensed the invisible codices governing our behaviour. We knew they longed to join in, to be initiated into our games and secrets and to gain Tree and Malachy's approval, but full access into our dominion was hard won. A few gained it. Children we chose not to like were excluded entirely.

By the last summer, Tree and Malachy were nineteen and eighteen. I was ten, and the youngest, and though I never doubted my siblings' love for me I was now sentenced to feel what those other children must have felt all those years. I stumbled, enmeshed in the unseen threads they'd woven. I couldn't see where to step, aware only that there were secret pacts and allegiances, mysterious games with rules I couldn't read.

Z

Zoe had hoped the change of location might help. A new bedroom and new setting, a new routine and different air and food and smells. But that first night she knew, as soon as she put down her book and switched off the little lamp by her bed, that she wasn't going to sleep.

The insomnia had started six weeks ago, just after her last visit to her parents' house. She'd never suffered from more than the odd bad night before, but now it was relentless: night after night, she found herself unable to imagine how she had ever fallen asleep. Sometimes she found herself screaming into her pillow.

It would never have been any better here, she realised now – in this bizarre situation, in this strange house full of strangers in a country she'd never visited before. It couldn't possibly be better after a day like today. The nerves that had accompanied her throughout her journey, the conversations she'd practised in her head, the new faces she'd watched and taken in over dinner. But she must stop thinking about that.

She didn't need to think about anything. She needed to do nothing other than breathe – not from her chest, which she'd been told could signal to the brain that she was stressed, but from her abdomen. Resting one hand on her stomach, she took a deep breath in and a longer one out.

And then she sat up, possessed already by the rage that never failed to surface each night, through these endless hours. There was surely nothing more dementing than concentrating on breath after breath after breath. Nor could she simply observe her thoughts, as she'd been told to do; they were far too demanding, a voice that insisted on being listened to. Bossing and over-confident, like the blonde woman she'd sat opposite at dinner, whose name she hadn't caught. Zoe's flight had been delayed and, arriving at the house late from Catania Airport, just as everyone was sitting down to their meal, she hadn't caught many names at all. She'd spent most of the meal trying to work out what relation each person had to the others. Only some of them were staying at the house, she gathered gradually; others were only guests for the evening, and would loop their way after dinner through the dark countryside she'd passed on her way here, back home to lush villas by the sea.

There were several children, who couldn't all have been Don's, ranging from about eight to twenty. There were many more women than men, their overall effect one of intimidating glamour: the over-confident blonde, who she thought must be Scandinavian; an older woman with black and silver hair scraped back and an accented, cigarette-gravelled voice, perhaps Hungarian or Czech; a tiny, birdlike Italian widow with a white chignon and swollen collarbones; three women she thought to be in their thirties or early forties, two of whom were uncomfortably attractive.

Zoe wondered what figure she cut among these people, crumpled and greasy from a day's travel. She hadn't dressed right. She had recently bought a small leather knapsack for hand luggage, with this trip specifically in mind; she'd thought when she bought it that it was the right thing for a setting like this, bookishly stylish. Now, greeting Don in front of this lantern-lit table full of strangers, it just made her feel like a little girl on a school trip.

She had first met Don in the London Library, perhaps one of the most surreally happy afternoons of her life. It had been novel enough to go into the London Library in the first place; she'd been awarded an honorary six-month membership along with ten other young writers of promise that year, so that walking through its doors she felt like she was there by special invitation. Then she had spotted Don Travers sitting at one of the desks, and seeing a mind like his at work had felt no less exhilarating than spotting a great whale emerge from placid water.

After an hour or so, noticing her watching him, he had beckoned her over to his desk and told her that a copy of her novel was sitting on his bedside table. He hoped she'd forgive him for not having started it yet; he meant to, as soon as he finished a great new Nietzsche biography he was working his way through. He recognised her from her author interview in the *Sunday Times*, it emerged, and it was an odd and charming thought, that someone like him would bother to read anything so rooted in the culture of the moment. Throughout their conversation, he never dropped his voice to a whisper; when other readers looked over, ready to shush, Zoe saw that they were silenced by their own sighting of the Leviathan.

Eventually, he took her address and said he'd write to her, before dismissing her elegantly and getting back to his work. She received a postcard three days later inviting her to lunch at the Garrick, where she met him and four others roughly her age: another novelist, a screenwriter, two doctoral students from UCL. She only got to speak to him directly for ten minutes or so, at the very end of the meal, when he told her he'd started her book and was enjoying it immensely.

The next lunch was another gathering of young talent, where she could hardly regret her lack of contact with Don because of the charmed sensation, enhanced by several glasses of silky and delicious wine, of having been admitted into a select committee of promising people. At the end, he rested one of his great hands on hers and told her she must come to Sicily. He said nothing else, as if Sicily were an event she should already know about, but two days later the invitation was confirmed by means of another postcard. He'd be delighted, he wrote, if she would join him for a week in August at Villa Frantoio, Scordia, Catania.

She'd relied on Elias, the screenwriter she'd met at the first lunch and a few times since, to fill her in a little more on what 'Sicily' denoted. He'd never been, but he knew others who had. She should prepare to be dwarfed by all the great and the good, he'd said. Artists would paint her in the nude; a publishing magnate would fall in love with her; she'd leave with her novel optioned for film and a lifetime of book deals.

He told her a little about Don's wife, too. Her name was Lydia and she was younger than Don, he said; he was pretty sure she was American; she was a housewife, not a writer or intellectual; she'd been ill that year and undergone cancer treatment, though Elias thought she was all right now. She was unremarkable, she wasn't at all what you'd expect. Presumably Don enjoyed other women on the side. When Zoe asked, 'Why presumably?' he smiled, tracing a finger down her shoulder, and said, 'She's no Marilyn.'

Sitting down to her first meal at Villa Frantoio, Zoe found Lydia even more surprising than Elias had conveyed. Sturdy, unmade-up, with her mouth closed in a pleasant smile that warded off conversation, she sat quietly at one end of the table with the youngest children. Her head was wrapped in a plain cloth. Zoe resolved to watch her during the meal – to glean more about her than Elias's stark picture – but it was as if she defied noticing. At some point, when everyone had moved from pudding on to coffee, Zoe realised that all the plates had been cleared and neither Lydia nor the younger children were there anymore. Their chairs were tucked tidily in.

Don had introduced Zoe to the table as a writer, which embarrassed her even as it was a delight to hear. She recognised at least one other writer there, Toby Dornan, and wondered what a man only a few years her senior but already with two novels, a handful of *New Yorker* essays and a short story collection to his name, must think to be classed in the same category as her. After her introduction, she was largely though not impolitely ignored. The only attention she noticed receiving was from the two eldest children, a boy and girl who were more properly young adults, and might have been twins. Beauties, both: thick dark hair and eyelashes, wide, freckled cheekbones. They watched her intently, not quite aggressively.

There were still sounds throughout the house now: the closing of a door, the echoing shake of footsteps above her, footsteps below, a muffled laugh somewhere. At one point, she thought she heard voices in the garden; she got out of bed and opened the doors to the little balcony outside her room, leaning cautiously out so that she wouldn't be thought to be spying. But she couldn't see anyone, and the voices had gone. She leaned against the railing, the air around her very warm, thick with insects. A thin crescent moon, the outline of trees shifting slightly against a dark sky. The faintest hint, she thought, of the distant sea – something in the swollen air, like the far-off rush of traffic. She imagined rocky black coast-line at night, the miles and miles of crashing, uninhabited dark. She stood there until a mosquito screeched in her ear, and then she closed the doors and switched off the lamp and lay listening, too hot, as the minutes turned to hours.

N

My mother was tired that summer. It didn't affect many things – not the mulish industry with which she worked in the kitchen, nor her involvement with all the children who passed through the house, so that it was most often her and not their own mothers who took them upstairs, cleaned their teeth, tucked them into bed – but I could see it clearly, even as I tried my hardest not to. I saw it in the way she sat down, the way she walked, the low grunts and sighs she made as she worked. I still hadn't got used to the scarf she wore around her head, nor the loss of hair beneath; I tried not to notice how her face had expanded and changed, which I know now was a result of the steroids she had to take. I thought that she looked old. With the scarf, she was like the babushka of one of our old books of fairy tales.

She is in just one of the photographs we have from that summer. In the centre are Magda and a couple of other guests, sitting at the lunch table under the oak; my father stands behind them, his large hands resting coolly on shoulders. My mother is in the picture only accidentally, at the very edge, eyes almost shut as she butters a roll. Her mouth set tightly, so that she looks closer than I ever realised she did to her own mother. There is a strong family resemblance in that clan, which Etta and I in particular have inherited: something ancient, Dutch or Germanic-looking. Brown eyes with deep lids, a strong jaw, thin lips. A long chin, so that I often think it wouldn't be hard to imagine we're toothless. In truth, in that photograph she looks like an old crone.

The mulish industry, too, she inherited from her clan. Her modesty and self-sufficiency. The impression we gleaned from my father – who was always intrigued by the strange, mean, paltry exoticness of her provenance – was that they lived more or less like Puritans. They wore home-sewn clothes. They were home-schooled. They ate only what they reared and grew within their land. They preached and prayed and worked. They married largely from within. I still marvel that my mother, with all her dedication and devotion and servility, managed to break out from a community as closed and traditional as that.

She left when she fell in love with an outsider, an Englishman visiting West Virginia. She was nineteen. He was a tutor at Cambridge University, a scholar of the American Civil War with a red moustache like a Confederate general. I imagine him bringing her back to England as just another historical curiosity, a quiet young virgin fourteen years his junior with her closed, perpetual half-smile. A souvenir from the Appalachian Mountains. How terrified she must have been.

Perhaps he was already tiring of her when he introduced her to my father, over tea on tin trays in the Fitzwilliam Museum café. My father – hailed by thirty-nine as a great writer, for whom both outcasts and strange communities were subjects to which he returned, again and again, in his work – was taken with her immediately. He asked his friend if he could interview her, fascinated by what little he'd heard of her family over tea; and in the series of meetings that followed he must have seen enough to decide that she would make a very good wife for a man like him. Quiet and tough, devoid of ego, hard-working, submissive, restrained. Emotionally modest, quite unlike the glittering jewels he counted among his many female friends. He had finally achieved real financial success with the latest of his novels; he could afford a house now, and children. They married two months later, with twenty years between them.

My mother never revisited her family and community after leaving. A total rupture. Growing up, I often wondered whether she regretted breaking free from their ranks. She must have, I thought, in the lonelier moments. Retreating to the kitchen of our London home and Frantoio as the rooms burst with loud, spoilt, outspoken people, each clamouring in his or her own particular way to be recognised as exceptional.

She seldom spoke of her first life to us. We only met the family through photographs. Still, elements of it were woven into the fabric of our home. The old-fashioned pickles and pies and preserves that we ate, unlike anything our friends' parents served. The abhorrence we all had towards lying, in spite of a great collective appetite for secrecy. And the odd puritan mottos that tripped off our tongues, the kinds you might find embroidered onto cushions.

Hold On and Hold Up.
The Tree Bears No Fruit Without Winter.
Kindness Is King.

Z

Zoe felt stale and swollen when she woke in the morning. It was awkward to make her way downstairs in a house whose rooms she'd never entered. Large glass-panelled doors opened out from the hallway into the garden; shyly she went through them, reluctant to present herself once again to a table of strangers. But there were only three of them there, scattered down the table around canisters of cereal and bowls of fruit and yogurt and pastries.

'Morning,' said the older woman with the black and silver hair. She was wearing heavy red-framed glasses now, and red lipstick that bled into the cracks around her mouth. 'Welcome to the medium birds. We are the more civilised of the breakfasters, not the very self-satisfied and worthy early birds and not the great lazy slobs still festering in their beds. Darling, what was your name again?'

'Zoe,' said Zoe, unable to think of anything witty or apposite to add, and the woman pushed a cup and cafetière towards her.

'I'm Magda,' she said. She looked expectantly at the other woman, one of the glamorous thirty-somethings from last night's meal, who was eating muesli behind black sunglasses. 'Faye?'

'I'm Faye,' she said, looking up. She had the nonchalant, slightly melancholy good looks of a well-bred animal – equine, perhaps, only with small, tidy teeth – and as Zoe took the woman in, she realised she was some marginal degree of famous. Zoe had seen that face before somewhere, lightly tanned under a Bardot fringe, all caramel hues. 'Magda, do we have to be called medium birds? It's a depressing title. A bit too close to home.'

'OK. Zoe, can you think of something better?' asked Magda.

Zoe used the pouring of coffee to stall.

'Egrets?' she said, eventually. 'They're kind of medium-sized, aren't they?' She heard that her voice lacked conviction.

'We get egrets along the canal near our house,' said the little boy at the end of the table, and she was grateful to have the conversation redirected. 'Don't we, Mummy?'

Faye looked vaguely down the table.

'Do we? Yes, probably.'

'I see he doesn't get his interest in nature from you, Faye.'

'Ha. No, that's another of Teddy's domains. Perfect Teddy. I'm afraid I don't offer much by comparison.'

'Darling,' said Magda. 'You're moving on from Teddy.'

'Am I?'

'Yes, you are. You will. Don't be so glum.'

'Mama, what's glum?'

'Dour,' said Faye. 'Down in the dumps.'

'What were you saying about Daddy?'

'If you've finished your breakfast, why don't you go and find the others? Where's your sister?'

'She keeps ignoring me,' he said, and Faye sighed, handsomely.

'Well, tell her not to. Or find little Nemony, where's she?'

The little boy looked down at the table. After a while he said quietly, 'I think I'll just stay here for a bit.'

They were joined, then, by the oldest teenager from dinner: the girl, who walked very upright, long legs swinging from a blue sundress, long black hair swinging down her back. She watched Zoe as she approached.

'It's one of the very lazy late toads,' said Magda, her face a picture of delight, and the girl kissed her on the cheek and sat down beside her. 'You're up early.'

'Thank you for the flattering intro.'

'This is Teresza,' Magda told Zoe.

'Tree,' said Teresza. 'Magda's probably the only person in the world who calls me Teresza. Magda and my mum.'

'Well, I named you.'

'Magda's my godmother,' she explained. 'My dad asked our godparents to name us. It's weird.'

Zoe recognised this patter as something they repeated routinely to strangers, and once again she found herself casting around for an interesting response. This was why she hated being around these kinds of people, she thought. It's always prickly or somehow sideways or facetious, you're always having to say something off-beat that you don't mean.

'You're lucky your godmother chose a nice name,' she said instead.

'You don't sleep,' said Tree, and Zoe laughed.

'Do I look that bad?'

'No – you're pretty,' said Tree, and Zoe wondered when she had ever been called pretty. 'My room's under your room, though. So I heard your footsteps during the night.'

'I'm sorry.'

'It didn't bother me.'

'I don't sleep either,' said Faye. 'Do you take something?'

'I find nothing really works,' said Zoe.

'Antidepressants do, somewhat.'

'Oh,' said Zoe.

'They slow the mind race, a bit. It's worth trying.'

'My doctor tried to put me on those,' said Tree.

'Darling, no,' said Magda. 'You're much too young.'

'And young people don't get depressed?'

'Oh, they do. They get magnificently depressed. But antidepressants deaden you. You want to wait until you're a bit older to become deadened.'

'I'll keep that in mind.'

Faye was watching Tree then, with some interest. She stood up.

'They don't all deaden you, Tree. In my experience, depression is the most deadening thing of all.'

'What's depression, Mummy?' asked the boy, and Faye exhaled, velvety lips puffed out.

'Being glum,' she said, 'dour,' and she smiled wearily at Magda and took her bowl, holding out her hand towards the boy.

'Come on, Timmy,' she said. 'Let's go and find the other kids.'

'It's too hot to go anywhere.'

'It's only going to get hotter, darling,' said Magda, and she turned to Zoe. 'It's going to be an evil one today, totally scorching.'

'But Krish is arriving later,' said Tree. She stirred milk into her coffee, licked the spoon. 'He's cool.'

N

There was something wrong with the whole day leading up to Krish's arrival at Frantoio that summer.

The heat was more oppressive than usual; there was not a breath of air. My father was in one of his moods. We could all read it in an instant, it carried like a smell in the air even before we could see it in the set of his shoulders, the tightness of his long and bony face. I could see its imprint on my mother, like the outline of someone's body on a bed. She wore his moods physically, she reminded me of a cat when their ears flatten down. I thought Tuva changed, too, when he was like that: she became louder, she fussed and organised, she took charge all the more.

I swam alone as the morning heat thickened and intensified. With a very histrionic kind of despair I pictured the empty day spreading out before me: a long, barren road, stripped of vegetation, prickly with dust, heat rising from earth to air in waterless rivulets. There is a boredom unique to summer holidays and unique to youth, whose sheer enormity I have not experienced since.

Then I heard the little boy, Timothy, calling out for me and I hurried out of the pool to hide. I was too old to play his foolish games, which were weedy and over-elaborate. Skin and hair dripping, I went to seek the cool of the old outhouse we called the Fort.

It was the ruined site of an old olive press, the *frantoio* that gave the house its name. Its ceiling was mostly coherent and must have been restored at some point, the beams a shaded resting place for pigeons or some other cooing bird. But the ground was chalky and uneven, splattered magnificently with bird shit, and the far end with its pale stony wall was coming down. The olive press itself – a huge stone circle like a wheel – was broken into two giant halves. They sat at the centre of the Fort on a round platform that looked like a well. It had a strange pull, a strange power; broken and ancient-looking and immovable, a great machine now defunct. One of us had lined up a ring of small stones and pebbles around it, as if it were a cultic altar.

Etta had got there before me with Timothy's sister, Alice. They looked up when I arrived and I could see that Alice was, or had been, crying.

'What's the matter?' I asked, and Etta shushed me, putting an arm around Alice's shoulder.

'Shall I tell her to go?' she asked Alice, and Alice sniffed no. 'You can stay,' said Etta, 'but be quiet.'

At moments like this I was filled with fury. I was sick of being treated like a child, there were only two and a half years between Etta and me. She had only just turned thirteen, only just acquired the teenage status to which she and Alice laid such unflinching claim. And I wanted to tell her that in any case I didn't need to be part of their world – that it wasn't so mysterious and important and tantalising as they seemed to think.

My fury was chastened a little by the resumption of Alice's crying. I went over to the corner of the Fort and sat on my own, shrouded in my wet towel, and I listened as she talked about her parents' divorce the summer before. She talked about the woman who was going to become her stepmother, and I marvelled at that sordid and seductive word, and Alice's real-life proximity to it, and the idea that Faye – my glacier-cool godmother, who I always imagined to be disappointed in which Travers daughter she'd been allocated – was being replaced. Alice's predicament, as it unfolded – the arguments between her parents, the time she and Timothy had to split between their two homes, the motorway service stations where they were swapped between their mother and father, and most of all this fact of a stepmother, until now the stuff of fairy tales alone – began to strike me as one of the worst a human could endure.

They tolerated me joining them as they sat cross-legged at the foot of the broken altar. As Alice's story unfolded, without my quite noticing it, I had moved closer and closer to them until I sat with a hand on her arm, which jogged up and down when she was overcome with tears. There was something somehow enviable about her grief. I thought it noble, it set her apart.

When Etta started crying too, it seemed natural – we were all three of us experiencing Alice's pain. But then her sobs started to outdo Alice's; in volume and ferocity they rose above Alice's cries, which fell silent.

'What is it, Etta?' she asked, her arm encircling Etta's shoulder, but Etta was so racked with tears that she couldn't answer for some time. She was taking Alice's pain too much to heart, I thought, it wasn't admirable. But then she spoke.

'I think my parents might divorce too,' she said before dissolving again into sobs, and as Alice leaned forward and hugged her, I sat back, horrified that she should lie like that. 'My dad doesn't love my mum,' she said. 'He doesn't even pretend anymore.'

'Do you really think he'll leave her?'

'I don't know. But I know who he'll turn to if he does.'

I felt the chill of the place. The decay of the chalky ground, burnished with those splatters of bird shit like tar. I longed now for the sunshine outside, even in the breathless heat of the day. I thought of my mother in the kitchen, of her quick hands folding napkins, piling them up ready to take outside for lunch.

'I think—' Etta could barely continue, consumed by her sobbing. 'I think of how lonely Mum must be,' she said, and in an instant I saw that her tears weren't false. Her words landed in my mind, and even as I recoiled – even as I wanted to shake my head, shake the shape of those words out of it – they made a horrible sense to me. As if the picture I had of my mother had been a jigsaw puzzle, and Etta had just completed it.

'She's still ill,' Etta said now, and though I wanted to put my hands to my ears I found that I couldn't move. 'She's really, really ill. This summer might be her last.'

She buried her face in Alice's shoulder and I moved, then; I stood up and ran from the cool white cavern of the Fort, and I ran through the garden, past the pool where someone was swimming, past the vegetable garden, past the fig tree where the young woman in the hat and Alice's mum sat reading. I ran to the steps down into the kitchen, just as my mother climbed them with a tray full of plates and cutlery and glasses and a large jug of lemon water.

'There you are,' she said. 'Lunch is almost ready.'

She walked past me and I watched her, my heart still whumping in my ears: the sturdy set of her shoulders, her elbows out by her sides as she carried the tray that would surely have been too heavy for someone really ill. I ran after her and took the cutlery from the tray, and I watched her as she laid the plates down between the places I set. I took her hand as she walked back to the kitchen, the tray hanging down from her other.

Z

Zoe didn't see much of Don that first day. She thought of herself as someone who survived well in unfamiliar situations, she supposed, but still it was surreal to find herself here, navigating her way around a large house and garden and people she didn't know. In Don's absence it was easy to feel as if she hadn't in fact been invited here – that she'd simply turned up to interrupt these people's holiday.

It didn't help that she kept getting things wrong. When she had finished her breakfast she stacked some used plates to take to the kitchen, but Tree frowned and told her no one expected her to do that. Cheerfully she insisted, carrying the plates away from the table and into the house. She found Lydia in the kitchen, whisking eggs in a large bowl.

'Thank you for a lovely breakfast,' she said, and thought that Lydia looked alarmed. She put her bowl and whisk down quickly, wiping her hands on her apron, taking the plates from Zoe.

'You don't need to do this.'

She frowned as Tree had done, and Zoe thought that it hadn't been alarm but irritation in her face.

'It's the least I can do. I'm Zoe, by the way.'

She reached her hand out and regretted it, since Lydia had to put the plates down in the sink and wash her hands and dry them again on her apron. The hand she gave was small and cool and motionless in Zoe's.

'Thank you so much for having me to stay with you all.'

'Thank you,' said Lydia, looking away quickly, and Zoe backed out of the kitchen she'd invaded.

As she made her way back to the grand central staircase, peering around some of the open doorways of the ground floor, she disturbed Toby Dornan in a sort of luxuriously decrepit library, sitting at a desk with what appeared to be a full-length manuscript in front of him. He looked up crossly, grunting a curt, cursory hello before looking back down at his work.

Back in her bedroom she unpacked her bags and considered simply staying there with the door closed until she was called to a meal, but that would have been ridiculous. Instead, reluctantly, she made her way back down into the garden, clutching a book in an attempt to legitimise her presence, and settled herself carefully in one of a collection of chairs in the shade of a large fig tree. She wondered if she was even allowed to be there – she wouldn't have been entirely surprised if someone had come and told her that those particular chairs weren't for sitting on, that the fig tree was out of bounds at that hour. Accepting Don's invitation had begun to feel like a ludicrous mistake. The mortifying idea started to creep into her mind that it had been intended only as a gesture; that it wasn't something he'd ever expected her to accept.

She only saw him hours later, at lunch, which he joined once everyone was already sitting. He sat at the head of the table, eating quickly and speaking little. Where she had only ever seen him expansive and relaxed, he seemed now to be remote and distracted, his rocky face solemn. She noticed that he excused himself as Lydia and some of the children laid a beautiful almond cake on the table.

Zoe had been talking to Tuva, the imperious blonde sitting beside her, but Tuva held up a hand to interrupt her, then leaned around people's backs.

'Are you going to work in your study?' she asked Don in a confidential tone, and when he frowned and said that he'd work outside – he needed the sun's fire – she said she'd send someone along with his coffee.

'Thank you.'

He stalked off, hands in his pockets and head bowed determinedly as if he were walking into strong wind. It was clear that their exchange had annoyed several of the teenagers: Zoe watched them watch Tuva as she carved out a portion onto a plate, filling a cup with coffee. She thought she saw something close to hatred pass over the face of the oldest boy, Malachy, as Tuva sent the little boy from breakfast, Faye's boy, off to take them to Don.

It might have been this – seeing another guest put a foot wrong, somehow, or miss a social cue – that allowed Zoe to feel more comfortable over pudding and coffee. It might also have been the wine she'd drunk, a couple of glasses now, which had gone to her head as it always did in the daytime, particularly when it was hot. Magda made her laugh, holding forth in the middle of the table about a play she'd directed once that had gone terribly wrong, and it occurred to Zoe from the volume of everyone else's laughter that they, too, had drunk a bit. That all these people were unfolding, in the afternoon heat.

N

I sat beside my mother at lunch. I watched her eat, I watched
how she glanced over at my father in his mood, I watched her
pick up Timothy's spoon when it fell to the ground. I noticed
actively for perhaps the first time that she didn't join in with
the adults' conversation. Etta's words in the Fort had made
my mother seem changed to me, or clearer. It was as if she'd
been unveiled.

There was a prevailing bad temper at the table, as if my
father's mood and the horror of Etta's words had encom-
passed us all. Alice's little brother Timothy whinged and
sulked; Etta and Alice sat together, puffy-eyed and conspira-
torial. Even Tree and Malachy, who were talking happily
enough with the other adults, had something strained about
them, and I thought that they were more openly hostile
towards Tuva than usual. Twice I noticed Tree interrupt her
as she held forth in the middle of the table; once to ask what
time Krish would arrive, and again ten minutes later to ask
whether he'd be getting a taxi or hiring a car. Tuva answered

patiently enough, I thought, though I saw a flicker of something pass over her face. Twice I saw Malachy roll his eyes when Tuva spoke.

I tried very hard not to think about what Etta had said about my father. I tried to bury her allusion to where he would go if he left. Taut and curt as he was that day, I still thought that perhaps her picture of my parents' relationship wasn't true – that she had exaggerated those things as a prelude to the real source of her sadness.

That real source was too horrifying to contemplate. After lunch dissolved, I spent the afternoon with my mother, in the kitchen. I grated cheese for the quiche she was making, I squeezed lemons. Perhaps I thought that if I helped her in these small tasks I could preserve her health and keep guard somehow against further deterioration. Or I was simply watching, seeking signs that she wasn't as ill as Etta had made her out to be. When she retreated into the games room for her break, I took a wet cloth and wiped the kitchen surfaces, stacked her cooking utensils in tidy piles, picked the paper of onion skins from the floor. She didn't say anything when she returned, but she smiled at me as she plucked tomatoes from a twig of vine.

'Can I help you, Mama?' I asked. She shook her head and I thought that she could feel me watching her as she washed the tomatoes, laid them on a dishcloth, rolled them onto the chopping board.

'If you like,' she said after a while, pulling secateurs down from a hook, 'I do need some peaches for the pudding.'

She held them out towards me and I took them, glad to be trusted with their frightening heft. I slid the safety catch back and forth with my thumb.

'I won't be a minute,' I said, an adult-sounding phrase, I thought, that rolled smartly like a marble over my tongue.

The heat pushed against my face and body, a wall of it. I was appalled by its immensity.

I trailed through the patch we called the orchard, really a motley place of fruit trees – peaches, lemons, figs – and lettuce and herbs, growing chaotically along a low and battered wall. In the heat of mid-August the herbs were ash-brown and desiccated. I hacked snips at them with the secateurs as I walked, dead rosemary and mint and thyme dropping onto tired earth. I bit into a pithy plum, discarded it, kicked clouds in the dust. When finally I reached the peach tree and stretched up to cut clusters of its fruit – they were snuffbox peaches, small and flattened like a bulldog's face – I found that I was too short to reach. On my tiptoes, jumping up and down, shoulders bunched with the effort of growing upwards, I could do no more than bat the lowest branch. It bobbed, as if we were playing a game.

I blinked in the savage light, and wanted to scream. I hated the tree. How I hated its branches that nodded and bobbed, the flat pink fruits dancing out of my reach.

Furiously I squatted down in the tree's shade to gather the dropped fruits instead. The air down there was thick with the stench of their bruised flesh; it hummed, too, with a great droning, and I saw that in many of the peaches there were three or four or even five dizzy wasps, working deep within the fruit's soft wounds. 'This is stupid,' I muttered aloud, 'this is useless,' because I felt ashamed to be so small and so power-less that I'd have to present to my sick mother peaches for her pudding that were squashed, and wounded, and rotting.

I quit my useless labour. I sat on my heels on the parched earth and squeezed my eyes tight over tears that were hot as they ran down my hot cheeks, and made me feel all the smaller, all the more powerless.

I seemed to cry there, sitting on my heels, for a very long time. I cried until I was exhausted with it, till in that mysterious way of childhood tears I felt absolutely nothing at all.

When finally I opened my eyes there was a creature there, poised militarily among the fallen peaches ahead. A scorpion, I was sure. Brown, the gelatinous misty brown of a certain kind of jelly bean. It was waiting; I felt that it watched me, its pincers held aloft. I swallowed, wiped the tears from my cheeks. I was conscious of my tongue in my mouth.

Slowly, silently, I laid the secateurs down. I shifted my weight to move closer to the creature, wincing as my sandals scuffed the ground. I stopped. Then I leaned forward onto my hands so that I could move forward like a cat, like a leopard. Small stones in the dry earth pressed into the flesh of my palms. I tried not to breathe. Something small crawled along the back of my neck. I felt brave tracking that scorpion: boyish, I thought, and alone, not afraid or in flight as I thought my siblings would expect of me. The child of the family, whom sometimes they called 'Nemo', *nobody*.

I would tell Malachy I had tracked it. I'd tell Tree.

I heard low voices coming, then, from around the corner. *Stay where you are*, I thought. *Don't come any further*. I lifted one foot off the ground, painstakingly, placed it close to my hands, lifted the other, placed that one down. I mustn't get too sure, I thought, even as I lifted my hand too quickly and the scorpion scuttled, quick as a dart, into a hole in the ground.

Still, I had seen enough to know what I'd seen. Enough to tell my siblings, I thought. I felt tense and brave, the impotent rage and humiliation and sadness all dissipated, and still on all fours I kept moving. Leopard-crawling, a hunter, stealthy but less stealthy than before, my breath freer now in my throat. Out of the tree's stinking shade the sun was formidable on the back of my neck. I would never lie and sun myself like Etta and Alice, I thought, not ever. I couldn't imagine anything more boring than lying there for hours like that, pretending to be adult.

That summer they had become thickly, impenetrably entwined. They whispered together, they linked arms, they leaned their faces into each other as they spoke, they erupted spontaneously into giggles and then back into measured silence. They seemed even to walk at the same speed, legs in matching denim cut-offs unfolding in time as they sauntered, metronymic and bored, from pool to house, house to pool.

Etta banished me from our shared bedroom during the long afternoons, when often they shut themselves in there and played music in the stuffy darkness, and talked – about secret, slithery sorts of things that I half-heard and was repulsed and enthralled by. I was entirely removed from their area of concern. To Etta I was irritating, but to Alice I was nothing – I think she barely saw me. And yet I was infatuated with her.

I thought that perhaps Alice might be interested to hear of the scorpion. Frightened, or impressed. I wouldn't lie, exactly, but I could say it had crawled across my foot. Its pincers raised, waving ominously, ready to snap shut, clack.

There was the distant drone, then, of something mechanical in the kitchen, and I thought that I must get back to my mother, explain that I had failed in my task. I went back to collect the secateurs, and as I straightened I heard the low hum of voices again, rising above the wasps' drunken murmur. A man's timbre, perhaps a woman's too. I edged my way along the hedge that marked the orchard's end, its dry leaves brushing my face, and then I pulled back, immediately. I didn't want to see.

And then I did want to see, just to check. My father's outdoor desk, and two chairs; my father and Tuva, sitting opposite each other. Their hands met in the middle of the table, on a pile of his papers, clasped together. Above their hands, their heads; their foreheads were pressed against one another as if they were praying, only I'd never seen people pray together in that way. Only their foreheads touching, and beneath their foreheads, their clasped hands. My father's eyes were closed; he frowned slightly, as if he were in pain. Tuva's were open, watching him.

Like a witch. She was like a witch. We'd always joked that she was a witch, but she really was, I thought. I had never seen my father look like that, I didn't know my father could look like that. My father, who never did what anyone told him to do, who was always the one who did the telling. He wouldn't have been sitting like that with Tuva if she hadn't made him, somehow.

I curled my fingers around the hot metal of the secateurs. I wanted to hurl them at the table and break that moment, break Tuva's spell and get my father to lean back and open his eyes and snap back to himself once again. An insect flew against my ear and I flinched, frightened, batting the air with my hand. I was desperate, then, to go and find my mother. I wanted terribly to cry again, but I wouldn't, I'd simply lie near her on the cold kitchen floor and say nothing. I'd say not a thing.

As I hurried back towards the house I frowned up at it against the sun, and I saw two faces there, Tree's and Malachy's, side by side in a little open window at the top. Their eyes were narrowed; I saw their lips moving in speech. As if they were whispering a spell of their own.

Z

In the afternoon everyone dispersed, and Zoe was reminded of the speed with which a lizard disappears into a hole. All the noise and motion of lunch had dissipated into thick, starchy silence, rampant with the scratching of insects. The heat was vast.

She was at a loss, again, for what to do. If she napped, she knew she'd further sabotage her chances of sleep that night, and yet the huge lunch she'd eaten and the three glasses of wine and the packed air outside – the absence of even a whistle of air, of movement – left her little choice but to retreat to her bed.

She lay there in her underwear, uncomfortably full, and stared up at the ceiling. She had managed to get hold of a fan, hauling it stealthily upstairs from a store cupboard Magda had pointed her towards, and now it whined and shuddered and clunked barely cold air at her as she lay there, her hairline sodden with sweat.

This wasn't, naturally, what she had pictured in London as she'd picked out her holiday reading, planned her outfits, folded her clothes eagerly into her suitcase and spritzed them, for God's sake, with perfume, because she'd read once that that was what Audrey Hepburn did.

She got up, pulled the fan closer to the head-end of the bed, lay back down. It didn't, now, seem unfeasible that she would spend the whole week this way: scuttling about awkwardly, emerging from her room only at mealtimes, borrowing a few minutes' worth of confidence from wine at lunch and then darting back to doze on this too-small and actually quite lumpy mattress. She had boasted about the trip to her colleagues, very slightly – she worked in publishing, how could she not? – and now she imagined returning to work and having to answer their clamouring questions about the whole week she'd spent in Don Travers's summer villa.

I spent it in my bedroom, she imagined saying, *sweating*.

Her parents, at least, she hadn't told. To her immense satisfaction they had absolutely no idea where she was, or with whom, because she hadn't spoken to them since she'd visited them six weeks ago, the visit from which her insomnia had grown and consumed her, a triffid.

She pictured them again, now, as they'd been that day: side by side on the sofa, her father's left hand resting on her mother's right, their shoulders subtly stooped so that their heads came forward from their necks. It had given them the impression of turtles. Their expressions were turtle-like too and so meanly placid, suggestive of such impassive endurance, that – along with their stooping stance and her mother's recent haircut – Zoe had been struck by the idea that they had become the same person. And as they delivered their speech, perched there together, braced against the space between themselves and their only child, their voices were eerily one.

'The publication has been very hard on us,' her father had started, and he'd looked at her mother, who nodded and looked down. 'Perhaps you didn't consider how it would look for us, or perhaps that simply wasn't important to you. Not as important as all the money they're paying you, or the attention it's got. The newspapers, magazines.'

'We haven't read any of that,' her mother had added.

'Your mother read the book through to the end, though.'

'Well, I thought I should. Your father wasn't sure he could stomach it. Not that he needed to read it, with all the people we've had come and tell us about it.'

'We just – we've no idea where you got all those ideas from,' he said. 'That's what we struggle with most.'

'It's all the questions we've had, from people who know us. I had Rosie Critton on the phone yesterday.'

'It's the childhood bits that are worst, of course. It's the woman character's childhood everyone asks about most.'

'That's why I read it through to the end, so I'd know what they were all asking about. I didn't want to, not because it's not well written – I'm sure it's that, you've always been very … talented – but because … Well. It's not easy reading the – dark, I suppose – nasty, really – the nasty things your own daughter has dreamed up.'

'Or, worse, experienced.'

'Yes, or experienced. That's the trouble for us, it runs our imaginations wild, wondering where you got all that dark, that – debauched, would you say?'

'Yes. I would.'

'That debauched material.'

'We're not going to ask.'

'We don't want to know. Not that it'd do any good anyhow, to know. It's out there in the world for all to see, nothing will change that.'

'There's the bits we recognise, though.'

'Yes, and, Zoe, you've hardly made an effort to hide those bits.'

'Using things that have really happened, to real people. People you know.'

'Writing about them as if they're your stories to tell. That's just – it's plain wrong. It's immoral.'

'I was disgusted, frankly.'

'Darling—'

'Well, it's the truth. I was disgusted.'

'OK. All right. But, Zoe, we did agree, your dad and I, that we'd look forwards now, not back.'

'We did. At the end of the day, what's done is done.'

'We can't change anything by ranting about it. But your father thought it right that we at least tell you.'

'It's too late this time, but maybe you'll think more carefully in future.'

'Maybe you'll at least consider our feelings—'

'Yes, our feelings, your own parents, instead of just – fixating on all the reviews and coverage you seem to crave so badly.'

'Chris—'

As she sat there across from them, she felt nothing; she just tried to store every word, so that she could write it down. But a little later, when she closed their front door and opened and closed their squealing gate and walked down their quiet street, she realised that she was deeply afraid. The hot, sweet smell of tarmac and rotten leaves rose up from the pavement, the same pavement she'd trudged up and down since she was a child. There was something of her childhood, too, in the fear she felt like a stone in her stomach.

It wasn't until she'd lain in bed that night, unable to sleep, that she'd realised that the horrifying thing she feared was simply hatred. She hated her parents. Yes, she despised them, she thought, sitting up in bed; she'd despised them for many years, perhaps for as long as she could remember. Listening to them that afternoon as they'd intoned, two mouthpieces for one mean, bitter perspective, the deep contempt she'd left unacknowledged all this time had just become too big to ignore. Its depths were dizzying, they were fathomless.

She didn't want to be someone made up of hatred. How could someone made of hatred ever produce anything great? And wasn't *Caged Creatures* in fact a nasty book, she thought, just as her mother had said; now that she considered it, wasn't her novel skewed and twisted by the hatred that lay at its author's heart?

She had thought, then, of Don. Since meeting him at the London Library she had found herself thinking of him often, wondering what he'd do in a certain situation, or what he'd make of a certain thought or action of hers – so that he had become a kind of internal barometer of what was honourable, what was admirable. His thoughts, and by extension his novels, operated on a level far above petty vices like hatred. They were expansive, they contained a nobility in their expansiveness that she – a mean creature, she'd realised, made up of bitterness and loathing just like her parents – would never attain.

But she was here, at least, she thought now. Her face had cooled a little in the fan's current. She took a deep breath, closed her eyes, tried to let her parents recede. Perhaps she hadn't pictured herself like this, hiding away in a dingy bedroom, dozy and sweaty and tipsy, bloated from too much focaccia – but she was in Don's radius, not her parents'. That was something.

N

'Mama,' I said. I lifted my head from the kitchen table, where it had been resting, the oak cool against my skin. 'How many more weeks until school?'

My mother blew out her cheeks and shook her head, scrubbing something in the sink.

'We go home in three weeks,' she said. I said nothing but dropped my forehead back onto the table, and as I did I thought again of my father's and Tuva's foreheads, pressed together. My father's closed eyes, Tuva's open and watching.

I shook my head and lifted it again, opened my eyes to watch my mother peeling the dark skin from a cucumber, revealing the pale flesh beneath, and I wondered whether I had actually seen anything at all. Or whether perhaps it was perfectly normal, or at least inoffensive, to do what they'd been doing. After all, they hadn't been kissing. For all I knew about adults, there was nothing strange at all about that embrace.

'Is it just going to get hotter and hotter?' I asked, and she shrugged lightly.

'I expect it will ease off.'

There were sticky footsteps, then: Tree rushing lightly, with a sort of chaotic control, down the steps from the garden. She paused for a moment in the threshold, a dark silhouette against the light outside, and then she was lolloping past the table in that way she had, the casual swinging gait that I thought half-leopard and half-gazelle. As she went she reached an arm out, ruffled my hair, and then she had plucked a cluster of grapes from the fruit bowl and was leaning over the table, elbows on the surface, eating them one by one.

'What's new?' she said through a mouthful.

'It's hot,' I said, and my mother whistled.

'Nemony's hot.'

'Poor Nemo.'

'And a touch bored, I think,' said my mother, smiling at me, and I nodded, watching Tree's face as she ate, but she didn't respond. Her thoughts were elsewhere. I could almost see them scrolling through her mind, too quick to catch, her gaze unfocused. I thought again of my father and Tuva. Tree had been watching too. She had seen them.

'Do you want to swim with me?' I asked, and though she turned to me her eyes were still unfocused – she was still not quite there.

'Sorry, Nem, not now,' she said vaguely.

'Please?'

But she didn't hear me, the bulge of a grape inside one cheek, eyes narrowing. Then she came to, spat the unbitten grape into her palm. She straightened, spread her hands on the table, looked over at my mother.

'Do you have time for a chat, Ma?'

'Yes,' said my mother simply, chopping swiftly, knife hammering the board like a woodpecker, and I looked from her to Tree and wondered what it was like to speak like that with my mother, as one adult to another. Then Tree looked at me, and I saw that my mother was watching me too, and realised that they wanted me to leave.

'Nem,' said Tree. 'If you head to the pool now I'll have a quick splash with you in a minute.'

I was up and out of the kitchen, then, swallowing hard because I was too indignant to concede again to tears, but I felt wretchedly alone, excluded from everything: from conversations, from understanding, from all the unseen and mysterious currents running under the world. I hated adults, I thought. I hated teenagers. Something incomprehensible and ugly happened to everyone older than ten and I didn't want it, didn't want anything to do with it.

I ran up the stairs to the room I shared with Etta. As I'd expected, it was locked, which struck me then as even more magnificently selfish than usual. I rapped the door so hard that my knuckles hurt, stepping back when Etta snatched open the door.

'What the hell, Nem? You frightened Alice.'

'Well, I'm sorry,' I said, squeezing my knuckles in the other hand. 'But it's my room too. You can't keep locking me out.'

She looked me up and down, holding the door open a fraction. Then she looked behind her.

'Well?' she said.

'Let her in,' said Alice's voice.

Etta opened the door.

'Hurry up.' She disappeared back into the gloom. 'And lock the door behind you.'

They had drawn the curtains and plugged in a cassette player, which was playing something haunting and catchy that I recognised. The low hum of music in the amber half-dark made me want simply to lie on my bed there, face down, and let the tears that threatened flow unnoticed into the pillow.

But I couldn't do that. I looked around. I hadn't expected to gain entrance so easily, and now I was in there I wasn't sure what to claim I'd come to get or do. I crossed over to my side of the room, opened one of the drawers.

'It needs to be something she can't ignore,' said Alice.

'Exactly. We've tried annoying her in the past, we've tried making her feel unwelcome – nothing actually gets through to her. It needs to be something bigger than that.'

I found my diary and a pencil and took them to the bed, sat on my pillow with my back to the wall, opened the book to a clean page and wrote the date. I hadn't written a single entry the whole summer.

17 August, 1999. Frantoio, Sicilia. Spotted a scorpion after lunch. Size: roughly 5cm? Colour: brown. Species: need to research!!

Half-heartedly I tried to draw it. I made the first cautious strokes with the pencil, a preliminary sketch.

'Let's write a letter,' said Alice.

'Saying what?'

'I don't know. An anonymous letter. It could say something like, *We know what you're doing, we—* Or hang on. Could it contain a threat? Could it refer to something she's done at home?'

'Like what?'

'I don't know. *We have reason to believe you are in trouble with important people in London. We will not tell anyone about it, as long as you leave these premises immediately.* Et cetera. She's sure to have done something bad, right? So she'll think it refers to that.'

'But it needs to be really convincing. Really ominous. Something to really scare her.'

'Is that blackmail?' I asked then, and they looked over.

'Butt out,' said Etta. 'We didn't say you can stay here if you're going to listen in on our conversations.'

'I didn't say don't do it,' I said. 'I think it's a good idea.'

Etta and Alice eyed each other.

'You don't even know what we're talking about,' said Etta.

'You're talking about Tuva.'

I let the pages of my diary fall against a finger. This was more exciting than seeing a scorpion, I thought. This was real life, a real danger. All at once, listening to them, I'd been struck by the wild sense that everything precarious and ominous that day, and that summer – Etta's tears in the Fort, the secrecy between my mother and Tree, my mother's illness, Etta and Alice's exclusion, my father's bad temper, my boredom, my loneliness – even the heat, somehow – all of that would be resolved, if only Tuva could be made to leave.

'I want her gone too,' I said. 'She's evil, she's even worse than we thought.'

'Why do you say that?' Etta asked. She looked hungry, I thought, too excited. I knew that look so well, I'd seen it so many times, and it always made me feel the same unique brand of unease. As if my footing had come loose, somehow.

'No reason.'

I closed my diary, stowing it and the pencil beside the bed so that I could leave the room. But then I pictured again my father's and Tuva's hands and foreheads pressed together; I pictured her open eyes, large and wet and radioactive blue, so close to my father's brain. I turned from Etta to Alice, who was watching me too. Her tanned skin, the neon yellow of her bikini, the deep nutty brown of her hair. Her expression was warm, like her skin. She was nodding at me gently as if I were a friend, a girl her age and not just Etta's little sister.

'I saw them together,' I said, 'this afternoon. And I think something evil is happening.'

Z

When Zoe woke in the early evening she swam, cool for the first time that day as she slid through the pool's oily water. Then she bathed and dressed for dinner. She chose a dark blue linen dress to wear, the only sophisticated piece of clothing she appeared to have brought with her. Combing her wet hair on the balcony of her room, she could hear the clinking of the table being laid. She put earrings on, and then took them off and put them on again.

She was the last to join the party outside and as she emerged from the house she was able to observe them all properly, as a group. Well dressed, somehow unmistakably moneyed, each holding his or her wine glass in the right way – lightly, casually, as if their fingers hardly gripped the stem. And yet there was just the right hint of something else, a certain scruffiness or insouciance or eccentricity – like the villa itself, with its stained walls and rambling garden – so that they could never have been thought quite bourgeois. She imagined seeing them through her parents' eyes.

Don turned to greet her, his grey hair combed back. He was tall, slim, eagle-elegant, in a linen shirt the same dark blue as her dress.

'Hello, Zoe,' he said.

'You're matching,' said one of his younger daughters, and Zoe felt as if she were somehow culpable.

'So we are,' said Don. 'Zoe, I hope you'll do me the honour of sitting beside me at supper.'

He hovered a hand at the small of her back, and as if Tuva were a maître d' awaiting a cue she now swept everyone towards the table, turquoise beads swinging from her ears, her hair swept into a majestic heap on the top of her head. For the briefest of moments her eyes passed over Zoe's face, and they were as hard and turquoise as her earrings. She smiled, turned to her neighbours.

'Do sit.'

They sat, and Zoe spread her napkin over her lap. It was starched and fresh. There was a glass vase like a goldfish bowl in front of her, filled with large, ripe, raspberry-pink flowers. Don's son Malachy sat to her right, Don to her left; Malachy filled her glass with wine, as Don gestured for her to help herself to the platter of ribbon-thin meat before him. And as she sat there amid the hesitant murmur of the meal's beginning, being helped to food and drink, cool in her linen dress, she felt soft and feminine, courteously solicited. It was novel, something she didn't think she ever expected to feel.

'I've been thinking about you all day, Zoe, wondering how you're getting on. I've had this wretched piece of work to finish; I regret that I've neglected you.' He laid some asparagus on her plate. 'Have you found everything you need?'

'Oh, absolutely,' she said, wondering what he might mean by this, and once again she had the feeling that she had missed the point of her invitation.

'There are some fascinating people here this week,' he said. 'I thought you'd get on splendidly with them all. Have you had a chance to swap ideas with Toby?'

'Ah – well, we haven't spoken much yet.'

'You will have spoken to Magda, though – she speaks to everyone. Did you manage to see *Chasm* before it closed last month?'

'Sadly not,' Zoe said, inflecting her voice with regret, though she'd never heard of it.

'Oh, it was extraordinary. Faye and I went together, actually, with Rob Jones and his partner Marcus. Marcus wrote the score for Bert Thomas's last picture; really, it made the whole film.' He looked down the table. 'If you haven't had the chance yet, you must get together with Faye. You'll know her from *Digs and Dictators*, of course—' and Zoe realised, now, why she recognised the woman. 'It's moved to Channel 4 now, hasn't it; you'll have seen that marvellous Alexander the Great episode, when she took the show to the Libyan border – but people often forget that Faye's not merely a brilliant presenter, she's one of the eminent classicists of her generation. We met when I was researching *Iphigeneia at Aulis* seven years ago, for a project – she's a

Euripides expert, among other things. Her husband's a barrister. Well' – and his voice was infinitesimally softer as he spoke now – 'they're recently separated. In any case, he's a barrister, in the same chambers as my cousin Matthew, oddly enough. Matthew Longley, he's the QC who represented the government in the landmark *R v. Hughes* case back in '82 ...' And so he went on, each person he mentioned flowering open into another connection, each name letting another name splutter into light, so that Zoe began to see London and Britain and then the entire world as one sprawling network, a city seen at night from an aeroplane flying high above, people and connections sparking like beacons.

If she could become one of those beacons, she thought. A person linked to another, linked to another. If the tight borders she'd always felt so close by were in fact only soft, ephemeral things – only mirages after all, dissolving like sugar.

She watched Don's face as he spoke, the deep lines etched there, the elegance with which he ate and spoke. His was an impeccable and old-fashioned courtesy. If it was elaborate, if it stepped lightly into disingenuity – the suggestion that he'd in any way selected the current crowd of guests with her in mind, for example – it was also natural, as natural and unthinking to him as the way he held his fork. How different would she be, if she had had a father like this. She felt Malachy by her side, self-contained, quietly assured, that same unthinking grace reconstituted.

'And now tell me about your work,' he said. 'Have you sent something over to your editor for the next book?'

'No,' she said. 'No, I haven't written enough to send them yet.'

'But you will. You needn't rush things. You'd be well excused for basking in the reception of your debut for a while yet. And what news there? Is Elias adapting it for the screen?'

How did he know that she'd seen more of Elias, she wondered, and not for the first time with Don she had the disorientating sense that conversations had happened; that she mattered more than she had thought, in some way she didn't quite understand.

'He hasn't read it, as far as I know,' she said. She had contemplated giving Elias a copy, but decided against it since he'd never expressed any interest. She wondered whether Don had invited Elias to that lunch at the Garrick specifically in order to set up a film opportunity for the book, and then she dismissed the idea as too ridiculously self-aggrandising. He wasn't her mentor, nor were those lunches in her honour. He facilitated connections, she thought, that was all. His great mind swooped down to visit such trivial affairs as hosting lunches and sending invitations and reading author interviews in the *Sunday Times* – and then it soared back up, producing novels that would continue to be read fifty, a hundred years from now.

'Magda,' he said, calling down the table. 'Who are the best young dramatists currently – who will you send a copy of Zoe's novel? It's made for the stage.'

'Oh, I think Boyd James is turning out brilliant stuff,' she said. 'I'm speaking to my secretary tomorrow; I'll get her to send him a copy.'

Zoe took a breath. Just like that, she thought.

'Thank you,' she said, but Magda had already turned back to her conversation. Don wiped away her thanks with a hand.

'It's made for the stage,' he repeated. 'Did you ever act, Zoe?'

'No.'

'But you've always written?'

'Yes, always.'

'And do your parents write?' he asked.

'No,' she said, and had to hold herself back from adding, *they're talentless*. The words appeared to her fully formed, guiltlessly treacherous, as if she'd said them many times before. 'And yours,' she asked, 'were they writers?'

It felt delightful, almost transgressive, to ask about his provenance.

'Not exactly,' he said, and the little girl sitting to his left spoke then.

'Daddy's father was a philosopher.'

'Yes, Nemony.'

'And his mother was an actress—' she said, but Don wasn't listening.

'Malachy, have you helped Zoe to the potatoes?'

Malachy asked someone for the potatoes and passed them to Zoe, and she was grateful for the distraction. She must think of something to say, she thought as she replaced the serving spoons – to justify her presence by Don's side tonight, but also in Sicily, on this holiday.

'Why did you choose Sicily for a summer house?' she asked. 'What first brought you here?'

'The history and violence,' he said without a pause. 'It's a barbaric place, don't you think? Only last month there was another prominent disappearance in Syracuse, not forty miles from here. A judge who'd passed a sentence against the wrong fellow. The right fellow, in fact, just not the kind you litigate against. But we also think of beauty when we speak of Sicily, don't we; we think of civilisation. You only have to look to Pindar. We have reason to believe he loved the island. How beautifully he writes about its rivers, about its nymphs. And yet he was bullied into writing those victory odes for the Sicilian tyrants. Theron, Hieron. Corruption and beauty, that's the fabric of a wild and ancient place like this ...'

And he continued, his words starting to gallop, and though Zoe nodded calmly as she listened, she was gripped all the while by an undercurrent of alarm. At some point the galloping would slow; he would ask her a question, and she'd have to prove she knew even the first thing about what he was discussing.

'Did you know it was only published posthumously?' he asked eventually, and Zoe shook her head, clenching the napkin in her lap. She hadn't been listening for the last minute or so; she knew that at some point since Pindar, Don had mentioned *The Leopard*, but she couldn't be sure that he wasn't talking now about a different book altogether.

And then his attention was caught by something outside the garden, along with everyone's, and it was with great relief that she was released. The sound of an engine winding through the dark quiet surrounding the house; headlights, flashing a semaphore as the vegetation along the road thinned and thickened. Zoe reached for her glass and as she drank she noticed Lydia for the first time that evening. She was sitting at the other end of the table, her hands in her lap; her mouth was drawn in a flat straight line, eyes blank. She looked small and grim and exhausted.

The car pulled in to the driveway, then. The little girl next to Don turned back to the table, smiling questioningly at Malachy.

'Krishna,' he said; 'Krish!' cried some of the other kids. Together they rose from their seats, and when a slim and handsome man in a suit with a holdall over his shoulder emerged, the children ran towards him and hugged him, followed by Tree and Malachy, followed by the little girl treading more shyly behind.

'What a welcome!' he said.

When he'd greeted the children, he clapped his hand into a handshake with Don; he strode down to the other end of the table, kissed Lydia on each cheek. She smiled with a quick and easy warmth that was a surprise to Zoe.

And then he approached Tuva, who was standing, and kissed her too – tensely, Zoe thought, with the stiffness of people being watched.

'What took you so long?' she said in a low voice.

'The car hire queue was as usual about ten hours long,' he announced to the whole table, sitting down in the empty seat beside Tree, 'with one extremely leisurely Sicilian manning the desk.' He poured himself a glass of wine. 'I expect I could have jumped to the front of the queue if I'd only known the right handshake. Don, you'll have to teach me for next time.'

'You just need a brick of Marlboro Reds,' said Tree, serving food onto a plate for him. 'They love a bribe.'

'As worldly as ever, I see, Tree,' he said, shaking his head, and Tree smiled. Zoe saw her eyes flicker very quickly to Tuva's and then away.

'Krishna's been busy advising the government on driving down domestic goods' price inflation; we're pinning our hopes on him,' said Don, and Zoe turned back to him, ready to pretend afresh that she knew anything at all about anything other than her work and herself and her small, unconnected life.

She was folding her clothes away, shortly after midnight, when there was a knock on her bedroom door. She opened it to find Tree standing there with those serious, dark-fringed eyes. Her long hair was dark too, and standing there in the gloom in black leggings and a cropped black T-shirt, the stretch of stomach between them yellowy white, she looked like a hazard symbol.

'Since you're not going to sleep anyway,' she said, 'I wondered whether you wanted to hang out.'

She held a bottle of wine and two tumblers between her fingers. Zoe smiled, though she was aware that this wouldn't help her sleep – that now she was only delaying further that elusive process.

'Sure,' she said. 'Why not.'

Tree came in and settled herself on the floor, long legs stretched out in front of her, ankles crossed. Her feet were bare, dramatically arched like a ballerina's, the soles filthy.

'I've never slept in this room,' she said, passing Zoe a glass.

'How long have you had the house?'

'Oh, it's not ours. Dad rents it every year because the first summer we took it he wrote *The Guild*, and I think he thought the house was responsible. I was ten that year – the same age Nemony is now, I guess. I remember not seeing him for weeks on end, he'd just emerge for twenty minutes every now and then to eat.'

Zoe felt a little pang of envy, then, for growing up in a household in which works like *The Guild* were created – to feel as casual as Tree did about that process. She thought of her own father when she was ten, and the main image she could conjure up was of his white, oddly hairless ankles and calves emerging from suit trousers at the end of a day at work. His work shoes gave him corns, he said. Wincing, he would remove his socks and roll his trousers up, and then he'd sit heavily down on the sofa and place his feet in a bowl of warm water and vinegar prepared by her mother.

'Dad says your book is very good,' said Tree. Zoe shook her head.

'I still can't get over the idea of your father reading my work, let alone saying it's good.'

'He's just another human,' said Tree, frowning. She took a sip. 'This wine tastes like piss. Anyway, Dad says you'll win prizes.'

'Oh, I don't know about that.'

'You're twenty-six, aren't you?'

'Yes.'

'That's very young to have written a prize-winning novel.'

'It hasn't won anything yet.'

'What's it about?'

Zoe hated that question. She hadn't learned how to talk about the book naturally, and so she had to stick to a script borrowed from her publisher. It was embarrassing every time, trying to recite that script in a way that suggested spontaneous speech.

'At its heart, it's about a relationship,' she said. 'It's about a man and a woman who have both in very separate ways found themselves rejected and damaged by the world around them, but who find some kind of acceptance in each other, for the first time in their lives. Then a random catastrophic event happens that throws it into jeopardy – and that's when the true damage is inflicted on them, only this time it's by each other. In their place of acceptance and solace, while it lasted, they learned all the tricks they'd need to hurt each other more than anyone else ever could.'

'It sounds good,' said Tree. 'Dark.'

Just as Zoe's mother had said.

'Yes, I guess it is.'

'How do they hurt each other?'

'Aha,' Zoe said. 'You'll have to read the book.'

'Oh, I will. I was annoyed that Dad didn't bring a copy out here. I've already asked to borrow it when we get home.'

Her earnestness was disarming. Zoe would never have had the confidence to speak with so little irony at nineteen. Even now she felt that it was difficult. And she let herself wonder, for a moment, about the context in which Tree and her father would have talked about her book, about her age, about her success or hypothetical success. It was almost too impossibly remote a thing to imagine. Don Travers discussing her with his student daughter suggested some other version of the world, in which the scales were all tipped and unaligned, an Escher graphic.

'It's interesting, what you were saying about damage. Last term we were studying the nineteenth-century novels, and I was starting to think that in a way all literature is about the harm we do to each other,' said Tree. 'Or the damage, to use your word. Don't you think?'

Zoe took a breath.

'All of my dad's books, for example,' Tree said. 'Or anything that's lasted. *Anna Karenina, Tess of the D'Urbervilles. Jane Eyre.*'

'And about redemption too, surely,' said Zoe then. 'Harm, damage, but also the redemptive acts humans are capable of.'

'Do you think? What's redemptive in your novel?'

'Well …'

She had thought about this a lot, since the last visit to her parents' house. She had spent many of her sleepless nights putting together a counterargument to her own self-accusation that the novel was mean and base, that its beating heart was simply hatred.

'I guess the fact the protagonists could find a place of love and compassion in each other in the first place. That's where the beauty is. Even if it's transient, it still saves their lives from bleakness and pain and hatred, just for that short time.'

'But don't those moments only make it all worse?' asked Tree. 'When your protagonists come to the end of their lives and look back at it all, will they be grateful that they found that happiness in each other? Surely beauty isn't enough. Doesn't it just make all the ugliness that happens afterwards all the worse?'

'That's a sad way to look at life, though,' Zoe said. 'That the good things only make the bad things worse.'

'Ah, but I didn't say life, I said literature,' said Tree. 'Although – there's an argument, isn't there, for extending it to life generally? The history of mankind is really just a long history of damage. Who vanquished who, who burnt down whose citadel, who poisoned or raped or pillaged who, etc. etc.'

'I'm not sure I agree. I think your theory attributes an intentionality to destruction that isn't always there.'

Tree looked away, and when she turned back to Zoe her posture had shifted: her shoulders had lifted, back very straight. Her crescent eyes too wide.

'I read something the other day about Russian soldiers in Afghanistan, which I can't stop thinking about. Some soldiers tied a mother to a chair so that she had to watch while her eleven-year-old son was raped by several different soldiers, one after the other. For several hours, she had to watch – she couldn't escape it, she couldn't stop it, she couldn't comfort him. Her own son.'

She hadn't dropped Zoe's gaze throughout her speech, had barely blinked or taken a breath. Zoe shifted and looked down at the glass of wine in her hands, relieved to break eye contact.

'And that's just one story, out of how many?' asked Tree. 'Tell me that's destruction without intention.'

She cracked a knuckle on one hand, then the other.

'And by the way – I don't believe women would have concocted that torture. If they would even have gone to war in the first place. Gone to war, taken everyone else to war. What do you think?'

'I don't know,' said Zoe.

'Those soldiers – isn't there something uniquely male in the total abdication of morality, of humanity? I don't know, how many women are ruthless enough for that? I just don't think they are. Doesn't their nurturing function – their role as mothers or would-be mothers – doesn't that rule it out? Pull them back from that kind of destruction?'

Zoe looked around, trying to think how to start answering this.

'I think mothers can be ruthless too,' Zoe started, but Tree held up a hand.

'I'm depressing you,' she said. 'Sorry.' She pulled her legs up, hugged her knees. 'But I still think my theory holds. History could just be called "stories of damage".' She took a deep breath and smiled, at ease again, and Zoe thought that it was as if a high wind had surrounded the house, shaken the windows in their frames, and then passed. 'I should have said that in my Oxford interview. They would have made a little note in the margins: *Warning: this girl is very bleak.*'

'So you study History?'

'History and English. I just finished my first year.'

'Do you like it?'

Tree made a face.

'To be completely honest, no.'

'Oxford, or History and English?'

'Maybe all of it? I don't know.'

She leaned her head back against the wall, so that she was looking down the length of her face at Zoe. At this angle her eyes were mere cracks, the lightly freckled bones of her face prominent, like her brother's.

'I find it difficult not to feel like a failure there, all the time.'

'Why would you feel that?'

'I feel stupider than everyone. Less informed, less articulate. Less – fluent. I don't think I'm made for a place like that.' She looked into the bottom of her glass. 'I can tell that my tutors have gleaned that I'm Don Travers's daughter, and are constantly watching for flashes of his brilliance. I can see them watching, and I can see them disappointed when they can't find it. And then relieved, perhaps. Like, even Don Travers can't just wave his genetic wand and produce genius offspring.'

'I really doubt they're thinking that.'

Tree straightened her head.

'I can't ask for pity,' she said. 'It's hardly the worst affliction there is.'

'Do you write?' Zoe asked.

'No. You wouldn't, if you had my father. Way too much pressure.'

'I can imagine.'

'Maybe one of the others will. Nemony's got a writer's eye, I think.'

'And perhaps she'll write about redemption, not damage.'

'Well, then she'll never get published,' she said, grinning. She took a large gulp of wine and winced again. 'In your novel, is it the man who hurts the woman the most, or the other way around?'

Zoe thought for a moment.

'I've never been asked that. I guess in a way it's the man who's the most destroyed, by the end.'

'Aha,' said Tree. 'That's refreshing. I feel like all I ever see in real life is men destroying women.'

She drained her glass, and Zoe tried to enumerate the men in her own life. Her male friends, left over from university. Her past boyfriends and lovers, the men she'd dated recently, the screenwriter, Elias. She'd thought him to be quiet and poetic, but he'd changed with each date, to the point at which she'd been grateful for this week away from London as a way to establish some distance. There was something cruel and hectoring about him, she thought; increasingly she felt that he hated her whenever she expressed an opinion about anything at all. And yet still, she couldn't imagine how he or any of those men could have the power to destroy her. She had a fleeting image of them all as Lilliputians, jumping and fussing around her feet.

'Have you ever had an affair with an older man?' asked Tree. For a terrible moment Zoe thought that she might blush.

'No.'

'How about a married man?'

Her expression friendly and blank, unblinking, as if it was the most normal thing she could have asked. As if she wasn't asking a near-stranger, who happened to have been invited on holiday by her married father.

'No.'

'No,' said Tree. 'I didn't think you were the type. I told Malachy, after you went to bed last night.' She peeled her back away from the wall. 'Well, I guess we should at least try to get some sleep.' She stood and reached out for Zoe's glass, still untouched. 'Thank you for indulging me. Good luck sleeping.'

'Goodnight.'

And she was gone. Zoe stood in the silence Tree had left in her wake, and then she turned, stepped onto her tiny balcony. There was the orchestral roar of insects. Resting her elbows on the rail, she wished she had kept the glass of wine that had been given and then taken away. She felt compromised, she thought, even somehow cheated. And a bit embarrassed too, she supposed, to have been chosen for a companion by the nineteen-year-old in the group. Perhaps that was a clear enough indicator of her standing here, of where the guests and family thought she ranked among them.

Surely that wasn't right, she thought; she might be young but she had been invited here by Don Travers, who had read – had even esteemed – her book. But why, then, had she clearly cared what Tree thought of her – why had it been the university student, in fact, who had directed that conversation, who had held all the authority? Tree had come along and taken Zoe into her confidence with her candour, distracted her with the bizarre rant about rape and Russian soldiers and destruction, got the information she'd wanted – and then left.

And it was humiliating, after all, to be told that she didn't seem the type to have an affair with a married man. It could surely only mean that she didn't seem sexually ambitious, or proficient; that she came across as an innocent, an ingénue, an overgrown schoolgirl with her new leather backpack like a satchel. Or perhaps that wasn't right. Perhaps an ingénue would be ripe for the picking, where she simply came across as dull, too sensible or sexless to seduce or be seduced. She thought again about Elias, his deadpan smile as he watched her getting dressed. She had held her T-shirt up over her breasts and stomach as she searched for her trousers.

'You don't like being seen naked,' he'd said, ignoring her when she protested. 'You're not sensual. You're not at home in your own body.'

Leaving his flat ten minutes later, she'd wished that she had told him that, with the doughy ring of flesh around his navel and the stiff puff of hair at the bottom of his spine, he'd do better to be slightly less at home in his.

And if she wasn't sensual; if she wasn't at home in her body, and it was an awkward body, all squares and straight lines and thick edges; if she wasn't the type to seduce an older man; if she didn't give herself over to Elias's fast and insistent manoeuvres, or gasp with pleasure as he seemed to expect; well, she still felt all the things that a woman and a body and skin and flesh can feel. She felt it all.

N

Tree and Malachy weren't twins, but they might as well have been. They were born eleven months apart and they were dedicated to each other. They spoke the same language, had the same humour, loved all the same things. I don't think I ever knew them to argue, though they must have done – each as obstinate as the other, each governed by an apparently immutable conviction in their own actions. And yet that isn't to say they were the same. Malachy spoke much less than Tree, though no one could have thought that Tree spoke for him. His energy was far more contained, a tightly sprung coil; hers was too much for people sometimes, I saw that it could be almost alarming. And I think life appeared more simply to Malachy: a straight path, so that he always seemed to see the destination clearly. Tree could become distracted; she could pour her considerable energy and purity of vision into what ended up being merely a detour. It cost her.

I got the sense that everyone was half in love with them, but I'm also aware now that I was never the best judge. I am clear-eyed enough, I think, about their faults – but perhaps I inflate their strengths. I have seen a look pass over people's faces when I've talked about Tree and Malachy, and Etta too; forbearance in some, irritation in others. Their private conviction that my siblings can't have been as exceptional as I credit them with having been.

But were they really not, I think, even as I try to see clearly. Can I really have invented it all? That final summer at Frantoio was the closest I ever came to being ashamed of them; and even then, disillusioned and disenfranchised as I felt for the first time, I still believed that they were made of something different from everyone else. The roll call of great people who filled the house, the philosophers and artists and pianists and Pulitzer winners – they were always cut from a drabber and coarser cloth.

Krish wasn't drab. As soon as he arrived that summer, he was a force of energy in the house. He joined the breakfast table early on his first day. I waited impatiently for him to eat his muesli and then I led him to the swimming pool and persuaded him to swim with me, dark and cold as the water was at that time of day. When he told me to get out of the pool, I listened; he flung a towel at me, then he marched through the garden towards the kitchen, his own wet towel slung over his shoulders, and giddily I followed.

Guests were usually unwelcome in the kitchen. We had had two middle-aged German sisters to stay earlier that summer – thin, white-blonde, giggling women we found immeasurably foolish. On their first night they announced that they'd provide lunch one day by way of thank you for the invitation to Frantoio. My mother demurred, my father demurred; they insisted, my mother demurred still further, my father lost interest and we all looked on, appalled, as they continued to insist. It was the least they could do, they said. They'd enjoy it, they'd love to think that my mother could take a break. She became silent and they seemed to take this as agreement, even as we all knew that she was at her most furious.

And of course, she didn't take a break. As they bustled their way around the kitchen the morning of their lunch, my mother stood by the worktop in the corner, watching them wordlessly as she started early preparations for dinner. Etta and I sat on the kitchen floor together, watching too, barely speaking. Their discomfort was palpable and delicious to me. When lunchtime approached, my mother started to look at her watch. Of course they hadn't managed to prepare a meal for sixteen people in time; only she knew how to do that. Eventually we all ate, an hour and a half late, and the sisters giggled less than usual and I don't think that we or my mother spoke another word to them for the rest of their stay. 'They won't be making lunch again in a hurry,' said Etta that afternoon as she placed a stack of dirty plates on the worktop, and when we laughed my mother shook her head. 'Don't be unkind,' she said, 'Kindness Is King,' but as she turned to the sink I am sure I saw her smile. Which was cruel, I suppose – all of it, really – except that I gleaned, only many years later, that the younger of the sisters had enjoyed a stint as one of my father's closer acquaintances. Another hidden crack in the floorboards I tramped on.

Krish was different. He was allowed in. That morning, I followed him into the kitchen and he sat at the table and my mother made him coffee and placed it in front of him and he talked and she listened. I don't remember what he talked about, but it was as if she understood his language better than she did other people's. She nodded and smiled and even laughed as she worked on lunch, topping up his coffee every now and again. At some point he left to get dressed, and when he came back and asked for her groceries list she gave it to him, willingly; she even added a few items. 'Come on,' he said to me, and I followed him out of the house and past the table, where Tree and Malachy and Etta and Alice were still eating their breakfast. With pride I got into his car, and I didn't even mind when Timothy joined us, sitting in the back of the car with his scratchy old rabbit in his lap.

With Krish there, I found it easier to forget what Etta had said in the Fort. Her imagination had run away with her; it had been an odd kind of day, we had needed a change of scene and company. My mother was fine, she was happy. She wasn't ill anymore, the treatment had worked, she wasn't lonely and my father wasn't going to leave her. If she was quiet – if she didn't laugh and opine endlessly like the other grown-ups, or linger with them as they sat drinking coffee and *digestivi* long after lunch had finished – that was only because she didn't want to. She didn't like those things, and besides, she was too busy to sit around. She, too, was made from a different cloth. You only needed the briefest grasp of her background to understand that.

When I was eight or nine, my class at school was assigned a project by our history teacher. We had to interview an older relative, an aunt or uncle or grandparent, about their childhood – what they ate, what transport they used, where they lived, how many siblings they had. The scaffolding of their youth. Of course, the project was really about change; it was about comparing our own time with one essentially expired, and in the comparison it was ultimately about privilege. How lucky we are now, the conclusion was pre-programmed to be. How easy we have it.

I didn't have any paternal grandparents, aunts or uncles; my father was an only child and fifty when I was born, his parents already long dead. My mother's might still have been alive, but that was immaterial since they weren't in contact with her, weren't in any case contactable in any practical sense, and presumably didn't even know of my existence. My father was in the middle of writing *Bones*, the novel that turned out to be his least successful though it took him the longest, and was therefore far too busy to talk. And so, taking his Dictaphone, a thrillingly official-seeming bit of equipment, I interviewed my mother.

My questions were not interesting. I remember vividly how curious I was, and I don't think that I was an unimaginative child; how disappointing, then, to dig out that school project many years later and find that instead of asking, as I might now, *Did you fear the outside world?* or *Did you know about space travel?* I asked only the most literal of questions. What did she eat for breakfast, what subjects was she taught, how many siblings did she have, what was her most common means of transport, what time did she wake up and what time did she go to bed? Still, the answers – *bran with cream; scripture and what your teachers might call domestic and agricultural sciences; eleven, though two were stillborn; the wagon; five o'clock; six o'clock* – couldn't fail to paint a sufficiently unusual picture that my teacher asked me if she might come in and talk to the class.

I never passed on that request. My mother had been paralysed by the Dictaphone alone. She'd flushed and stammered, become muddled, so that what might have been a fifteen-minute interview took up over an hour of tape. She would never have agreed to come and talk about herself to a room full of people, never mind that they were schoolchildren.

It was many years later, when my father came to sell our family home, that I found the tape, sorting through boxes of my old schoolwork and reports. I sat down against the wall of my old bedroom – a twenty-year-old woman, surrounded by undeveloped camera films and Polly Pockets and old diaries, all the defunct detritus of my childhood – and closed my eyes to listen.

A buzzing, at first, a rumbling background whir; the clunk of a glass being placed on a surface close by. My voice, piping and stupidly well-spoken, stating the time and date. And then my mother.

Do I talk into this bit?

No, just talk to me normally. OK, what did you wear to school?

Oh … A dress, usually. We didn't go to school.

Did you have a weekend job?

No, not a weekend – well, there were jobs … We didn't have weekends, exactly.

Did you hear the news on the radio or the television?

Oh – I don't recall. We didn't have a television. I don't think I heard a radio.

Did you have a pet?

I suppose the chickens were my favourites.

That's not a pet, Ma.

She sounded so young. And indeed, she would only have been thirty-eight or so: a mother of four, the keeper of a large household, a woman who at the age of nineteen had left her life and family behind for a man she didn't even know. Who within a few months had married a second unknown man, in a city almost 4,000 miles from home.

And yet that hesitant voice, barely audible. Those bungled and halting answers, so that I could hardly bear to listen.

What did you do for entertainment or comfort?

What do you mean?

Well, what did you do when you were bored, or ill? Or
  lonely?

It was excruciating now, to hear the impatience in my young
voice. How roughly and quickly I spoke, how imperiously.

There were long pauses before all of the answers on that
tape, but here the silence stretched on and on. The grand-
father clock chimed twice, waiting for her answer. I sighed,
grandly. The sound of paper rustling. Something heavy being
lifted and replaced; another sigh.

We were too busy to be any of those things, she said eventually. She was speaking so softly by then that it was hard to
make out the words. *We were too tired to be lonely.*

That's when I switched the tape off, and threw it away.

That's what comes back to me now, when I think of our
last summer at Frantoio.

In the supermarket, Krish gave me a list of items and then set
a timer on his watch – a smooth, liquid-looking thing with a
caramel face and glossy walnut straps.

'Ten items, ten minutes. I'll give you five thousand lire if
you can do it. Go!'

I sprinted down the aisles. I knocked things over and
righted them. I became stalled behind an elderly couple in
the freezer section and sighed loudly, tapping one foot on
the ground, while they reached shakily into the very corner

of the exact freezer I needed to access. The stress was exhilarating.

Ten minutes for ten items wasn't enough time, for a
ten-year-old. It was thirteen and a half by the time I found
Krish again, picking out cooking chocolate with Timothy by
his side.

'Not bad, my friend,' Krish said, breaking off a piece of
chocolate from one of the bars in his hand and holding it out
towards me. I took it hesitantly, wondering if it was permitted
to eat something before you'd paid for it. The chocolate was
almost black, and very bitter. 'But you don't get the five thousand lire.'

'Can I try again?' I asked, breath still ragged in my
chest.

'Not enough items left. But I tell you what. If you track
down icing sugar, you can have four thousand. I can't find it
anywhere.'

He gave me the money, though I didn't find the sugar –
and some to Timothy too, which I thought undermined the
whole thing. Still, I felt good as we travelled back to Frantoio,
the windows wound down, hot air blasting into my face, a
paper bag filled with sweets in my lap and several leftover lire
sitting quiet and still in my shorts pocket.

For a good few hours I had forgotten all about the letter.
I didn't remember it until the car burst onto the gravel at
Frantoio and I glimpsed a flash of colour through the hedge
alongside the driveway: Etta and Alice, on their way to the
pool, I imagined, to lie interminably in the glare of the sun.

I had sat with them in our gloomy bedroom the afternoon before, the same haunting ballad on repeat in the background, as together they'd composed it.

We have reason to believe you're in trouble. Please know that if you show this to anyone we will know. We know everything as we have eyes and ears everywhere. As you will know the island of Sicily is run by Mafia and many of these people are close associates of ourselves. Who owe us favours and will be only too happy to share information with us if they hear of anything untoward. We have them to thank for delivering this very letter.

Luckily for you we will not tell anyone about the terrible thing you have done, as long as you leave Sicily IMMEDIATELY. We know you have the money and wherewithal to fly home from Sicily now. We strongly advise you to act in accordance with the instructions contained herein hereupon reading this. Only then can you maintain the good reputation you pretend to deserve. Otherwise REST ASSURED: your secrets will out and your job and marriage will be in trouble not just the reputation already mentioned.

Lastly do not try to find us, we are everywhere.

I had lain on the floor beside them as they'd written it, Alice's right knee jogging up and down without pause beside my head. She'd let me try her bracelets on; I'd turned my wrist over, admired the beads and plaited threads. And in the locked half-dark of the bedroom, pulled for those few hours into Alice and Etta's confidence, I had not doubted the letter's necessity and ingenuity. It was as if I too had come under a spell.

Now it struck me as a reckless idea, and naive. Tuva wouldn't believe that anyone but we had written a letter like that. She would show it to Krish, they'd show my father. I wished that I hadn't told them about my father and Tuva in the garden. Their strange, loaded not-quite-embrace. I had embellished the details – to impress Alice or validate myself, somehow, to Etta – and now I couldn't go back.

I closed the car door behind me and watched Krish as he unloaded bag after bag of shopping from the boot. The lire sat there in my pocket; the bag of sweets hung from my hand. That settled it, I thought. I would have to make them destroy the letter, not only because it was reckless, but because I couldn't do that to Krish. He was my friend.

I left the driveway and made my way grimly towards the swimming pool to confront them. They were lying there already, sharp-tongued lizards on their loungers. I stood beside Etta, took a breath.

'We mustn't deliver that letter,' I said, and Etta pushed herself up onto her elbows. She eyed me over her sunglasses.

'Duh,' she said finally. 'It wasn't for sending. It was just a purging exercise.'

She pushed her sunglasses back up her nose and lay back down.

'A what?'

'A purging exercise,' said Alice, not even bothering to open her eyes. 'We do them at school when someone's been a real bitch. It's just a way of getting your feelings out. We never actually send the letters.'

I stood there staring at them, willing one of them to bother to open their eyes and look at me. We had sat there in that room, all together; for once, they had included me. They'd pulled me into their furtive scheme, and hadn't even seen fit to tell me the most important thing about it.

I turned to the pool, where a dragonfly skated. I would never understand them, I thought, pulling my T-shirt over my head. I would never be like them. I glanced back at Etta, lying there smugly in her sunglasses. Even Alice seemed in that moment to have lost her allure. I held my nose and hurled myself into the pool, and hoped that the radius of my splash would be large enough to get them.

Z

Somehow, Zoe had agreed over dinner to visit a Roman villa in the morning, with the other women.

Don had put her forward, having overheard Faye and Tuva discussing the extraordinary mosaics at the Villa Romana del Casale. Zoe had pretended to have heard of the villa, though in fact all the classical sites she'd read about in her guidebook had merged into one as soon as she'd set the book aside.

Still, she had agreed to join them. If nothing else, she'd thought at the time that it would be interesting to spend the time with Magda and Faye and Tuva. She regretted it bitterly in the morning, waking after only four hours' sleep to the alarm she'd had to set. And, facing the prospect of a long drive and a ponderous slog around the site, trying to deduce even a scrap of truth or life or meaning out of *mosaics*, of all things – which seemed to her to be even more oblique and unpromising than the hot stumps of ruins – she felt furious. Furious with Tree, whose swift bullet of a visit to her room had left her so wired that she'd been unable to sleep until past four that morning. Furious with the women for having arranged something educational on holiday, so that she had felt compelled to feign interest. And, ultimately, furious with herself, for that compulsion to prove her curiosity, her culture. When would she grow out of that, she wondered; would she ever? Would she continue to feel beholden to others, to fail to make her own decisions, as if she'd never grown up at all? When Don had asked Toby Dornan if he'd be joining the women, Toby had simply said that he couldn't, since he would be working. It never would have occurred to her to say that, to have felt so little compulsion to play ball. And so here she was, trying to revive a face both drawn and bloated from yet another tortured night's sleep, clumsily hurrying because she was already late, already keeping those strangers waiting. And she felt a fresh stab of fury with her parents then too, for the bitter tandem diatribe that had resulted in all these endless, fitful nights.

It turned out that none of them seemed very happy to be going. Tuva drove. She wore several bracelets, which jangled every time she changed gear. When this happened Faye exhaled, loudly. She was formidably reserved; she gave only the barest of responses when spoken to. Even Magda was quiet. She sat in the back beside Zoe, resting her head against the seat as if asleep behind her sunglasses, and when Tuva asked her a question she held a hand up and said she'd have to be excused from speaking for just a moment; last night's grappa hadn't agreed with her. Tuva's questions continued, focusing on Zoe instead, and appeared to be motivated not by any kind of interest in her answers but by an aggressive, dogged kind of social propriety. Where do you live, Zoe? And what do you do for work, aside from writing? How large is the company, where are the offices, do you enjoy it, how long have you worked there, and on and on as the dry Sicilian plains whizzed past.

But in the cool, hushed light of the Roman villa all the bitterness of the morning slipped away. Zoe drifted away from the other women. She wandered alone, calmed by the church-like echo of murmurs and footsteps against stone, the muddy espresso she'd drunk at the site's entrance working itself into her bloodstream. Her irritation and weariness dissolved, all that churlish chafing. Visiting a place like this wasn't dully educational. The mosaics weren't oblique; they were vivid and extraordinary, the co-existence of permanence and decay. Don had spoken to her of human violence, of corruption by ancient tyrants and modern Mafia – but couldn't he also have meant the violence of time, she thought now, the relentless and brutal corruption of obsoletion? She was struck then by an image of Lydia, her stillness at the far end of the table as everyone had waited for Krishna's car to approach. The visible weariness in her face, in her silence. An elderly woman who could hardly be a day past forty.

Magda and Tuva stood a little ahead, and Zoe stalled to let them move on. She didn't want to talk to anyone, not when she finally felt as if her mind was working again. She leaned forward to examine a charging bull with human figures before it. They wore tunics, and were either stabbing the bull with staffs or pulling it on ropes, she couldn't quite tell. The artistry was both extraordinarily good and quite bad, even silly; the human faces were squiffy, the proportions not quite right. How noble and pathetic it all was. How admirable and foolish and touching, the smallness of human endeavour.

'The tiger's my favourite,' said Faye, appearing beside her. Zoe had seen her on television, doing just this: laconically flirty, cut-glass commentary; khaki shirt and linen shorts; hand combing through leonine hair. 'She's so commanding, such a beast, and she's a mother too; look at her breasts.'

She turned, waiting, and Zoe blinked.

'Right,' she said.

'She's nursing.'

'Oh yes.'

'You want her to break free from her harness, don't you? And sink her teeth into the little squirts trying to restrain her.'

'I'd say she's got the odds on her side,' said Zoe. 'She's twice their size.'

'She's a mother,' Faye said again, gazing furiously at the tiger's breasts. The sides of her mouth drawn down, the off-hand sexiness all gone.

Magda and Tuva were waiting for them in the next room. It was called, a sign explained, the Chamber of the Ten Maidens on account of its magnificent floor mosaic, which portrayed nine and a half lissom, almost-naked women, throwing balls and holding weights.

'We need you, Faye,' said Magda. 'Our tour guide. Who are these irresistible creatures?'

'They call this one the Bikini Girls,' said Faye. 'Its real name is the Coronation of the Winner, and it's one of the only classical depictions we have of women competing, or even just playing sports. Achieving something. And people call it the fucking Bikini Girls.'

'I'd rather die than play sports in a bikini,' said Zoe, and she felt a flutter of pleasure when the others laughed.

'Oh, traumatic,' said Magda. 'Though these young ladies don't seem too shy about it.'

She and Faye drifted from the room, and as they did Tuva turned to Zoe, leaning in conspiratorially. She smelled of something crisp and fresh like fennel.

'I'd say they're positively coy, compared to some young women.'

She smiled, cat-like.

'Wouldn't you?'

They stopped for lunch on the way back from the villa: tomato salad and sardines and oily focaccia in a near-empty restaurant on a yellow piazza that was blanched almost white in the midday heat. The bright scent of basil leaves, too bright; yellow wine, the hot smoke from Magda's cigarettes. Afterwards, Zoe slept in the back of the car. The silvery jangle of Tuva's bracelets drifted in and out of her dreams.

She awoke as the car pulled into the driveway at Frantoio, and over the crackling of insects and of gravel under tyres there was the steady distant thud of a beat.

'A party in our absence,' cried Magda, as they unfolded themselves from the car. 'Beastly creatures!'

'For God's sake,' said Tuva. 'Don in the middle of a crisis with this wretched manuscript, and they think it's OK to make a din like this.'

She dropped the car key, muttered an expletive as she bent quickly to collect it from the gravel, grasping it too quickly and dropping it again. She was genuinely stressed, Zoe thought. As if the manuscript and the crisis were her own.

The music was coming from the pool, cut off from the rest of the garden by hedges and a gate, so that when they entered the poolside they took the whole scene in at once: three semi-naked, Italian-looking teenagers sitting at the pool's edge with Malachy, their legs in the water; the youngest kids doing handstands in the shallow end; Etta and Alice, sitting up from their sun loungers and hiding wine glasses; Krishna and Toby Dornan, playing a sort of tennis with plastic bats and a ball, cigarettes in their free hands; and the inane, repetitive beat of trashy club music pulsing from a hi-fi just out of reach of the kids' splashes. The paving was littered with pitchers of wine and cartons of cigarettes and large packets of cheap crisps.

The entire scene was so unsophisticated, so unglamorously sexy and perfectly at odds with what Zoe had envisaged for a holiday at Don's villa, that she felt as if she might still be asleep.

'Welcome back!' cried Tree, her face and neck emerging white from the dark water; and as she rose out of the pool she was spectacular, long and sylph-like and naked but for a pair of gingham bikini bottoms. Her hair even longer with water. She wrung it with one hand, and Zoe had the peculiar sense, then, that the entire scene revolved around that one gesture. The black hair, heavy as wet linen; the deft motion of her hand as she twisted and wrung; the weight of the water as it struck the stone. The bare inevitability of gravity. She heard Elias's words, clear in her mind: *You're not sensual. You're not at home in your own body.*

'What did I say about the Bikini Girls?' Tuva muttered, leaning in again as she had at the Roman villa, and Zoe stepped away.

'How was your trip?' asked Tree, largely to Magda. 'Have some wine – we've had too much. Only because we missed you.'

'No you didn't, you wicked thing,' said Magda. 'I'll have a glass, and then I'm leaving you young people to it. Darling, you're wonderfully naked.'

'It's Lucia's influence,' she said, gesturing towards the beautiful Italians by the pool. The girl was topless, tiny elegant breasts above a flat brown stomach. As Zoe looked at her, all the while trying not to look too carefully, she could only think that her own breasts would have sat there, too boxy; her nipples were too large; she wouldn't have looked elegant at all, but indecent, embarrassing, on display.

In fact, she thought, everything about her in that moment – she could just imagine how she looked standing there fully clothed with her knapsack, face composed in an encouraging beam to try to show that she was neither prude, nor voyeur, nor envious spectator – felt paradoxically indecent and embarrassing and on display.

'I've gone European,' Tree was telling Magda.

'Is that what they call it?' said Tuva, and Tree smiled.

'Too shy, Tuva?' She blinked. 'Won't you have a swim?'

'Not right now. I need to check on your father – did you think about the fact that he must be able to hear this from his desk?'

'God forbid,' said Tree, and she turned and walked to the pool's edge and sat down beside Malachy. Zoe watched the faces of the Italian boys as they watched Tree approach; she saw Krishna and Toby look swiftly and busily away, concentrating afresh on their game; she watched Malachy press a towel to Tree's hands to dry them, hand her a cigarette, light it.

What a thing, to be looked at like that. It was hard not to feel some envy – but Zoe felt admiration, too, for Tree's immaculate boldness. It radiated. Zoe might never have that body but she, too, could have something of the boldness, if she wanted. If she just claimed it.

She thought of Tree's words – 'All I ever see is men destroying women' – and smiled. Men were mere comets in Tree's orbit, she a whole planet. Surely she knew that.

The atmosphere at dinner that evening was much more relaxed than it had been so far. When Zoe had left the poolside she'd spent the rest of the afternoon stretched out on her bed, reading. She had washed and dressed with care, tied her hair back, painted her lips red like Magda's, and in the cooler calm of evening she felt refreshed and clean and emboldened.

She sat again at Don's end of the table, but the pressure of his presence was diffused by the others. Toby, who had seemed intimidatingly terse and remote until now, was rendered more ordinary and approachable by an afternoon of drinking. Magda had apparently taken a liking to Zoe after their trip to the Roman villa, and was warm and familiar. Krishna was warm too, teasing Zoe with the same casual, fraternal intimacy with which she saw him treat everyone. And so she found herself easy and articulate, no longer indecent or embarrassing or on display, and released from the stricture of constantly watching her words. She laughed along with the others. She even made them laugh, noticing with a little pleasure that the other, much quieter end of the table looked over whenever this happened.

'This Roman villa sounds fascinating,' Toby said, and Zoe noticed that he had said 'fascinating' several times. His elbow had slipped from the table once, causing him to right himself with a clumsy jerking motion. These things made Zoe feel something like fondness. 'I've read about the mosaics – it's the largest collection in the world, isn't it?'

'One of them,' said Don.

'I'm annoyed I had to miss it,' Toby said. 'These edits have come at a bad time.'

'Well,' said Zoe, 'you were of course terribly hard at work when we got back.'

She smiled, to show that it was a joke. For just a moment she worried that she had overstepped a mark, but he shrugged and Magda cackled.

'This one has a wicked tongue,' she said. 'Where did you find her, Don?'

'Zoe's going to be very famous,' Don said, and Zoe busied herself passing a bowl of salad to Krishna. A jolt of joy and something more dangerous than joy went through her; she tried to keep it from showing in her face. She could feel them looking at her.

'I won't forget to have a copy of your book sent to Boyd,' said Magda, and Don nodded.

'It'll be great on the stage. I'm sure it will be a film too – it's only a matter of time.'

'What's it about?' asked Krishna. Zoe took a breath, ready to launch into her laboured précis, but Toby spoke first.

'It's a "Lives of Quiet Desperation" novel.'

'A what?'

'Oh, it's a term my friend Rudy coined.'

'Rudy Becker,' said Don, and Toby nodded. 'But he didn't coin it, of course. It's a Thoreau aphorism: *the mass of men lead lives of quiet desperation.*'

'Ah, Thoreau,' he said quickly. 'Yes, of course. But as Rudy points out, it defines a certain kind of novel very well. The "Lives of Quiet Desperation" novel. You know the one – a small handful of suffering characters, doing their best to find their way through the darkness. Plenty of self-flagellation and yearning.'

Zoe's fingers curled into her palms, nails sharp. She thought of her characters, of the diligence with which she'd borne testament to their pain and, yes, she supposed their yearning. It's envy, she thought, watching Toby's face as he took a large sip of his wine, a base and obvious barb in response to her teasing; and yet even as she was thinking this she saw her characters, suddenly, for what they surely were: tired tropes. And how pathetically earnest, her testimony to their pain.

She had only read one thing by Toby: 'Midas', a sparse, wry short story in which a young man trudges around London wearing a coat. He is obsessed with the coat. He has lost his job, his girlfriend has broken up with him, he's struggling with urinary incontinence; and yet he becomes convinced that his coat is a totem, a lucky charm of some kind protecting him from further harm, and that if he removes it he will lose everything. Among other things, it becomes soaked with urine. Only now as Zoe thought of it did she see the meaning of the story's title. Of course, he literally made everything golden.

It was a dry, brilliant little story. Tight, precise sentences like neatly stacked cubes. She would never have dreamt up an apparently foolish premise like that and been able to turn it into something of literary worth, she thought now. She would never have paired incontinence with monomaniacal obsession. Nor would she have made the object of obsession a coat. Its bathos was playful and assured, its mythic undercurrents lightly worn. In an instant, her novel struck her as girlish, basic and overblown, the next step developmentally from a teenager's journal.

She must not have kept the desolation from her face because he added quickly, 'It's been successful. You must be very pleased.'

There were a few beats of silence.

'I'll be sure to read it,' Krishna said, and Zoe knew that he wouldn't.

'Who doesn't love some quiet desperation,' said Magda. 'It's certainly the genre du jour in the theatre.'

'And is Rudy still writing for the *LRB*, Toby?' asked Don, and the conversation moved on.

Zoe ate in silence, no longer tasting the food, aware already of the particular shape her insomnia would take tonight. It would take hours, to disentangle everything packed into those three or four casual sentences. She would nurse her new hatred for Toby and all the young male writers like him, their artful little stories squeezed of warmth – even as she knew that lack of warmth was a feeble criticism, not even necessarily true. She would explore the fear, already creeping around her now as she ate, that Don's view of her talent might be swayed by Toby's barb, that he might be embarrassed by his original conviction in her work, and be moved to revise it – and that, if Toby dismissed her novel so easily, others of literary worth and taste must too. And more than any of that, she would come back, time and again, turning this way and that in the hot, crumpled bed, to the devastating suspicion that his indictment might be right.

The conversation crackled again into laughter, but she took no pleasure now when she saw Lydia and Faye and Tuva look swiftly over. She watched Toby's curling smile as he repeated something about an actress they all seemed to know, and heard Don laugh afresh. No one seemed to mind the repetition, or that Toby leaned back in his chair, swinging it gently back and forth in the way a child does. Probably no one had noticed the dark wicks above his lip, little winged stains from his red wine like a devil's horns.

His ease here was palpable. He belonged in this terrain. Intimately he knew these people's language, the poems they quoted and wines they drank and plays they'd seen. This holiday wasn't his big break, his grand entrance; he was already enmeshed in Don's network. She could guess exactly the kind of parents he'd have: liberal, subtly wealthy, fearsomely educated. She knew exactly the conversations and debates that would have encircled the dinner table when Toby was a boy, moulding and kneading and honing him as he grew, all so that he could be the kind of person who could swing casually in a chair while talking to Don Travers. Who needn't be embarrassed, for spewing out a Thoreau aphorism without knowing its provenance.

She finished her food, laid the spent cutlery down carefully on her plate, at the correct angle. It was a sequestered world, she thought, all of it. It was fenced off. There was a gate separating her from the rest of them, and it didn't just swing open for people like her, like it did for Toby. Those lunches at the Garrick, being invited out here to Sicily – the leather knapsack, the sales figures – none of it, she could see, was enough.

N

If Krish's arrival brought energy into the house, I began to see that it brought other, less welcome changes too. Tuva – acting, as she'd always done, as a self-appointed social delegate for my parents – organised a fresh influx of lunch and dinner guests, which I imagined at the time to be largely for Krish's sake. The parties were long and very boring for us; and whereas in the past I'd had the pleasure at their end of dissecting and bemoaning the guests with my siblings – had they smelled the breath on the old professor with the long thumbnails, was the Salvadorean woman an alcoholic, wasn't the countess exactly the type to keep children locked up in some wing of her castle – in our new more disparate formations this didn't happen.

Perhaps it was unusual that we had ever discussed these things. I've never really worked out whether our constant analysis of people was normal for children or an inevitable inheritance from our father, whose appetite for it was so cold and keen, who did it with such quick and dazzling alacrity. I've occasionally watched someone carve a chicken – someone who really knows what they're doing with the knife, so that the bones are almost licked clean – and thought of him.

The other changes in the house were subtler but no easier to ignore than that sudden relay of parties. Tree paid too much attention, too visibly, to Krish. Perhaps I was too young to recognise this quite for what it was, but I understood that it wasn't appropriate, it wasn't well judged. I didn't like to see her try to court someone. She, who never seemed to me to have to change herself for anyone. I noticed clearly Tuva's irritation, as well as the interest it piqued in our other guests, and found myself pleading inwardly with Tree to hold back. Worse, I became aware that my mother felt the same way. Small things that no one but our family would have noticed: the low, repeated clearing of her throat when Tree addressed Krish, yet again. Tidying away the plates a little more loudly, as if she could redirect people's attention. I hated to see these efforts from my mother, whom unconsciously I'd always considered to operate outside social nuance.

I began to watch Malachy with new eyes too, wondering what he made of it, and I noticed now where he looked, the easy and assured interest he paid to girls and even women, even those as unreachably adult to me as Faye. I hadn't paid enough attention, I thought. At some point, my focus absorbed elsewhere, I had missed some crucial and seismic change.

I wasn't oblivious to sex. I don't think I had ever spent much time thinking about it as a physical act – I knew little more about that than what I'd been taught in biology – but I was aware of and intrigued by it as an impulse, as most children are. And yet, until that summer, I had never imagined its maleficence. Now I became aware – tenuously, and without recourse to words – that it was a governing force, quite real and incredibly powerful, and that it could make people do things they wouldn't usually do. I could see, I suppose, that my siblings had each stepped off a launch pad into new water. They were busy swimming there. I was still standing blithely on the launch pad, thinking it the whole world.

When I thought of that, I became immensely sad and also jealous. I felt a prudish horror that Tree and Malachy might already have lost their virginities. Jealously I noticed the lovely curves of Tree's long body under her clothes; primly, I registered how scant those clothes always were, mere slips and scraps of things. I had always assumed Malachy to be the very handsomest of boys, something that had given me great pride – the same innocent, boastful pride I felt when he and the others did well in sports or their studies. Now it scared me. I saw that I had no claim over his beauty, it was nothing to do with me. It was something for other girls and women to notice and love and claim as their own. In that way, my brother's and sister's allure compromised us. It invited the world in.

*

We had always been rude to Tuva. We were probably rude to many of my father's guests, but none in the easy and guiltless manner in which we were rude to her. It was a time-honoured tradition, something we considered our prerogative, given the meddling parental tone she took. If she had always over-stepped certain marks with us, we could naturally, with a clear conscience, overstep in return. But the lunch party with the mussels was different from anything that had come before.

Etta set the tone, from the outset. When Tuva held forth, yet again, about her speed-skating past – we had several new lunch guests she must have been keen to impress – Etta clinked her glass with a fork, as if gathering silence for a toast. The adults paused, their attention momentarily held. When they saw that it was only a thirteen-year-old child, some resumed their conversation, perhaps imagining it a mistake, but not everyone. There were enough of them still listening when Etta announced, in a ridiculous voice with a Swedish lilt just like Tuva's, her hand held sentimentally to her chest, chin lifted in the exact way Tuva lifted hers, 'Ladies and gentlemen, have you ever heard about all the *exceptional* competitions I have won?' She always was brilliant at imper-sonations.

'Etta,' my mother hissed. Krish smiled faintly, though I wasn't sure he looked pleased. I watched my father resume his conversation as if nothing had happened, but I knew well enough the subtle shape of fury in his features. Tree and Malachy's eyes had widened when Etta spoke. They looked impressed.

The next thing was a game Alice started, which at first didn't seem wildly worse than anything we'd done before. 'Bluuuuuuh,' she'd say loudly, every time Tuva spoke. But then Etta joined her, and finally even Timothy, whom we'd always dismissed entirely as a weed but who must have been caught up in the thrill of it all. Sitting together, a wild troop at the far end of the table, their groaning became louder and louder. No one stopped them. Alice's mother was at the other end of the table, with my father. My mother, talking to a half-deaf old woman whom Tuva had seated next to her – as she habitually did the guests no one else would want to be lumped with – could not detach herself fully enough to work out what was happening. But Tuva understood. Every time she opened her mouth to speak, the loud and atonal chorus would start up. It was obnoxious; as a form of intimidation, it lacked any finesse; but its vulgarity seemed wonderful and shocking to me. I could see Tuva struggling to concentrate on what she was saying. I could see how embarrassed she was in front of the grand Sicilian man she sat next to. Of course it was embarrassing, to be so clearly the object of such hatred. I felt only pleasure in that fact, even if it was laced with fear for Etta. She was surely pushing it too far this time.

That fear was soon realised. I was coaxing a mussel from its bed with a spent shell, an involved and sticky business I enjoyed, when I saw something fly above me, and looked up. A mistake, surely, a one-off. But then there was another: a mussel, spongy and lurid, flying through the air across the table towards Tuva. And a bubbling silence from the girls, as they launched one mussel after another. The first five or six missed; if Tuva knew they were landing near her, she did a good impression of not noticing. But then one found its target. Wetly it landed, on her breast.

She stood up, pushing her bowl away.

'You are behaving hideously,' she said.

The table fell silent, and then my father spoke.

'Children, you're embarrassing us all. Leave the table.'

He seldom got involved with us. He seldom intervened in anything we did. Very rarely we found ourselves, individually, the focus of his interest – but it was a detached, forensic kind of interest, and didn't last long.

'You don't like to step on the cracks between the tiles,' he'd observe suddenly, looking up from the kitchen table at home to fix his inky eyes on me. 'Tell me why.' I'd try to tell him, as quickly and efficiently as I could – floundering for words, tense, so tense, as if I'd been asked to speak to a room of strangers – and all the while I'd see him become bored with my response, his thoughts already occupied by something else. The sense that I'd missed something, some vital opportunity that might never present itself again, would haunt me for whole days after.

But his detachment from us did not preclude anger. His fury, when he was forced to notice us, the childish mess of us, was formidable. We all saw it now, sitting there in the flickering shade of the oak tree. Alice stood, looking down at her feet; Timothy's eyes had filled already with tears. But somehow Etta didn't seem to care. Oh, she was glorious, her eyes flashing. She pushed her chair back slowly, staring steadily at Tuva as she stood.

'None of you are coming to Scordia,' Tuva said then, and Etta turned to my father.

That was surely too much. It was the festival in Scordia that night, an annual event in which the whole town dressed in white. We took a large table at our favourite restaurant, we danced afterwards in the square where there was live music, white balloons floating up from every building. We had attended it every year we'd gone to Frantoio, which was every year of my life. To ban Faye's children and Etta from going was unthinkable.

But my father nodded.

'You heard Tuva. Now leave the table. All of you,' he added, turning to me, and when I made to object, he placed his hands on the table and started to raise himself up, as if to stand. 'I said all of you.'

He sat back down and returned to the young man at his side, face rigorously calm, and asked him a question as if nothing at all had happened.

The injustice of it smarted, like I had been slapped. I knew him well enough to know that was the end of it. Even Timothy and Alice, whose mother was staring blankly at her plate, knew his word was the only one that mattered. We walked away as one, making our way to the Fort, disbelief and shame and anger gathering like a storm around us.

*

As far as I knew, Etta's anger towards Tuva was twofold, its extent the same as mine: the historic animosity we'd always nurtured, catalysed by what I'd told her the day before – and then this unprecedented punishment, the diktat over the festival. As an annual event, it was on a par almost with Christmas; it was the apex of every summer. We were, of course, horribly spoilt. We felt the withdrawal of the festival not only as a tremendous loss but an insult, an inexcusable withdrawal of our liberty, out of proportion to any crime we were capable of committing. I am ashamed even now, remembering the depth of our outrage. I have often wondered how our fierce entitlement sat with my mother, once a girl who wore home-sewn clothes and milked cows before breakfast, for whom humility and acceptance were paramount.

I didn't understand yet that there was more to Etta's outrage – that what I had seen in the garden was only one of many moments she had glimpsed. I only pieced that together much later. That summer Etta understood enough, finally, to start questioning our parents' unusual arrangement. They had become lazy, Tuva and my father.

'We'll speak to Mama,' I said in the Fort. 'She'll let us go.'

'No, she won't.'

Etta was pacing angrily, hands in pockets and chin tucked into her chest, the way my father did when his work was going badly. As usual, Timothy was crying. Alice sat glumly by the olive press, her arm around her little brother's shoulder.

I knew that I should think it pathetic that he was crying, but I wanted badly to join him.

'She will.'

'She can't. Tuva's the one in charge.'

She hurled a stone up at the rafters. There was a hurried thud of wings, anxious throaty bleating from the pigeons before they resettled.

'Tuva's a fleck of dirt on the floor compared to your mum,' said Alice, and I found her anger on my mother's behalf – or perhaps her loyalty, the vehemence behind it – too much.

'What's Mama got to do with any of this?' I asked, and a look passed between them.

'Nothing,' said Etta.

'Tuva's gone too far,' said Alice. 'She can't call the shots like this.'

'We need to bring her down, once and for all.'

'Let's write another letter,' said Alice then. 'Saying everything we want to say. Timmy, go and get paper and a pen.'

Timothy ran off, his tears forgotten.

'You're not going to write another letter to Tuva,' I said, and Etta frowned.

'It's just a purging exercise.'

'So you won't send it.'

Etta put her arm around my shoulder then, pulling me close into her body. She hadn't hugged me or held me for a very long time, perhaps years. That wasn't the kind of relationship we had.

'This is bigger than you, Nemo,' she said softly. She was clammy with heat, smelled of sun cream and sweat and herself. 'You're still little. There's a lot you don't understand. You will when you're older, OK?'

I was still smarting from the injustice of being swept up into their crime, and their punishment. To try now to calibrate the gross disparity between Etta's kind voice and gesture on the one hand and her baldly patronising words on the other was too much for me. To my shame, my eyes filled with tears.

'Don't cry,' said Alice, leaning in to tuck my hair behind my ears, and in the smell and heat of her I had the fleeting sense that if I tried I could cross over into her body, I could become her. She took my hand, rolled one of her bracelets over her own until it hung from my wrist.

'Go and find Mama,' said Etta, the sugary kindness already fallen from her voice. She dropped her arm from around my shoulder to take the pen and Barbie-pink paper that Timothy had brought, skidding back into the Fort, but my hand still rested in Alice's.

I didn't go, and Etta let it pass. I suspect she saw the merit of disciples, as we arranged ourselves before the altar of the olive press, cross-legged, she at our head.

'Tuva Brøvig, you're overweight,' she started, writing it in her flamboyantly grown-up cursive. The words were upside down for me as they curled, fluid, from her pen.

'You make us sick,' said Alice.

'Your eyes are revolting,' said Etta, when she had written Alice's words. 'You think they're your greatest asset, but they make you look like a startled, slimy frog.'

'You wear loose, wafty clothing and pretend it's because you're chic, but really it's because your stomach is out of control and you're trying desperately to hide it.'

'With your skinny legs and fat stomach, you're even more like a frog.'

'You shouldn't be allowed to wear a swimming costume.'

'You're so full of yourself.'

I looked from one of them to the other as they took turns, a volley of insults I thought sophisticatedly cruel. And so quick, slowed only by the time it took Etta to write. Beside me Timothy breathed heavily, his bunny in his lap.

'The way you worship Don Travers is pathetic.'

'Women hate you.'

'Everyone hates you.'

'Your husband is way too good for you.'

'He doesn't love you.'

'He's going to cheat on you.'

'You're a show-off.'

'You have cellulite.'

'You're disgusting.'

'You're a slut,' I said loudly, and they looked at me, as shocked as I was.

Until I'd said the word, I hadn't known its meaning. It had simply slid out from between my teeth, and as soon as it had I knew incontrovertibly what it meant, from the sound and feel of it alone.

'Good,' said Etta then, nodding firmly. Alice bumped her shoulder against mine, congratulatory. And so we continued, the air between us thick and electric.

When finally the letter was finished, Etta folded it and, with great ceremony, tore the folded paper into four pieces.

'Ah,' she said. 'Much better.'

'Why did you tear it up?' asked Timothy, but we ignored him, standing and stretching. I watched Alice and Etta as they brushed dust from their shorts, and I looked down at my own legs and did the same.

'What we need now is a swim,' said Etta.

'Shall I fix it?' asked Timothy, but Etta was already tucking the torn pieces under a rock.

'No, Timothy.'

'We need Sellotape!'

He squatted down beside the rock. Etta rolled her eyes at me, a most delicious thing.

'Leave it, Timothy,' I said in the tired voice Etta used. 'It's just a purging exercise.'

'Forget about the letter,' said Alice. 'You can play with Bunny now.'

She threw his rabbit into the corner of the Fort and then she linked arms with Etta and left the Fort and I followed behind. I walked in time to their footsteps, trying to spring up from the balls of my feet as they did. Alice's calves shone, I thought, like polished wood.

I felt different as I walked. I was part of something. I was light, and elated, and powerful.

All of that fell away as I stepped down into the kitchen. My mother stood entirely still before the worktop, her hands on the surface. Her fingers were outspread and taut, like a pianist's poised to play. She stared blankly into the space before her, eyes as wide as a fish's eyes, or a shark's. Her face was fractionally turned, as if she had just heard something behind her, or was listening out for something, or her mind had been caught on the loose thread of a thought. It wasn't a moment of repose, nor even quite stillness, though there wasn't a quiver of movement. The clearest impression I had was of motion arrested, as if someone had pressed pause on a video.

'Mama?' I asked. She didn't move immediately. Then her shoulders dropped a little, and her fingers, and she turned to me.

'Nemony,' she said, as if to herself. And she was my mother again, quiet efficiency in low, square movements, lifting and lowering a tower of stacked lunch plates into soapy water, returning to the worktop, wiping her hands dry on her apron. She took a paper bag and upturned it. Fuchsia-pink radishes rolled and bounced into a dish.

'Can I have some water, Mama?' I asked, but she was silent, slicing the radishes against a mandolin.

'Can I help you, Mama?'

She laid down the mandolin, swiped the paper-thin slices into a bowl.

112

'Is that a salad?' I asked, laboriously cheerful. 'Mama. What are you doing with the radishes?'

'You children will have to eat something for dinner,' she said. 'Since you're not going to the festival.'

'Etta doesn't like radishes,' I said, to divert her from the topic of the festival, and she closed her eyes, her body still again. 'Mama,' I said desperately. Her motionless face was terrible.

'What?'

'Etta doesn't like radishes,' I repeated, and she opened her eyes.

'It doesn't matter what she likes. She'll eat what she gets.' She was furiously angry, I thought. 'You weren't brought up to be spoilt.'

She shook her head and looked down into the salad, and I thought that she might cry. I waited, appalled. I had seen countless women cry: friends of my father's who had drunk too much wine and become maudlin, or come to our house to confide in him after a break-up or divorce or bereavement. But just as women and children cried, men and my mother didn't.

She shook her head again and turned to take a chicken from the fridge, laying it down on the worktop. The slap of its loose white flesh on the chopping board, the cool click of the scissors as she cut its strings.

'You embarrassed me,' she said finally.

'I didn't do anything.'

'When children behave like that, people look at their mother. I suppose you didn't think of that.'

'But I didn't do anything. I wasn't even part of it.'

'People will think what they choose about the other things. We mustn't mind all that, it can't be changed. But I never wanted anyone to think ill of any of you.'

'Mama,' I said, pleading.

'My children.' She closed her eyes, opened them. 'You four are the only thing I have in this world to be proud of.'

I can still see those words now. I can see the letters, the shapes of the words, as if she hadn't spoken them but had typed and printed them out and laid them down in front of me.

'The only thing,' she repeated, and I ran then from the kitchen, down the stone corridor and up the stairs to the hot and sordid gloom of the bedroom.

Z

By the time Zoe had stopped vomiting, the darkness outside had changed. Violet crept in around the edges. The stars were fewer. Her neck hurt, the tendons of it strained from retching. She didn't look in the mirror because she didn't want to see her face, but she wiped mascara from her eyes and cheeks, and she cleaned her teeth, and then she stepped into the bathtub with the russet stains running down from the overflow and held the showerhead above her. Cool water in her hair and down her neck, down her back.

When she stepped out of the bath she barely dried herself. It would help her in the hot room to let the water cool on her skin. She picked up the dirty white jeans and white blouse from the floor, scrunched them into a ball and put them into her suitcase. She imagined unpacking everything when she got home that evening, washing her clothes and replacing her toiletries into her own bathroom and bedroom. She would do all of that and she imagined that somehow, back in her own bed again, she might really sleep.

The room didn't spin anymore. After all the vomiting, she felt sober and clear and purged. It was a relief to be on her own, and to know that she would go home tonight and stop having to make an effort all the time.

'The trouble is that you feel like an impostor,' Don had said to her after dinner in Scordia. At that point he was sitting alone with her at the table; everyone else had peeled off to dance with the Sicilians in the square. She thought now that it had been the sexiest and most exciting moment of her entire life so far.

Terrible Italian pop music was playing; everyone was drunk, cacophonous and flushed in their white clothes, the alternating disco lights rendering them pink and then blue and then red; and then there was this eagle of a man beside her, one of his long legs resting firmly against hers so that she could barely concentrate on his words. A dramatic change had taken hold of him. He was no longer the paternal, elaborately polite figurehead of refinement she'd come to recognise. She was dizzyingly aware for the first time of all the dangerous, rapacious, incisive power of his brain. Gone was the perambulatory course of his usual conversation, the elegant and fluid and ultimately, she realised now, oppressively boring catalogue of artists and cultural moments and novels and politics and historical events. She was speaking now not to the man she'd met in the London Library, but to the author of his books.

'What do you mean, an impostor?' she asked.

'You know what I mean,' he said, swiping her question

away with a hand, and she nodded. 'You have to learn to stop questioning yourself. It's a symptom of youth, and of your sex too, I'm afraid. You waste crucial time questioning yourself. Gradually you'll learn to stop, and then you'll produce your most powerful work. You can't rush that process, I'm afraid. You'll have to wait and see it out. For most women of talent, like you, it happens in their forties.' He leaned forward a fraction, and smiled darkly. 'That's when you'll get really interesting. I hope I still know you then.' He leaned back, looking around into the crowd, and his leg moved away from hers. 'Now, let's see who's still sober enough to get in a car home.'

He stood and she watched him, needle-sharp and upright as he stepped into the crowd. She didn't see him again after that. He and Tuva and the older houseguests went home. Toby and Krishna and Malachy and some other young men came to join her at the table with bottles of limoncello and tiny glasses, and then Tree joined them, her long hair in plaits that were coming loose.

At some point, Zoe found that Toby's arm was around her shoulder. He pulled her face towards his with one hand.

'I'm kind of fascinated by you,' he said, and she asked why – but it was never satisfying to chase a compliment, she knew that even as she asked. It always evaporated. In Toby's case, he said nothing at all. He made her drink another shot of limoncello, even though the young Sicilians at the table had told them that it was supposed to be sipped.

'I want you.'

'With "quiet desperation"?' she asked, ruefully, but he looked blank.

The next thing she knew they were all back at the villa, in the silky dark water of the pool, and she remembered only snapshots of things from then onwards. Toby kissing her in the pool. All of them dancing, still wet from swimming, on sofas in the dingy games room by the kitchen. Someone telling them to turn off the music, and moving as one back outside, with bottles of wine. The last thing she remembered was Toby's arms around her again, his hands too insistent, and the contempt on his face when she told him she wouldn't go upstairs with him, that she needed to go to her own bed. Then with great relief she had found herself to be arched over the lavatory in her own bathroom, vomiting repeatedly with an odd barking cry like a fox.

Sober now and calm, entirely lighter, she was ready to go back to London and fast-track the maturing process Don had forecast for her. He had been right, she thought, in everything he'd said except for one thing: she wasn't just another of the young women of talent he knew. She wouldn't wait until her forties to stop feeling like an impostor.

She would do it all now, starting by shedding everything worthless in her life. That included her parents' small, mean world. It included her hatred for them, which she saw now as the legacy of their smallness. And it included men like Elias and Toby. She saw their easy insults now for what they were. Fear, nothing else.

Because she was powerful, she had power. Don saw it in

her. Others must too. Leaning over the railing into the brightening dark, she pictured again the sprawling network of lights and beacons he had conjured up for her at the beginning of the week. She had stepped out of her parents' cramped world into this other one, she would transcend their petty limits; she too could spark and flash. She could destroy them all, if she wanted to.

The sky was pink. She closed the doors, and when she lay down on the bed, her hair wet on the pillow and cold around her neck, she realised that she was going to sleep.

N

I remind myself that there was much about that final summer at Frantoio that was happy. Those memories are vivid, when I search them out.

My mother cutting my hair under the fig tree, one quiet afternoon. I remember the bowl of water, its surface shifting as she dipped and removed the comb. Quiet, methodical work, the cool of the water in my hair, the movement of the shade on the grass, the silver of the scissors, the quick blunt snap of their blades by my ears. The sense of her concentration behind me.

Malachy teaching me how to dive, after he had overheard me pleading with Etta. I was aware at every moment that his time was a rare gift, something no one else had the patience to give me, and I kept waiting for it to expire, but it didn't. My nostrils hurt by the end of the afternoon; I was dizzy and sunburnt. My happiness safe inside me.

Tree holding me in her lap at dawn, when the whole household had woken to wave off a particularly well-loved guest, a childhood friend of my father's. We sat in a chair in the kitchen and I pretended to be sleepier than I was, speaking only in croaky murmurs, barely able to open my eyes. In this way I could get away with snuggling into the maternal warmth of her body as I did when I was a much younger child. Her arm around me; her hand, resting lightly on my elbow. The smell of her, the hum of her chest when she spoke.

T

Malachy knew to say nothing. There was comfort simply in the sight of his veined hand on the wheel. The round, prominent wrist bone that sat above his watch. There was comfort even in the watch itself, a scuffed Casio Tree had seen so many times it was almost impossible to notice. But if these things brought flickers of comfort – because it was just about possible to imagine that, if things were at least the same with Malachy, then nothing could be too badly damaged – they were only fleeting. Then dread would rise up again, subsuming everything.

Malachy had tried to stop her. Apparently it had become sufficiently clear, at a certain point in the night, what was going to happen. Clear to him, and therefore clear to everyone there. She groaned quietly, held a hand up over her face, and she felt his concern, felt him glance over at her.

As they approached the sea the first families were already arriving. Malachy had to drive slowly along the final stretch, making way for parents with hampers and inflatables, children in jelly shoes with towels rolled up under their arms. They had slept all night and woken up early and breakfasted. Whereas she had not slept at all, and could taste only the bitter, furry scum of a night of smoking and drinking.

'It's too busy,' he said, and she shook her head.

'It's OK.'

They left the van and walked slowly across the shingle to the very end of the beach, and then they sat down and she buried her face in her arms. She wanted him, now, to say something. It was starting to occur to her that his silence might not be a sign of his understanding, but of the wholly unspeakable nature of what she'd done.

She groaned, again.

'Fuck.'

Still he said nothing, and she tried to imagine a single thing he could say that would make any of it better, but the only thing would be to tell her that she'd imagined it all. It had been a hallucination. Like a child, she indulged a desperate fantasy simply to wish everything away. There was no Krish, he wasn't at Frantoio this summer. Or if he was, she'd drawn the line at flirtation. Or, if she'd crossed that line, Tuva hadn't come downstairs and found them. Or finally, if Tuva had had to find them, by some miracle she wouldn't tell their father, and their father wouldn't tell their mother. But all of those eventualities had already unspooled from the first thread, from the plane that brought Krish to Sicily. If her mother didn't already know, she was perhaps finding out at this very moment, as they sat here on the pebbles with the early sun rising, indomitable, already too hot on their skin.

'This is going to pass,' he said finally.

'He's married. They're married. I did that.'

'Tree, stop.'

'I'm just as bad as her.'

'You're nothing like her.'

She squinted against the sunlight glancing on the water.

'It was awful.'

'Tree.'

'Fuck, Malachy.'

Because it had been awful. It hadn't at all been as she'd anticipated it. In the dull, too-familiar light of the games room, each sobering up a little, it had felt suddenly awkward to look at each other. Impossible, suddenly, to see Krish as anything other than the avuncular figure she'd known for far too long, virtually family. But things had progressed too far by then to stop. At least it might be quick, she had thought when they started – but it hadn't been. It had gone on and on, Krish desensitised from a night of drinking, so that any sensuality or romance or tenderness had been pumped away. Repetitive, mechanical motion. Dull and ugly slapping noises, so that she had become falsely vocal, trying to drown them out. The noises had made her feel like meat, or one of the hollow-eyed girls in the pornographic videos her ex-boyfriend Doug had made her watch with him. And just like in those videos, it had all seemed grossly anatomical, devoid of the thrill of desire that had been building for days and should never have been anything more than just that, desire.

'*Fuck*, Malachy.'

'I know.'

He lit a cigarette, and she reached out for a drag. Her hand was shaking, the way Magda's did before she'd had a drink.

'You haven't eaten anything, have you?' he asked.

'I can't.'

'We'll get you something. You have to try.'

'I feel sick to my bones.'

'I know.'

'I want to go somewhere and hide, forever.'

'It will pass. I promise.'

'Mum will know by now.'

He said nothing.

'She'll never get over this.'

'She will. She loves you.'

Her throat constricted. She wanted to be a child again, to hide her face in her mother's skirt and be clean and unimpeachable and invisible to men. Something awful had taken possession of her. Alcohol, and her fury towards Tuva, but more than anything, too, her vanity. The hollow, compulsive drive to be desired.

'I never meant to let it go that far. I just wanted to make Tuva feel like an idiot. I meant to stop there.'

'I know.'

'I feel fucking disgusting.'

'Tree, please.'

'It's always like this,' she said. 'I'm in control of it all, and then suddenly I'm not. I – forget what it is I wanted in the first place, I become erased. Men can sense it in me, they can smell it.'

'Tree.'

Malachy had heard all of this before, several times. She would call him from Oxford in the dark night or the pallor of another inexorable dawn, and his sleep-cracked voice was the only possible antidote to the wild, all-consuming loathing she felt when yet again she had compromised herself, given her body over to things she'd never wanted to happen, not in the ways they ended up happening.

It was the same every time: the thrill of being wanted, the thrill of transient power as she felt these men entranced by her. And then the shift that happened, inexorable too. The spell fell away and each boy – each man – caught on somehow to the fact that she didn't, in fact, have any power at all. As if in reaching inside her body they learned with a redemptive jolt that there was nothing there: no substance, no strength, no conviction. A vertiginous hollow.

But Malachy's warm voice, as familiar as a heartbeat on the other end of the phone. His refusal to loathe or condemn her as she loathed and condemned herself.

'I'm not like other women,' she said. 'I learned it all wrong, somehow. I've never got it right.'

'*Tree.*'

'Sorry.'

Because it wasn't fair, she knew: making him carry it all for her, yet again.

'What we need is a plan,' he said. 'What are you most worried about?'

'Mum. I can't bear for her to have to look at me.'

'It won't be as bad as you think it will. We'll go back soon, as soon as you're ready, and I'll make sure you have a clear path to her. You won't have to see anyone else.'

'But I'll have to see them sooner or later. I'll have to face Dad. Can you imagine? And Tuva – she's not going anywhere, is she? She's part of our lives.'

'Slow down. We'll take this one thing at a time.'

'But we can't. We don't have that luxury. What's going to happen with Tuva?'

'I don't know,' he said, too loudly. 'I don't know, Tree,' he repeated, more gently, but she could hear the weight of it all in his voice. 'You have to stop talking so I can work it out. I'll work it out. We're going to go back now, and you're going to speak to Mum, and then you need to sleep. I'll take you to the airport if you want. My student loan's come in, we can get a flight to – I don't know, France, Greece, home, wherever. Anywhere. Just concentrate on yourself, eat something, get some sleep. Leave the rest to me.' He took a deep breath. 'I'll work it out.'

Z

When Zoe woke, nothing seemed as straightforward as it had when she'd gone to sleep. To begin with, she felt evilly hungover. She emerged from the house late, missing break-fast, and passed Don as he was stalking past. He greeted her briefly and automatically but he was cold, implacably formal, and she wondered for a terrible moment whether she had misjudged their exchange the night before. It seemed now so brazen as to be scarcely credible, that she had allowed her knee to rest against Don Travers's, leaning in close enough to smell him. She remembered Tree's question at the beginning of the week, her face tilted. *Have you ever had an affair with a married man?*

She sat at the cleared breakfast table, where Faye and Magda sat drinking coffee and looking dismal.

'I'm a late toad today,' she said, but Magda looked blankly back at her and it occurred to Zoe that she had been crying, her face puffy behind sunglasses. Neither woman spoke.

When Don approached the table, they sat up straighter.

'Is there anything we can do?' asked Magda, and he nodded.

'Faye, I could use your car to take Tuva to the airport,' he said. 'She doesn't want to go with Krishna, evidently, and Teresza and Malachy have escaped somewhere with our van.'

'Of course.'

He nodded again, eyes dark and liquid.

'We can leave today too, if you need us to,' said Magda. 'Or I'll stay, if I can help.'

He nodded again but said nothing. Zoe and the two women looked up at the house, then, as Krishna emerged quickly in sunglasses, carrying his holdall, his head bowed, and though Don didn't turn it was clear from the tightening of his jaw that he knew who they were looking at. Krishna disappeared into the driveway. They heard the quiet thud of car doors and then its engine starting up.

Of course, thought Zoe. Krishna and Tree.

Other snapshots came to her, then. Krish and Tree had been intertwined variously, throughout the night: a hand on a back, on a thigh, around a waist; hips nestling casually into a lap, whispered words in an ear. Friendly, familiar and then too friendly. Their final disappearance together, drifting into the darkness in the direction of the house, just before Zoe told Toby she needed to go to bed.

There was a shift in the silence Krish's car left behind. Zoe looked up to see Tuva approach the table, a piece of bright pink paper in her hands. Four torn squares, joined together with Sellotape.

'This, now,' she said, placing the paper in front of Don. 'On top of everything.'

She turned and walked away, and Zoe watched as he scanned it briefly, holding it far away as people of a certain age do, and she watched the anger take over the muscles of his face. He slammed a fist on the table, and then he scrunched the paper into a ball in his hand and strode back to the house, and she didn't see him again until eight months later, when his strangely silent wife had died and, after a private service, they held a large wake in their beautiful, rambling London home. He greeted her then as warmly and courteously as ever, and congratulated her on the extraordinarily lucrative film deal for *Caged Creatures*, which had just been reported in the *Bookseller*. There were a great many people there that she must meet, he said, one of his hands resting very lightly on her back as he led her towards the drinks. She must tell him all about her second novel, how it was coming along.

N

Of course, I was the last to understand what had happened that night.

As a child, I took guilt very much to heart; I became almost physically sick with it. My childhood is laced with guilty memories, tiny things that plagued me, that I couldn't share with anyone. A triangle I cut in the hem of a summer smock. A small scribble I made on the last page of one of my father's books. A silly lie I told, about seeing a different face in the moon from the one everyone else saw. I spent a disproportionate amount of time turning over these secret crimes, haunted by the knowledge of them and the fear that they would be discovered – so that, viewed in a certain light or a certain mood, my childhood seems to me to consist of few other emotional states than those of dread and guilt.

And so the horrible silence that took hold of the house the day after the festival – the closed doors and tears and hissed whispers, the slamming of car doors as people came and went – made sense to me at first simply as an extension of Alice's and Etta's crimes at the lunch table the day before, in which I was inextricably implicated. Until halfway through the day, it didn't occur to me to suspect that anything more dire had happened than the throwing of the mussels.

It was only when I saw Tree running into the house that I realised there was something much worse.

'Mama,' I heard her cry, before she closed the door from the garden to the kitchen. It had never been closed in the daytime before. And I hadn't heard Tree cry like that, or call my mother 'mama', since she was a young girl.

I went into the house through the main French doors and started down the long corridor leading to the kitchen. I walked slowly, lingering, standing with my back against the wall in the cool darkness; and I knew as I stood there that something irreversible had happened and that once I discovered it I wouldn't feel the same as I had before.

A muffled sound of sobbing came from the games room. I was, I remember, very afraid, edging my way along the wall and then crouching in the dark to peer through the cracked door.

My mother was sitting on the little sofa she sat on to do her word puzzles. Tree knelt before her, her head in my mother's lap. My mother stroked Tree's long hair with one hand; the other she held in front of her eyes, as if she was too tired to see.

'I never meant for it to go that far,' Tree was saying. 'I just wanted to make her suffer, for everything she's done to you.'

My mother groaned, moving her head from side to side, her hand still pressed over her eyes. I saw that her head-scarf had become untucked, the end trailing sadly down her back.

'Kindness,' she said. 'Kindness, and never revenge. Nothing good can ever come from revenge.'

'I'm so sorry, Mama,' Tree said, crying again. 'I'm so, so sorry.'

I hadn't grasped yet what had happened. But I knew the flavour of it: I could taste all the shame and violation and ignominy as my own. That is how it is, with girls. From the earliest age, these things are planted. They sit inside us.

Quietly, I stood and stepped back into the gloom. I walked back towards the light at the end of the corridor, and there I found Etta sitting at the bottom of the stairs in front of my father, who held the crumpled piece of pink paper in one hand, its patchwork pieces slick with tape.

*

In one sense, my siblings achieved their goal. Tuva left that day, chased out of the house by their sordid, heroic, botched collective cruelty. But in truth they succeeded only in making things worse. Tuva did leave, but she left with my father. They took a house together in Liguria, and he only returned to our London home some weeks after we did, greeting my mother with as much careful civility as he always had. For us, he reserved implacable silence. I suspect he never really forgave us – neither for the hit his work must have taken, precious focus and momentum lost, nor the ugliness in which he'd been forced to become involved.

My father wrote brilliantly about ugliness – miasma, and the foul mess beneath human endeavour – but he wanted no real-life involvement in it. For that, he had delegates. My mother. His publicist, his agent, his publishers, his women, all his dizzily devoted friends. And Tuva, of course. I can see now that she would have had no easy time of it, that hers was no golden ticket. She was just another deputy, taking care of the base business of everyday life so that Don Travers could serve the higher purpose in which he had such unflinching belief.

It was in a miasma that we left Frantoio for the last time. My mother shut up its doors, its faded shutters. Helped by Malachy, she packed up the van. It was a long, hot, silent journey back home, she and Malachy taking turns to drive, Tree like a fevered invalid in the back of the van, sighing and wordless and drifting in and out of sleep.

And so it isn't the quiet, peaceful moments that come to mind when I think of that summer. It's only with searching and effort that I access those. Instead, I picture Tree on the floor before my mother. The quivering letter in my father's hand. My mother standing frozen that day in the kitchen, poised as I imagine her contemplating all the things she could feel unravelling, clattering out of her grasp: her husband, her children. The continuation of her firm principles in the four of us, her life's work. The equilibrium she'd achieved, in the strange arrangement – surely painful, perhaps humiliating, but at least undramatic, at least consistent – that she and my father maintained. And then her health, her life.

But of course, she might not have been thinking any of that at all. She might have been looking much further back, into the bolted fortress of her past. I didn't know then what course her thoughts were taking, nor do I now. I'm not sure that anyone ever did.

LONDON

'Then it will have to be a summing-up. Which side will you come down on? Violence, or charity?'

A Wreath of Roses, Elizabeth Taylor

N

There is a wild stretch of heath to the northeast of Blackheath where the ground drops to form a sort of bowl, veined with badly kept pathways and wooded with clusters of the kinds of close and scratchy trees that are almost impossible to move between. The grass grows very long. As children we would run down into this bowl shrieking like hunters. Unlike the grand and open heath, where people jog and walk their prams and dogs, made safe by the sight of the steeple at its heart and the high smart houses along its perimeters, there is a steady suggestion of malice in this forgotten stretch. In the way that children do, we responded to its wildness by becoming wilder ourselves; that we called it Cowboy Land was as much a nod to its remoteness and desolation as its thrilling sense of lawlessness.

Once, returning to it as adults, my siblings and I found evidence of that lawlessness we'd imagined as children: two used condoms, little empty baggies, some blankets and disparate items of clothing and a pair of black knickers twisted around a thin, snappable branch. One of the condoms was smeared with something dark that made Etta vomit, since she was pregnant with her second child. We found all of this entertaining, clearly still suggestible as adults to depravity and disorder. But I was happy to leave the bowl, walk back out of it onto the level ground of the common. The tone of our conversation was light as we left but I knew that beneath our wry sense of regression was a profound bleakness. It was bleak to be back there, no longer wild-hearted and no longer cowboys, no longer with Tree at our helm as she would always have been. And even as I was glad to walk away, I felt the ghostly pull of the place. I was seized by an urge to run back down into it as I had as a child: ululating, out of control with speed, my heart full with a sense not just of how dangerous the world might be but how dangerous I might be, too.

Perhaps it was that same urge that drove me back there a few years later, when I had my own child. At that time George was a four-month-old baby who had colic, so that feeding him one bottle could take two hours of screaming. Hungrily he would scream for the bottle; hungrily he would gulp it, only to be repelled by the wind he'd gulped. He would thrash and arch and scream all the more, pain added to his hunger. It felt, largely, that his cry was the only sound I heard.

He also only slept in his buggy, and that only when the buggy was moving – which meant, since all I seemed to think or care about at that time was whether he was sleeping or not, that I spent hours and hours walking round and round the park and heath and streets.

I was demented: underslept and obsessive and almost shrill with loneliness. All I wanted was to escape; to be on my own; to have time stop, for just a moment; to have silence, peace, open space.

I'd never been to Cowboy Land on my own. I would never have dared to as a child, or even teenager – my imagination was too sprawling – but now, driven by a sort of weary, punishing bravado, I steered the jostling buggy with its filthy treads through the grass and down the sides of the bowl. Immediately I realised my mistake. Not only was there a man lying on his front under a bush, asleep with one hand crushed under his crotch and two empty-looking bottles beside him, but there was no way to keep the buggy moving steadily enough to keep George asleep. The ground was uneven, the path meandering and overgrown with knobbly roots and fallen branches and large sticks, for which the buggy wheels, even with their thick treads, were no match. I swore quietly, watching the man. Obsessed and single-minded as I was at that time, my horror was almost evenly placed between the hysterical thought that I might be attacked and raped on the one hand, and that George might wake up, on the other.

The buggy had lost its motion for a matter of seconds while I stalled, trying to work out how to turn and push it back up the slope, but already I saw George's eyebrows rise and then knot into a frown. His head moved from one side to another. I knew what this meant. Before he had even woken fully he was screaming; I plucked him from the bassinet and held him to my chest but he pulled away to scream in the direction of the sleeping man, who woke and raised his head and looked at us with hatred.

Holding George to my shoulder, I tried to steer the buggy one-handed along the tangled path. His body bucked and bolted. His little hot head rammed my chest, as if he were trying to break down a door. And all the time, the appalling sadness of his cry. I thought at that time that I could feel the cry in my body: very tangibly, I felt it in the cords of my neck and in my sternum too. It was a wound and an accusation. 'Go away, go away, go away,' I found myself repeating in a whisper, and I wasn't sure whether I was saying this to the stranger in the grass or to myself or to George.

His head rammed my chest again and then the noise stopped, all at once. There was total silence. I looked down at George, at his face pressed against my shoulder. Already it was less puce; his eyes were no longer screwed shut, they had softened; he was silent, he was asleep.

He was asleep. I inhaled.

But still, there was the man. I turned to find him watching us, still with the look of hatred. He was very large, with big sloping shoulders; his face was broad and uneven, his eyes too bulbous. His nose was a lumpy mound, like the botched papier-mâché face of a doll I'd made when I was eight and given to my mother. She'd kept it in a nook in her kitchen, by the narrow window she opened to let out steam and smoke.

I gave the buggy another futile push.

'Asleep?' he barked, thickly, and I nodded. 'That makes one of us.'

144

He scratched the matted mass of his beard, looked around.

'I've got kids myself,' he said, and I nodded again. 'Don't believe me?'

'No, I do. Of course.'

'Two boys. Good boys, big, strong boys. Last time I seen them.' He cleared his throat. 'They're with their mother now, God help them, they …'

He trailed off, blinking grimly, staring now into the space before him, and I wondered if he saw the faces of his boys as he blinked and stared, or whether the space was a void. He came to with a sniff, took a coiled stub of a cigarette out of a pocket, lit it.

I stood there, waiting for my heart and breath to slow. George was quiet, George wasn't crying. What I most wanted to do was to get him back into the bassinet without waking him, but I knew that wouldn't work. Even if it did, I would still be stuck in the bowl, unable to manoeuvre the buggy up and out of it. I would have to wake him, because I couldn't stay in this filthy hidden place with this man, who had now picked up one of his near-empty bottles and was draining its clear contents. And yet I was frozen again by the prospect of that ceaseless cry.

He rolled the bottle under the hedge and threw his cigarette into the grass.

'You're scared of me,' he said, and when I shook my head, he laughed. 'Calm down, I'm not a monster. I'm only bothered if he's screaming his head off like before.'

I didn't move. He laughed again, held his palms up to show no harm. His huge fingers chalky white, they were so dry. I was conscious of all the primness and injustice of my clean hands, my mostly clean nails.

Then he lay back down on his front with a forearm for a pillow, his face turned away from us. I watched him for what felt like several minutes, and then – with the distinct sense that I was prioritising my own needs over George's safety, that I was deliberately overriding whatever maternal instinct I was supposed to have – I sat down at the foot of the slope, next to the buggy. I eyed his lapsed form in the grass, unsure. But I was being precious. My fear was little more than prejudice, and I was ashamed of that. He wasn't interested in us, I told myself, why should he be. I would let George sleep for ten more minutes, and we would be perfectly safe, and when ten minutes had passed I would have the energy to face his cry and get us out of the bowl and back home to battle with the bottle.

When he was asleep against me like this I could imagine that I was getting things almost right. His breath was the most peaceful sound there was. We were warm against each other, May sunshine dilating and retracting, quick clouds. I imagined my own mother, holding me as she'd held my siblings before me. She was already well versed in children by the time she had Tree, with a brood of younger brothers and sisters. I imagined her as a young girl, dressed in the old-world smocks from her few family photographs; sifting bran in a bowl with a baby on each hip, toddlers wrapped around her legs. These simplistic images all I had.

And I thought of Tree. There was a time when she held me like I was holding George. There are photos somewhere. A proud eight-year-old gazing down at the furry creature I was; another in which she stares gravely into the camera, my newborn pliancy stark against the careful tension in her arms. In another, she has broken into a smile, two large front teeth that her face has not yet grown into.

A breeze moved through the trees and messy hedges around me, the same hedges I used to duck into to hide. I was by default the laggard in our games, younger and therefore slower and smaller and more confused than the others. I remembered falling there once, straining my ankle as I ran down into the bowl to catch up with them. I lay on the ground with my face in the dirt, and the tears came in part from the pain but much more from the hot, blinding fury that had been building up throughout our games. The humiliation and injustice of being constantly behind, constantly flailing to catch up.

But then there was Tree beside me, panting. She pulled me up gently and held me against her, where I sobbed into her lovely warm chest. She held me while I cried and then she indulged me by asking what hurt and how much. When I clutched my ankle she examined it gently, as a doctor might. And then she stood and I watched – no longer crying – as she started to tear her T-shirt. She tore a thick band from the bottom of it, all the way around, so that it hung to just under her ribs, baring her boyish stomach. Very white, like the flesh of an apple. I watched as she squatted back down beside me and wrapped the cotton around my ankle. Malachy and Etta stood squinting nearby.

'A bandage,' she said. 'It'll have to do for now.' Then she lifted me, carefully, to my feet. 'Does that make it a bit better? Do you think you can walk now?'

I took a tentative step, having to pretend it hurt more than it did – because in truth it no longer hurt at all – and looked up at her with what I hoped was a brave face, wincing but stoical. Etta rolled her eyes and left us to run off again, but Malachy held out his hand and together he and Tree helped me over the knotted roots and bumpy ground, until I had forgotten that I was supposed to limp, absorbed back into the business of being a cowboy or hunter or witch, absorbed back into trying to catch up.

George sighed, and I shifted gently. My shoulders ached from holding him and I wanted to recline against the slope, but didn't dare disturb him. I should call Etta, I thought for perhaps the fourth time that day. I had had three missed calls over the last few days, and a text message asking how George and I were. But I couldn't face speaking to her. I couldn't face pretending that things were going all right, nor could I admit that they weren't.

'I'm in love with him,' I'd told her when we last spoke, which was true – but then, 'It makes the sleep deprivation manageable,' which wasn't.

'Is the feeding still going OK?' she'd asked, and I'd said something non-committal. I hadn't been able to admit to her that I wasn't breastfeeding; that I hadn't been since the third week, when I had become convinced that my milk was the cause of George's colic and in a tortured act of abdication had stopped and let the milk dry up. My breasts had become clogged and hard and angry, glands clumping and twisting like the gnarled roots of a tree. I'd watched it happen as if to someone else: a distant friend, a colleague. I'd changed each bra and shirt that became sodden with milk, all the while suppressing a mounting horror that I was losing something I could never reclaim.

'And is Liam helping?'

'Of course.'

'Actually?'

'Yes, Etta.'

I rested my lips on George's head now. His hair was thick for a baby's, and soft as butter – a dark, woody brown, like Liam's. Liam, who wasn't helping, not at all. He had come home from work – a collaborative exhibition in a disused industrial space in East London – at six that morning, just as I was making George's bottle. 'I couldn't leave earlier,' he'd said. 'It would have been career suicide.' Red-eyed, unsteady and yet somehow magisterial, in spite of the state he was in.

I'd told him in a low voice to get away from us. I told him, too, though he was a decade older than me, to grow up – and in my sexless dressing gown, with hair unbrushed and face unmade, shaking our baby's bottle, I felt like a stereotype of a desperate, nagging mother. We had promised we wouldn't be like that. We'd planned to be easy parents, not perfect and regimented like Etta, or grim and snapping and harangued like the parents in the apartment beneath ours, who talked of nothing but how exhausted they were. But I couldn't be easy, not when I was underslept as I was, not when he was in a position to choose to forego sleep. The galling luxury of that enraged me.

Our flat was on the main road, where there were five lanes and huge European lorries passed constantly, thundering up the approach to the A2 where they'd thunder onwards to Dover. We had made it a thing of beauty, I thought: low furniture, minimal clutter, its white walls bare canvases for Liam's paintings. But it was tiny, a fact I only really realised once George had arrived and the two streamlined rooms become filled not only with the endless kit a baby seems to require but those cries, too, relentless and deafening. Liam had taken to cursing our home, muttering expletives as he tripped over toys and dirty muslins and the handwoven Moses basket we'd been given by Etta. Each of those expletives, I thought, intended indirectly for my father's ears. Liam – happy for his tough childhood to show up mine for all its flippant and easy privileges – had nonetheless always balked at the paucity of the deposit my father had put down for our flat, pointing out that Don Travers could have afforded to buy something twenty times the price. But he had missed the point, my father's point. He had never tried to understand him.

The man stirred, lifted his head from his arm, fixed me again with the look that was hatred and something else, too: something more impenetrable even than hatred, so that the smallness of my suffering and the stale luxury of my having a home, and bemoaning its size and clutter, and despising, just for those early hours of the morning, my baby's father – all these things felt ridiculous and hateful to me too.

With a heaving, rolling motion he sat, then stood. He was very tall. He twitched a shoulder back twice like a dog, a kind of tic.

'Fucking baby woke me up.'

He spat, still staring, unfocused but intent, and took a step heavily towards us, and another. He stood there, swaying, and then he took another step, another. I could hear nothing, not a bird, not a whisper of breath in the trees, not even the white rushing silence. I simply sat there, clutching George to my shoulder, and as I did I watched my fear form as I had watched my milk dry up. As if it belonged to someone else.

He stepped again and stopped, steadied himself. He stared and I stared, my heart galloping as fast as George's.

'Your *fucking* baby.'

There was spit in his filthy beard. A tear became unloosed from my lashes, ran fast down my cheek.

And then, with another twitch of his shoulder, he turned. Dumbly he kicked an empty bottle and walked away, leaning backwards as he went, and eventually he stopped in front of another bush and started unfastening his trousers to piss. I laid George down in the bassinet, and as his brow creased into its frown and his little mouth yawned open to bellow, I pushed the buggy with all my might; I steeled myself against the slope and pushed it again, and the gradient made him slip all the way down the bassinet but still I pushed, and then we were up over the edge and back onto the flat heath and I was marching, as fast as I could without running, back home.

Tree thought that I was the brilliant one. She told me that, many times. I was brilliant, and I would go on to be brilliant. There was nothing hypothetical in her belief; she was assured of it. But it confused and unsettled me. In truth, I could see that I was clever enough – I didn't doubt that I had the ingredients for some kind of success. But I knew I wasn't brilliant. I knew my limitations. The gulf between those limitations and her expectations for me has been a perpetual source of shame, a guilty secret I still hold now.

I can understand how she became mistaken. I was so self-contained as a child; I was thoughtful, I listened and observed and made note. Privacy and silence and thoughtfulness are useful traits. They are intimidating, in their way. They make those without that capacity for restraint feel oafish, somehow slovenly or loose, out of control. Tree was powerful, but she lacked control. That was where her own shame was allowed to bloom and flower.

I have never felt as far from brilliance as I did in George's first year. My career, if it can be called that – I had stumbled sideways into a position as a research assistant at King's College London, collating data for a large-scale research project into antidepressants, Selective Serotonin Re-Uptake Inhibitors specifically – a project for which, as a literature graduate with a PhD in Folklore, I could not have been more inappropriately matched – was something accidental and temporary, a way to tread water and earn money after my years as a nascent career academic had become too financially deleterious to continue. I had two degrees and a doctorate, I had always been a first-class student. And now I was on maternity leave from a badly paid position that had nothing to do with anything I knew or cared about, sifting through archives and data, through impregnable terms like 'serotonergic' and 'norepinephrine transporter' and 'junctional rhythms'.

Liam, conversely, was very successful. He had a name for himself, which is more than can be said for most painters. But, like most painters, he had little to show for it financially, so that between us the bills and mortgage payments were a tortuous balancing act. In that climate, I should never have got pregnant. Even Malachy – uncensorious both by nature and principle, passionately respectful of personal choice – had warned me against having a baby before our situation had become more stable. Probably charged with the task by Etta, he had called me from his new life in San Francisco – a life I couldn't envisage because I still hadn't made it out there, too afraid of acknowledging that his move was final – and he'd urged me in his unhectoring way that I should wait, prioritise freedom for now. There was still time, plenty of time.

But I listened instead to Liam, who had an extraordinary knack when he was excited about an idea of making anything seem possible. Parenting wasn't hard, he said, pacing as he did, his dark eyes behind their glasses large with emotion. People made it hard. We were different. We would remember to hold on to the joy of life, always. We would desire each other still. The baby wouldn't get in the way – it would be a manifestation of our unity. Our love for each other was different from other people's, we relished and protected each other's liberty. Having a baby wouldn't change that.

Pushing the buggy around and around the streets of Greenwich and Blackheath – those frenzied, interminable perambulations – I thought, *What liberty?* I couldn't imagine a way out of any of it. The cramped spaces of the flat, the vice-like strictures of our debts and bills, the bitter, humourless barbs Liam and I spat out at each other before he escaped to his studio. The hours upon hours in which I ministered purely to George's needs, every minute squeezed of space to think about anything but money, and Liam's absence, and sleep, and the next bottle.

Each day as I walked, Tree's unwavering vision of me – of all the Travers siblings, the one who'd be really brilliant – seemed to walk beside me, just a fraction ahead, just out of reach.

When I got home from Cowboy Land that day I made George his bottle, and when I fed it to him and he started to recoil with his colic, finally I called Etta.

Over his cries, I said that I couldn't do any of this anymore. I told her everything: that Liam wasn't helping me, that he spent all day in the studio and barely engaged with George, that I hadn't slept for more than two hours at a stretch for as long as I could remember, that George cried when he was hungry and cried when he fed and cried when he was tired, that Liam hadn't come home that night because he'd been at a lock-in that had gone on until the morning, that I was a useless mother who had gambled her baby's safety for ten minutes' silence. That I felt I was going mad, truly, with no identity anymore, so that I laughed bitterly like a stranger and screamed in the empty flat and struggled, sometimes, to recognise my reflection. That I missed her and hated the distance that had grown up between us.

Liam, who must have been woken by George's screaming but hadn't come out of our bedroom then, emerged when he overheard my words. He stood in the doorway, trying to look angry but looking mostly like a schoolboy in trouble.

'I can't hear you,' said Etta. 'It's a terrible line. Can you put George down so I can hear you better? Are you OK? Are you crying? Start again, tell me again.'

I took a deep breath.

'Can you hear me now?' I shouted over George.

'Hello?' said Etta.

I hung up, and Liam came then and took George from me. I watched him, shushing and jogging our baby as he'd watched me do so many times. His face was tender as he looked down at his son. He reached for the bottle.

'Here,' he said gently. 'Let me try.'

*

It was one or two in the morning when, unspeaking, he reached for my body. In the dark, under cover of the white noise I played to cajole George into sleeping, we had sex. We had barely done so in the months since his birth, whereas previously sex had been omnipresent in our relationship, the solution to every problem.

'I'm going to be better at all of this,' he whispered afterwards.

'OK,' I said.

'I'm just afraid, I think,' he said, 'of being like my dad.'

I waited.

'But I'm not going to be. Do you believe me? I'm not going to get caught up in all of that.'

'OK.'

I kissed him. He fell asleep with his face pressed to my chest, and as his breathing slowed into sleep I heard George stir and start to whimper. For a moment, I vacillated between which of them to hold. I was needed, I was necessary; I felt, for perhaps the first time, truly like a mother. I shifted away from Liam and took George from his cot, held his yielding body against my shoulder. For now, he was silent. I felt his breath on my skin, warm and tenuous.

The living room was flickering blue when I entered it: an ambulance or police car on the road below, sirens silenced. There was the guttural splutter of a lorry's engine juddering back into motion. George turned his head and whimpered again and I moved over to the window, leaned my forehead against the glass, letting my breath turn it to mist. Three more lorries passed, wheezing, and I imagined their great trailers empty inside, on their way back through caffeinated darkness to the countries they came from to fill up again, with fruit or flowers or machinery or cheese or whatever it was we in the UK were missing, to come back again via the same roads, to pass by our dark windows again in a few nights' time, an endless loop.

I saw a shape, then, moving in the darkness beyond the road. It had the mournful gait of a bear, slow-fast; it had a bear's sad and hunted menace, the same impression of privacy interrupted. The heavy shoulders and long arms. As he turned to the road I saw the face of the tramp from Cowboy Land: the botched nose and round, unseeing eyes. From one hand hung a bottle; from the other, a large soft bundle. Clothing, I supposed, perhaps bedding. I wondered if he slept outside, or whether he had somewhere to go, or whether he simply lumbered through the night as he was now.

I pictured the dark, lonely spaces of Cowboy Land at night. As I turned from the window to make George's bottle I wondered whether there was anyone there now in the long grasses, where we four once played. Or just foxes, limping and lolloping among our ghosts.

The next evening Etta came for me.

Our doorbell buzzed and Liam answered the intercom and winced as he listened – a siren was at that moment screaming past the house, so loud that it felt like an act of violence, almost – and when he put it down he shook his head, already grabbing his jacket.

'It's your sister. Did you know she was coming?'

'No.'

'Fuck's sake.'

Etta and Liam had never got on.

'She's just a bit – tritty trotty,' he had told me after the very first time they'd met, and I knew what he meant, of course I did. He was so defensive, and she was so tautly together in everything, an elastic band of a person.

He took his keys and phone, patted his pockets, and then – like an afterthought, as if he might easily have forgotten – he came over to where I was standing, jiggling George mechanically against my shoulder to try to extract one of his agonising, tortuously elusive burps. He kissed my forehead.

'I'm heading to the studio. Don't wait up.'

I laughed at that, our door slammed behind him, and I flinched as another siren wailed past. And then the door yawned open and there she was: my sister Etta, modestly sleek in her suit. For a split-second I saw her as a stranger might see her. I saw the kind of woman who runs a marathon every few years and doesn't much refer to it, who holds her own in boardrooms and mixed doubles and teacher–parent meetings alike.

'Hello,' she said, and held up a bottle of red wine. 'You need this.'

Already she was standing before me, opening the bottle – somehow she knew, in her Etta-like way, exactly where the bottle opener was kept, and our wine glasses – and pushing a glass across the worktop towards me. She reached out for George. Heavily, with the very heaviest kind of relief, I handed his mewling body over to her.

'Sit,' she said. 'Drink.'

'You look amazing.'

'Shut up.'

'You didn't need to come,' I said. 'I'm fine.'

'No, you're not.'

I watched her as she perched on one of our stools and with her infinitely capable-looking hands placed George face down on her lap, rubbing his back. Almost instantly, he burped. Then he became still, his breath calm and constant as the shhh of the traffic outside. I exhaled.

'How did you do that?'

'They need different hands sometimes. They're not supposed to spend their whole time with one person.' She eyed me. 'You're supposed to have support.'

I held a hand up over my eyes, a low sob in the back of my throat.

'I'm no good at it,' I said, when I could speak.

'No one is.'

'You are.'

'I'm not. And I certainly wasn't at the beginning.'

'Of course you were.'

'Hell no. I was a total fucking mess. When Lila was a newborn I was full of rage, all the time.'

I wiped my eyes and cheeks.

'I don't believe you.'

She shrugged and took a long sip of wine, and then she rested her hand on George's back again. He was asleep. I thought I could feel everything in me loosen: muscles, sinews, even my skin.

'I threw things,' she said. 'Constantly. Do you believe me now?'

I smiled.

'What things?'

She exhaled.

'Anything. Not Lila, obviously, though honestly I came close. I'd put her into the cot and my hands would literally be shaking with rage and then I'd reach for the nearest item.'

'Like what.'

'Sometimes I had the wherewithal not to pick something up that would break, but often I didn't. I broke loads of things. Ask Mark. Toys, my phone … a sugar pot I really liked. I still think about that pot sometimes – it was so nice, just the right size, from this tiny shop in Girona of all places. A small tragedy.' She cocked her head. 'I smashed Mark's bicycle pump, which was actually quite satisfying. And cups of tea too – cold tea, always, because you can never just sit and drink a cup when it's still hot, can you?'

It was a platitude and beneath her wit but I laughed, a tiny bit.

'No. Literally never. I hate cold tea.'

'It's the pits.' She looked down. 'I kicked a door once, so hard that the handle cracked a hole in the wall beside Lila's cot. It's still there, at the end of her bed. We've never plastered it over. Yeah, it felt like I was angry all the time in those first few months, with Lila. Not Maeve. It was a whole different hormone cocktail with Maeve, more a kind of woozy – melancholy, I'd say. But with Lila it's like something went off in my head, some rage nerve became exposed. It was terrifying, actually.'

'I didn't know that. You make being a mum look like the easiest thing in the world.'

'No, *our* mum made it look easy. But it's bloody hard.'

'Mum made it look like the loneliest thing in the world.'

Etta grimaced, barely perceptibly. She hated it when I said things like that, I knew. To her there was no point.

'Why didn't you tell me you were struggling?' she asked.

'Why didn't you tell me it was so hard?'

She smiled.

'Well, I mean, we're not the best at asking for help, are we.'

'He doesn't sleep,' I said. 'He just does not sleep.'

'Does Liam help at night? Does he give him a bottle so you can sleep a bit?'

'No. He doesn't even stir.'

Anger. The tiniest flicker of an eye roll, something no one would have known to see except me, because I knew Etta in the same way I knew walking, placing one foot in front of the other.

'OK. Come with me now. We can get a cab to mine. We'll put you in the spare room, we'll put George in the playroom in the loft. We'll put in a routine, we'll do some gentle sleep training. When Mark and I are at work and the kids at school you can have the whole house to yourself – you can have some space, some quiet.'

Some space, some quiet. Her offer sounded like the most wonderful thing I could imagine.

'I'm not leaving Liam.'

'It's only temporary. Two weeks, three max. Just long enough to sort out the sleep.'

'It's not just the sleep. It's the feeding, too.'

'I have a brilliant paediatrician I saw about Maeve.'

'We can't afford it.'

'I'll pay.'

'I can't just take your money and live in your house. I can't freeload off you.'

'I'm your sister, it's not freeloading. If it makes you feel better, you can pay me back at some point. It won't cost much.'

'Etta. I'm not leaving Liam.'

'It's only temporary. It'll help.'

She reached over to top up my glass, and as she did I watched her face: the translucent eyelids, the half-moons of skin beneath them pigeon-grey, like mine. The blue of veins, ticking coldly beneath the surface. In his sleep, George exhaled.

'Sometimes men need to remember what they've got to lose.'

'But—'

I closed my eyes again. I imagined Liam at the warehouse party that had kept him out so late the night before last.

Standing in a darkened, pulsing room, his hands moving as he spoke, animated, to attractive people about things that excited him: art, the breadline, Freudian theory. Things we used to talk about, and which now seemed so impossibly remote and unconnected from me and from the small tunnel into which my entire life had burrowed and narrowed down. That sighing, oblivious creature on Etta's lap, which was the only thing I could see.

'He wouldn't realise what he has to lose,' I said. 'He'd just relish the freedom. After two weeks of that, he'd be the one leaving us.'

'Nem, this is how you get trapped with a man. You live in perpetual fear that he will find something better. You live paralysed by the conviction that he's better than you.'

'I don't think that,' I said, which wasn't true. 'And I'm not – trapped with Liam. There's nothing wrong with us. We're fine. I'm just exhausted.'

'I know you are.'

'I'm utterly, utterly exhausted.'

'I know, Nem. It's torture, virtually. I promise it won't last forever.'

She watched me, and sighed deeply, and I could see everything in her wanting to find a solution.

'I know,' I said, to keep her quiet, and she gestured at my glass.

'Drink.'

*

When Etta had to leave I went out with her, laying a waking George down in his buggy.

'I'm only taking you as far as the park,' I said as I locked the door, and she smiled.

'I know. I'm not going to bundle you into a cab against your will.'

'No abduction.'

'No abduction,' she said. 'I get it. You're not leaving Liam yet.'

'Yet?'

'I've made my peace. For now.'

The park was cool and dusky, the day's warmth thinning against our faces as we walked, and I watched George for signs that he might be cold, stopped to tuck a blanket in over his chest.

'I should turn back,' I said, but she flapped a hand.

'He's fine, it's warm. Walk me as far as the Observatory. Come on, move aside. I'll push.'

Gently, firmly, she manoeuvred me away from the buggy, and as we walked I looked at her hands on the handle and marvelled that they were the hands of an established mother. It always struck me as incredible, that that was what she was. It was always, somehow, a novelty.

'God,' she said. 'I still know every tree in this place. Every pathway. Every dogshit bin.'

'Is that their technical name?'

'I mean, what are they called, actually? They're like repulsive little post boxes. Though actually, I heard once that people do post poo into real post boxes too, like actual Royal Mail letter boxes. Can you imagine?'

'Etts,' I said, watching George as he frowned.

'The things people do.'

'Etts. I should head back.'

She eyed me, not unkindly.

'Stop … flinching. He's fine. Let's sit for five minutes.'

We reached the viewpoint by the Observatory and sat down together beneath the stern, rook-black statue of General Wolfe. It was quiet. A teenage girl leaned over the railings, smiling into her phone. Her hair dark and very long, like Tree's before she shaved it all off. A little dog yapped, white and fluffy, with mucky-looking eyes, and a woman dressed in bright Buddhist orange squatted to the ground to kiss it.

The sun was setting over London, the tips of the office towers in Docklands and the City shrouded in a milky haze. Unlike the trees and the pathways and the dog bins, very little of that view was familiar from our youth. The city had proliferated into something much smarter and slicker and more real than anything I remembered from our childhood, so that whereas the viewpoint had always felt somehow homely and even scruffy, a place where teenagers used to gather after school – Etta in their midst – to smoke and eat crisps and flirt, it felt as bossy and impersonal now as any tourist site in any city.

'I don't know how you can bear to live here.'

'Wow, thanks,' I said, and she grinned.

'Sorry. But I mean it. It makes me feel weird, being here. In such proximity to our youth, but unable to touch it.' She pressed her forehead with her fingertips, as if to iron out wrinkles, and then she looked sideways at me. 'No wonder you're depressed.'

I blinked.

'I'm not depressed, Etta.'

'Of course you are.'

'No, I'm not. I'm just tired.'

She smiled vaguely, looked away.

'Etta?' I said. 'I don't have depression, Etta.'

'Of course you do.'

'I'm happy, I'm really happy.'

She laughed.

'*So* happy.'

'Etta. I'm just tired.'

'It's nothing to be ashamed of. It doesn't mean you don't adore George. It's a totally reasonable response to new motherhood – probably the only reasonable response, actually. The very rare occasions I come across a new mother who doesn't seem a bit depressed, I presume she's either mentally or emotionally deficient in some way, or both.'

'You can't mean that.'

'Oh, a hundred per cent I mean it. The hormones ensure it, but the circumstances too. Don't get me wrong, I loved a lot about those first months – particularly in retrospect. Mostly now I remember the magical bits more than the bad parts – you know, when you gaze at them when they're sleeping on you, their perfect little everything. The fingers, the smell of their neck. The first smile. I remember feeling literally high on the joy of it, sometimes – but when I wasn't high I was anxious, irrational, insomniac … full of rage. Depressed, in short. Like you.'

I shook my head. There was nothing I could ever do in the face of her brisk, breezy sureness, her irrepressibly Etta-like certainty.

'I really need to head,' I said, and she nodded. 'He's getting hungry.'

'OK.'

'Etta Travers?'

The woman in orange had approached us. She had dark, greying hair cut short with a fringe, so that her face was very starkly framed and looked somehow like a television. Standing straight in her bright tunic, arms behind her back, one leg pointed outwards, she was like an acrobat or a clown, someone in costume. I thought that perhaps there was something familiar in her face, but it was all too far away, words in another language.

'Yes.'

'God, I thought so. And Nemony, isn't it? I thought so. I can't believe it.'

She smiled, but not quite warmly – more a smile of satisfaction that she'd guessed correctly, I thought, than a greeting. She nodded, taking in our faces as if we were a painting in a gallery.

'You won't remember me,' she said finally, reaching her hand out to shake ours in turn. 'Zoe Goodison.'

'Ah, yes,' said Etta, and I smiled alongside her, but I would never have put that name with the woman before us. I had started reading one of Zoe's novels once, interested because we'd had her to stay that time at Frantoio, but some other book had got in the way and I'd never finished it. Of course I'd watched the film they made out of her debut – everyone had watched it, though in that moment I couldn't begin to remember the name.

'Do you live here?' asked Zoe, tugging the lead as her dog snuffled away.

'Nemony does. I'm just visiting.'

'And this is yours?' she asked, peering into the buggy. I cleared my throat.

'That's George. He's mine.'

'Isn't he gorgeous,' she said, and she looked from me to Etta. 'You two are so alike,' she said, smiling, and then she frowned. She became still.

'I was devastated to hear about Tree.'

'Thank you,' I said, and already I imagined Etta loathing this woman.

'And your mother, of course. She was a truly lovely woman.' The dog yapped, twice. 'Life is a real fucker.'

'Yes, well,' said Etta, her voice squeezed of warmth. 'It can be.'

A disembodied voice rang out then, echoing amont the trees behind them; a bored male voice on a tannoy, the park was closing, we must start to make our way out. We stood.

'So you live in Greenwich, Nemony?'

'Yes, over on Shooters Hill Road,' I said, 'near the Esso. How about you?'

'Just over there,' said Zoe. 'Crooms Hill Grove.'

'That's where we grew up,' said Etta, 'on Crooms Hill,' and as she said it I saw that Zoe already knew.

'Yes, the beautiful house on the left,' she said. 'About half-way up.'

'That's right.'

The voice on the tannoy rang out again, accusing and weary.

'I have to get all the way back to Hampstead,' Etta said, glancing at her watch. Zoe nodded incuriously, still scanning our faces in that strange way, a visitor in a gallery.

'I'm so glad I bumped into you both. I'm so glad I recognised you.'

'Yes.'

'Can I give you my number, Nemony? I'd love to meet up.'

'Of course,' I said. 'That's a nice idea.'

But it was an odd idea, I thought when we all parted and I walked away, tracing my route out of the park, past Cowboy Land, back to the close walls of the flat. It claimed something unearned and too casual, not quite intimacy or ownership but something similar. As if Etta and I were an object or curiosity, something to be observed but also laid claim to, and I thought that perhaps that was just how it was with writers. I'd seen it in my father, countless times: that unceasing mode of acquisition, so that he was seldom truly present, a part of his mind forever recording and taking, sifting for use. It was ruthless and parasitic, I thought as I walked, an addiction. People credit great writers with such humanity, but to me there was something sociopathic, something truly anti-empathetic in our father's ability to see another's subjectivity as just another subject. An hour into my mother's wake, I had gone upstairs to use the loo and as I'd passed his study I'd seen him in there, at his desk. He couldn't wait, I knew; he'd seen some facial expression or heard some snippet of a conversation that he needed to get down before it was gone, and it didn't matter that it was his own wife's funeral, and that he had four newly motherless children downstairs.

My visits to Zoe Goodison's house coincided with two things. The first was the dissipation of George's colic, which ended as abruptly as it had started. He turned five months old on the fifth day of June and, suddenly, there was silence. That silence was so absolute, such a dramatic cessation of sound, that it seemed artificial, as if a button had been pressed.

He no longer cried throughout his waking hours, puce and tormented. I was no longer stalked by that cry. I learned what it was for us to watch each other. As if there hadn't been time to see each other clearly, until now. I sat and let his gaze scan my forehead, my teeth, my hairline, my eyes. At some point in the new silence, I stopped flinching.

I thought that his huge brown eyes were astounding. The beetle-red lips that moved even when he slept, the mollusc centre of his ears, the dormouse fur on the lobes. The perfect pointed tip of his chin, like the end of a leaf. As is usually the case with a young baby, he looked exactly like his father.

The second was that Liam's own father, Hal, became very ill. We received a phone call from Krystyna, Liam's mother, who told us – not without satisfaction, I thought – that Hal was 'raddled' with cancer.

'He's been told we can expect two, three months, maybe a little more. Maybe less. It's all up for guessing.'

Given the years of relentless bullying she'd endured, I suppose she could hardly have been expected to engage in any greater emotion than relief. But still, I wished that Liam might have been allowed a softer delivery. He hated change, he hated sudden discoveries. He always responded particularly badly to his mother's unflinching frankness.

If I had lost Liam in the raging storm of George's colic, I saw now – with sorrow for him but also, irrepressibly, a guilty, steady resentment – that I would lose him to Hal's illness. Since I had called Etta, since I'd screamed my litany of complaints into a phone call she couldn't even hear, Liam had been a different father. As was his way, he'd thrown himself into his resolution to improve, coming back from the studio early enough to give George his bath and cook our supper, delaying work in the morning to give George a bottle, let me sleep a little more.

But now, as was also his way, he was gone. I saw it the minute he ended his mother's phone call. That was what I was thinking as I crossed the park to Zoe's house that first time: that George and I were on our own again.

Her house was expansive and bright, lit through with sunshine that poured in through the high windows at the back. She was smaller than I'd thought in the park but solid, with the upright musculature of a body hewn by Pilates or gymnastics. As clean-looking as the house, and I thought, this is what it would be like to earn decent money and live on your own: time to do exercise, to iron your clothes, to blow-dry your hair properly and arrange your home exactly as you like.

'I'm so pleased to have found you,' she said as she took me through to the kitchen. She pumped levers on a chrome machine – even those levers looked as if they had just been polished – and there was a rumbling and pressured hissing and then the lewd trickle of hot coffee into a cup. The white dog had joined us. It sat now by her ankles, watching me.

'I couldn't believe it when I recognised you both. But of course, you're clones of when I met you in Sicily, albeit grown women now. Your face in particular is almost unchanged.' She looked at me quickly, and then back at the coffee. 'Exactly like your mother.' I shifted George from one hip to another. 'Now, you head straight out to the garden. Go on, I'll follow. I think we'll be warm enough, don't you? No, go ahead, I'll take the cups, you have your hands full. How old is your little man? I'm afraid I'm no good at gauging these things.'

I liked her better than when we'd met in the park a month earlier. I had walked away from her then feeling examined, compromised, but watching her closely now I couldn't see any of the writer's avarice. Instead I saw someone self-contained and calm, not hungry.

But if her welcome put me at ease – her busy chatter and familiarity, her almost maternal solicitousness – I saw too that she was not casual, that indeed a great deal of thought had gone into my visit. She had borrowed a bouncer from a neighbour – 'I'm told they like to sit in these' – and toys, which she'd arranged on the lawn. There was a blanket over each of the chairs, another next to the bouncer for George. A plate of shortbreads, a vase of pale peonies from her own flowerbeds.

'Make yourself comfortable,' she said. 'I'll get milk and sugar. Don't worry about Mildred, she's too shy to bother you.'

I knew this stretch of gardens so well: vivid lawns reaching out behind a terraced cul-de-sac, like a mews. As a child I had played often in the garden two doors down from hers with my nursery friend, Ralph Thomas, whose house I still visited frequently in dreams. I would have looked out, from the branches of the Thomases' great pear tree, over the very lawn on which I was now laying my baby down. George looked up at me, blinking in the spring light.

'Where do you come from?' I asked him, as I often did. His gaze was so dazzlingly foreign to me. Mildred settled down at a safe distance, her head on her paws, blinking.

This was how I had pictured being a mother. A happy baby kicking fat little legs in the sunshine. A blue June sky above us, striped with vapour trails. I watched a bee as it hovered over a stem of lavender, inspected it, flew drunkenly to the next. And this sensation, too, I supposed: something approaching calm and warmth and even belonging, with which this stranger Zoe – with her plate of biscuits, her solicitude, her blankets and borrowed toys – had enveloped me. The feeling wouldn't last, I thought, but that I felt it at all made me hopeful. I had been in a state of alert for so long: always vigilant, always braced.

'You know these streets better than I do,' she said when she returned.

'Yes, I suppose I do.'

'I fell in love with the area when I came …' She paused. 'When I came to your mother's funeral actually, her wake. Sorry.'

'No, don't be.'

'Something about the streets around here just snapped me up. And all the trees! It was the first place I thought of when I was looking to buy, some … Gosh, nine or ten years later.'

She pushed the plate of biscuits towards me, cleared her throat slightly.

'It was a beautiful wake,' she said. 'Your mother's. A beautiful tribute.'

Had it been, I thought? I supposed it might have seemed that way to adults.

'And your house was so amazing. I was young – younger than you are now, I'd guess.'

'I'm thirty.'

'I would have been twenty-seven – it was the spring after I stayed with you in Sicily, wasn't it? And God, I was a very unworldly twenty-seven. My own background's nothing like yours,' she said quickly. 'No. I'd never been somewhere so – full of character, I suppose. There was something on every inch of wall, I remember thinking. And sculptures! I'd never been in a home strewn with sculptures like that.'

My own memory of the wake is in fragments, three or four. In one, I am sitting in the corner of the drawing room next to my favourite sculpture, if that is the word for it – it was a mask, Congolese I think, white stripes cut into black wood, an open mouth like an 'O', eyes closed as if in bliss. I sat next to it in my new black dress and watched adults drinking and spilling wine, talking about books and politics and people they knew, occasionally remembering to mention my mother in quieter tones, and I wondered what on earth any of it had to do with her. If she had been there she wouldn't have joined them. She would have been moving ghostlike between them instead, removing dirty glasses and replacing them with clean ones. I traced the top ridge of the mask, where a feather-light layer of dust had formed. She would never dust it again. She would never clean anything in the house again. I pictured her face against the pillow just ten days before, the wide bones devoid of flesh, her sparse and shallow breath. My mother, the mule.

I remember sitting under a table in the kitchen, too, so that all I could see were feet. And then there was Tuva, the seething sense of her even before her ankles and emerald shoes emerged, her voice intoning above as she directed the caterers.

And I remember Tree. Her arm around me, stiffening or pulling me closer as people approached with tilted faces, eyes round and full of pity. Malachy clinked a glass and said some words at some point, low, gentle words about my mother that reminded people why they were there. Tree sat beside me as he spoke, staring down into her lap. I glanced up at the new brush of cropped hair covering her scalp, not even a centimetre long. Her oddly nude neck, and a glimpse of the tiny square letters she'd had tattooed across the span of her shoulders only a few weeks earlier.

K I N D N E S S I S K I N G

'George is something else,' said Zoe. She cocked her head, like a bird. 'Look at him, watching us. He really takes you in, doesn't he?'

'Yes, that's what I think.'

'They're such fascinating creatures. He *knows* things. People think of babies as empty vessels waiting to be filled, don't they? But they're not, they can't be. Look at him, full of some unreachable wisdom.'

Well, I loved hearing that.

'I think so too. But I'm not the most impartial judge.'

'I am. I impartially judge him to be adorable.'

When Zoe spoke, she made small, flicking motions with her fingers and thumbs that I hadn't seen anyone do before. As if she were clearing crumbs from them. It was odd, this compulsive restless motion in a body in every other way still and ballet-poised. She reached one of those lively hands forward now – 'May I?' – and cupped his cheek, with the tenderness of a mother.

On the train to visit Liam's father I held George in my lap and watched my husband as he watched the high-rises pass by. His sinewy face was tight, his narrow and muscular shoulders pulled up towards his ears. He was like a lightweight boxer dancing about the ring before the bell goes.

When we reached his childhood estate he walked quickly with his head down, hissing at me to hurry up. The very first time I met him he had told me about the estate, how he had never fitted in there, had never been able to fall in with the rules of the place. He both loathed and revered it.

'Fucking lift's still a piece of shit.'

We clunked slowly upwards in that dingy box that stank of urine, metal creaking and clanging as we went, and I started to feel as if it would never stop and release us. I laid my hand on George's forehead to keep it still, watched Liam's unfocused and impregnable stare. Finally, the doors shuddered apart. I hurried to push the buggy behind Liam, whose quick light steps in his trainers made squeaking sounds on the floor.

Krystyna opened the door and embraced Liam and then me. She held me very tight, as she had never done. I felt the bones of her shoulders.

'My little boy,' she said, taking George and holding him up in the air before her. I noticed her hooded grey eyes, how they brightened. Then she gestured us into the grim chaos of their living room.

Hal rested lightly on the brown sofa he'd always dominated. Formerly a handsome, barrel-chested man, not tall but somehow immense with that chest and his crackling baritone of a voice, we found him no sturdier or less ephemeral than a butterfly. Like a butterfly, he appeared poised for flight. The warm brown of his skin was yellow now, and tight.

'Well now,' he said. 'Well now.'

'How are you doing, Dad?' said Liam, and he clapped a hand on Hal's back as he always did, but when he did I thought that they both seemed to wince.

'Not too bad,' he said. 'Not too bad.'

We sat down. No one spoke. The television was on, a refurbishment show I half-recognised. The screen demanded our attention, though I saw Liam's gaze flicker quickly to his father's small new face and back again.

'Well now,' said Hal again, after a while. 'Let's see the boy, then.'

Krystyna stepped forward from the doorway, relinquishing George to me, and Hal glanced at him briefly and then blinked, turning back to the television, as if the sight of the baby was painful.

'Good lad,' he said, his hands on his knees, and Krystyna left the room.

'You know what?' the woman on the television asked the couple in front of her. 'Our amazing team is going to sort all of this out for you. Think of us as your knights in shining armour.' A tense-looking man and woman stood huddled together, grinning back at her. 'Your rescue team.'

I tried to catch Liam's eye, and then I glanced at Hal. He blinked often, slow, effortful blinks. I thought that he was stunned by his own frailty. For the first time I felt pity, along-side the anger and repulsion I always felt for him. There are many different kinds of sorrow, and the sorrow I held for Hal ranked low. He bullied his children. He bullied and terrorised his wife. And yet … there is something particular about the diminution of a once-powerful man. All that heft, all that force, and then an infant again.

A faceless narrator had taken over from the woman now, introducing in jovial tones each member of the couple's rescue team. George started to squawk loudly, his new trick, and Liam and Hal looked over at me.

'Can't you take him out?' said Liam.

Krystyna was smoking by the window of the small kitchen, and when I came in she straightened, threw the cigarette out, waved the air with a tea towel.

'Sorry, darling,' she said.

'It's fine.'

'I started again, but only one, two a day.'

'That's fair enough,' I said. 'Are you OK?'

'Oh, you know.' She shrugged, switched the kettle on, dropped teabags into cups. 'What about you? Not getting any sleep, are you?'

'Hm,' I said. 'Not much.'

'Eating?'

'When I have time.'

'You must eat. Look at you, thinner than me now! You look like you're going to fall down.'

'Thanks, Krystyna.'

'Yes, just topple down right there. I could blow you over, poof!'

'You're too kind.'

'I don't know,' she said, shaking her head, eyes glinting. 'Pale, pale face. Those black bags under your eyes. You could be hobbling up Wood Green High Street holding out a bowl for coins. "Please, sir—"'

'OK, OK,' I said, laughing. 'I get it.'

'But look at this one,' she said, and she smiled down at George. 'You two made such a good baby. Give him here. Sit down, take a break.'

I did as she said, and thought how strange it was that they were related by blood. My plump little creature in her thin, almost blue-white arms.

'How is your family?' she asked.

'They're OK, I think.'

'You haven't seen them?'

'I've seen Etta a bit. But you know, Malachy lives in California now.'

'Ah, yes. That's very, very far.'

'He's coming over next month for Dad's birthday,' I said. 'It's his eightieth.'

Krystyna nodded. I always loved how little interest she paid my father.

'Will he stay long?'

'Less than a week. His life is over there now. Etta doesn't think he'll ever move back.'

'You miss him.'

'Yes. He loves it there, but it's still – strange, to be so far away. I mean, he hasn't met George yet.'

'Don't I know it. I haven't seen my sisters for, huh, ten years? More? Agnieska's sick as well, the youngest. And three of us grannies now, it's not believable even.'

She tugged a bunch of her hair out from George's fist. Then she leaned forward, smudged one finger gently under my eyes. First one, then the other.

'Darling, someone needs to look after you.'

Her kindness more painful than Liam's silence.

Malachy had resisted moving to the States for a long time, even though his work – the company's head office was based in San Francisco – obviously called for it. I understand now, which I didn't at the time, that he stayed in London as long as he could for Etta and me, in the aftermath of Tree's death. Even so, self-referential with youth, I felt betrayed when finally he left.

Shortly before he moved, there was a brief time – the summer I finished my undergrad – when Etta and Malachy were my friends, in London. Not siblings, but friends. We went to each other's parties. We were absorbed into each other's groups. Previously I'd either been too young to join them, or we'd all been too embroiled in the long, cold, messy business of grief. I see that short summer like a little pocket of something approaching lightness, even carelessness. The dark rocks above us lifted, just a fraction.

And then Malachy was gone. Without him – and perhaps with the arrival in my life of Liam, whom I met that same summer – my friendship with Etta couldn't continue, not in that way. Without Tree and Malachy, we were the stumpy end of the stick, our relationship faltered, we fell into our old patterns, deeply ingrained. She was too fast, too busy, I was too finely tuned or impractical. Too watchful. Or, I don't know what, actually. I was too something, for Etta.

The night I met Liam, I was out with Malachy. He had urged me to join him at a gallery party in Soho – the gallerist's daughter was a friend of his – and told me that it was time to let loose, since I had just finished Finals. I must stop thinking so hard, for just a moment.

As was usually the case, I lost sight of Malachy soon after we arrived. The gallery floor was teeming and humid with people. And so, instead of letting loose as I'd been instructed, I stood in the comparatively emptier basement, beside a table spread with food. I took a wary refuge in examining its contents. The food was Danish, like the artist. Herrings, pickled cucumbers, hard-boiled eggs hairy with dill. Inevitably, I thought of Tuva. She'd encouraged my mother to pickle herrings once and we'd all found them disgusting on principle, grey and wet and slug-like.

I filled my plate and then I stood in the corner eating and watching people from the outside, Banquo-like, as they spoke and laughed and touched – that constant touching: a hand through someone's hair, a palm resting lightly on a forearm or a shoulder, on the small of a back. At times like that I could feel entirely foreign and detached from other people, along with an almost dizzy sense of disembodiment – so that not only the people around me, but even parts of my own body – the hand clutching the plate, the gullet closing around a bolus of bread, the teeth knocking against the wine glass – all of it could seem as disconnected from me, or from whatever it was that looked out from behind my eyes, as those grey and humid herrings.

After some time the feeling passed, and with a sort of rushing sound the noises of the room came back to me. I found that I had made my way through my plate of food. The room was too bright. I felt, suddenly, very tired. And then there was Malachy in all his easy, warm, solitary grace, descending the gallery stairs.

'I think I'm going to head off,' I said when he approached, resting his elbow on my shoulder. He looked down with such light fondness that for a moment I could imagine what it might be like to feel at home in a place like that, to feel absorbed into it.

'Don't go. Let me catch up with a couple more people and then we can head off together and grab dinner.'

I glanced at the empty plate in my hand – it was one of those plates with a special clip on the side for a wine glass, so you can hold a fork in the other hand – which I've always hated, it's horribly awkward to stand and talk and eat a plate full of food at the same time – and he laughed.

'You must be the only person here who's actually eaten any of that. Well, you'll still have space for a cocktail somewhere. Please stay, it's been months since you had any fun.'

'Years,' I said, and he squeezed my shoulder.

'Just fifteen, twenty minutes, I promise.'

It wasn't just twenty minutes, of course. It became clear as I watched Malachy move through the party that he had set his cap at sleeping with the gallery owner's daughter, his friend. It would be churlish, to hurry him up. I was used by now to Malachy's constant and fluid, somehow blameless engagements with women; I understood that they needed to take their course. I suppose they were his way of navigating his world, as retreat from it was mine. And so I found a half-hidden place – a cloakroom-like area, partitioned by a curtain, adjacent to a loo – and pretended to read something on my phone.

When after fifteen minutes or so a man emerged from the loo I thought that he looked as sheepish as I felt, and caught out. He was holding a plate in one hand and an empty wine-glass in the other. A fork, his fingers laced around it.

'Excuse me,' he said.

'I wasn't waiting.'

'I was—'

He laid the plate and glass and fork down on the floor, straightened up and scratched the back of his neck. He was older than me – thirty, early thirties, I guessed – and though perhaps he wasn't conventionally handsome I thought that he looked amazing. A bony, heart-shaped face, shiny black eyes behind glasses, long eyelashes. His cheeks were grooved lightly with acne scars, which I have always found beautiful.

'I hate having to stand and eat,' he said, the sheepishness all gone. His expression was severe now, he was a wolf. 'The toilet's the only place you can sit in silence and eat properly.'

'Well,' I said. 'I was reading a pretend article on my phone so I didn't have to talk to anyone.'

I showed him the unlit screen. He looked at it and then at me with that severe, almost schoolmasterly expression behind glasses, professorial hair upright and unkempt. And then, as if a decision had been made – I suppose it was – he broke into a broad smile. I thought that even his teeth were lovely.

'I'll leave you to it,' he said, not moving, and I shook my head.

'I finished the article.'

He sat down beside me there in the cloakroom, our backs against the wall. He told me that it wasn't just that he hated standing up to eat. Food or no food, he often spent most of a party locked inside a toilet cubicle, with a glass of wine. How I loved that. There could have been nothing I found more charming. As he spoke, I watched his hands. I was fascinated by their gestures, which were both tense – he could have been gripping a lectern – and fluid, dancer-like.

And he was funny, he made me laugh. At his own expense, often. As the hours passed he unfolded his life story for me, piece by piece. He had been a weedy little boy, he said, which hadn't gone down well with his macho father or on his macho council estate. Little Lord Haringey. He wasn't self-pitying when he spoke about his father. He'd been bullied and beaten by him, yes, but he'd also been tended and watered like a beloved plant. Smacked and coddled by the same broad hand. His parents' paltry salaries had gone straight into paint-brushes for the Fauntleroy son, he said, much to his mother's and brothers' dismay. I wasn't surprised when he said he was a painter. With that combination of tenderness and hatred I thought he must be capable of creating.

Passionately he'd always loved two things other than painting, he told me that night: football and women. Those were the things he'd always found most beautiful. As an adolescent, his love for them had just about kept him out of the reject pile that he was, with his thick spectacles and slight physique and artistic sensibilities, in every other way socially destined. Women, I remember thinking as I twirled my empty glass by its stem. Beauty. As if he read my thoughts he pushed his glasses up the bridge of his stern nose and elaborated. He wasn't interested in conventional beauty, he said. His hunger was for the kind that was harder to see. Oh, he got me. But I also think that he meant every word of it all. He was never anything other than true to his values, impossible as they became.

*

That was what I thought about when we left his parents' flat and walked in silence back through Liam's estate, down his childhood streets. I tried to take his hand but he moved it away, not quite gently. When we got to the station, he told me he'd meet me at home later; he needed to go straight to the studio. I watched as he walked off to find a bus, his hands in his pockets, shoulders back up near his ears – that defensive, rolling gait I imagined him having since he was a boy.

With George on my lap I made the slow journey back through the outer stretches of North London, as grim and endless to me as South London was to Liam, and felt about as irreparably distant from the father of my child as I did from the sick man on the sofa. I looked down at George's face, the deep-set eyes he and Liam had both inherited from Krystyna, and tried to remember Zoe's words. An unreachable wisdom, she had said. Some unreachable wisdom. George beamed, reached for my face, scratched my cheek with his little nails. Perhaps it's just us now, I thought, and I felt shocked by that formulation, by the ease with which the words had sounded out in my mind.

I swiftly grew to love Zoe's house. Even now, it is what I picture when I think of a beautiful home. The chequered flagstones that clicked under Mildred's claws, the creamy Aga and plain white walls of the kitchen. She did colour very well: a huge turquoise dresser she kept her plates in, a butter-yellow kitchen table and orange Mora clock in the hall. All Gustavian antiques, she said. I liked that she presumed I'd know what Gustavian denoted – I couldn't have said who or when Gustav was – but also the name conjured up Sweden, and inevitably then I thought of Tuva. But there were other pieces to distract me. A huge, ominous Victorian birdcage. A lute, propped up on the mantelpiece. A series of tiny square canvases spaced evenly along one otherwise empty wall, like the square letters of Tree's tattoo. *Kindness ...*

Upstairs was sparse: pine furniture, clean lines, little colour. Low beds, a tidy desk. Liam – an almost-obsessive proponent of psychoanalytic theory, who saw metaphor in everything – would have said that that represented a character focused on external appearance, putting all her decorative efforts into the rooms visible to strangers and none into the private. He might even have gone as far as to have said that there was an emptiness to Zoe, an absence of internal life.

That wouldn't have been right. Zoe had a great capacity for self-appraisal – she told me things about herself that surprised me. She spoke almost ruthlessly about her strengths and weaknesses as a writer and also about her alienation from her parents, the cruelty she felt she'd shown in her increasing awareness of their class and in her own, self-denying snobbery towards it. Her snobbery – her contempt for what she'd considered her parents' provincialism – had stemmed from weakness and vanity, she said, very matter of fact. Weakness, vanity, the coldness of ambition.

I had never encountered candour like hers. In response, I – always such a private person – found it unusually easy to talk.

In many ways, Zoe rehabilitated me over the course of that summer. She got me taking an interest in food, whose presence in my frantic, aimless days as a new mother had dwindled to functionality. I hadn't seen friends for a long time: I'd joined none of the local mother groups, which struck me as desultory, and I avoided the friends I already had, citing George's colic as an obstacle to any kind of meeting until the invitations dropped away altogether. Now Zoe's calls gave me a place to go and a time to get somewhere. They were a reason to brush my hair, to present myself with at least a measure of thought. And she got me talking to people again. I heard myself speak to her friends when they visited with some degree of eloquence, or at least I remembered that I knew about things: books, a little history. I was like an archaeologist, brushing away at dusty earth to find the sturdy foundations of something. Something that used to be real, a real thing.

But if the introduction of Zoe into my life served a rehabilitative function, Liam remained a strong competing force. In the complex grandeur of his grief – Hal being, with each week that went past, swiftly sicker and weaker – Liam was even more impossible than he had ever been: impatient, self-important, terse. But I can't blame Hal's illness. With Liam I suppose I had always sunk into the role of solicitous assistant to his ego: his arrogance and his churning, tortuous self-loathing.

Around the tidal edges of his moods I was rendered a second-guessing creature with no solidity, no clear outline. I am ashamed to think of it. My conviction such a shrunken thing. Even the sex was never quite right with us – prolific as it was before George, it always felt somehow ponderous, an unanswered question. God, that was a terrible relationship. In almost every way it could have been, it was terrible. A dazzling failure, I suppose, were it not for the creation of George, who emerged from our crooked union independently of us and our errors and base frailties.

We never spoke about Frantoio, Zoe and I. Nothing more than the lightest of references, and those only from her, never from me. But sometimes when we were together I tried to recall her as she'd been that summer.

I did remember her arrival, I thought. Yet another woman we vetted for signs of interest in my father. I remembered, too, that we quite swiftly exonerated her from being a potential threat – he was too absorbed that year, in any case, with Tuva and his work.

And so in fact the only clear memory I held of Zoe was really a memory of Krishna. They were sitting together on the chairs under the fig tree, reading while I whittled sticks in the dry grass. I glanced up at them occasionally. Krish was in fresh white linen, I think, Zoe in a crumpled dress and a sun hat. She looked, I remember thinking – not without that particularly confident brand of disdain that children do so well – very self-conscious in the hat. The brim drooped sloppily at one side, so that she kept plucking at it as she read. It was the hat of a scarecrow, it made me feel sad.

And Krish lifted his eyes from his magazine and said something casually kind about it, about the sun hat. That is what I remember. It was a light remark, nothing overt enough to patronise. Perfectly judged, like everything I'd ever seen him do, up until the final night of his trip.

After all of that, Krish disappeared from our family. But he did become very prominent in public life – a household name, in a certain kind of household. One of the great financial brains of the country. Tenaciously I avoided any coverage of him, so that I only saw his face once again, after Frantoio.

He hadn't come to my mother's burial or wake, which struck me as unfair at the time because he was perhaps one of two family friends I could ever remember her really talking to. He had neither sidestepped nor patronised her, as everyone else had done. On the other hand, I couldn't have borne his presence. Tree was changed enough as it was, and not just because of her shorn hair and tattoo – though the effect those physical changes had on me was immense. I had recently turned eleven, and there can be little of more significance to a pubescent girl than appearance, particularly that of her female idol, a young woman known and celebrated for her beauty. I felt humiliated on her behalf, by the disappearance of that black and wild Rapunzel hair. I felt humiliated by her naked neck.

The behavioural changes were hardly subtler than the new hairstyle or my mother's old puritan mantra, stamped across her back. She had become so dark and still, that is all I can think when I try to remember. She seemed to stand in shadow. All her fizzing, crackling, barely controlled energy – that energy that both infected and unsettled other people, and had always released and uplifted the three of us, her siblings and disciples – had been subsumed into silence. She had become a full stop. Everything stopped in her. Dialogue, laughter, noise. She, the loudest of the four, now muted us, a finger held up to our lips. I only learned much later that she'd been prescribed lithium at that time and was in the medication's initial throes.

It was many years after her death that I saw Krish, in the South Terminal at Gatwick Airport. I was tired after a cheap dawn flight from Greece, barely looking as I stepped onto the escalator to go down to the baggage carousels – and then suddenly there he was, narrow face and shoulders filling a huge TV screen. He was handsome as ever, with a slight silvering of his hair now. I turned my head, climbed back up a few steps to keep myself level with him.

He was being interviewed outside Lehman Brothers, in whose uppermost echelons he'd worked until its collapse that morning. The TV was muted, but there were subtitles and a red headline scroll sliding across the bottom of the screen: *Investment Bank Lehman Brothers has filed for bankruptcy …* I don't remember what his subtitles said. I have never been interested in these things. They come and go, they pass so quickly. I didn't care about any of the banks in 2008, I knew I should be angry but it all seemed self-evident to me, of course they had played foul, of course it was unfair, of course it was disgusting, surely everyone had always known that. I didn't grasp what it would be to be truly impacted by such a crash. Instead I watched Krish's face, craning my neck as the escalator pulled me down and away from him. He looked animated, charged by a sort of furious euphoria, his tie loosened and hair a little dishevelled so that he was like a schoolboy, released for the summer holiday.

When I reached the bottom of the escalator I looked back up, a woman tutting as she had to move around me, and then Krish's face was replaced by a moving image of anxious men and women walking out of the Lehman Brothers glass doors, clutching their cardboard boxes like dunce hats. His juniors, stepping giddily into their uncertain fates. He, naturally, would be fine.

As I stood with all the other tired strangers in the baggage hall I pictured Krish's animated face on the screen again and thought, *I wonder if you still like to sleep with nineteen-year-old girls*. But that, too, was unfair. I was trying to push him into a mould he didn't fit but that made him easier for me to hate. And why should I hate him after all, that episode hadn't been responsible for Tree's death.

I couldn't bear anything that had caused her pain or humiliation when she was alive. The small failures of her life have always been unbearable to me.

Z

She tells Zoe things.

She has a reticence about her that is unusual. It would be natural to take her for a closed book. But then, relatively easily, with a few gentle pushes, she tells Zoe things.

She says that she distrusted adults as a child.

She says she was always conscious, as a child, of getting things wrong. Particularly around her father, from whom she seems as far removed as Zoe had imagined when she stayed with them that summer.

She misremembers the house in Sicily. She places the great fig tree on the left as you approach the house from the garden. She describes the walls as yellow, but they weren't. It was all white.

She remembers Zoe, she claims, though Zoe is unsure. She says Zoe wore a hat, a sun hat, but Zoe isn't sure she did.

Zoe can tell that she doesn't like talking about that summer.

She says she felt dislodged when she had her baby. Dislodged – Zoe likes that word, its precision.

She worships her siblings. She holds her oldest sister up as a tragic heroine or martyr, but she isn't ready to talk much about her.

She returns questions more often than she needs to. She takes great care not to appear uninterested or self-involved, to be talking too much about herself.

She says that of all the siblings she is probably most similar to Malachy, though Zoe cannot see the resemblance. Zoe remembers him as steady, grounded. She is cleverer, probably, but she rattles. Or rather: there are loose and painful things in her that would rattle, if you took her by the shoulders and shook.

She is defensive of her siblings. Zoe can see that she holds criticism for them within her, but she will never voice it.

One day when she comes she has burnt her arm on the oven; she strokes the blister gently as she talks. The tenderness of her self-touch is unexpected.

She talks about her PhD, which was on kindness and cruelty as motifs in folklore in literature. Zoe keeps a straight face. The things people study.

She doesn't like talking about her partner, the child's father, whom Zoe has in any case googled and judged to be a slippery sort.

Zoe can tell that she dresses well for her visits, that she has put care each time into her choice of clothes. She is usually understated but looks good one day in a pair of wide trousers that are zig-zagged, black and white, altogether louder than anything Zoe imagines their owner has ever said, or done.

Her visits are frequent now: two, three times a week. She is becoming a presence in the house, unobtrusive but present, like Mildred. She learns where the mugs are kept, the washing-up gloves. These things please Zoe in a way she wouldn't have expected.

She strokes the baby's cheek or fingers or the soles of his feet as she talks, she never lets him go long without eye contact. Sometimes when she is talking to Zoe she addresses the words to the baby instead, with a smile and wide-open eyes, so that he is included.

She worries that the baby won't like her, or that she hasn't done right by him somehow. That she needs to give him more, more. She doesn't say that, but Zoe can tell.

N

I hadn't enjoyed alcohol since I'd become a mother. It was another way I felt that Liam found me changed, as if I'd crossed over into a new, constricted place. But with Zoe, I started to taste it again. She waited until six o'clock before she drank, calling it The Hour, rising from her seat in the garden to go inside and return with a bottle and glasses and a corkscrew shaped like a snake.

'It was your father who taught me the difference between OK wine and really good wine,' she said one day, busying herself with a bottle. She had never mentioned my father before, I didn't think, though we saw each other often now. I watched her as she poured the wine: a misty rosé, the same very pale pink as the sky.

It had struck me a few times as strange, that she had maintained no contact with him. He was always assiduous – more than that, even quite brilliant – at maintaining friendships, including those that had strayed into more than friendship. In nearly all of his former protégées, the talented, promising, illustrious reams of them, he had managed to inspire total devotion. Genuine affection, genuine loyalty.

'He's snobby about rosé,' I said.

'I'm sure he is. But it can be subtle. Try this.'

I took a sip and nodded, as if she were a waiter.

'I still remember the wine he served in Sicily – really thick, pungent stuff I wouldn't have thought I'd like. But it was a revelation.'

That would have been Tuva's choice, I thought.

'And then he used to take me and some other writers my age to the Garrick. He made it a bit of a mission, I think, to educate my palate.' She smiled. 'I imagine he was appalled by my lack of finesse.'

'My palate remains uneducated. He never made me his mission.'

I laughed, as my siblings and I customarily did, careful to show that we were wry about his foibles. But as I did so it occurred to me how strange it was: he spent all that time fostering young talent, a kind of patron of the arts, and missed us out entirely.

'And your mother?' she asked. 'Was she a connoisseur?'

I watched her face carefully, then. Surely the question was disingenuous, I thought; she must have known that my mother was not a connoisseur of anything. The word felt so far removed from her as to be humiliating.

But Zoe's expression was unironic, uncharged.

'I hope you know,' she said, 'you never have to talk about your mother if you don't want to. I know how hard it must be, even after all these years.'

'No, I don't mind talking about her. I'm just surprised, I

suppose – she didn't really drink, I don't think. I suppose she never really got the hang of it. She was brought up in a community.'

She leaned back, nodded in that way she often did: impartial and knowing, more psychotherapist than friend.

'Tell me more about that.'

I was used to people asking me about it. People were naturally fascinated. There was a comic line I could do, which I'd heard each of my siblings rehearse at one point or another: our inbred cultic provenance, cross-eyed hillbillies eating curds. Or there was a salacious version: our virgin mother's escape from brainwashing, from a cult. Whenever I had told the story as one of those two extremes, I felt wretched afterwards, as if I'd sold her.

'They called themselves the Fabelhof. I don't know a huge amount about them – she didn't talk much about herself.'

'But she told you certain things?'

I thought again about that bungled interview I did, the tape with its long, whirring silences. *What time did you wake up*, for God's sake. *What did you eat for breakfast.*

'My dad told me most of what I know, actually. It was a closed community, as in, closed off from modern life – they practised traditional medicine, hardly used electricity, that kind of thing. They made or grew everything they consumed, everything they used. Clothes, furniture, machinery, food. Everything.'

'And it was religious, rather than … progressive.'

'Oh yes. Very religious. I know prayer was a huge part of

her childhood. Prayers and songs and fables, moral tales. Fabelhof, the Fable House.'

'Fables, as in animal stories?'

'Animals, and other things – like the wind, or my mother used to tell us one about trees.'

'Go on.'

'A man goes into a wood and asks the trees to give him a small branch, just for a gift. So they do, out of kindness. And then the man fits an axe-head to the branch, and uses it to cut all the trees down.'

Zoe nodded again in that way she had, as if she could never be surprised by anything at all.

'Meaning: don't give your enemy the means to destroy you.'

'Yeah,' I said, and sipped my wine. 'You're right. Though I think I always interpreted it more simply, as just an indictment of human beings. What perfidious shits we can be.'

Zoe laughed.

'Well that's certainly true. Did your mum speak negatively about it – the Fabelhof?'

'No.'

'Really? Never?'

'No, never. Why?'

'Well, she left the place.' She frowned then; a flicker of something like concern. 'Tell me if I'm intruding, by the way.'

'No, you're not,' I said. 'She didn't fall out with them. It wasn't – acrimonious. She left because she fell in love, or thought she did, I suppose. She didn't run away, not in that kind of way. I think she was happy enough there.'

But as I said it, I heard my mother's quiet voice on the tape. *We were too tired to be lonely.*

'Ok,' said Zoe.

George started to fuss. I picked him up off his stomach, held him onto my lap, one hand over his warm belly.

'What did your father make of her background?'

'He's always spoken about the Fabelhof as an anthropologist might – he was curious. I'm sure he would have liked to write about them.'

'But he didn't.'

'No. He was respectful of her background. Or her privacy around it, I guess.'

She nodded.

'Did he respect the Fabelhof itself?'

'Elements of it, sure. He's – obsessed with hard work, anyone who works hard. He liked that they were grafters, I think. And I remember him saying once that they had a great emphasis on charity.'

'Right.'

'There's that saying – Mum quoted it sometimes – *Do all the good you can, by all the means you can, in all the ways you can.*'

'Yes,' she said, nodding, 'John Wesley.'

'You know everything.'

She smiled, holding out a hand to Mildred, who came and kissed it.

'But it wasn't a Wesleyan community,' she said.

'No. I don't think so. I don't know.'

'What did they make of your parents' marriage?'

'Hm. I don't know that they ever knew about it. She didn't keep in touch. My impression is that there would have been … no space for her there, once she'd left. But I'm sure she could have visited, if she'd wanted to.'

She nodded, but I thought that she looked unconvinced, and I realised that I was tired of talking about it.

'It was perfectly amicable,' I said.

'Still. She must have found it all very painful.'

I didn't like that. My mother's pain was mine to hold for her.

'Sorry,' she said. 'I'm overstepping. That wasn't my place to say.'

'It's fine. Don't worry.'

But none of it was fine, I thought. I hadn't held my mother's pain for her when she was alive. I never asked the kinds of questions Zoe was asking now, fundamental questions. I never asked her how much she missed the siblings she'd left behind, the ones she'd cradled in her arms as babies. Or whether she felt shame in the godless path she chose, the failed love affair with the historian, the godless marriage in which she ended up. And then, finally, the godless children who let her down that summer before she died, and who had perhaps – in different ways, on different scales – been letting her down ever since.

'I'm intruding,' said Zoe. 'Sorry. I go into interview mode sometimes, when I'm really fascinated by something.'

'It's fine,' I said again. 'I'm just – I suppose I don't know that much about it, truthfully.'

She waited.

'I suppose I feel embarrassed that I don't.'

'You were so young,' she said. 'I remember you at the wake. Still a tiny thing. Tiny, watching everything.'

She looked down at the dog and then sternly back up.

'It broke my heart, actually.'

Liam was brooding when I got home. I knew immediately; his face became wolfish with it.

'Where have you been?'

'At Zoe Goodison's.'

'Just you and her?'

'Yes,' I said, holding George out towards him. He hesitated, then came over to us, took our little boy in his arms.

'Hi, big man,' he said, but he was too distracted to engage with him properly, to swing him up in the air and make him smile. 'Aren't you a bit late for his bath?'

'It's fine,' I said. 'We're not that late.'

'I didn't know where you were.'

'Why didn't you call?'

He didn't answer, but as I undressed George on our bathroom floor he came in and put the lid of the loo down and sat on it, watching us. He looked handsome: imperious and tortured, dark shadows under his eyes, little bolts of silver bursting out in the dark curls on his temples.

'I went to Dad's chemo session,' he said, and I felt the accusation in his tone.

'Sorry. I didn't know it was today.'

'Yeah.'

'It must have been really difficult.'

'It's not even doing anything,' he said. 'It's palliative. It's buying him another – I don't know, month or two. What's the point in that?'

'I'm sorry.'

'It's pointless.'

I lay George down in the bath and let the water shine on his round little belly. His womanly thighs.

'Why are you spending so much time with that woman?' he asked, and I concentrated on rubbing soap into the folds of George's neck. That soft throat, I thought, every time I did it. There is a violence so close to a mother's gentle touch, just the other side of the line. I thought, *How fragile we all are*.

'Nem?'

'Well, what else do I have to do?'

'See Sophie? She's on mat leave.'

'She lives in Chiswick.'

'Your other friends?'

'They're at work.'

'Why doesn't this woman work?'

'She does. She's a successful author.'

'Is she a lesbian?'

I laughed.

'What?'

'Is she coming on to you?'

'Don't be ridiculous.'

'If it was a man you were spending all your time with, it'd be inappropriate.'

'Would it?'

'Of course it would.'

'Well, she's not – coming on to me. I suppose we're friends.'

He snorted, lightly.

'Friends,' he said. 'She's twice your age.'

'She's not twice my age. She's late forties, if that.'

'Old enough to be your mother, virtually,' he said, and I shook my head, exhausted. One of his knees jigged up and down, ceaselessly; his hands were clasped together as if in a knot.

'Actually, no one comes on to me anymore,' I said.

I smiled sideways at him and he looked at me and the knee stopped jigging. He softened, a little. Jealousy did this to him. It made him sulky and then it brought him closer to me.

'Don't be stupid. I do.'

'Hm.'

I lifted George's slippery body from the water, wrapped him in a towel. Liam stood and as he passed us he rubbed a hand over the back of my head.

'I'll put some food on while you put him to bed,' he said. 'I'll pour a glass of wine.'

I found him brooding in the kitchen again once I'd put George down for the night, frowning at the traffic below. There was more to come, I thought. We would be locked into a fight now, tussling and tugging until whatever it was finally came to the surface. I closed my eyes, and thought how much I'd like to sleep.

Then I opened them and saw that he had turned to me, his expression soft again. I exhaled and he walked over and reached for me, held my hips under his hands. Whatever happened, I thought, his hands were things I could not imagine I'd ever stop loving. An artist's hands, practical and agile.

'I love you,' he said, and kissed me.

'I love you too.'

Still he had something he wanted to say, I knew, and so I waited. I rested my forehead on his chin, so that he wasn't being watched. Any pressure, any sense that he was being pursued, and the words would recoil, snail-like.

'I think I've failed you in certain ways,' he said. He cleared his throat, took a breath to speak. 'I always resolve to change and be better. I come home from the studio and all the way on the train I'm so excited to see you and George, I'm so full of good intentions and patience, and then I walk through the door and as soon as I'm stressed – by anything, even the tiniest thing – all my good intentions just ... I don't know, they – it's as if my head is in a vice. When I feel stressed it's like every single one of my nerves is on fire and all I can do is get away, be on my own again.' He laughed drily. 'Maybe I'm not cut out for a family. Maybe that's it. Maybe I'm like my dad, and I should never have had kids. Maybe that's why he was always so fucking furious all the time, because he was like me, he had his head caught in a vice too.'

I thought about the excitement with which he had persuaded me we should start a family. We were so stupid, I thought, so unbearably stupid. I pulled away from him and took a deep breath.

'You are cut out for a family. And you're going to be a wonderful father to George. We'll work through the stress stuff.'

But I didn't believe what I was saying. He might well not be a wonderful father, I thought with a coldness I didn't recognise. And in fact I was furious that he could pronounce so flippantly that he might not be cut out for parenthood, after all. Maybe I'm not, either, I could have said. Maybe no one is. But it was academic at this point, at least for me. I didn't get to opt in or out, depending on whether or not I found it to suit me.

I didn't say that. I had learned very early in our relation-ship that, however badly he behaved, whatever wrong he committed, attacking Liam achieved nothing. My job instead was to coax, to persuade. I took a breath.

'You're an artist. It's famously hard, to marry creativity and parenting.'

'You're the expert,' he said, and I regretted my use of the word 'famous'. How he hated to step into my father's lofty shadow.

'No, you're the expert. You're the artist. And you're under a lot of pressure. We both are, but you've got the show coming up and now your dad, too.'

'It was fucking horrible, sitting there with him in the

chemo unit. He's so—' He waited for the word, rubbed one of those lovely hands over his mouth. 'Tiny.'

Then he pulled me close again, and his voice cracked as he spoke. He had spent his whole life, he said, longing to be stronger than his father. He had fantasised, throughout his adolescence particularly, about seeing him afraid, laid low by fear. He'd even fantasised about killing him. Now, finally, he was the stronger of the two. Finally he had seen, in the depleted figure perched in the hospital chair, the behemoth of his youth cowed. And it had only been painful, only terrifying. I listened, and I stroked the back of his head as he spoke, but my anger hadn't dissipated. I didn't feel as moved as I should have. There was that coldness again, I thought – in me, who'd always felt Liam's pain as my own, often more acutely than my own.

And so instead, now, of contemplating his plight, I wondered whether anyone had accompanied my mother to her chemo sessions. I imagined her in a hospital chair with a cloth tied around her head, a book of word puzzles on her lap. A biro in her square right hand. Her feet and knees placed neatly together. The little bony bird she'd become, by the end.

We had sex that night. Before Liam went to sleep he kissed my forehead and told me that he felt close to me, for the first time in a long time.

'I feel close to you too,' I said. I lay there watching the passing lights on the ceiling, and then I sat up and watched our baby outstretched on his mattress, fists coiled either side of his head. And I thought: *I don't feel close.* All I had been able to think as he'd moved above me was that I was missing out on precious sleep, and that it would make George's night wakings more difficult.

As I watched George's stomach rise and fall I wanted to be back at Zoe's house. I didn't want to be sitting there on our crumpled bed next to Liam, in the close fug of our room. I had the strange thought that I wanted to be lying alone on Zoe's spare bed with its crisp sheets and the shadows of trees flickering against a bedroom wall, with her asleep in her own room just down the cool, clean corridor. I wondered if her hands and fingers still moved lightly, those restless picking motions, as she slept.

But it wouldn't do to think like that, I thought. I didn't want to have to wonder what it meant, I was too tired to wonder about anything. Instead I turned from George to Liam, who was curled on his side like another baby, and I thought of the scrawny adolescent who'd wanted to kill his father – that huge, bombastic, bullying man – and in that way, with a little effort, I could generate tenderness in myself. I lay back down and rested my hand on his ribs, felt them shift and slide with his breath. Liam as a little boy, cowering in the corner of their kitchen. Or as an adolescent, flinching in the door of his parents' bedroom, shouting at Hal to leave Krystyna alone, skinny arms and teenage acne and a breaking voice, trying to be a man. Little Lord Haringey, brave and terrified. I pictured that, and I imagined my tenderness as something tangible inside me that I could pull out, let unfurl into the room and curl around his sleeping body.

My father sold the Greenwich house when Etta and I were at university. He called us each to tell us, and then, as was his way, he managed to enlist various friends to pack the house up for him. So that when we came home for the weekend only two weeks later, the contents of the place were already largely boxed up.

I moved from room to empty room and already it was foreign to me. There were dark squares on walls where paintings had been taken down, dimples and pockmarks in the carpet where furniture had sat. In the absence of blinds and curtains, the rooms were washed with a cold and wistful northerly light.

Only our own bedrooms remained to pack up, everything else was done. So I never had another chance to open those drawers where, since my mother's death, a few of her things had been stored. A handful of books, which had always looked colossally uninviting. Her dresses, pressed and folded, vinegary with mothballs. Her sewing kit in its carpet bag. And a tin box, whose lid had become deformed and no longer fit, which we understood her to have taken with her when she left the Fabelhof. That box I had opened many times, half-hoping always that I might find something new inside – some fresh insight – but of course it was always the same sparse relics from her childhood: the few photos, some neatly folded cushion cases, and a child's diary with a padlock that opened, 'My Diary' printed on the front against hazy watercolours. The kind of thing a little girl loves, not a nineteen-year-old brave enough to run off with an older man. And it was empty, save for her name written painstakingly on the first page. An empty diary! What a metaphor Liam would have made of that, had I told him. As far as I knew, they were the only things she ever took with her when she left America.

The morning after I'd spoken to Zoe about the Fabelhof, I woke up with the urgent sense that I must see all those things again. I wanted to hold them. Zoe's barrage of questions – or perhaps more accurately my halting answers, the glaring lacunae in my knowledge – had uncentred me. I felt as if I'd left my suitcase on a train, or lifted my foot to climb a stair where there wasn't one.

I made coffee, and then standing in the kitchen with George on my hip, his plump hands batting first at the scalding cup on the worktop and then the phone in my hand, I composed an email to my father. It was particularly long and laborious. I was very keen to introduce him to George, I said, though I wasn't. I'd enjoyed his recent piece in the *NYRB*, though I hadn't actually made the time to read it. I was sad to see an obituary of his old acquaintance John Peterson, though I'd been unmoved. And then, finally, I asked if I could come over to have a look through my mother's belongings. It must have been the first time either of us had mentioned her to each other in several years.

I sent it, put the phone down to take a long sip of coffee, and before I could set the cup back down on the kitchen surface there was a whooshing sound on my phone.

Will have T find the things you're looking for.
Best etc., D.

That was all.

I started to read Zoe's novels. I read them in order of publication, and as I did I thought I could detect the trajectory of her writing maturity alongside her personal maturity. It was a way to get to know her. The first was the best – snappy and dark and cosmopolitan – but I preferred the later ones, particularly a novella called *Strange*, which was just that, strange. It was short and spare, more a meditation on eccentricity than a story. And not the self-announcing kind of eccentricity I perhaps knew better than most – the tiresome, trilling people who'd filled our home and holidays, at pains in their outfit choices alone to announce their distance, wealth aside, from the bourgeoisie – but the quiet strangeness of those who approach life differently, who can't or won't quite enter the game or master the rules. Outcasts, vagrants, loners. That book taught me to think for the first time of my mother as an eccentric. Her lack of self-regard began to strike me as a radical act.

I wanted to ask Zoe about her books, but it felt like an invasion to do so. More than anything, I wanted to ask how she wrote so convincingly about motherhood, or even childbirth. *Strange* opened on an operating table, unseen hands rummaging inside a mother's abdomen, and then without ceremony a mewling baby tugged out and held up, up into the blinding air, the theatre's violent white. That was how I had experienced it, after thirty-six hours of labour. The violence and safety of that operating theatre, its terror and calm. A heartbeat, a heartbeat. That was all.

I didn't ask Zoe, but I got my answer to the question one evening when I'd put George to bed upstairs, in her spare bedroom. I had taken to doing that a few times a week: bathing and putting him to bed at Zoe's, eating supper with her in that peaceful garden. Then when it was dark and I was soft with wine I would lift his sleeping shape from the bed in the darkness and walk home, my warm, just-solid baby against my chest.

The flat was always empty when I got back. At that time, Liam barely came home for anything more than sleep. I caught snatches of him in the morning, the odd evening, or creeping into bed beside me in the flickering dark of night. In the lead-up to his show, all of his work and all his focus had become subsumed into one major project: a huge portrait of his father. The biggest, the most ambitious and most difficult portrait he'd ever done, he told me, though he wouldn't say any more. He was locked inside it. He could barely see George and me when he was home. Like my own father, he'd ask a question and disappear back within himself before I'd had time to answer. Charged and monomaniacal and underslept, he had perhaps never been so handsome to me – but in the way that a stranger is handsome, or a man in a daguerreotype. I felt I had no access.

That evening it was only Zoe and me in her garden, the dog lying between us on the grass.

'And are you happy?' she asked.

What a question. I exhaled, stretched my neck.

'No, let me ask you something different. Put aside everything else, I'm just talking about you in your new role. A mother, as of – almost six months now, isn't it? Do you feel fulfilled, is it what you expected?'

'It's not,' I said. 'I could never have expected any of it – no, nothing could have prepared me for how it's been.' I looked up at the back facade of her house, at the window of the spare room in which my baby slept. 'I feel full,' I said, to avoid the word 'fulfilled', a state of being that I could no longer, in fact, begin to imagine. 'The love I have for him is crazy, and sort of alarming. It's even more than I could have anticipated.'

She took a quick, sharp breath, and I wondered whether she had wanted children of her own, and whether it hurt her that she hadn't had them.

'But that's not to say the love is always enough,' I said, to mitigate the hurt. 'Or rather, it is enough, but that doesn't cancel out how hard I find it, frankly. Yes, even with the colic gone and with him sleeping better, I still find it the hardest thing I've ever done.'

'Of course it is,' she said. 'It's impossible. I know. I had two.'

My eyes must have widened. She looked down, reached her hand out to Mildred, who snuffled her palm.

'A son, Zachary. A daughter, Matilda. I didn't bring them up. It was out of the question. No, I couldn't abide it.'

I think I laughed, then. I didn't know what else to do.

'Oh, don't worry, I know how it sounds. I know what people think, and they're right. Men, women – most people are horrified when I say it. But I couldn't, I couldn't abide it; it almost killed me. For whatever reason, whatever lack there is in me, I couldn't do what other women do.'

She exhaled, with a whoosh. Filled my glass, and then her own.

'When they were three and one, I hit a wall, I really did. I remember the moment – I was trying to feed the baby outside a museum café in the South of France, can you imagine? In St Paul de Vence, of all places. The toddler was asking me questions – always those questions, that constant running stream of inanity – I'm talking as if all I had was contempt but I didn't, I also loved and was interested in those questions sometimes, but only sometimes – and there was no high chair and I was trying to shovel that dreadful baby mush between clamped lips, kneeling on gravel in front of an adult chair that the baby kept trying to hurl himself out of. The idiocy! Partly I couldn't cope with that. For my own shortcomings, I know, not theirs. They were only children! But I couldn't—' She cast around, picking the air in that funny ceaseless way. 'I couldn't be the one cushioning their idiocy, their inanity, their *total* inability and inexperience and ignorance and – incapacity … I thought, at that moment, pinning the baby – Zachary – back in the chair so he wouldn't hurl himself into injury, *There is no end to this. This is how it is now. I have to get these half-formed things up and out there into the world, and it won't even stop when they're eighteen, they'll still need me, they'll still understand so little, so terribly little.* I mean, look at me, I was still hard at work stumbling in the dark, and I was thirty-seven! How could I be their crutch, their torch through all that darkness?' She shook her head. 'No, the toddler asked me one more question – something she'd asked twice already in the past thirty seconds – and I realised it, cold and stark as light: I had to get out.

'"Take them," I told Sam, my husband – Sam Bennett, the architect – and I went and stood alone in front of a huge Chagall mosaic that I hadn't even noticed until that moment. I'd been so frantically meeting the kids' needs, I hadn't even noticed a wall-high Chagall, right there, bang in front of me! I hadn't even seen it. You can't – *see* – when your mind is down there in the pit. The dark, dank, messy pit. It's like you're in the orchestra, and the rest of life is up on the stage.' She shook her head again. 'No, motherhood is for other women to do – God, I admire you – but not for me.'

She leaned back in her chair, and I did too. I was stunned.

'It's refreshing,' I said, after a silence. 'To hear someone talk about it so honestly.'

That was a platitude, and also it wasn't quite true. What she said, how she said it – it alarmed me. The truth of all that she said, alongside her clear revulsion – those two things I found threatening, I couldn't see how to marry them.

'It was my writing, more than anything,' she said. 'I couldn't write, and that was crippling me, it was suffocating me. How could I think anything worth thinking, create anything worth creating, when my brain was forced into those endless, repetitive, *repetitive* logistical loops of thought – what time will this one need to eat, when will I get a chance to clip this one's nails, have I got dinner for them both, how long do we have until the next nap-time, how will I get this fucking stain out of my trousers because the baby's thrown Bolognese all over everything, on repeat, on repeat, on repeat. Other people manage it, somehow – look at you, you're not a frantic mess the whole time – but I was.' She took a deep breath. 'Yes, that's what it really boiled down to. I could see only two options left to me: either I live as a frantic, frazzled ball of rage, all the time, or I enter a place of bovine incuriosity, of total stupidity, of the indifference and calm that accompany stupidity. I would write nothing of any worth in either of those states. I thought I'd just have to give up writing. I'd have to do what every woman seems to do. I would simply have to efface, to subjugate every idea and impulse and will of my own.'

She leaned back again, shook her hair back from her face as if shaking it all away. Her fingers plucked, plucked, and then stilled on her knees. A pigeon had landed on the lawn, mauve and plump, and Mildred lifted her head from her paws and watched it. We all watched it, and as I did I wondered which state I'd entered. Did she see me as bovine? I had been frantic and frazzled for so long at the beginning of George's life, through the aftershock of birth and the constant war of his colic. But now that I was calmer and better-slept I approached a new, careful kind of happiness at times, in spite of the freedom I still mourned. In spite, too, of my distance from and disappointment in Liam.

And it's true, that happiness when it came was a kind of stupidity. Calm, earned at the expense – the conscious shutting-down – of curiosity.

Zoe could always read me.

'Whereas you,' she said kindly, 'you can subjugate a certain amount of will for George, but you can also hold on to something of your own, can't you?'

I thought, *Can I?* The truth was, I had no idea what was my own anymore. I thought that I hadn't seen clearly since George was born.

'I'm too selfish to be a mother, you see,' she said, and she leaned forward in her chair and kicked the air, quickly, so that the pigeon jumped backwards and hopped and flew away. 'That's what I realised. That's what it all boiled down to. I believed in my work. I believed in my *self*, in my autonomy. I couldn't give everything up. I tried, but I couldn't. I wouldn't.' She sat back. 'That's how it happened. You'll be horrified, you'll think I'm terrible. Most people do, I know. Selfish, immature, unnatural. Heartless.'

'No, I don't,' I said, though I wasn't yet sure that I didn't. 'I admire you, for knowing what you wanted. For being able to see clearly.'

She smiled faintly, stroking Mildred's head.

'What did you do?' I asked.

'I left them. I literally left them there, in France. Oh, I went back to the hotel with them that day, after the museum.

I pitched in for the rest of the afternoon, I helped Sam put them to bed in the evening. I remember Zachary, the baby, he was more difficult to put down than normal, he cried and cried and cried. The way he clung to me – it was as if he knew. And sure enough, that night I packed my suitcase and at first light I left. I said I'd see Sam in London, and I did, but only briefly. He still thought it was temporary, but I knew it wasn't. The divorce itself was quick. It was terrible, of course – it was very painful, for all of us – but it was also the best thing I could have done. For us all. The kids were better off with him, by far.'

We sat in silence for many minutes in her peaceful garden, and truly I was at a loss for what to say. I couldn't work out what I thought of what she'd done. I was arrested, I suppose, by her frankness – by the detached, entirely undefensive frankness with which she'd laid her crime bare; because it was a crime in my eyes, it was true that I was horrified, she was right about that. I thought of the baby, clinging to her as she tried to put him to bed. I imagined the toddler waking up in the morning to find her mother no longer there.

But there was something else I felt, undone as I was by her honesty: a kind of relief, on her behalf. Even in the worst moments of motherhood – the roiling storms of frustration, isolation, claustrophobia – leaving George would have been no easier for me than removing a limb. It was simply unfathomable. We were conjoined.

And so I was glad for her, I suppose, that she didn't have that. That she'd never had it. If she was able to leave a baby and a toddler and live her life without them, she was never conjoined with them in the way I was with George. Even before she left them, she was free. She had been trapped, like I was, by the external shackles of motherhood, but not by the shackles generated from within, which I found most confusing of all. How desperately I wanted freedom, and how desperately I clung to George, how almost physically painful it would have been to be apart from him. That paradox created a push and pull, a flux, a tension and constant movement, so that even now when I look back to early motherhood I see myself like a sailor freshly aground, still with her sea legs. There could be no stillness.

If I felt wary of Zoe in the wake of that fevered confession, it also brought me closer to her. It was impossible for me not to admire the honesty with which she'd carved out her life. She was ruthlessly true to it.

That was the evening I first spoke to her about Tree. She listened quietly and seriously when I told her about Tree's depression, its evolution and escalation and the increasing starkness with which she veered between her two extremes. On the one hand the manic, too-bright energy: the emboldened and misdirected ideas that carried her off, careering like a derailed train. On the other the absolute – injury, I suppose it was. The word 'depression' no match for how violently injured she was, when it struck.

I told my version of Tree's story: why I thought she dropped out of university to knock around London's underbelly. How muted she became on medication, how too-vivid she was when she was off it. I know she experimented with drugs. She lived in squats and disused, unorthodox places, she lived what my parents would have called a wild kind of life.

Finally, she stopped taking any medication or recreational drugs or even alcohol. In that final year she became palpably calmer and more present. Best of all, she took to visiting home every Wednesday, waiting for me outside the school gates and taking me to a café for tea. I was fifteen, she the wonderfully sophisticated age of twenty-four. She'd buy me a pancake or waffle or milkshake or whatever sickly treat I'd request, and she'd sit opposite me with her spidery fingers wrapped around a cup of coffee and ask me about my life, about boys and subjects at school and my future.

Those weekly teas came to overshadow everything else. At the time I hated school, where I found the classroom harsh and huge and remote, and I was lonely at home. It was many years since Tree and Malachy had moved out. My father had long since jettisoned Tuva, of course he had; their partnership could never have survived long without my mother's presence as its foil and buffer. He could never have shared his life with someone as vivid and vocal, who took up as much space, as Tuva. But he hadn't yet met Tabitha, his second wife, so girlfriends came and went unpredictably. Etta was mostly absent, absorbed in the bewitching business of popularity. And so for those two hours every Wednesday afternoon I basked in Tree's attention, longing for my classmates to walk past the café and see us. She looked amazing, with her pixie hair and high cheekbones; she had become a woman at some point. A grown-up. I liked to pretend, sometimes, that she was my mother.

She was walking me home from one of those teas when she first told me she was going away.

'For how long?' I asked.

'I'm not sure yet. A good few months, at least.'

We had just passed through the main gates of Greenwich Park and I stopped, panting, and leaned against the wall. We'd been walking fast and I'd eaten too much at tea, too quickly; I was winded suddenly by a stitch that felt like a knife in my lung. I bent over. I pressed my fingertips into the soft flesh under my ribs, and as I did I felt my eyes fill with tears. A good few months, I thought, and was flooded with such enormous hurt that I was grateful for the stitch, so that I didn't have to look at her until I could gather myself.

'I'm going to Appalachia,' she said. 'Are you OK?'

I grunted.

'A stitch.'

'I'm going to start the trip off at the Fabelhof.'

'What?'

'Mum's community.'

'I know, but – why?'

'I want to meet her family. Our family. I want to try to understand things a bit more, I think it'll help us.'

'I don't need help,' I said.

'Maybe I do.'

I took a deep breath, the stitch blooming cruelly.

'I'll see how that goes, and then I might go off and explore a bit. All those weird places – the Rust Belt, the Bible Belt.'

'On your own?'

'On my own. It kind of needs to be.'

I wiped the tears from my eyes. I was still bent over, staring at my scuffed school shoes.

'Are you sure you're OK?'

I nodded, swallowing painfully.

'It's just a stitch.'

'Maybe you'll go too, when you're older. I think it's important.'

'Why?' I asked, but what I really wanted to say was that staying near me was important too. With Tree's weekly visits, her new calm an umbrella above me, I'd been happier than I could remember being since my mother's death.

'It's important to understand where you come from.'

'Why?'

'Oh Nem, come on. I want to – I don't know, I guess I want to find my roots.'

'You're the Tree,' I said, and my voice was shaky. 'You should already know where your roots are.'

She laughed and put her arm around me and kissed my temple.

'Come on, invalid. Let's hobble home.'

The Appalachia trip was where I ended, when I spoke to Zoe that night. I couldn't take Tree's story further than that point. I didn't yet tell her that she died out there, in West Virginia.

She had a minor chest infection; she had an allergic response to a medication she was given; she died from anaphylaxis, four minutes before the paramedics arrived.

That was it. A last swollen breath, a life, and then. Tree's avoidable, irreversible end.

She should have gone out in a blaze of glory. She was all those things that build towards a glorious death: wild, flawed, beautiful. But in the end she was just another person, subject to life's grinding arbitrariness.

'I suppose it was a pilgrimage,' Zoe said, 'the trip to your mother's hometown,' and I liked that she understood it as that. Even more, I liked that she said and asked very little. She didn't try to put voice to her pity.

We sipped our wine, we sat in silence as the minutes passed in her cooling garden. I wondered what Zoe was thinking about. Her face never struck me as that of a woman at rest. When she was still, hers was the ready, listening stillness that accompanies active thought.

'Can I ask ...' she said and paused, stroking Mildred's face. 'This might be a painful question. But what is it that you miss the most about your sister? I suppose by that I mean – what was she, to you?'

It was a painful question. Intrusive too. But that was one of the things I relished in Zoe's company: her conversation was never small, never cursory; she was never going through the motions. There was a fastidiousness to every word she chose, whatever she was talking about, even if it was only food, or weather, or clothes, even if it was a question about my most private loss. And so, as I had come to do – meeting her frankness with a measured frankness of my own – I answered.

I missed the feeling I had when I was around Tree, I told her. It was indefinable, but if I tried my best I could see that with Tree I felt supported, but also I felt pushed. She had that crackling, propulsive energy. It electrified me. Even now, I am sure I would have led a different life if her energy had remained to propel me.

'And, of course,' I said, trying to lighten things, 'she was beautiful.'

'Oh, she was. Very.'

'Not that that's something to miss, exactly.'

But in truth, I did miss it. Everyone always says people they've lost were beautiful. Their mother was a beauty. Their grandmother – they've seen a black-and-white photograph from when she was a young woman – was beautiful. Well, my mother wasn't, nor was my grandmother – either grand-mother – but Tree was. I knew it shouldn't matter, it was no achievement of hers, it wasn't even what people found so attractive about her. But still, I missed it. I suppose I missed basking in it.

Until that evening I hadn't mentioned Tree's trip to Appalachia to anyone. I couldn't bear to. I didn't even speak of it to Liam, who was happy to leave the stones of my past unturned. Since Tree's death, I'd had an almost super-stitious feeling – it wasn't conscious, I didn't consciously subscribe to it, but still it held me tight – that if I spoke of

what had happened to her it would become real, and until I
did it wasn't.

That night, as I got into my empty bed beside George in his
cot, I googled Sam Bennett, architect. He was co-founder of
a firm I was sure I'd heard of, Bennett Tomlinson. Sleek,
expensive-looking office buildings, an art gallery somewhere
in Scotland, various high-end commercial projects. They had
won a number of awards. He must be rich, I thought. And all
as a single parent.

He had an unsatisfying, one-paragraph Wikipedia entry,
which referenced his two children. I looked at Zoe's much
longer entry, which I'd read a few times before, this time
scanning it for mention of the children, but it was as I'd
thought, they weren't there. Then I googled Zachary Bennett
and Matilda Bennett and in 'Images' I picked out the one
photo that was clearly of them: nice-looking, besuited young
teenagers flanking their father at some kind of function, some
architects' gala in which Sam had been nominated for something. I felt a strange, jealous admiration for them that I can't
quite explain even now, a kind of jealousy *over* them. In an
irrational way I wanted to know them, I wanted them to like
me. I tried to scrutinise their faces for accusation, or some
sign of damage from their abandonment, but they looked
intimidatingly grounded, stable. The boy in particular I studied, picturing a younger Zoe trying to get her baby to sleep,
comforting his crying, knowing that she was about to leave
him.

I put my phone aside and looked at my own baby boy. *To efface, to subjugate every idea and impulse and will of my own.* Was that what mothers did, the two billion mothers across the world? I considered the mothers living in dire poverty, subjugating every impulse to keep their children fed, their children alive. But my own mother hadn't lived in poverty, far from it. She could have had something of her own, and still she hadn't. For the first time in my life I felt something like anger towards her. *Why* hadn't she taken something of her own, why had she effaced herself? Was it for us, or my father, or both? We never asked for it. Not consciously. I wanted to reach back and shake her, tell her to take something for herself so that I didn't have to live with the guilt of it all. Her lack of self-regard wasn't a radical act, I thought; it was apolitical, irresponsible, it was even somehow selfish.

But I couldn't stand to feel anger, or the pain of its alternative. She must have had something. She must have kept something, she must have had a secret will and ideas and impulses that she kept and nurtured within her. Tree wanted her to have had them, too. That was what she was looking for, I thought, when she made her cursed pilgrimage to Appalachia. The secret things that made our mother a person, not a mule.

Z

His small buttocks swinging flatly, she writes.

She deletes *flatly*, writes:

His flat buttocks swinging.

She sits back and looks through the window beyond the laptop screen. Beneath, her garden; beyond, the flats and slopes of the roofs of other houses. She thinks there is little she loves as much as green leaves against the solemn grey-brown of London bricks.

This morning the sun slanted so coolly on the kitchen floor that she did something peculiar that she's never done before: she found herself on her knees with her arms stretched out before her, palms flat on the stone, a yawning kind of stretch pulling through her shoulders and then down her waking spine. She was struck by a sort of love for the floor. For a moment, she felt quite euphoric. She felt something like, *This is mine. I earned it. On my own, I got all of this, for myself.*

She couldn't convey that euphoria, quite, when she told the girl about Sam and the children the other day. It would perhaps have been insensitive, to speak of the freedom she gained. But the fact is that, just two days after leaving them, she'd found this house – it had been on the market only a week – and she'd known immediately, as soon as she walked through the front door, that it was absolutely right, what she'd done. In spite of all the recrimination and pain that her leaving had caused, would cause. To have found this place, which would be hers and hers alone.

The pain, she'd told herself, would pass. Sometimes she was afraid of it – it would catch her at moments, a little wild panic when she woke, so that she wanted to go back home to her baby's room and lift him from the cot and feel his soft, full cheek against her lips. Or she'd imagine the toddler, uncertain, standing on one leg in their bedroom doorway, asking for her in the middle of the night. It was as if something fell out of her stomach, then. It was very nearly too much to bear. But the day she first entered this house, following the estate agent through the cool empty rooms, she'd seen – as already, really, she'd known – that it was worth it. It was necessary.

She paid for it all herself. She has always paid her share of the children's costs. The film they made out of her first novel made that possible, but even if it hadn't she would have found a way. It had to be her money. She had decided in walking away from them that everything she did now – everything she wrote, everything she spent, every moment of time she apportioned to things – would be achieved and decided by her, and her alone.

It is like that, still. Which isn't to say things have come easily. Over the years her novels haven't done what she wanted them to do. They have been well received, they have done well and earned money, which is hardly a given – but she has been unable to penetrate the world with them as she did with the first three and as she might have continued to do with the patronage – even just the cooperation – of someone like Don.

But never mind Don. Regardless of him, everything she has is hers. Everything she does is hers. That is why she had that peculiar moment, stretching out like a cat on her kitchen floor.

She watches a real cat now, poised on the high garden wall, sniffing the air. It is as if she has conjured the creature up. She thinks that she is sniffing the air too, at moments like this. Gauging the balance of things: how things have added up, what might be lying in wait. She still feels that old pain, at times. It tugs within her, where her womb is, she supposes. But she was right, it did pass. It does pass.

On the screen, she swaps the words again.

His small buttocks swinging flatly, she writes.

N

'Your father's in Edinburgh,' Tabitha told me when I arrived at their house. She kissed my cheeks lightly, and when we parted George reached out to her. I was beginning to suspect that he might be a friendly, easy-natured child, which amused me given my and Liam's temperaments. I liked it in him. He could be a fern growing out from under our dank shade.

'Oh,' she was saying then, her face soft with delight, 'oh, he is gorgeous, aren't you gorgeous, just gorgeous,' and I followed her into that scented, somehow leafy-feeling hall that was grandly tasteful and restful in a way that our crowded childhood home had never been, all creams and soft greys. It purred, I thought, that house on that exquisite square with the hush of privacy about it.

Tabitha settled on the carpet with George, and I had the jarring thought that she made a nice grandmother, sitting on the floor beside him, graceful and warm.

'You'll find it all in the street-side room on the top floor,' she said, facing George, which spared me the awkwardness of acknowledgement. 'Your father had me get it down from the attic – I hope it's what you're expecting.' She turned to look up at me, an unobtrusive smile. 'Take your time, darling.'

As I climbed the quiet stairs I thought that unfortunately she was very nice. Sometimes in her absence I tried to vilify her – I could frame her as pretentious, or manipulative, or acquisitive – but in her presence it was impossible because I don't really think that she was any of those things. Or at least, no more than anyone else. And yet – if she had come on holiday to Frantoio as one of my father's female friends, we would have made a ready villain of her, of course we would. We would have done it easily, like peeling a tangerine. I wondered briefly whether Tuva was ever as bad as we thought she was, and then I put the thought out of my head.

Tabitha had left my mother's things out for me in one of their many spare rooms, which was otherwise stacked with redundant author copies of my father's novels. Towers and towers of books, unopened and unread, faintly sun-bleached – Don Travers, Don Travers, Don Travers, shouted their spines – and then on its own in the middle of the room were my mother's belongings, reduced to one cardboard box. On the side, in handwriting I didn't recognise, was written 'LYDIA EFFECTS'. Someone who knew her well enough to write her name, but not well enough to write 'things' or even 'stuff' instead of 'effects', which as a word I found brutally funereal. Her belongings, packed into a box by someone I didn't know, pulled down from the attic of a house my mother never lived in by a woman she never met. Now gazed at by a daughter she hadn't known for two decades.

For a moment, as I stood there gazing at that box, death struck me as the very most ludicrous of all the things humans do.

I sat down beside the box and then I found myself folding my body over it, almost hugging the thing. Its sharp corners pushed against me, it was as if I was inconveniencing it somehow, but still I clasped my arms around it, nestled my head between shoulder and cardboard. 'Mama,' I said. The street was so quiet, the sunlight so soft in the room. I could hear only birds and the distant, distinctive chugging of a black cab. Then I sat up and rubbed my arms – they were furry with dust – and opened the box.

Her dresses were at the top. They were so plain and dismal, I could barely look at them. The tin box, with the cushion covers and diary and those old photographs inside: stiff, formal photographs, my mother staring out from a crowd of siblings. I looked at every one of those kids, who ranged in age from the eldest brother, a sturdy teenager, to the baby in my mother's arms. A tiny scrunched thing, a newborn, raggedy neck in the nook of my mother's elbow.

At the bottom of the box were the books that had always defied investigation, but which I now turned over with a degree of interest. Alongside a very old Bible there were three slim educational books: biblical commentaries, all. *Proverbs, Ecclesiastes, The Book of Job.* I opened them, I let their pages flutter. I had never, I didn't think, seen my mother read anything but a recipe book, or hunched over her editions of word puzzles. And yet these commentaries were scored throughout, as diligently as by someone studying for an exam. Pencil marks and the neon brights of highlighters. So she hadn't eschewed religion when she left the Fabelhof, I thought, nor when she married my father, who was the most avid atheist I have ever known.

I heard a squawk from downstairs. George, who sounded happy but would need me soon enough. I set the books down and shuffled a few large manila envelopes: Health Insurance, National Insurance Docs/Passports, and finally Health Records. I opened the last, pulled a thin wedge of paper out.

Her GP record was a sparsely populated timeline, from around the time she married my father to the year she died. A raft of immunisations near the beginning, which my father presumably urged her to get since she would have missed them all, growing up in the Fabelhof. Then, eighteen years later, the cancer diagnosis and a sudden proliferation of prescriptions and appointments and test results. Between those two events, there was almost nothing. Almost.

In the autumn of 1993, when I turned five, she was prescribed a medication I recognised instantly, given my research position. Fluoxetine, commonly known as Prozac. The dosage high.

I laid the paper down, looked up. Across the square, the branches of a beech tree waved slowly, very slowly.

Fluoxetine. My mother, who never once said that she felt low, or unwell, or sub-par. Who never even spoke of sadness.

We were too tired to be lonely.

I slid the papers into the envelope and sat back on my heels, tried to let the truth of it settle in my mind. But it was impossible, actually, to imagine what it must have taken for a woman of her character, and provenance, and wariness towards medication, to go to a doctor and ask for help. To take, after that, a pill every day to help her to survive. It must have been nothing short of a crisis, I thought, a major depressive crisis.

It wasn't good enough, trying to piece her together like this. I didn't have enough. I never got to speak to her as a woman myself – as someone who knew anything at all, however limited, about the world. Of all the things I missed just then, it was the opportunity to address her as Tree had done, one adult to another. I thought of that day in the kitchen in Frantoio, before everything became undone. *Do you have time for a chat, Ma?*

All the thousands of things I would have asked, if I could have had my mother beside me now.

I was only a child when I knew her. There wasn't enough time.

I felt an impostor's shame. I was little more than a stranger, sitting there on the soft, faintly stale carpet in that magnificent home of my father's, with these fragile parts of my mother's identity spread out before me.

*

As I made my way from their house to Holland Park Station, my mother's books and photos and health records in a bag that slapped my side as I walked, I got a message from Liam.

I love you, you know.

I stopped. The street so quiet beneath the birdsong. I stood there beside a knotted mess of white roses, their myriad heads reaching out from a house's black railings as if yearning, and I read the message again. We never sent those messages anymore, not since George's earliest days. I had just been thinking, starting out on the long journey home, that we were further apart than we had ever been. I wouldn't be able to tell him about the antidepressants, or show him the photos. I wouldn't even tell him that I'd gone to my father's house.

But perhaps that wasn't right. I remembered his voice cracking as he spoke to me a few weeks earlier about his own father – it had been him reaching out towards me, him needing me. It seemed just possible, I thought as I started walking again, that when all of this ended, whatever it was – the show, and Hal's illness, and I suppose in some abstract way George's first year, or at least my maternity leave – we would come together again.

I didn't want to lie beside Liam's lapsed post-coital body, infinitely vulnerable, thinking that we were separate and not minding that we were. I didn't want to be unmoved by him. It was urgent, I thought then, not to let things unspool any further. To close the gap between us and not drift into the coldness of not caring, anymore, whether we were united or apart.

With George I made my way to Liam's studio, not home. We would make, George and I, a triangle of London, from South to West to East to South, and in this way we would make things connect again.

We were greeted by Nat, the sculptor who shared Liam's studio space, and though I had known her for a few years I had the uneasy sense – as, smiling, she let us into the studio – that she had forgotten my name.

'Liam's out for a breather,' she said. 'He'll be back soon. But hello, mini Liam,' she said to George. 'Bloody hell, the apple didn't fall far with this one.'

I nodded.

'He's definitely Liam's son.'

'He's his twin! It's uncanny. But you're not here to chat to me, Nemony,' she said, and I could tell by the way she used my name that I'd been right, and she'd only just managed to conjure it up. Liam didn't talk of home, I thought.

'There it is,' she said, looking over her shoulder. 'The main event. *Father*.' And she gestured, with real awe, towards the massive painting at the far end of the room.

My first thought was that it would make us a lot of money. It was brilliant. I hadn't seen anything so brilliant by Liam, not ever.

I had imagined, for some reason, that the portrait would be of Hal as he had always been, but instead it was the Hal we found the day we visited Liam's parents, just after we discovered he was ill. I stood before the huge canvas, moved, and there he was: tiny, jaundiced Hal on their brown velvet sofa. The left-hand seat of the sofa dipped substantially from years and years of his weight, his robust and solid body. How poignantly his new lightness sat in the bowl hollowed out by his former frame.

His hands rested on bony knees, as they had when we'd seen him. His shoulders high and uncertain, his collar too large around his neck. But the most strikingly effective thing of all was his expression: stunned, exactly as it had been when we'd visited, as if he was confronting for the very first time in his life the intractable fact of his own fragility.

I started, gradually, to look around the figure on the sofa. Beneath his feet in slippers, that worn-out carpet. A plastic bottle lay on its side there beside the remote control, a Sports Direct mug half-full of coffee, the TV guide. A pill packet, the little hollows spent. And then – stark and bold and full of life – a luminous violet flower that I recognised to be a *Cyclamen cyprium*, Cyprus's national flower. Again, I was surprised and moved. Liam had never produced something so personal, even autobiographical.

I looked up at the shelves and shelves of books above Hal, behind the sofa. They, too, had been captured perfectly. Hal the autodidact, who read and read and read, so that their entire flat, small as it was, was always bursting with books in chaotic stacks. He read non-fiction, omnivorously, and as I started to recognise certain titles I'd seen on those shelves before – Alfred Russell Wallace, a Caesar biography, an Ernest Shackleton biography – I began to notice, too, my father's name on many of the spines. For the second time that day, DON TRAVERS – clear enough to make out, even if the words had been painted more as shapes than distinct letters. His name, the titles of his works; as I scanned the painted shelves I saw them over and over, threaded in and among the non-fiction I knew to be Hal's, so that the impression became oppressive; the more I looked, the more it seemed to me that Hal was weighed down by Don Travers, that Don Travers's books were hemming him in, burying him, pinning him down on that sofa.

I turned away, a metallic taste in the back of my throat like the smell of Brasso.

'I'm going to wait for him downstairs,' I said, turning back to Nat, who was sitting gallantly astride her potter's wheel.

'OK, love. Come and see us again. I want to spend some proper time with this little one.'

Whose name you don't remember, I thought, and as I watched her I wondered whether she and Liam had ever had something. I realised I could smell it, somehow. She was tall, perhaps taller than him, and I noticed that her arms and shoulders were very lovely: slender and strong, like his.

She wiped her hands on her overalls as she stood and wandered over, all too slowly, and then she hugged me between her elbows, clay-wet palms kept aloft to keep me clean, George buoyant between our bodies. She smelled of work. Held there, I had the urge to cry into her neck like a child.

'Bye,' I said brightly.

I stepped out of the studio and then I moved down the corridor and the stairs as quickly as I could, shoes ringing out on the gridded metal, my head full of things I didn't want to start to contemplate. All I would let myself think for now was that, as far as I knew, Hal had never read a single one of my father's books, and certainly didn't own any. He didn't like fiction, he'd even told me a few times that he couldn't understand novels, to him they were just stories. The stuff of children.

I wouldn't think any further than that, I told myself as I walked to the station. I'd go straight home, and I'd wait until I was there and George was fed and bathed and in bed, and only then would I let myself start to contemplate the painting, this fact of my father and Liam's father. And then finally, worst of all, this other fact – this surely unavoidable fact – of Liam's fury. Because if it was a moving and intimate portrait, it was also a furious one. That was why I burned, why I felt burnt and wounded and humiliated. Furiously, unavoidably, I realised, Liam hated me. He hated us.

I couldn't go home, knowing that.

Zoe's house was full. I heard the hum of many voices as I approached the door. Someone I'd never met opened it when I knocked, and then Zoe came through to greet me.

'Oh,' she said. 'Hi Nemony. I'm having a little gathering – join us. Does George need to eat?'

She gestured, not quite brusquely, for me to make my way through to the kitchen, and then she stopped a man who was walking past with a glass of wine, rested one of her hands on his arm as she spoke to him.

'Charles,' she said.

I waited for her to return her attention to me but she didn't. She guided the man towards the orange Mora clock I so loved, their voices receding as they moved away.

In the kitchen I mashed a banana with formula for George, and knelt on the floor before him as I spooned it into his mouth. I had started to introduce some food around his bottles and so far he'd loved everything I'd offered, huffing and flapping greedily as I lifted the spoon. But now, too distracted by the commotion to eat properly, he shook his head from side to side, lips sealed, and I felt a miserable fury rise up in me.

'Just fucking eat,' I whispered, deploring the words as I spoke them, and I remembered suddenly Zoe's confession about her own children – about the day at the museum café in France, 'shovelling baby mush' – and I removed his bib and wiped his mush-smeared mouth and held him to my body.

Z

Zoe watches the girl sitting on the edge of a group. She has drunk a bit too much and looks bitterly on as they talk among themselves, and Zoe thinks, *Poor child, I know that look, I remember something of that bitterness and uncertainty.* It is for the most part directed at Zoe this evening. The girl feels Zoe has wronged her somehow, left her out, betrayed her, something. Perhaps she wants Zoe to herself. Or perhaps that is overstating it. Either way, it is endearing and Zoe would like to walk over and hold out her hand to the girl and take one of hers, give it a squeeze, say something to pave her way into the group's conversation, give her the status of which she seems to feel, obliquely, that she's been robbed – simply because she wasn't invited, Zoe supposes – but at the same time Zoe is absolutely not going to do that. It isn't her job to protect the girl. She's thirty, for God's sake, she's a woman, she can't have someone to hold her hand. No one ever held Zoe's.

Her third novel, *Heron's Rock*, had just been published when she turned thirty. In the wake of *Caged Creatures* she'd written the next two quickly and easily, riding the debut's swelling wave, and though she wasn't foolish enough to rely on continuing success, she felt very confident at that time. She felt sure-footed.

Thirty was also, and she cannot help but be amused by the irony, the age she started to meet the girl's father on her own. For the first time, Don invited her to long lunches at the Garrick with no one else, no illustrious retinue. People looked at her differently when she dined with him alone. She had clearly graduated from his circle of acolytes, those young stars-to-be held at arm's length; she was a woman now, she was being recognised as a woman. At times, walking through London streets to meet him, dressed in the bright block colours she had made her signature, charged with the anticipation of his lust and esteem, she had felt something truly close to invincibility.

The night he spoke to her about *Heron's Rock* was at the Francis Hotel in Bath, where they'd each been put up by their publishers, having each spoken at a literary festival in the day. Her event had been full; it had gone very well. She had felt articulate and assured, and her audience – clever-looking and smart and bookish – had discussed *Heron's Rock* with a level of respect and seriousness that made her feel truly established. An established author.

And so she felt as if she were thrumming when she met Don in the hotel bar, conscious as always of the hushed glances they received. Conscious, too, of the two empty hotel rooms upstairs. Two large beds, waiting.

'I finished *Heron's Rock*,' he said, when they sat down at a little table in a nook in the corner of the bar. His knee was pressed firmly against hers. 'It's good,' he said, sipping his whisky, and she tried not to look too thrilled. '*You're* good, actually very good. And one day you'll write something great.'

She felt her cheeks colour in an instant. The maddening heat of blood under her skin. Those words from a writer of his status should have been a huge compliment to her, but all she could hear as he continued to talk was *you're good, not great – you're good, not great* – so that even when he pushed their drinks elegantly to one side and leaned across the table to take her face in both of his long hands and kiss her – this moment they'd been advancing towards slowly, slowly, and then swiftly – she could still hear it. *You're good, not great*, she thought as his lips pressed and opened against hers, so that it was impossible to give herself over at all.

Over the years she had spent fantasising about kissing him, her mind had always gone a bit blank over the actual reality of his age. The mouth that was somehow stiffer than a young man's; the looser, coarser, more absorbent skin of his chest and arms, the muscles there which even in a man who kept himself in good shape like Don would inevitably have slipped and sagged. An elderly penis she couldn't even begin to imagine. And so she had simply blurred those parts in their imaginary liaisons, fixating instead on the things she found easily erotic: the way he looked at her, his hands on her, his palpable desire. She had presumed that in the moment's reality the age gap wouldn't be something to contend with. It would be absorbed into the eroticism.

But it wasn't. It did feel odd to kiss a mouth like that. It was different from a younger man's, just as she'd thought. And when he removed his shirt – it was as she'd imagined, his body, and she felt saddened and embarrassed by it. Embarrassing too was his lack of self-consciousness as he stripped off – his apparent obliviousness to the disparity between her flesh and his. How was he so heedless of the idea that she might not find his attractive. How did he feel entitled to paw at her firm chest, when his own was so flat and low above his ribs. It was ridiculous. It was so ridiculously, complacently male.

And finally she found that she was appalled by the silly valiance of his erection, which strained away like a young man's. It was humiliating, for a man who wrote those books – who celebrated and castigated and crystallised humanity as he could – to have this thing charging forth from his pelvis with such eagerness.

The expert way he handled her – inevitably this was a man who knew what he was doing – went some way towards distracting her, particularly when she closed her eyes, but even the expertise was a bit uncomfortable. As if he were a brilliant mechanic, and she an engine. It was undignified, a man like him having put such work into acquiring a skill as complex and carnal as a woman's pleasure.

She had a sudden, unexpected orgasm, which happened almost in spite of her actual experience of his touch. And when with a great quaking he finally came, she observed it as dispassionately as if he were an animal she was watching on television. He lay extravagantly back on the bed, spent, his quickened breath a bit alarming, and she closed her eyes again so that she didn't have to look at him or say anything, didn't have to dissemble.

She made a mistake, then: she kept her eyes closed for too long. When finally she opened them, he was watching her. She smiled, but he didn't return it. He turned to look at the ceiling, his expression unknowable. Then he stood up from the bed and walked to the bathroom, flagrantly naked, his small buttocks swinging flatly. He shut the door. As she picked her bra and knickers up off the floor she heard the forceful, horse-like runnel of Don Travers taking a piss.

Good, not great, she thought as she returned to her own hotel room, stepping into the shower and looking down at the naked stomach and hips and thighs and breasts she knew so well and that now Don Travers knew, too. And as the water warmed on her skin she remembered a moment four years earlier, at that long shady table in the garden in Sicily. Don's wife had served stewed peaches, their syrup making amber rivulets in whipped cream. When Zoe had murmured to her neighbour at the table that the peaches were delicious – an unthinking comment and not sincere, since she'd never much liked cooked fruit – Don had said quickly, 'Well, they're good, not great.'

The comment was quiet – it was almost under his breath – but nonetheless Zoe had looked down the table at Lydia, her impenetrable face with its high flat forehead. Unmistakably, she'd seen the woman flinch.

N

That old feeling grew upon me, as Zoe's party progressed.

I saw people as if through a layer of something, I heard their conversation as if it were on a television in another room. That I could be counted among them, as another living human, was implausible. It was laughable.

I was drunk before an hour had passed. Somehow I put George to bed – he went to sleep so well in Zoe's spare room, I think he too loved that house – and then I moved around the party with a glass in my hand, on the edge of things. I had no access to Zoe, I understood that I didn't mean much to her. Of course I didn't. She had this other life, these philosopher friends, philanthropists, professors, wealthy people. My father's kind of people. Whereas I was just an unsteady new mother, using Zoe's home as somewhere to relearn how to walk.

I told myself that I should take George and go home. But there was the fact of Liam, who might be waiting there already. There was the portrait – *Father* – which I was starting to understand as both a betrayal and an accusation, and then there were all the many, many problems that proliferated beyond that specific problem: a sprawling, living, heaving network, a colony, like bacteria. The relationship was rotten, I realised as I drank wine in that calm, unrotten garden.

I felt a hand on my shoulder, then, and my first thought was that Liam had come to find me. I turned.

'Nemony Travers,' the man said, a half-question.

'Ralph?'

We hugged, my childhood friend and I. Like that, the disembodied gloom dissolved – quickly, as things can with alcohol. It was such a relief to see him, as familiar in spite of the lapsed decades as the street itself.

'Zoe told me I'd find you,' he said.

'I didn't know you were here.' I looked over his grown-up face, flushed and stubbly, a hint of jowl. 'This must be surreal,' I said, nodding towards the garden of his childhood home two fences away, and he smiled.

'It's nice, actually. Like coming home.'

'How do you know Zoe?'

'She and Danny worked on some project together, for the BBC.'

I thought of Danny, his older brother, as I remembered him: short, naughty, scrawny.

'Is he here too?'

'He is.'

'And your parents?'

'They live in the sticks now,' he said, which I supposed meant a large country house. 'They moved away ages ago. But they know Zoe too. I think maybe everyone does.' He looked over my shoulder. 'Here's Danny now,' he said, and I saw a well-built man in a silky bomber jacket that was too young for him striding out of the house towards us. 'Look who I've found,' he called out.

'Oh, mate,' said Danny as he approached us, his arms swinging. 'Definitely a Travers girl! Hang on.'

He stood before me and scanned my face, narrowing his eyes. He'd become handsome, I thought.

'It's either Nemony or Henrietta,' he said, and I felt the missing space of the other Travers girl. I could almost see her name beside ours, crossed out.

'Nemony.'

'I knew it,' he said. 'All grown up! What are you doing here, Nemony?'

'I met Zoe recently—' I started, but I could see that he wasn't really listening, his eyes flickering over the people behind me. He was moving while he stood still, brimming with an extrovert's bold energy. *I hate Liam*, I thought with a rush of clarity and relief. I wished he could see me standing there between those two men.

With Ralph and Danny and the people they knew and spoke to, I stepped in from the outside. I stepped wholly away from myself. We toasted our childhood, we knocked back rancid shots of vodka. I rested my hand on Ralph's shoulder, I took him away from a tiny red-haired woman he spoke to, and in a compulsive whir I talked: first about foolish things we had done as children and then, encouraged by his laughter and surprise, about other, more personal things. I knew that I was talking too fast and too openly – I was aware that I was drunker than him – but wilfully I ignored my habitual instinct for silence.

It was extraordinary, what I unlocked in myself that night. As others joined and left us, I reeled off memories of Tree, memories of my mother, allusions to my father's philandering. I joked crassly – perhaps even cruelly – about how obvious Danny's crush on Tree had been, how we had all laughed about it because even at eighteen he was two inches shorter than her. And then I was flirting with Danny, who was standing now beside me. I leaned into him, I teased him, I brushed the full muscles of his arms as I spoke. I referred dismissively to Liam, I hinted at deficiencies in the relationship. Finally – intent on shocking and impressing both brothers with my flippancy – I bemoaned becoming a parent. Macho, I mourned the inconvenience of it all, the constraints on my liberty and autonomy, all without telling them that I loved George. That George was the most worthwhile and beautiful, the most perfect thing I knew.

Danny's arm was around my shoulder by the time Zoe came to find me. She sat down on the grass beside us, limber and sober in an expanse of uncrumpled chartreuse silk. I pulled away from Danny, just slightly. I realised where I was and what I was doing. The fire I'd felt had burned itself out some time ago; drunk and silent, I'd been sitting there on the edge of conversation again, this man's fingers stroking the skin of my arm.

'All OK?' Zoe asked, and I nodded. There was a chill in the lantern-lit garden. I couldn't feel the shame yet but there was a whisper of it, a scent carried in on the breeze.

'Fine.'

'We've just been talking to our old friend Nemony here,' said Danny, moving his hand from my arm and running a finger down my back. 'Our old neighbour.'

'That's right,' said Zoe.

'I knew her when she was a little tyke.'

His finger stopped and tapped, a sort of Morse code, and then it continued its journey down, down.

'Well, I'm sure she was never a tyke,' said Zoe. 'But actually I knew Nemony as a child too. What were you that summer, Nemony – ten?'

'Yes,' I said. 'Zoe stayed with us in Sicily once.'

'You went on holiday with the Travers family?' he asked her. His hand now on the flesh where it rounded at the very base of my back. 'How did you pull that off?'

'I knew Don.'

'Aha,' said Danny, and Zoe twitched, a tiny shake of her head.

'I was one of many guests,' she said quickly. 'The least illustrious.'

'So modest, Zoe,' he said, and with his spare hand he pushed back his hair. It was ungovernable, a curl popping back from behind his ear as soon as he'd tucked it there, and as I watched him tuck it back again I began to feel nauseous. Something rolled in my stomach.

'No, really. The other guests were people like Faye Cope, Toby Dornan.'

'Don't forget Tuva,' I said, turning to Zoe.

'That's right.'

'And Krishna, of course.'

She watched me steadily. We had never referred to Tuva, or Krish, or anything that had happened that summer.

'Krishna Gupta?' asked Danny. He was drawing a circle now at the base of my spine, under the fabric of my shirt, and the steady repetition of it made my nausea swell. 'The billionaire who set up the Summits Foundation?'

I nodded.

'He's a friend of yours, isn't he, Zoe?' he asked, and as I turned to Zoe her eyes darted to me. She straightened her shoulders. A silent, acrid bubble burst in the back of my throat.

'No,' she said.

'Didn't I see you together at Soho House a while back?'

The nausea was overwhelming. I wondered how I would make it inside. I stood carefully, I tried to hurry discreetly across the lawn, but the retching started as I went. I made it into the loo just in time and slammed the door and vomited harshly, repeatedly, my whole body seizing up to empty itself, like a cat.

When I had finished I sat back against the wall. Here was the shame, then, creeping steadily into the space around me.

And George, asleep upstairs.

When finally I opened the door of the loo, Zoe was standing there with a glass of water.

'You'll have to stay the night,' she said.

I nodded and she followed as I trundled myself up the stairs.

'Drink some of this,' she said on the landing outside the spare room and I took the water from her, drank it all. 'I'll get you more.'

She disappeared down the corridor and I opened the door to the room, crept in beside George. I was so cold. I shivered under the duvet, marvelling at how cold my fingers were. The warmth emanated from his sleeping body. The curls at his temples were moist with it, like breath.

Zoe came back in and placed the glass on the bedside table.

'Thank you for letting me stay,' I whispered, and she shrugged.

'I can't let you go home like this.'

I felt a surge of rage, then, that took me by surprise. I hated for her to see me lying there disgraced, next to my clean little boy, and I hated her for not having invited me to her party when we had been seeing each other twice, three times a week, and then witnessing my reckless and stupid performance. I hated her, too, for not telling me that she knew Krish. But most of all I hated her simply for looking so unknowable as she stood there in the open doorway, the light from the landing cloaking her face. She had let me down. I didn't know how, I only knew that somehow I felt let down, and that I was unutterably alone.

'I don't trust you,' I said.

The words spoke themselves. It was perhaps the most baldly confrontational thing I had ever said to anyone outside my family, or Liam, and it was exhilarating. It was like hurling a glass bottle against a wall.

And yet there was no response, nothing but another shrug.

'I've never asked you to.'

'You're so cold.'

'Go to sleep, Nemony.'

'You're like an old schoolmarm.'

'Go to sleep,' she said again. 'Before you say another foolish thing you'll regret.'

She closed the door with a click. George stirred and whimpered and curled onto his side, his back to me, and I lay there with my eyes open in the dark room, listening to the voices rise and fall in the garden outside.

George punished me with a restless night. He cried on and off and then he woke for good at six o'clock and whined unrelentingly, the sound beating into my head. I took him to the bedroom door, shushing him to be quiet, and Zoe appeared.

All I had wanted was to leave the house without seeing her; the prospect of it had been a torment as I'd lurched in and out of sleep. But there she was, crumpled and oddly childlike without make-up, in her dressing gown.

'Give him to me,' she said, eyeing me sternly, but unlike the night before there was the hint of a smile. 'I'll give him breakfast while you bring yourself back to life. Go back to bed for a bit. There's Solpadeine in my bathroom cabinet.'

'I can't—' I said.

'Yes, you can. He'll eat banana, won't he?'

'Yes, but – are you sure?'

'Yes. Though we're not going to make a habit of it.'

She took George, who was quiet now, watching us with interest.

'I'm so sorry about last night.'

'Shush shush. We'll talk later.'

I walked with thudding temples to the bathroom and sat on the loo with my face in my hands. I groaned, quietly. The stupid things I'd said the night before passed in and out of my mind, like voices on the radio. The brash and boastful creature I'd become, for those few hours. Tree, I'd spoken to strangers about Tree. I'd made jokes about my father. For the first time since I met Liam, I'd leaned into the warmth of another man's body.

I stood up and flushed the loo and bent over the sink, cupping cold water into my hands, lowering my face down into it. I wished I could simply stay like that: my face submerged, eyes closed, world paused.

George's cries came up through the floor. He needed a bottle, not banana, he needed me. I dried my face and hands and as I walked down the stairs I switched on my phone. There was nothing from Liam. Of course there wasn't – he didn't initiate contact when he'd been caught out. His instinct when he felt under attack was resentment first, contrition only much later. I wasn't surprised and yet I was frozen by it, the brutal cold of it.

That is why, when I entered the kitchen and Zoe asked me, glacially unperturbed by George's grizzling, if I wanted a cup of tea, my response was finally to cry.

'Oh, silly child,' she said, the words not quite at home on her tongue. I took George and bounced him to keep him quiet, and then, a silly child, I wept.

Zoe said nothing. She made a cup of tea, set it before me. Took a tissue, laid it next to the cup.

'I'm sorry,' I said eventually, 'I was so rude to you.'

'Forget it.' She batted a hand. 'You were rude, but it could have been worse.'

I don't trust you, I thought, *you're like an old schoolmarm*, and I grimaced.

'It was bad.'

'Look, we've all had a stupid night like that,' she said. 'Actually, I was thinking about it when I woke up this morning. I was remembering one of my own stupid nights. It was in Sicily, on holiday with your family.' She laughed. 'I even vomited, like you. And I almost slept with that intolerably smug – specimen, Toby Dornan.'

'You mentioned him last night.' Instantly I regretted saying it, since we'd also mentioned Krish, and I didn't want to confront that yet. 'Toby Dornan … No, I don't remember him.'

'Another writer.'

'I don't recognise his name.'

'He was rather a hot shot at the time, but I suppose there's no reason you'd have heard of him now. He's a bit – esoteric.'

Krish's name sat there in the space between us.

'I haven't drunk more than two or three glasses since before I was pregnant,' I said. 'My body's not used to it.'

'Let's not make excuses,' she said, wryly parental. 'You drank too much. Though you should be glad you were sick. It stopped you from making a very stupid mistake with Dan Thomas.'

His name was the last thing I wanted to hear. I held a hand over my eyes, but George's fingers tried to peel it away. His dark, shiny, infinitely lovely eyes gazing up at me, all the humour and belief in them. When I was old and George a grown man, I thought, I would look back on moments like this. I would reach back and try to grasp them and it would be hopeless, my fingers would have no purchase.

'What's happening with Liam?'

'That's the real problem,' I said. 'That's why I came over here last night, actually.'

I took a breath to speak.

'You don't have to tell me anything,' she said. 'Not now, anyway. You can stay here. Just for a little while, while you work things out, you and George can stay.'

*

Zoe's days were regimented. She woke and showered very early, before even George wanted to start the day, and then she shut herself in her study and wrote for several hours. The rest of the day always followed the same pattern: boiled eggs or lentil salads and green juices, brisk walks with Mildred, exercise, a militantly short nap, emails and editing at the long kitchen table, a cup of coffee by her side. Finally came The Hour – 6pm, her glass of wine.

It was so ritualised and efficient and uncluttered. What discomfort George and I, with all our mess and noise and unpredictability, must have constituted. But she didn't allude to discomfort. We were welcome, she said. She never elaborated much, she didn't embarrass me with kind words or any real reference to how desperate the situation with Liam must be, she said simply – and she repeated it many times, over the fortnight we ended up staying there – that we were welcome.

For the first few days, Liam said and did nothing. That meant – though I knew he'd be hard at work denying it to himself – that he felt guilty, that he knew he had betrayed me, with that portrait. But it didn't take long for his guilt to veer into anger, of course it didn't. I had taken our boy away from him. I'd even gone into our flat when I knew he was out, to remove the belongings we needed. That I felt betrayed at the public indictment *Father* was going to make of my father – and by extension my family – was not, I knew, enough to justify that. And yet I, who had spent my life worrying about which side of right or wrong my actions fell, and perhaps more maddeningly those of the people I loved, found now that I didn't much care about justification. If Liam was raising a battle cry against Don Travers and hadn't seen fit to tell me, it was only confirmation of what I had already been gathering: we had become separate. A tether had snapped.

That is what I realised, those first few days in Zoe's house.

And I realised this too: if George's birth had made extinct the person I'd been before having him, it had also made extinct the former terms of my relationship with Liam. The hurt I felt over the portrait had less depth, less purchase than it would have before.

On the third day he called, as I was walking through the park. I told him that the situation was temporary, I just needed time to work out what had happened to our relationship. And help, too, with George, since I had effectively been raising our baby alone.

He didn't listen. He never could. When he was too angry to speak, he hung up and sent a string of messages instead.

I can take you to the police.

This is child abduction.

You're doing this when my dad's dying.

You've taken my own child away from me because of a portrait of my dying father.

We'll never come back from this.

This, from the man who'd said we set each other free.

He'd said it just hours after we first met – a text message that said simply,

I felt very free tonight.

Malachy had come to find me at that party – finally he had given up on his conquest – and Liam became immediately cold. He and Malachy knew each other vaguely; I supposed Liam presumed Malachy to be my boyfriend, that that was why we were leaving together. But when I told him we were siblings he became colder still.

Liam could never stand that I was Don Travers's daughter. On the dusty floor outside that gallery loo, beside the hush of hanging coats, he thought he'd met an ordinary girl. Someone with origins as plain and simple as her appearance. The kind of beauty that was 'harder to see'.

I didn't yet understand that, leaving the gallery party, walking through Soho with Malachy. I felt rebuffed by Liam's sudden distance. What repellent thing had he suddenly seen in me, I thought as I walked, my arm linked onto Malachy's, and then I looked at my phone and there was that message, from the mercurial stranger. *I felt very free tonight*.

I thought of those words now, sitting wearily down on a bench in Greenwich Park, watching a sleek crow rifle through the grass. Its fat swagger was abhorrent to me. When it hunched its shoulders and spread its wings out and left, another, even fatter crow took its place. I watched as it tugged a worm from the soil.

This is child abduction.

You've taken my own child away from me because of a portrait of my dying father.

We'll never come back from this.

All fair things, all true enough, more or less. All things I might have said in his place.

I stood, and the crow flinched and hopped.

I didn't reply to the messages. I had no interest in a battle of words.

Z

The writing is going well. Probably it shouldn't, with the girl and her baby in the house, but it does. She can see new connections between her two protagonists and the weak, powerful men who shape them.

Don himself once told her: never write fiction as a means of revenge. She had been telling him about her parents, who kept taking form in her stories, even as she tried to keep them out.

She remembers, or thinks she does, that they were in a theatre bar when he told her this.

'Of course, you're using your work to commit parricide. Most of us try it. But it seldom works, don't you think?' Perhaps he had twisted a glass between long fingers, or tipped the rim of the glass towards his nose. 'No, never write fiction as a means of revenge. The revenge will take over, it will burn up the truth of the thing.'

But, Don, she thinks now. *I'm still writing truthfully. Don, with this novel, I think that I might manage both.*

N

It was Etta, not Liam, who came to find me. I received a message ten days into my stay at Zoe's, as I sat drinking tea at the butter-yellow table.

I'm in Greenwich. What's Zoe's address?

I didn't like that. I cast my eyes over Zoe's kitchen with my things in it: George's bottle, George's flip-book, my headphones, the wire looping around a coffee cup. George, propped up in an amphitheatre of cushions on the floor. It was his new trick, this tentative sitting, and another way in which I felt that I could see him more clearly. That he was emerging, into the world.

She's working. Let's meet by the station.

Etta embraced me quickly, her hair very faintly wet and shampoo-sweet as it brushed against my face. She was never one for physicality. A greeting hug or kiss from her always seemed to me to be an embarrassment or inconvenience, something to be dispensed with.

'Doesn't that thing destroy your back?' she asked, touching the sling that carried George, and I thought: *she disapproves of it, she thinks I am babying him too much, I'm letting him become too attached.*

'I like it.'

She shrugged.

'I could never make them work for me.'

She leaned forward to look into his eyes.

'You're huge! Aren't you? Aren't you a huge boy?'

I thought that she was awkward with him, as if she hadn't had two babies of her own. When she turned she added quietly, 'He's perfect.'

We walked in silence beside the Thames, brown and stolid, and then we stepped down onto the gravel of one of the grim and stinking little beaches. On the pier someone was throwing breadcrumbs at gulls; there was a flurry of them, frantic, hovering and snapping forwards and diving for the food.

'Urgh,' she said, and I nodded.

We stared out across the water at the Isle of Dogs.

'I remember hearing once that the Isle of Dogs has more CCTV cameras per square mile than anywhere else in the UK.'

'Really? Why?'

She shrugged.

'God knows.'

'That's so sinister.'

'I know. Although, I'm not sure if it's true, so.'

She gave a quick sigh, so quick it was barely a sigh at all. I knew her, I knew her so well. We had preambled enough; it was time to talk.

'Come on, let's sit.'

We settled on the gritty shingle, cross-legged. Ahead of us a boy and a girl squatted in wellies, collecting stones, their father waiting beside them.

'We don't like you staying at Zoe Goodison's.'

I watched the little girl stand, holding a stick aloft.

'We?'

'Me and Dad. We think she's after something.'

'You've spoken to Dad about this?'

I have a memory of the long table at Frantoio. An earlier summer, when I was six or seven. I was sitting on Tree's lap, her arms around my middle. Etta, beside me, sat on Malachy's.

Etta and I had been to a puppet show in Scordia. Some guest or other had taken us, we had eaten ice cream, it had been a great excitement. We were bubbling with it, we spoke over each other, we couldn't get the sentences out quick enough to recount our story. And then my father, squeezing his eyes shut, frowning – his great, Zeus-like thunderclap of a frown – levelled one great hand at Etta and opened weary eyes to look at us.

'Henrietta to do the talking, please. In the interest of everyone's sanity.'

And Tree squeezed me, silently. I had thought, when he'd said it, that he'd picked one of us at random. He could just as easily have chosen me to speak, it wasn't personal. Tree's squeeze told me that it was.

Those incidents are so tiny, they're so inconsequential. Except that, of course, they're also not.

'Nem, a few years ago Magda got in contact with Dad.'

'OK,' I said.

'She said she'd been in an email exchange with Zoe Goodison.'

I stared ahead of us. The children watching their father skim stones, the cool hop of each stone across the scuddy surface.

'Dad wasn't on speaking terms with Zoe anymore – he hadn't been for some time. He didn't go into that, but in itself it's weird.'

Which I had thought too, many times. But I didn't want to agree with Etta.

'You're sure they didn't just fall out of touch?'

'No, I mean they fell *out*.'

'She's never alluded to a fallout.'

'Well, that's hardly surprising. But you can imagine – maybe she got needy after they slept together, or something,' said Etta. 'I don't know. He didn't elaborate, clearly. But anyway, Magda called to say that Zoe had got in touch with her out of the blue, under some pretext or other –

congratulating her on a play, or something. Magda remembered her from Frantoio, so she sent a friendly reply. She'd read one of Zoe's recent novels. They started emailing.'

'OK.'

'That's when Zoe started to ask questions about Mum and Dad.'

I shifted on the dirty shingle. The pebbles beneath me needling, a blinding grey glimmer on the water.

'She told Magda she was researching religious communities in the US,' continued Etta. 'I mean! And she'd just, poof, remembered that Mum had come from one. So she asked Magda various things – what was the Fabelhof called, where was it based, things Magda could barely remember, I mean, why would she. But she told Zoe what she knew – she didn't immediately smell a rat. It was when Zoe started asking questions about Dad too, and about that summer with – well, Krish and Tuva. That's when Magda started finding it odd. She told Zoe to fuck off, basically. I mean, you know, not literally. In a wonderfully direct Magda way though, I imagine. She told Zoe she should get in touch with Dad directly.'

Stop, I thought. I didn't want it, I didn't want it.

'And Zoe fobbed her off and she never heard from her again.'

George, who had been listening attentively, had fallen asleep. His cheek and breath were too warm against my chest.

I felt trapped, sitting there. I felt hunted. By Etta, with this theory she'd cooked up with my father and which they would force upon me – which would force me, too, out of this place of comfort, of relative stability, that I had been enjoying in Zoe's home, the first moments of safety I could remember since George's birth. By Liam with his hatred, his portrait that prised its fingers into my life, my family. And by George. Twenty-four-hour, doting, endless George.

'Nem, it's weird, don't you think,' – and as she spoke I found that I wanted to hold my hands over my ears, just like I'd wanted to in the Fort all those years ago, as Etta told Alice about my mother's illness – 'that she's so interested in our family. That she was asking about the Fabelhof, and about that summer with us. That she got in touch with Magda what, twenty years later? And that now she's so desperate to be your friend. That she's offered her home up to you, for God's sake.'

I frowned.

'That's a nice thing.'

'What?'

'It's a really nice thing, to have offered it.'

Etta exhaled a laugh, dry and harsh.

'For fuck's sake,' she said. '*I* offered it. *I* offered for you to stay with us. Twice! And you said you couldn't. You wouldn't leave Liam. I'm your sister, and you say no to me and yes to a total stranger.'

'She's not a total stranger.'

'I don't even know what's going on with you and Liam. Are you guys separating? What's going on? You haven't told me a thing! You don't answer my calls, you've never once let me help you, all this time with George. I *know* how lonely it is, I know how hard and lonely the beginning is. I've banged my head against the wall trying to help you. And instead you turn to – fucking – Zoe Goodison!'

Etta didn't cry. I couldn't remember the last time I'd seen her cry, if there had even been a time at all since our mother died. Tree's funeral, surely. Which was a terrible day: violent in contrast to the too-civilised calm of my mother's, the church clanging with the horror of Tree's absence, pews too small and bony to contain her messy, multifarious friends, each one scrabbling to claim her as their own; and the high walls and vaulted ceiling of the church – no place, in any case, for Tree – warped, as if bulging, with too much breath. Too much personality, too much vocalising, too much, too much. I hated every person there. I felt my lungs warp and bulge with panic.

I had just turned sixteen, so Etta was eighteen; she sat beside me, her jaw as tense as a jaw could be so that her mouth was mean with the strain of grief. She held my hand in hers: not tenderly, but in the way a person grips a steering wheel, driving through slashing rain. It kept the panic from engulfing me.

It kept me.

She must have cried, I thought.

Malachy did. Exquisitely, purely, he cried. That was agony to see; I couldn't watch. My father's face beside him, impenetrably blank. I had the sense that for him the whole thing was simply vulgar, an unwanted intrusion into his private life.

Etta wasn't crying now, but I thought that the shaky voice was the closest she would come to it.

'I'm sorry, Etta.'

'You're an idiot, you're such an idiot.'

She crossed her arms across her chest, stuck her legs out in front of her. I'd forgotten that I had the capacity to hurt her. I always forgot; it was too hard to imagine. I made her bullet-proof in my head, but she wasn't. Of course she wasn't.

'I'm really sorry. I didn't think.'

She shook her head.

'It's done. It's not even the point.'

I waited.

'The point is, she's writing about us.'

'What?'

'Oh, come on. Look at all the signs. What is this "research" she's doing into religious communities? Who else has she contacted, apart from Magda – who else of our family friends?'

'Probably none of them, Etta,' I said, though I was thinking of Krish. And Ralph Thomas, Dan …

'OK. Well, how about all the time she spends with you?'

She likes me, I wanted to say, but as the words formed in my head I realised I was entirely unconvinced. *Did* she like me, actually? What did she like about me? I pictured all the assured and colourful people at her party and thought that there was surely nothing, really, for someone like her to like about me.

And then – even now I can see this moment, the clouds seeming in an instant to gather ahead, the view's sunken greyness intensifying so suddenly into dusk – those small children and their father, still skimming his dark cool stones – I thought: *How many times have I asked myself that same moronic question?* From the moment I had recourse to words, the moment I became a halfway socialised creature:

Do they like me?

I am sure my father never asked himself that, not once.

I rubbed my hands down my face, over its plain straight planes, and turned to Etta with the great weariness of someone who finds herself stuck, truly stuck.

'Etta, Zoe and I are friends,' I said.

'Zoe's not the type to make friends.'

'You're wrong, she's very sociable.'

'That's not the same thing.'

'This is – Dad narcissism, Etta. Why would she write a book about us?'

'Because we're a story.'

She picked a stone up and threw it, a lame shot.

'And – I'd guess – because she hates Dad. It would be the perfect revenge.'

We stared ahead, not speaking. Etta's theory made sense, already I could see that, but still I couldn't believe it. No one would dare to violate a family in that way. Zoe wasn't so cruel. She had morals.

And yet still I felt uncomfortable, I felt not right. She might not be cruel, or immoral, but she could be ruthless. I knew that about her.

'How much has she asked you?' said Etta.

'She doesn't ask me things.'

'What, not even about the family? Or about Frantoio that summer?'

'Why would she ask me about that summer? She was there. Why would she want my take?'

'Because you can give more insight into – I don't know, our problems.'

'What problems?'

'Oh, Nemo,' she said, eyes narrowed, face deadpan and tilted like a puppet's. 'Come on.'

But I had meant it, my question, it wasn't disingenuous. The things that had soured that summer – they weren't problems, surely, they were anomalous and unfortunate, just a bunch of kids getting things wrong. Shamefully wrong, in Tree's case. The only underlying problem I could see in it all was that it was my mother's last summer, and no one could have changed that.

'So you haven't told her anything she could use?'

'No,' I said, but with a steadily creeping dread I was thinking of the many things I'd said. Tree's death, our grief. Tree's depressive episodes and her manic ones, the years Etta and I effectively parented ourselves, my mother's loneliness, my mother's mythical bolt from her commune. Even, and I was amazed now to think I'd spoken of it, the presence in my childhood of fear. The indomitable fear of his opprobrium: the great and terrible opprobrium of Don Travers.

'I haven't told her anything about us,' I said. 'You know me, I'm hardly one for opening up to—'

'Strangers.' She smiled bleakly, shaking her head. 'Exactly what I said she was.'

'I wasn't going to say strangers. I told you, we've become friends.'

I looked down, took a deep breath. The Thames stank. I got up, dusting grime from the back of my legs, and I had the strange impression as I stood – it was palpable – that my feet and ankles were tangled, so that when I took a step I might trip.

'I've got to go,' I said, planting my feet carefully. 'We can talk about it again tomorrow night, with Malachy. What time does he land?'

'I don't know. The reservation's at seven.'

'OK. Let's chat more then. I have to go, I need to get this one back for his dinner. He's not supposed to be asleep, bedtime will be a farce.'

Etta nodded and then she looked up at me, squinting in the falling light. She looked so like Etta that for a second I wanted to go with her, wherever she'd take me.

'I love you,' she said.

'I love you too,' I replied, and God, how I did. My busy, bulletproof, not-bulletproof sister.

'I really do.' She reached up, brushed the tips of my fingers with hers, then looked back ahead of her, at the river. 'I don't think you know that.'

*

A friend of mine once said that her mother's personality – she'd been a stage actress, quite well known – was so large, so dazzling and magnetic, that she, my friend, had never felt she'd had the space in which to express herself. As long as her mother was around, there was no air in which to make her voice heard. She was like the tiny shoots on the rainforest floor, she said, where the sun couldn't reach, feeble below the high, fantastic canopy.

With us it was the opposite. Our mother couldn't even stretch a few branches over our heads. She was only ever the soil beneath.

There were too many directions in which to grow. We could shoot upwards, like Malachy and Etta, or down. We could grow towards each other, or apart.

Z

It won't last, this companionship they have struck up, and yet Zoe enjoys it. It is a source of curiosity to her – she is curious simply to share her home with someone again, it has been so long since she let someone become a regular visitor – and it is also, sometimes, a source of irritation. The wet cloths in the kitchen sink, the bibs left to dry, the shreds of wet Weetabix that harden and stick. But pleasure, too. There is pleasure in coming home, turning her key in the front door and thinking that the girl and her baby will be there in the kitchen or the garden, making mess and clearing it, constantly making mess and clearing it. That, it sometimes seems to Zoe, is all that being a mother is.

The girl asks Zoe what she's working on, and Zoe tells her that she's writing a novel that she feels good about. The most personal novel she's ever written, something she has wanted to write for many years. And Zoe does feel a bit uncomfortable, because she knows that at some point she is going to have to talk to the girl about the novel and the material behind it, but – she is sure she'll be able to talk the girl around. Zoe could probably talk her around to anything at all.

Not because she's weak, actually. She is rudderless, but she has too much composure and privacy, is too much of a loner, really, to be weak. It takes courage and a certain conviction to be a loner in the way that girl is. She doesn't pretend at anything.

She says things that interest Zoe and afford her little insights. 'My hands are like Rumpelstiltskin's hands, all angry-looking,' she says. She tells her she can't eat toast because she can't abide all that chewing. And, when Zoe played Beethoven, 'This is such brave music.' In comments like these Zoe catches a certain oddness, an old-fashioned scent: a whiff of her mother's community, those faux-Wesleyan forebears.

The girl still cringes about the things she said to Zoe when she was drunk: that Zoe was cold, and a schoolmarm. She doesn't realise that Zoe has been called cold all her life. It means nothing anymore, even if it once did. It is par for the course, if you are a strong woman, if you are a woman who doesn't need people. Particularly, if you are a woman who doesn't need children or a man. You are unnatural. You are disruptive, you have subverted the order of things. You are certainly not to be trusted.

She is nothing like her father, the girl. She has his intellect, but there are blind spots, blunted corners. She has none of his rapacity.

Zoe thinks of Don often these days, inevitably, and when she feels anger it is cool and not fearful but it is wary, nonetheless. Because he is quite the adversary, Don Travers. After they slept together, a handful more times after that first vacant and mechanical tussle in the hotel room in Bath – after he became a human in her eyes, and not a god – his contempt was formidable. A drawbridge came up; she saw right away that it would never lower back down. This from a man who famously kept up brilliant friendships with the many women he bedded.

Not Zoe. She was too unadorned for him, she thinks. She couldn't dissemble. He understood immediately what she saw: that in spite of all the brilliance he was an ordinary man. And, like an ordinary man, how he hated her for seeing it. With what self-righteous scorn.

She doesn't think he actively sabotaged anything for her – her books, her career. He didn't have to. When the scales fell from her eyes she had taken a step sideways, and just like that she'd stepped out of his great, glittering network. That sequestered world she'd worked so hard to pass into – the world of the Magda Dabeczes, the Krishna Guptas and Faye Copes – how quickly she found herself back outside its gate.

Because if you wear the contempt of a man like Don Travers, people can smell it. It carries a subtle stench. For Zoe, falling from his grace was enough to change everything. Fewer book proofs sent to her home, for her kind consideration. Fewer invitations, lower book sales, less media coverage.

The phone calls dwindled, the review spaces. The lunches, launches, parties.

And so of course she hates him. Of course she holds this anger. Of course she still thinks of him, often.

But his youngest daughter is nothing like him. Zoe will be saddened, when the girl and the baby move on. She will be glad in some ways to reclaim her space, but it will be a loss of a kind, not to have something of them to bask in. The girl's ordinary oddness, her sort of accidental self-sufficiency. And the boy's bright eyes. The way he has started to reach his arms out towards Zoe.

N

It was very easy to find. I had to wait until Zoe left the following day for Mildred's lunchtime walk, and even then I found myself procrastinating – delaying George's nap, folding up our clean laundry, the countless little socks and bodysuits I'd washed using Zoe's washing machine, Zoe's detergent, Zoe's tumble dryer. If she was a traitor, I thought, so was I.

But once I stopped delaying – once I stepped into her sacred study, as sick with nerves as I'd been walking into my Viva – it was so ludicrously easy. That was how much she trusted me, or how guileless she thought me. No lock on the door, no passwords on her documents. I nudged her computer awake and opened Documents and there it was: a folder, 'The Gatekeepers', filled with files.

I opened her current draft to read from the beginning, and it was more than I think even Etta expected. There we all were: there was my father, there was Tree, there were my siblings and me – some names altered, most not. There were the Sicilian olive trees, the Sicilian high sky, the dust rising from the road as a car moved along it. There was my mother, bowed beneath a heavy tray. There was our laughter, glinting through the trees. There were Tree's long, swinging legs. And Tuva.

I read until I reached Tuva, just a few pages in, and then I closed the draft and blinked, several times, as if I had spent hours and not minutes in front of a screen. With shaking hands I emailed the contents of the folder to myself and to Etta, and then as I stood to leave the room I saw the box files, running the length of one shelf. One for every novel she'd written, starting from *Caged Creatures* and ending with this, *The Gatekeepers*.

I took it down, rested it on the desk, opened it up. There at the top of a wedge of papers, in Zoe's tough, quick, practical handwriting:

THE GATEKEEPERS (working title):

Two women – Teresza and Zoe. Names to be changed.

T: 19 years old, beautiful, all the uncertainty of youth, sleeps with charismatic older man. Swept up in his magnetic power, just like:

Z: 26, uncertain too, still working out who she is, swept up in D's success and interest in her.

What is the legacy of these powerful men …?

What does withdrawal of their favour mean for the two women?

The joke of power.

> T's death in Appalachia (*WILLIAMSON, West
> Virginia, research (opioid capital of world!!) etc.). Where T
> ends up on pilgrimage. (Mother?)
> Z character – her own journey, how to step out from
> shadows of D's contempt.
> * Change Sicily to Greece? (Ruins)
> * Make family bigger – more siblings? (Religious
> element??)
> * Change youngest sibling to boy (Jack)? Or get rid?

I swung shut the lid of the file.

I left her study, and then I moved around the peaceful perfect house scooping up our scattered things. Quickly I packed them, feeling all the while as if I had caught Liam having an affair. I was pulsing with something like jealousy: the victorious, terrible, almost erotic thrill of betrayal. How dare she find in Tree's actions a mirror to her own, in which her own troubled story was reflected. How dare she claim Tree as her foil. Tree, *my* sister. Her mistakes were mine to claim, not Zoe's. It was our story, it was the Travers' story, it was ours, it was ours.

I woke George and strapped him, confused and mewling, onto my chest.

'We're going,' I said, trying to keep the anger and the blinding hurt from my voice. 'We're going, we're leaving.'

I pulled the front door quietly to, I left the mews on quick feet, unobtrusive in spite of the heavy bags that hung from my shoulders. I was like a burglar. And as I rounded the corner onto Crooms Hill and walked straight into a man, I was seized by an illogical pang of wrongdoing. As though I had just committed a crime in Zoe's house, and this stranger would be called upon as a witness.

I had to look right up. He was very tall, and wide, so that I had the childish impression that he was blocking the daylight out. And in the same instant that I recognised his face – it was the homeless man from that day in Cowboy Land, whom I had seen and noticed a few times since, around Greenwich – I was struck by the reek. Urine, laced with alcohol, and more than anything else the daily, filthy accumulation of being.

He looked down at me. He took a while to focus on my face. I think I had muttered 'Sorry' – a reflex, even though the collision had been his fault as much as mine, and as he focused on me his top lip pulled up, a sneer of loathing.

'Slut,' he said.

I blinked, I moved away. I left him there on the pavement, I hurried quickly from his stinking shape. And as I hurried up the hill, the word 'slut' replaying in my ears, I pictured his face with its pockmarks and unhappy eyes: a father to two sons, he had said, from whom a complex mass of unknown misfortunes must have alienated him, misfortunes I couldn't imagine. I pictured, too, Zoe's expression when she arrived home to find us gone – self-possessed, no doubt, unflinching in all its careful pride. All the carefully laid bricks and mortar of the life she'd made. And all I could think was: how fucking sad. How impossibly lonely and furious and far away. How impossibly far away we all are.

My phone rang and I stopped, catching my breath.

'Malachy.'

'Hey,' he said, and asked me how I was, and I burst into tears. For a long time I stood there on that quiet street, weeping into the silent listening space of my phone. My kind older brother, listening. The sun was warm, it moved and flickered on my face and the ground before me.

'It's OK,' Malachy said, after a while. 'It's OK.'

When I could speak, I told him that Etta had been right about the novel, and that I'd tell them more at dinner. His flight had landed that morning, he was in the same city as us, he could be somehow real again. That evening we would be together, all three.

'It's OK,' he said. 'Don't worry about this woman's book. We'll work it out.'

I told him about the collision with the man from Cowboy Land, and he was silent for a moment – and then there was a sound that was as much a surprise to me as it was deeply, enchantingly familiar: Malachy laughed. He laughed, and laughed, and so I did too, until my eyes were watering once more.

'And he recognised you?'

'I don't know.'

'Slut!' he cried, and I could imagine him wiping tears from his eyes. 'Why slut? Oh Nem. This kind of thing only happens to you.'

By the time I ended that phone call, I was as light as a cat. Just then, in the delicious afterglow of our laughter, I felt that nothing was far away, after all.

I was standing directly across the road from our old house. Usually, climbing that hill, I averted my eyes when I passed it. Primly I'd look up and away; I'd fix my attention on the trees encircling the convent across the street, or a car that was passing, or the phone in my hand. A few years before I started visiting Zoe, I had seen a young man emerge from the house and been flooded, then, with such intense emotion that it took me some moments to recognise it as rage. It was as if I'd been smacked; my eyes smarted, my face throbbed.

The habitual way in which that man swung the front door closed behind him. His casual gaze, which slid over me as if I were merely another passer-by. How I hated, how I loathed him; how in that moment I could have scratched his face and torn his hair, just for living there. And – passing me by with so little consequence – for erasing all the years that we had lived, slept, breathed, fought, grown, been born, run in, snuck out. We hadn't died there, none of us had died in that house. That was the only thing we didn't do, even if my mother gave a good go at it.

Now, though, in the blank calm I felt after that phone call with Malachy, I let myself cross the road and approach the door. I even rested my hand on the doorknob: cool, ridged, paling bronze. Once, a thousand times, I thought, Tree touched this. My mother touched this. Etta. Malachy. Me, once I was tall enough to reach it. And then I thought: my father and all his friends and lovers, they touched it too.

Slut.

But my memories of that house – they didn't include my father, mostly. His many absences – his days out and nights out and all the trips abroad, the book tours and retreats and visiting fellowships and award ceremonies, and then of course all the time that he was home but shut off from us, typing and thinking and frowning and creating – always, and God forbid we interfere with it, *creating* – all those many absences merged and fused together to make one large, near-constant absence in my mind.

I sat on the low wall before the door, gazing up at the white facade. The ivy, the many asymmetrical windows, like trinkets.

'This was my house, George. This was our house.'

Looking up, I invoked all the places inside it that I had loved the most – the parts that would always be ours, in spite of all the years since the last of our boxes were cleared out. The tooth-like enamel of the bathtub, on which Etta knocked out her two front teeth. The cool pantry, rich with secrets if you knew where to find them, which naturally we did – candied diamonds for decorating cakes, Brazil nuts, geological clumps of ageing brown sugar. The tiny landing on the top floor; I remember sitting there in slanting sunlight, dust motes rising. And my mother's high oak bed, the knots of flowers carved into its headboard. It was my father's bed too, only mostly it wasn't. Much of the time he slept upstairs, on the large divan in the spare room next to his study –

particularly when he was in the thick of a novel, at his most unreachable. How I loved those times. Her bedroom walls were green, a very dark green, and I would creep in there in the night and lie between the yellow coverlet and the duvet and we'd both pretend, my mother and I, that she didn't know I was there. Her breath rose and fell as she slept, the little lamp on her table hummed. She – who was brought up in a rural commune that barely used electricity – left a light on when she slept, she never slept in the dark. I never thought to wonder why.

I asked Malachy and Etta that night. Sitting around a table in the dim, warm light of a French restaurant Etta had chosen. In a pause in conversation, it popped up to the surface of my mind like a bubble.

'Do you remember how Mum used to sleep with the light on? Don't you think that's weird?'

Etta frowned.

'No she didn't.'

'She did. That lamp on her bedside table, it was always on. Do you think she was scared of the dark?'

'I don't remember that,' said Malachy, and then the waitress came to take our orders, and that was that.

But she did. She did sleep with the light on. *It doesn't matter*, I thought, *but she did*.

I never mentioned the Fluoxetine, after that. If we each held a different Lydia in our minds, I wanted to keep mine intact.

And in any case, she wasn't the point of that evening. The past was not the point. We had come together again as ordinary siblings, the three of us who remained. In that modest restaurant – for all Etta's ability to bulldoze, I could see that she'd chosen a place where I wouldn't be humiliated by the bill – we ate steak and drank red wine and talked about the present, even while my discovery of Zoe's novel sat in the air between us. Etta had her hair tied back in a new style, very straight and flattened and chic, and Malachy had grown, somehow; he was slim as he'd always been, but fuller – there was an Americanness to his physique now, it was clear he spent time in the gym, and his teeth were very white. I looked from him to Etta – it was the first time I'd seen them both together in well over a year – and I thought about the cell renewal process, how each cell in our body will have died and been replaced every seven years. Ten, at the most. Like the Ship of Theseus, its planks each replaced, one by one, so that over time it is an entirely new ship altogether. Or not, Liam had once argued, because he believed in essence, he wasn't literal about anything.

But that was what I asked myself that night, watching my siblings as they talked and laughed and ate. Were they new, or were they the same? And if they were new, if with the piecemeal replacement of each of their cells in the decades since Tree's death they had become entirely new physical entities, then she had never known those two people across the table. She had never known me.

At moments, which is the painful thing, which is the really unbearable, almost unmentionable thing, it could seem as if Tree had never really existed at all.

I had arrived at the restaurant still shaky from the discovery of the novel. I assumed it would be all we would speak of. But Etta made clear from the outset, from her manner alone – as relaxed as she could ever be – that it could wait.

And so gradually we uncoiled, we relaxed. We rehearsed our usual patter: revisiting memories that made us laugh, memories that showed one of us up in a way that only the rest of us could understand. We spoke about the kids, Lila and Maeve and George. Malachy had never had children, and I didn't think he would. He had never settled with a partner for very long. After Tree, I don't think he could ever really attach himself to anyone at all. And we spoke about our father – in the only way we ever did, wryly and with what sometimes struck me to be a dry and essentially hateful awe.

Only when the desserts came – the part of a meal I always most associate with my mother; of all the things she cooked, it was her area of true glory – did we come to speak of Zoe.

'I can't believe – I couldn't, I don't know what—' I started, and Etta waved a hand.

'You don't need to worry,' she said. 'Now we've got it, now we know what we're dealing with. That book will never see the light of day.'

I laughed.

'We can't stop it being published.'

'Don't you know who your father is?' Malachy asked me, and though it was a joke I saw that he was serious too. I turned to Etta.

'She's written seventy thousand words,' I said.

'I know, I read it.'

'You read it all today?'

She waved a hand again.

'I skimmed it.'

A quick twitch of something passed over her face, before she corrected it. It wasn't even pain, I thought, it was agony.

'Don't read it, Nemo,' she said then, looking up. 'Either of you, actually. The more I think about it, the more I think it's poison.'

'Poison how?'

'Just promise me you won't. Delete the email you attached it to. I don't want another pair of eyes to skim over that ... shit.'

'God, what did she write?' asked Malachy.

'It doesn't matter what she wrote. It's irrelevant.' She nudged a wedge of lemon tart with her fork. 'We just need the right people to know the right thing. Luckily for us, the literary world is very small and unsurprisingly corrupt. She'll be blacklisted from every event, publication, paper, if she goes ahead with it. No publisher will touch the manuscript. Not with Don Travers's veto. No one will dare.'

'He can't veto a book.'

'It's already done. He gave his agents the go-ahead to make calls this afternoon. Nothing official exactly, just ... *persuasive*.'

'God,' I said.

'Trust me, no one will touch it. No one's willingly going to make an enemy of Dad.'

'How much of him is in it?' asked Malachy. 'Would he have a libel case?'

Etta laughed.

'So American!'

'I'm serious.'

'There's – a lot of him in it, in every sense.' She gave a little whistle, a mock shudder. 'Things I'll never unsee. But no, no libel case – she obviously knows what she's doing, there's enough distance to make it legally OK. It is a novel, at the end of the day. She's fictionalised plenty of it, made things up here and there. But God, there's no mistaking who everyone is.'

I looked at Malachy, who was looking down, twisting a teaspoon between his fingers. His eyes at this angle – thick eyelashes fanning out in an arc – were so eerily like Tree's.

'How do you both – *feel* about it?' I asked.

'I feel nothing,' said Etta.

'I don't know. I mean, I haven't seen it.' Malachy paused, shrugged. 'I don't plan to.'

I looked from one to the other.

'OK. But I mean – is sabotaging it OK, morally?'

Etta pushed her plate and fork away and leaned forward, arms crossed on the table.

'Nemony, the woman's been sneaking around speaking to old friends, unpicking things, digging up graves, sniffing around our lives, our memories.' She almost laughed. 'Courting you, for fuck's sake! And she – dares to write about our lives as if we're fiction.' She sat back. 'No, I feel just fine, morally.'

'Etta's right,' said Malachy, and I found myself nodding too, but still I felt a creeping sense of discomfort, the sticky business of wrongdoing.

'Nem,' she said, touching my forearm quickly with her hand. 'Consider the whole thing done. Please can we never think, or talk, about that woman again. Ever.'

And she gave me a final look on the matter – a small quick smile, a look of decision but also indulgence or kindness, as if I'd been forgiven for some silly and childish transgression. And that is when the full humiliation of it hit me. Blithely, vainly, I had walked around seeing nothing, suspecting nothing. Believing that Zoe and I were friends.

With effort, then, I smiled back at her, at my not-bullet-proof sister who could have grabbed my shoulders and shouted *I told you so!* and railed at my stupidity, but who instead was trying to change the subject.

'What about you, Nem?' asked Malachy. 'Do you feel OK about it?'

'I guess so,' I said, though I didn't know what I felt. 'If you both do. There's something else, though.'

'Oh God,' said Etta.

I took a breath, and then I told them about Liam's portrait of Hal as I had read it: a boy immigrant from a ruptured once-British colony, impoverished and crushed and dying under the weight of our father's intellectual imperialism.

'Jesus! Why does everyone want a piece of Dad, all of a sudden?' said Malachy, and the lightness of his response was a shock to me. I turned to Etta, who was stirring a drop of milk into her decaf, and she looked up and shrugged.

'Fuck it,' she said.

'You don't think it matters? He's taking a gun and pointing it at Dad and – everything he represents, and he's firing it.'

'No, I mean – it matters, in that I care about how it affects you. It's horrible for you. But in terms of firing a gun at Dad—' She tilted her head to one side, mouth in a deadpan crease, nostrils flared.

'Etta,' said Malachy, and she laughed.

'I mean. It's true!'

'What's true?' I asked, and I felt like I did that summer in Sicily. The others had a secret language, they did, and I would never understand it.

'Well, no one will care,' she said. 'Sorry, but it's true. A few reviews in some hipster zines, maybe one broadsheet, max, and then poof, it'll be forgotten. It's only art.'

'Only art,' said Malachy, laughing now too, shaking his head. 'Jesus, Etta.'

'But you know what I mean.'

'Well—'

She held her hands out in front of her, palms upwards. She made them wobble slightly, like weighing scales.

'Liam Ersoy,' she said, gesturing towards one. 'Don Travers,' she said of the other, letting it drop right down so that the hand that was Liam pinged upwards, towards the ceiling. And then she raised the same hand still higher, and looked over my shoulder, catching someone's eye. 'Can we get the bill?'

When I got home that night, back to the flat Liam and I still owned together, I found Krystyna asleep on the sofa in the darkness, her face bathed in the moving lights of the traffic.

I took my shoes off and went into the bedroom to look in on George, lying on his front – wholly, slackly absorbed in the blank totality of sleep. It was the longest I'd ever spent apart from him, and there he still was, existing.

I went back to Krystyna, knelt before her, rested my hand on her elbow. She blinked awake.

'Sorry, sorry,' she said, sitting stiffly upright. 'I haven't been sleeping well these days. What time is it?'

'Eleven,' I said, and she looked around and nodded. I could smell her breath, sleep-sour.

'I'll go,' she said, nodding again, taking stock.

'You can stay.'

'No, no.'

'Thank you so much for babysitting.'

'Any time. Really, any time.' She leaned her head to one side. She looked so sad, I thought, like a dog. 'What is going to happen, with you and Liam?'

'I don't know.'

'Has he cheated?'

'No. Well. I don't know.'

I had returned that afternoon from our weeks away at Zoe's house to find the flat empty and clearly unlived-in, fridge bare, Liam's drawers only half-full. It was a shock, to find that he hadn't been there all that time as I'd imagined he had; but I found, moving around the vacated flat, preparing a bottle for George with water from a tap that spluttered after a period of unuse, that I didn't much care where he had been staying. Or with whom. An image of Nat, her clay-caked hands held gracefully aloft, passed briefly through my mind and was gone.

There was a kind of conscious cruelty in my indifference, something I didn't recognise in myself. I respected it. We don't have to remain attached to people, I was starting to think. We can become unattached. Ropes can become unloosed.

Krystyna shook her head.

'He's like his father,' she said. 'Those men don't know how to …' She looked around her. 'They don't know how to share themselves. They – break good things. They can't help it.'

I nodded, though I felt deceitful because I was letting her believe a certain narrative. I didn't even know what narrative would have been right; I only knew that it wasn't only Liam who was breaking the relationship.

'He'll come back to us soon,' I said. I believed that, at least. 'Then we'll talk. We both needed a moment to – think.'

She looked at me with those deep-lidded eyes that were so like Liam's. Eventually she turned, bent over heavily in spite of her tiny frame to pick up her handbag, her jacket.

'OK. You take your moments, however many moments you need.' She nodded her head towards the bedroom, towards George. 'Just as long as I keep seeing that boy.'

'Of course,' I said. 'Always.'

She reached her arms out and held my body to hers, which was physically awkward since we were the same height, our arms hinging at exactly the same place. Her hair against my cheek smelled of oil and heat, and some version of home that wasn't mine but that still let me close my eyes, drop my shoulders. I felt my breathing slow and deepen. 'Sometimes I think – I should have been different, with Liam. A different mama. It was always so hard, I was so tired always. But, I don't know.' Gently she pushed me away, looked at me, shrugged. 'Maybe it would have made no difference.'

She kissed me on the cheek, and she left. I moved to the bathroom, wiped away mascara, eyeliner. As I brushed my teeth I stared into my eyes, Etta's eyes, my mother's eyes, and then I opened the mirrored cabinet so that I no longer had to see all those women.

Z

It is childish, simply to run away without an explanation, however brief. A confrontation of some kind, a reckoning. It is not Zoe's style.

She sighs as she shakes peanuts into a small bowl, chooses a wine from the fridge, takes the bottle opener, arranges them all and one wine glass on a tray to take outside.

She had been looking forward to talking to the girl about a volume of essays she bought this afternoon; she read the first one quickly, standing against the bookshelves in Waterstones towards the end of Mildred's walk. It was about our fascination in art, literature and film with the prostitute figure, and women's transactional value. The essay started with the gorgeous Toulouse-Lautrec portrait of a collapsed trollop on a bed, in black stockings. Anyway, Zoe had been looking forward to hearing the girl's take, because at some point the essay dwelt on Thumbelina, the tiny fairy-tale creature who is bartered at every turn in the story for coupling with some predatory male creature, and of course she is the fairy-tale expert.

Irritatingly the essayist also mentioned, in passing, Don's third novel, *Girl of Joy*. She called Don's rendering 'exquisitely nuanced', which Zoe concedes it probably was.

Zoe wondered briefly whether the essay had any relevance for *The Gatekeepers*, for either of its female protagonists, but decided it didn't.

Now she will have an evening alone. But that is fine by her. And here is Mildred, after all, trotting up to sit beside her, not looking around for the girl or her baby.

She has run away, childishly. Not unlike Thumbelina, in fact, who flees the bad old mole's home on a sparrow or swallow or skylark. That renders Zoe the bad old mole, she thinks, and smiles, but she doesn't feel light and the smile drops. She holds her palm out towards Mildred. The evening is gloomy, there is an unsettled sadness and a gloom in the scented air.

No explanation, no reckoning. That is not Zoe's style.

N

My father's house was on one of those squares in London with a huge Elysian garden in its centre for the square's residents to use, when their large back gardens do not suffice. It is a place of soaring plane trees and clean benches and grass so green it could only be English.

It took me a while to find the entrance; I had to walk three sides of the square until I found it, on the fourth side. But it was locked. I stood there in my dress with a bunch of flowers in my hand and George against my chest and I saw them all. Malachy, standing beside my father with his hands in his pockets, head inclined courteously to listen. Tabitha on one of the blankets with Etta's two lovely girls, the pages of a children's book flowing open on her lap. Etta and Mark holding hands, her head on his shoulder. They made a beautiful picture.

I called out, but no one turned. They were too far away, and it wasn't a place for shouting. I called their phones, one by one, but they would all have been on silent or tucked considerately away, an unspoken condition of being in my father's presence. And so for several minutes I stood there, watching, until eventually he happened to look up and across and catch sight of me. We studied each other for a moment: my eighty-year-old father, his youngest daughter, a great expanse of grass between us. Two strangers, I think.

And then he bowed his head and started his long, still-vigorous, still-decisive stride towards me. When he reached the gate he took a key from his pocket, fitted it into the lock, turned.

'Nemony,' he said.

'Happy birthday, Dad.'

He smiled sagely at me in that way he could when he wanted to be generous and polite. He could switch it on: just a hint of twinkle in the eye, to convey warmth. He gestured at my stomach.

'You were rather bigger last time I saw you.' He glided down to my height for a kiss, which was really just the sliding of our cheeks against each other's. 'And this is George,' he said. 'We meet at last. A handsome boy, Nemony. Congratulations.'

We stood in silence, and I vowed not to break it. He hinged slightly at the knees, pushed his hips out. His thumbs tucked into his belt, his shoulders straightened. He was already bored and a bit put out, I thought, the twinkle fast receding.

'And is it suiting you, motherhood?'

It was a foolish and loaded and utterly complacent question, I thought – I might even have gone so far as to call the complacency behind it truly pernicious. How immense, his ability to trivialise. But I played the game, as I always had. I didn't say: in the pure gaping blackness of labour and when George was finally cut out of me and in the hunted months afterwards I was pulverised. A wrecking ball swung and smashed me – my body, freedom, identity – into shards, and slowly I have been collecting those shards back together, those that weren't too finely smashed to fix. I have been rebuilding them into something.

Instead I said:

'It depends when you ask. At 2am – not so much!'

Exactly the dull and docile quip he expected from his dull and docile daughter – that mould he had created and in which I was inexorably stuck – and he received it graciously, with a bored smile, and then that was it, my time was up. I'd had my half a minute and now his attention was gone, gaze sliding away towards the people who deserved it more. And yet – looking up at his long nose, his wild white eyebrows, creased forehead, creased cheeks, the combed and old-fashioned hair that was still quite thick, at eighty – I couldn't help but admire him.

I could never help it.

'Come,' he said, gesturing towards the others, and together we crossed the grass.

They took me into their fold. I let George down from his carrier and Malachy stepped forward to meet him, taking him and swinging him up in the air so that my baby's laughter came out in little simian whoops, irrepressible. I was embraced by everyone in turn – my nieces, my stepmother, my brother-in-law, Etta.

'Hello, Nemo.'

She even ruffled my hair.

'Well, this is idyllic,' I said, and she smiled, looked round.

'Isn't it.'

'I always wondered how much people use these gardens.'

'Oh, often,' said my father, standing tall beside Etta, and he threw his head back, inhaled the fresh green air, studied the high swaying branches above. 'How useless the plane tree,' he quoted, and we nodded. One of the countless fables deeply implanted in our family, our collective vernacular. 'It bears no fruit.'

'Serves only to litter the ground with leaves,' continued Etta, sing-song.

'Well,' I said. 'The tree bears no fruit without winter.'

My mother's words, too firmly hers. There was the sigh of silence, the shifting of feet. My father looked down, nudged an empty snail shell with the toe of one shoe. And then – just when we needed it – there was another glorious peal from George as Malachy threw him up, up. My George, I thought, and something wonderful surged within me. His leaf-like face, the buttery black curls a halo above it.

'Nemony was describing the toils of motherhood,' said my father, and Etta looked up.

'Oh yes?'

'Just the night wakings,' I said. 'The 2ams.'

'Ah,' said Etta. 'But that's only one of the many, many toils.'

'Hm,' said my father. 'I can't understand the fuss that's made out of the whole business.'

Etta raised an eyebrow, and I saw it start. One of their crackling volleys, the air packed with it.

'What business?'

'It strikes me you can't move for another book or article about how hard it is,' he said, 'how this woman had postnatal depression, this one had psychosis, etc.'

'And you, of course, took motherhood entirely in your stride.'

He grinned.

'Ha. No, naturally I can't understand all that it entails. But it strikes me it must have got much harder, somehow, than it was when you were all babies. I don't remember women *talking* about how hard it was all the time, the way they do now.'

'Oh, then they must have found it easy.'

'Don't be contrary.'

'Well, you know, some people posit that things have changed a bit since then. Women have something to lose now when they have children, not just their sanity. Careers, opportunities, freedom. We can even give voice to the experience! We're basically spoilt.'

'Women have had a voice for some time, Henrietta.'

'See? We're spoilt.'

'Don't be banal.'

'You're being banal. "The world's going to hell in a hand-basket,"' she said, adopting perfectly his frown, '"the younger generations are going to the dogs, we're going to rack and ruin"—'

'I do love these gentle conversations we have,' he said, chuckling, and she smiled, nodded.

'You live for them.'

I had a feeling of total desolation, standing there beneath the plane tree. It rose up inside me like nausea.

It had been decreed that my father's eightieth birthday would be a modest affair. A simple lunch, no fuss. No phalanx of decorative, bright-feathered friends; just us.

A young man in a waistcoat appeared to usher us from the gated garden to my father's hushed and gorgeous home, along with two young and unobtrusive French women – girls, really – who appeared out of nowhere to look after the children, so that the mess and noise of them might not intrude.

Tabitha had arranged those French girls, just as she'd arranged for the whole simple lunch to be catered. She swept us through into the creamy drawing room and, creamy in caramel silk, she moved between the waiting staff and the five of us, uttering *sotto voce* commands, nodding subtly towards a glass that needed filling or a canapé offered. As I watched her I thought that it was sensible that she did things like this: spending my father's money on staff, rather than striving for days over dish after dish of elaborate home cooking, as my mother would have done. It is decisions like that

that have one woman moving calmly around in soft silk and another bowed and strained and silent. With money, you don't have to be a mule, which is something my mother never learned.

The presence of staff opened up a space, though, that made it all more stilted than it would have been otherwise. We stood around awkwardly, formally. None of us could retreat into the opening of a champagne bottle or the fetching of a spare glass. I began to feel desperate for an excuse to do something. That, of course, was one of the reasons my mother never chose to stop moving.

My solution was to drink, very fast.

And then my father was beside me again, voluntarily, which seemed almost alarming in its novelty.

'I hear there's another show in the running,' he said. 'For Liam.'

'Yes. In September, the White Cube,' I said, though I knew he didn't care about that.

He cleared his throat.

'I hear it might cause a little stir.'

I swallowed.

'I'm sorry about all of that.'

'Oh,' he said, wiping it all away with a hand. 'Let him have it. A way to garner a little publicity, presumably.'

I watched him. Zoe's novel hovered there in the air, between us.

'And your work?' he said, looking around the room. Their garden glowed beyond the high windows, trees stretching skyward, pristine lawn hugged by roses. He didn't even know what I did for work, I thought.

'I'm still on maternity leave.'

'Ah, yes. Yes.' He cleared his throat again. I waited. 'And – did you find what you wanted, the other day? Among your mother's things.'

'Oh,' I said. 'Yes.'

He said nothing, though he nodded faintly. I finished my glass of champagne, and took another from the young man hovering behind us.

'Dad, did she become unwell at all, when I turned five?'

My father turned to me, blinked, and for a moment I had the sense that he didn't know who I was talking about.

'What year was that?'

'1993.'

'You might remember,' he said slowly, turning back to the room. 'She did her back and neck in at that time. The road accident. You had that girl Daisy come to look after you all.'

'Daisy?'

'I think that was her name. Young girl, an orphan if I remember correctly.'

'You mean Poppy?'

'That's it, Poppy. Androgynous young thing.'

'The one who looked after us at Frantoio a few summers.'

'Not only Frantoio,' he said, shaking his head. 'She took care of you at home too, for three or four months while your mother was away.'

'Mum went away?'

'She had to rehabilitate, in a clinic.'

It is extraordinary, the way we can do it: bury memories that are as vivid and intricately formed as ammonites, when we unearth them. I barely had to brush the dust away to rediscover Poppy's sudden, constant presence at the house on Crooms Hill, giving us breakfast every morning, cutting sandwiches for our school lunch, tucking me into the lower level of the bunk bed I shared with Etta, singing Edelweiss in a queer reedy voice like an oboe while I tried my best to remain awake. She had a way of setting out our school uniforms at night that I loved: laid out on the floor in the form of a person, sleeves outstretched like arms, tights outstretched like legs. Like snow angels, or children who'd been mown flat.

'She stood in for Mum, all that time?'

'Yes. Yes, your mother needed a lot of care. Rehabilitation.'

'Did we visit her?'

'It wasn't appropriate.'

I shook my head.

'I don't remember an accident. She never spoke about it.'

He nodded, eyeing me, and something passed between us.

'One can be too literal about these things,' he said finally, and then there was a young pretty waitress in uniform by his side, gazing up at his greatness.

'Ah,' he said. 'Time to eat.'

*

The lunch was what my father would call exquisite. Elegant wine, intricate salads, shellfish decked with lemon quarters. A complicated, hard-won simplicity. I imagined it through Liam's eyes, or rendered by his paintbrush: the curlicues of kale, the prawns with their shiny black eyes like tiny pearls. A year earlier there had been riots in Notting Hill, only a short walk away. The smoke and sirens had reached the house, and my father and Tabitha had locked up and left for the countryside. When Liam heard that, he said he would never visit them there again, on principle. I thought of that as I looked down the table at my father, robust for his eighty years, and I pictured Hal, sunken in that sofa, the Sports Direct mug and the *Cyclamen cyprium* and worn carpet and my father's name on those spines, again and again and again. A little stir. A little publicity.

He was holding a glass up now, commanding our silence with just that gesture.

'It strikes me I should say a word or two,' he said. 'We don't get together too often now, particularly with you off in the deepest darkest Americas, Malachy. Well.' He looked down at his hands on the table, grave now. 'Our path as a family hasn't been a straight arrow.' Just enough of a pause. He looked up. 'But I am fortunate, to have you lot here now. And still working, at eighty – that is more than I hoped for. I am fortunate. Thank you.'

That last 'thank you' as if in acceptance of an award, and yet effortlessly, laboriously modest. His face lightened then – enough earnestness, it seemed to say – and he tipped his glass to Tabitha.

'You've put on an immaculate lunch, as ever, thank you, darling.'

That was it. Eighty years old, fourteen novels, countless prizes, a lost wife, a lost child, three surviving children he'd done his very best not to raise – and that was it, all the words that were needed. Everyone raised their glass and took a sip, and I took an enormous gulp and felt about as bleakly depressed as I'd ever felt in my life.

Etta's glass dinged, then, her knife ringing out against it, and as I looked across the table at her – she looked handsome that day as I never felt, in spite of our similarities – I almost laughed. It came to me so clearly: Sicily, the lunch with the mussels, Etta standing up, her glass dinging, her chin tilted, the Swedish rounding of her vowels as she spoke. *Ladies and gentlemen, have you ever heard about all the* exceptional *competitions I have won?* The dread and tension I'd felt at that lunch, watching as her rebellion against Tuva unfolded, but also the thrill of it. Even if I had no idea what she was doing or Tree or Malachy were scheming, even if I was out of my depth with all of it, we were unified in whom we hated and whom we loved. We had our clear governing principles. We were one, all four of us.

'… be the first to confess you aren't always the *easiest* company, of course,' she was saying now, 'but then there's nothing easy about what you've achieved, Dad, and …'

Malachy was looking down at his plate, his tanned face serene, and I couldn't bear it anymore, the homilies or the platitudes or the acceptance: of my mother's absence, of

Tree's absence, of how utterly unwild we had become, my wild siblings and me. I couldn't bear how completely eradicated they were, those children around the dappled table in Sicily.

'Are you going to throw mussels at Tabitha, now?'

Etta stopped, Malachy looked up. For once, everyone was staring at me, even my father. I had his attention.

'What the hell, Nemony?' Etta asked, in a very low voice.

I swallowed.

'Do you have something to say?' asked my father.

Already I could make it out: the subtle shape of fury in his distinguished, distinguished face. I took a breath.

'I was joking, Dad,' I said. 'One can be too literal about these things.'

I didn't wait around long after that. We moved back into the drawing room for port and cheese, Tabitha touching my arm graciously as she guided me into an armchair, and I drank my port quickly and sat for as short a time as I deemed acceptable and then I stood to leave. Liam had messaged, I said, he had forgotten his key and was locked out of the apartment. My father barely looked up.

I went into their cool conservatory, where George lay on his stomach, smiling, a straight line of drool hanging luxuriously from his lip onto the mat beneath him. His cousins were stroking him like a puppy.

'Time to go,' I said, picking him up, and the girls clamoured and protested, jumping around my legs.

'No, don't go!'

'We love him!'

'Let him stay!'

'Please!'

'I said time to go,' I snapped, and I was ashamed to see their smiles drop, their jumping stop. The French girls looked up from their phones to watch me. 'Next time,' I said, strapping him into the carrier, and I thought that all I wanted in the world was to go somewhere and drink more wine and sleep.

Silently I stepped down the hall, but when I opened the front door someone grabbed my upper arm. I turned, the leafy street waving behind me. It was Etta, her face tense, fingers tight.

'That wasn't OK earlier,' she whispered.

'Sorry.'

'Are you really still so angry at Dad?'

'Are you not?'

She waited, watching me, and then she shook her head.

'No,' she said, and I realised with a hot jolt that I believed her. 'No, I'm really not. You know, Nem – no one can ever pretend he was a perfect dad. But he's had a fucking hard time of it.'

'Hard?'

'Nem.' Reluctantly, in the lowered voice she always used when she felt obliged to speak of the past, she said, 'He lost Mum and Tree too.'

'He's never acted like he did.'

'That doesn't mean anything. He was destroyed. His wife and his firstborn, Nem.'

'But we were destroyed too, and we were children, and he never offered us one – shred of comfort.'

'He was grieving. And anyway he's complex, Nem, you know that. He's not an ordinary man. You insist on – I don't know, expecting ordinary things from him. But he's not like that.'

'Too extraordinary to be a father,' I said, and my meaning was sardonic, but she nodded. Angrily, I thought. Defiantly. She was defending him, not me.

'Yes. Exactly that.'

I looked down at her fingers, still gripping my arm, and she loosened them and then dropped her hand. When it was level with mine she held it in hers, one of her stiff attempts at showing affection.

'I'm not saying it wasn't hard on us. But I think you need to—'

She paused, looked around for the words.

'What?'

'Move on. Or rather: look forward, stop reliving the past. Like the other week – Dad said you asked him to get all of Mum's stuff down from the attic.'

'Yes.'

'Why go through all that, Nem? What were you hoping to find?'

'I discovered a lot.'

'Like what?'

'That she had a breakdown, around my fifth birthday.'

She nodded, letting go of my hand.

'And?'

'You knew?'

'Well, I mean. I worked it out a bit later. She was in that clinic for months.'

I exhaled. How the world moves on around us.

'Incidentally,' she said, 'do you think that was easy for Dad too?'

'The poor guy.'

'I mean it. He had to get her through that.'

'No, Prozac and hospitalisation and childcare got her through it.'

'OK, Nemo. Stick to that version.'

She leaned against the wall, upright and cool, arms folded in front of her chest. When she was like this I could see her as the schoolgirl she once was: the quick, effortlessly popular girl at Sports Day, ponytail swishing, short shorts, taking a bored break between races.

My infuriating older sister.

'What caused it, Etta? The breakdown.'

'You're obviously assuming it was to do with Dad. Rather than – God, I don't know, her fucked-up childhood, perhaps?'

I watched her, and as I did I thought of my mother's bedside light, keeping her vigil through the nights.

'You know things that I don't know, don't you?'

'Nem, please,' she said, unfolding her arms. 'What's the point in picking through all the bones?'

'Because I want to know the truth. I can't stand not knowing these things about our own mum.'

'What does *truth* mean though? Whose truth? Fucking – Zoe Goodison's?'

'Why do you say that?'

She took a deep breath, batted the air as if at a fly.

'It doesn't matter. It's nothing, it's irrelevant. That novel is poison, like I said.' Lightly, she rested a hand on my arm. 'The point is, I think the past can loom too large. Nem, I think you should – I'd love for you to move forwards, now. Stop nursing Mum's and Tree's wounds. Or what you perceive as their wounds.'

'Fuck off, Etta.'

That shocked her. I pulled my arm away.

'I'm sorry,' I said, but we both knew I wasn't.

She studied me for a long time. We heard Malachy's laugh bubbling up from the murmur of their voices.

'Dad's old. He won't be around forever.'

I shrugged.

'Why don't you concentrate on what you've got now? The people you have now, not just the ones you've lost. We're *here*.'

'But Dad's not. Not for me. He never has been, actually. Concentrate on what I've got – well, I've never had him.'

She didn't have a response to that. I turned and pulled the door open and then softly closed behind me, a thudding in my chest. For the first time in our lives, I walked away from an argument with Etta without resolving it. Oh, we'd fought

– many, many times – but it had always settled as swiftly as it had flared up. We had never been the kind of siblings to fall out in any lasting or meaningful way, none of us. It was one of our unspoken but sacred principles. Walking away from a conflict – it wasn't honourable. It was for people linked by a weaker chain than ours.

The ugliness of that haunted me as I made my way home, sobering up in a tube carriage that jolted and popped and rattled. I had the sickish sense that follows confrontation, and as the wine receded so did the conviction I'd felt at lunch, so that I no longer felt defiant about insulting Tabitha and my father. The comment about the mussels seemed appalling to me, in the sallow light of the tube.

I didn't want to agree with Etta about my father. I didn't think that I ever would, and actually I was furious at her defence of him. Him, against me: that seemed to me to go against our rules. And then it struck me, so starkly as I stood there, swaying with the motion of the tube, pressed against the fake leather of a stranger's jacket in that crowded carriage: those rules were defunct. I was the only one who remembered them. I was the only one who'd enshrined them. Devotedly I'd maintained this allegiance to the past – regressive, I saw now, even pitiable – only to realise that no one had ever actually asked it of me.

How uncanny, the sense of repetition. This had all happened before, our lives were simply pouring like water into a gully formed long, long ago. I was still that child in Cowboy Land, the laggard in our games, the runt of the pack, cheeks hot with effort and humiliation as I struggled to keep up. I was the child in Sicily that summer, realising with a start that her siblings had launched off into the world of adults, and danger, and sex.

I tried to imagine what the rest of the world saw, now, when they thought of the Travers siblings. And perhaps it was simply this: a disparate and ordinary quartet. Malachy and Tree – certainly, they had had an aura when they were young and beautiful. I wasn't the only one to have seen it, I saw so many succumb to its supernatural pull. But perhaps it was just youth, just beauty. Things they couldn't control, however powerful they seemed, and which jeopardised us all.

And in the end – what was Tree to anyone else now, all these years later – wasn't she perhaps just a dropout, a troubled young woman killed by the wrong dose of antibiotics, of all things. And Malachy – he was a womaniser like his father, a bit bloated with too much protein and American muscle and money and, perhaps this too, perhaps self-regard. Etta was successful – like Malachy, she was accomplished – but still she was so ordinary: tense and thin and too busy, forehead already out of whack in the first rounds of Botox. And as for me. Well, I think that really I was nothing, yet.

But not in Zoe's story. The doors of the tube shuddered open and I thought, with a torrid, crackling, creeping feeling: in Zoe's story, we held our magic. Those pages held our wild heart – even just the five or six pages I had read. They held all the wild that remained of us.

316

Our cleverness, our laughter, our oddness, our energy, our cruel vigour and compassion and honour, our youth. More than anything, our bond. We were inimitable together. Apart, we weren't.

Zoe's story, which might not, after all, be poison.

At Cutty Sark, I got out into the falling light of the evening and opened the message she'd sent me that morning:

Please let me come and see you.

OK, I wrote. I'm free now.

Z

The flat is not what Zoe expected. Much nicer than she imagined, in spite of its size. Charming, considered details, like an old wooden chest for a chair and a blue porcelain vase of dried leaves. The girl wears a spotted dress that Zoe has never seen her in before, short and swishy, almost flirty, which is also unexpected. She is usually plain shapes, androgynous, understated.

'Where's George?'

The girl stares back. Not hostile, quite, or sullen, but off limits – it is as if she stands behind a screen.

'Asleep.'

Warily she takes the wine bottle from Zoe, and the flowers, and then she takes two glasses from a cupboard and goes to the sofa and drops down into it. Zoe opens the bottle, pours it into the glasses. She sits down, gathers herself.

It is uncomfortable. But she's at an advantage. She doesn't mind a fight, whereas she imagines the girl can barely abide it.

'May I talk frankly?' she starts, and the girl nods.

'You tend to.'

Zoe takes a breath. She has practised these lines.

'I deeply regret that I've upset you with this novel. Not only have you become a friend, whose closeness I value, but you're also going through a very tough time and I don't want to add to your feelings of isolation and betrayal. So: I deeply regret your upset. But I also want to be clear that I'm not here to apologise for writing it.'

The girl blinks, twice. Zoe thinks that her cheeks – which are almost grey with tiredness, as they mostly are – start to colour.

'I can't choose what I write,' she says, following her script. 'You of all people know: this is what writers do. Stories inhabit us, they catch our imagination in their net – and that's it, we write.'

The girl shakes her head, and Zoe can see it coming: anger, rising to the surface. In a way, she's glad to see it.

'You don't agree?'

'No,' she says. 'No, I don't. You say it's just what writers do, as if that justifies it. But I don't believe it does. It's parasitical. I always thought that about my father, and I think it about this too.'

Zoe nods. She was wrong: here the girl is, fighting. The thought strikes her that perhaps the girl has had a few drinks already.

'OK. Maybe you're right – maybe it is parasitical, to use someone's life as material. But we don't differentiate between real and fictional. It's all material.'

The girl is shaking her head again, but Zoe continues.

'I have to write what's authentic for me, what captures my interest; I can't choose what that will be.'

'It's so narcissistic.'

Her cheeks are flushed now. Zoe waits.

'You all talk about writing as if it's this sacred and inviolable thing, as if everything else must fall down before it, everything else is secondary and dispensable – it's all just collateral damage in your great higher cause. But the only other people who live their lives like that are religious nuts. Using a grand higher purpose to justify abhorrent acts. It's exactly the same thing. Writing is your god.'

'Fair,' says Zoe. 'I think you're probably right.'

The girl lifts the glass of wine – Zoe brought the inexpensive white she knows she likes best – but sets it back down before drinking.

'It's just such an extraordinary violation. Can you imagine reading about your own family, written by someone else?'

Zoe tries to imagine a book about her parents. She wonders what it would be called, what the cover image would be.

'I think I'd quite like it,' she says. 'I'd be curious.'

'But you'd also feel violated. And, you know, we're not a normal family. We're a family blighted by loss. Perhaps that shouldn't change anything, but I'm afraid it does. I keep thinking – that's my sister you've been writing about. My mother too.'

'They won't be called Tree and Lydia, in the final version.'

'Come on,' she says, smiling bitterly, and Zoe is embarrassed, actually.

'I'm sorry,' she says. 'That was glib. I do understand that you feel violated. I understand that they're sacred to you, because of your loss. Again, I do – deeply – regret that I've made you feel like this.'

'But you won't apologise.'

'Do you need an apology?'

The girl stares, then closes her eyes, opens them. She wears the tiredness physically, like a coat. She has worn make-up today along with the dress and it has loosened, melted a bit. It makes her clear and Spartan face look crowded.

'Nemony, I would be very sad to lose your friendship.'

The girl nods, says nothing. Zoe looks around her at the flat again. It is impossibly small, really.

'These are Liam's?'

She gestures towards three huge and handsome paintings: a portrait, a huddled group of men under umbrellas, the tired aftermath of a party. They dominate the walls and make the space even smaller, somehow bullied.

'Yup.'

'They're great.'

'Yup.'

'I can imagine the father portrait better now,' Zoe says, and regrets it. 'I suppose that's yet another violation, isn't it.'

'You know, I feel less violated by that portrait than I do by your novel. Even though Liam's my partner, the father of my son.'

'This novel's really hurt you.'

'Not hurt, exactly.'

'Angered you.'

'Not that either, really. It's betrayal, more than anything.'

'But you must feel angry too.'

She shakes her head.

'It's strange. I don't really feel angry at you or Liam. I was thinking on the train leaving my dad's today, I don't think I really have the energy for anger. I can't seem to sustain it.'

'That's a shame.'

'Why?'

'It might do you good, to be a bit angrier. And you know, I don't think it's true that you're not. I think you've just learned very well how to hide it, even from yourself.' Zoe tries a gentle smile, to see if she is allowed. 'I can see it, though. I see it when you've had a few drinks, it glints beneath the surface. I saw it when you stayed over at my house that first time when you told me you didn't trust me.'

'I was drunk and rude. Although – I was right, wasn't I, not to trust you?'

'I suppose you were. I should have told you about the novel. I wouldn't have stopped writing it, but I should have told you – that was secretive. It was dishonest, I suppose. I can't stand to be dishonest.'

'Is this an apology then?'

Zoe smiles again.

'Yes, I suppose it is. I apologise for keeping the thing a secret.'

'That is the worst thing, now I think about it. I feel sort of – tricked. Like you were an undercover officer trying to get information out of me.'

'Oh, Nemony – I wasn't doing that.'

'That's not why you invited me over in the first place?'

'No! No.' Zoe leans forward, to show that she is serious. 'I'll admit that I was curious to get to know you in real life – one of my subjects!' She hadn't been able to believe it, when she'd seen them in the park. Like two Fates, hunched there side by side in the fading light. 'But by the time I met you and Etta, I already had all the material I needed. I'd already written most of the thing. Surely you can see from what you've read – I haven't used a single thing you've told me. I wouldn't do that.'

'Oh, you draw a line there.'

'Yes, I do. I haven't been tricking you into revealing anything. My novel is a separate thing entirely from our friendship.'

'But it can't be, because it's about my fucking family.' She looks away. 'I haven't read it, by the way. I don't want to.'

'Oh. Well – fair enough, I suppose.'

The girl looks back at her, frowns. She looks so like her mother.

'If you really haven't used anything I've said, what have you based it all on? Is it all just invention?'

Zoe shakes her head. This is the delicate part, she thinks. This is the really delicate part.

'Well – no, I can't say it is. When I write a story, I research it – thoroughly. I interviewed a lot of people when I began writing this – friends of your sister's, your family's, your mother's.'

'My mother didn't have friends.'

Zoe sighs.

'I always visit a place, in order to write about it.'

'Right.'

The girl waits and Zoe sighs again, shifts in her armchair. It is a horrible armchair, lined in the cheap, bubbled nylon of a train seat.

'I went to West Virginia,' she says, and the girl's lips part. 'I spoke to people there,' she continues, before she's interrupted. 'I always research a story thoroughly, it's how I work. I looked at photos, read some letters, conducted interviews.'

'You went to West Virginia.'

'Yes.'

The girl gives a grim little laugh.

'That's fucking creepy, Zoe.'

And actually, Zoe does cringe. She hasn't done anything wrong, she does believe that, but still she can see that it must feel intrusive. That naturally it will seem as if she has overstepped certain lines.

'You have to stop thinking of it as me researching your family,' she says, 'and see that I was just researching a story, same as every novel I've ever written.'

'Not *a* story. Our story.'

Zoe shakes her head again.

'I'm afraid I don't believe that. I don't believe that we own our stories. There are only thirty-six stories in the world –

you're the one with a PhD in fairy tales, you know that better than I do.'

'Folklore.'

'Fine.'

'You interviewed Krish.'

This, too, feels uncomfortable. She nods.

'Magda.'

'Well now I feel like you're my husband,' she says, trying to joke, 'grilling me about an affair I've had. How many times? Where? Which positions?'

The girl doesn't go with it.

'Tuva,' she says, looking sick.

Zoe is glad to say no, not Tuva. What she doesn't add is that, of all the people she contacted, Tuva was the only one who refused to engage. *I don't entertain ghosts*, she said on the phone, and ended the call.

The girl drains her glass and looks away while Zoe refills it.

'I just don't believe you haven't used anything I've said.'

'I really haven't. You know—'

'What?'

'Actually …'

She pauses again. She must step gently here, too.

'What?'

'A lot of what you've said in our conversations doesn't line up with what I've learned.'

'You're telling me you know more than me about my own family.'

'In certain ways, yes. You have your own version of the story, but that's all it is, a version. And of course, you're entitled to protect it, if it keeps you safe.'

'Oh, thank you. Isn't that what you call "bovine incuriosity"?'

'No. I think most people would call it survival. But – I do think you're strong enough to question what you've been told. Interrogate it a bit.'

'You're so patronising,' she says.

'You see, you are angry with me.'

'Only when you treat me like a child.'

'I'm sorry. You're right, I guess I was.'

The girl lifts her glass and takes a long, long drink of it, as if it is water.

'What else angers you?'

'You asking that. Acting like my analyst.'

Zoe smiles.

'Fair enough.'

They sit in silence, then, and Zoe watches the girl's face as she thinks. She has gone somewhere, this conversation has sent her somewhere. Tentatively, Zoe can feel the focus start to shift from the novel. The slight letting-up of pressure.

'And my dad,' the girl says, then.

'What?'

'You asked me what angers me; my dad does. I'm furious that he wins everything. He lives his life by his rules, and he always wins. Even today, he won today.' She lifts her glass, drinks more. 'And I'm angry that my mother had nothing.'

'She had you four children.'

'That's just the consolation prize given to mothers though, isn't it? You knew that. That's why you left your children. No, my mother never – *claimed* us. She never claimed anything, really. She was entitled to, but she never did. I wish she had. I wish she hadn't subjugated her will.'

'I'd say you children were much more than a consolation prize.'

'My dad humiliated her with his affairs. She was constantly undervalued, passed over, underestimated.'

Zoe thinks that they are getting somewhere now. They are really getting somewhere.

'You see your mother as a victim but you know, I think she was wise. She was canny, she made a good transaction when she partnered with your father. Perhaps it wasn't without pain or humiliation, but—'

She leans forward again. The girl is really listening.

'We all have to find a way to navigate these currents we swim in. Your mother's way was strategic, she found a strategic partnership. She swam in someone else's slipstream, and that way she kept herself and her children safe.'

'We were only safe until she died,' she says. 'We weren't safe after that.'

'Oh, Nemony.'

And then she cries, Nemony. Silently, head bowed, she is racked with it. Zoe remembers the small and silent creature that she was at that funeral: a little scrap with moon-wide eyes. She was too young.

Zoe stands and sits beside her on the sofa, puts her arm around her shoulder for the first time. It occurs to her that she almost loves this girl.

'I read something in one of my mum's Bible books – Proverbs, I think,' she says finally. She wipes the tears from her face and moves away from Zoe, puts distance back between them. 'The one about the perfect woman, the perfect wife. And there was this one bit she underlined, that just killed me. It says: *Give her the rewards she has earned. Let her works bring her praise at the city gate.*'

'OK.'

'*Let her works bring her praise.* She underlined it, for fuck's sake! In pink highlighter. I can't bear it, I can't bear it.' She starts to cry again, and then stills. 'What rewards? No one sings my mum's praises at the fucking – city gate. Or rather, no one would listen if we did. Don Travers's name will live on, but Lydia's means nothing.'

'But you know,' Zoe starts, gently. 'You're going to accuse me of patronising you again.'

'Go on.'

'Well, life isn't a fable, it doesn't have a moral. Or if it does, it's this: the underdog doesn't win, in real life. The hare wins, not the tortoise. The powerful win. Men, by and large.'

'That's so depressing. What about vulnerability? And compassion?'

'Ah, your King Kindness. It was your mother's mantra, wasn't it?'

Nemony's eyes narrow, but Zoe continues.

'You know, I was thinking about your PhD the other day. Kindness and Cruelty in Folklore, was that it? And I think you got it wrong. I'm not patronising you, I promise – I'm sure it's a brilliant piece of work, you're far cleverer than me – but still I would argue your focus is wrong.'

'How?'

'It's not kindness versus cruelty. It's power versus weakness – all of life, all the stories we tell. No, I don't find kindness to be King.'

While she waits for a siren to pass beneath the window she sips her wine, which is warming.

'Your father, for example, he's not *unkind*. What I would say, rather, is that he knows how to use power. He's not sentimental about it.'

'He's a fascist,' she snaps, and there it is, the anger again, unhidden. 'That's how I feel about his use of power.'

Zoe waits for more, and Nemony looks sharply at her.

'You think I'm over the top.'

'No. I don't think that. I'm curious. Tell me what you mean.'

'He's a fascist,' she says again. 'Not politically, obviously, and not in his work – oh, I know,' she says, and she shifts her voice lightly to imitate someone, 'it has a moral force, it shines a light on the terrible inequalities in human experience, etc., etc.' She shakes her head. 'But in the way he lives, he's a fascist. In our family, he is. Our dictator, and the most insidious type because he doesn't even suppress opposition forcibly. He does it through the sheer persuasive force of his approval, on the one hand, and on the other his opprobrium. Those are the strings he controls us with. Us, and maybe everyone in his life.'

Don's daughter is becoming something, Zoe thinks. She cannot help but wish she had her notebook, and a pen.

'I don't know what to believe anymore. Which version, as you say. I heard a few things today that made me think – I have been fed a sanitised truth. A sweetened cup.'

'You were young when very painful things happened. Two tragedies, in pretty quick succession. I can see why you were given sanitised versions of events.' She pauses, takes a breath. 'Your sister's death, for example—'

Nemony gives her a look of such furious warning that Zoe steps back from this. She must tread carefully, around this more than anything.

'Those sanitised versions, though – they were stories. Fables. Perhaps you were told them out of kindness – yes, there we go, kindness – but I don't think it's kind at all. I don't think dishonesty is ever kind.'

Slowly Nemony shakes her head, looks down at her lap.

'I don't know what to think anymore.'

'Read my novel, if you want clarity.'

Nemony rolls her eyes, but there is the palest spark of humour there. There is a ruefulness that makes Zoe think, *She isn't forgiving me yet, but she will.*

'I'm serious. Obviously it's a novel, but – I haven't fabricated the events themselves. Crucially, I haven't – I haven't fabricated the ending. I've only furnished it, imagined some details.'

'I don't know. I don't know if I'll read it. I'm not sure I can bear to.'

Nemony finishes her wine, sits right back, rests her head on the back of the sofa.

'You know,' says Zoe, refilling the glass again, 'you can ask me to change things you're not happy with. I'm not saying I'll definitely make the changes, but I'll do my best. I don't want you to feel exposed when it's published.'

'Well, about that,' says Nemony. 'About it being published.'

'Yes.'

'I should warn you. Dad's agent has already called around. Etta says no one will touch it. Publishers, newspapers—'

So Don knows. This is a thrill to Zoe. She would clap her hands, if it weren't distasteful.

'Nemony, they're shooting for the moon. This isn't ten years ago, even five. Men like Don Travers don't hold the keys anymore, not in the same way. A novel connected to someone as revered as him? It'll be published, and it'll get its coverage too. Because of its subject more than its calibre, which is galling since it's really a pretty bloody good novel. I think maybe my best.' She smiles to hint that she is not as arrogant as she might seem, but she means it. It is good. Perhaps even great. 'Oh, some papers might be cautious, but others will take it. I mean – and this isn't why I wrote it – but you have to see that for the media this will be a story. Don Travers the letch. The irrepressible groomer.'

Nemony frowns.

'Is what they'll say, I mean,' she adds. 'Some people.'

'I don't know that I want that for him.'

'Oh, he'll come off fine, overall. One paper's letch is another's Don Juan.'

And it's true. Because it won't be uncomplicated, the novel's reception. It will be published, but for every scrap of interest it garners it will also incite indignation – not just from his friends and allies and all those who owe him something, but from all the countless people who fear either their own unearthing or that of the men they know, the men they've protected. She will be accused of brazenness and wile, of using Don's fame to gather her own.

But she's ready for that. She's prepared. She believes in what she's written, in what Don Travers would call the truth of the thing.

Nemony has leaned forward. She rests her elbows on her knees, her face in her palms.

'He'll come off fine, Nemony,' Zoe says again. 'He's one of the world's winners, you said that yourself. He wins things.'

She raises her grey face from her hands.

'I need to work out what I think about all of this.'

'Of course.'

'You, your novel, my dad. How we all come across in what you've written.'

'Sure.'

'But not now. I've had a really, really long day.'

Zoe stands.

'Of course. Take your time.'

Tentatively, she rests a hand on Nemony's shoulder.

'You know, I really have come to care about you. And your gorgeous boy. I don't want to hurt you.'

Nemony snorts, lightly.

'I mean it,' Zoe says. 'I care about you both.'

'OK.'

She lets her hand drop from Nemony's shoulder, takes her phone from her pocket, scrolls quickly.

'While you're letting the dust settle on all of this,' she says, 'can I suggest something?'

She shows the screen to Nemony, watches her face for recognition.

'The house in Sicily is on the market, look.'

'You're not going to fucking buy it.'

'No!' She smiles. 'No, I'm not that – creepy, as you say. Or rich! But I am going to go there and look around it. It'll be very helpful, for the first part of the book.'

Nemony takes the phone and swipes from one picture to the next: the high hallway, the olive groves, the pool.

'Come with me. I'll pay for your flight – consider it compensation for upsetting you with all of this.'

'I don't know,' she says, but Zoe can see she wants to. She hands the phone back.

'If nothing else, you and George could do with a change of scene,' she says. 'Don't you think?'

N

Liam came home that morning, in the early white of a summer dawn. Possibly Krystyna had told him we'd moved back in, but I don't think so. I don't think he expected to find us there, and certainly he didn't expect to find me awake already, perched on the sofa with my laptop beside me – unopened, because I hadn't yet gathered the courage to start reading. Before he had time to see me – for the split-second before he could compose his face into one of anger – I saw a tired boy, sad and lost.

'What are you doing?' he said, ramparts back up. All the bunched fury and assurance of the man he'd had to become.

'I don't really know,' I said.

Tree was there with me, that morning. I had woken up tingling with the sense of her presence, as if she had just left the room. And so, instead of what Liam and I had or hadn't done, what would be lost or was already lost between us, I had Zoe's words in my head as he stood there. *I haven't fabricated the ending.* Tree's ending, which I was starting to suspect I didn't know.

Liam was biting his lip, shaking his head, all clenched with vindication. I stood and walked over to him and he flinched as I took his hands, but I held onto them nonetheless.

'It doesn't matter,' I said, and truly it felt an anachronism, his anger.

'You mean, taking my son from me, you mean moving out without a word—'

'Please,' I said. 'Let's not go into all of that. Not yet. Let's just be here for a second.'

I could see that he wouldn't let it go, of course he wouldn't, but I could also see that a large part of him wanted to. So there was still love there. It just wasn't enough, not to keep us going.

I leaned into his body and kissed him, and in the leaning into him and the kissing him I felt his resolve give and soften. I knew that the softening wasn't permanent. It would last only as long as this moment, and then it would all come back, all the exhausting mess of us.

But just then, for that small moment, he let it go. We had sex for the last time, on that sofa, with Zoe's novel waiting on the laptop beside us, and the trucks quaking and shuddering below.

Liam took George out, when he woke.

'I could do what you did to me,' he said before he left. 'I could just fuck off, and not bring him back.'

As I watched him get ready to leave – that interminable process, getting ready to leave anywhere, with a baby – as I watched him drop a nappy, swear, pick it up, find that there were no wipes in the pack, stride sighing to the cupboard to find a fresh pack, swear again, spill formula powder on the surface, drop the bottle lid, pick it up, all while George sent out a tattoo of long, atonal whinges, I thought: *Of course you'll bring him back.*

When they had gone I leaned back into our sofa and carefully, very carefully, I set Liam and George to one side – very simply and coolly and cleanly I drew a curtain over them – and I opened the computer and I started to read.

WEST VIRGINIA

'It came out of the cold night; I did not think such anguish possible.'

William Styron, *Darkness Visible*

Tree's first impression of the Fabelhof was that this was, frankly, a collection of the greatest nerds she had ever come across in her life. She wanted to walk straight back out.

She had touched down in Charleston, West Virginia, at four-thirty in the morning and waited outside the airport for the coaches to start, sitting atop her huge backpack in the tentative morning, a cooling coffee in her hands. She watched the dawn open up into a high, white-blue sky.

When her coach opened its doors she was the first inside it. She dozed as slowly it filled, and when with a great rumbling it set off from the airport she sat up, awake. She pressed her forehead against the buzzing glass and tried to think: *I am coming home, in a way.* Even as the country unfurled either side of long and alien roads.

They passed signs for places called things like Sod and Pilgrim and Comfort and Seth. A grey-haired woman fell asleep on her shoulder, and when she awoke she apologised to Tree and in almost the same breath she listed the names of her grandchildren, all sixteen of them, illustrating her catalogue with photos. She gave Tree biscuits to eat and an apple and didn't ask her a single question, not even her name, had absolutely no interest in her life whatsoever, which was perfect.

The coach stopped, finally, a little way outside Williamson. Tree dismounted as a fleet of motorbikes roared past. Twelve, thirteen, fourteen of them, glinting in the morning sun. There surely couldn't have been anything more American than that.

She hitched a ride the rest of the way, driven by a taciturn young woman with a hard chin and a thick, bolted scar running the length of her forearm. Tree sat in the back between a baby and a four-year-old boy. He climbed onto her lap and explored her face with sweaty fingertips. She felt alone and precarious, which just then seemed glorious things to feel.

But now, standing in the front yard of the Fabelhof, all the exhilaration of the journey and landscape's strangeness dissipated into something like low panic. The familiar embarrassment of making a bad decision, even if she was the only one who would ever know.

Everything she saw looked drab, devoid of energy: the tired buildings, the unmade faces, the fleeces and cagoules and long shapeless clothes, the spectacles and beards and knapsacks, the inspirational slogans and sagging washing lines. And the badly drawn posters tacked to the walls, depicting things she'd seen a thousand times: doves and candles, multiracial hands reaching around the Earth.

The community had modernised significantly since her mother's day. They no longer looked like eighteenth-century Methodists. They had a box television in the main lobby, a barbecue area around the front. If the women wore their hair in scarves and the long, pleated skirts her mother had always favoured, they were paired not with quaint billowy blouses but with ill-fitting Aertexes, buttoned to the neck. Tree had come here wanting to retreat into the past, but this was the present: modernised and low-tech and unpicturesque, unappealing to her in every single way. Shaking hands with them all, one by one, standing in the glare of their smiling gaze, all she could think was that coming here was a terrible mistake.

A young woman called Sammy showed her around. This was where they made their crafts – dreary, irrelevant things – which they sold in town on a Wednesday, giving their proceeds to the local hospital. This was where their rota was kept, with its complex colour-coded system. This was where the young ones played, this was where they studied. Much was made of the barbecue, which was in fact four or five different barbecue devices and surprisingly new-fangled, and in which they clearly placed a lot of faith and emphasis. Sammy stole cautious looks at Tree throughout the tour. She eyed her black jeans with their torn knees, the huge leather jacket, her cropped hair and multiple earrings. She seemed relieved when Jon arrived to take over.

Jon was in his fifties, Tree guessed. He was slim but wide-hipped, with a neat dark beard at odds with the white hair on his head. A still man, softly spoken and, she thought, not very friendly. They had all mentioned him as soon as she'd arrived: it was Jon who would know who her mother was, who knew everyone who had lived in the Fabelhof.

'You'll have to excuse me,' he said when he took her into his office. He moved with the slow, elaborate calm of a person used to being in charge. 'I've spent a long day in the hospital.'

He gestured for her to sit down, and then he rolled up his shirtsleeves and washed his hands carefully in a sink in the corner.

'Are you a doctor?' she asked.

He smiled as he shook his head, as if this was a question he heard often.

'Not at all. No, I'm on the board. Most of what we do here, we do for the hospital. They've nursed many of our family, brought many of us in and out of this world. It's a good place, Williamson Memorial – that's the hospital – but a troubled place. Lots of troubled folk, lots of sickness. It needs help and money.'

He dried his hands with a towel and then held it to his face, inhaling the damp cloth.

'Now, Teresza,' he said, sitting down opposite her, 'you've come to find out more about your mother. Gwen and Peter Weber's second daughter, Lydia.'

'Did you know her?' Tree asked.

He smiled serenely, privately, and shook his head again.

'Not personally. She left five years before I arrived.'

Tree had thought everyone was born into the community, not that they arrived and joined. She'd thought, too, that they didn't use hospitals or doctors. Her mother had told her that their babies were born on a kitchen table. That their old faded and expired in hushed bedrooms.

'But I knew Gwen and Peter. And I knew Lydia's siblings.' He nodded. 'Your aunts and uncles. Melly, May, Susan, Mike, Dora, Nora, Kieran … let's see, who else, Kristen … Joseph – yup, I've known them all. But none of them belong to the Hof anymore.'

She felt something drop inside her. A lightness, turning to weight.

'No, they all left some time ago. A lot has changed. We've had to remodel the Hof, bring it into this century. You don't get many communities anymore, living like the Hof did back then. It was a – solid community, self-sufficient and simple, it respected the traditions of our ancestors. But, well, it needed cleaning up. There were some problems.' He cleared his throat. 'The world around us is different now. We can't live in the past like we used to. We have to respond,' he said, clicking his fingers, 'we have to react. There are many troubled folk,' he said again, 'and it's not our duty to keep ourselves shut off from them. That's not what our brother did.' He eyed her. 'Jesus.'

'Right,' she said.

'He taught us that it's our duty to help them,' he said, watching her. 'All of them.'

'Right.'

It transpired that Jon's family had arrived from a related community in Ohio, and that it was Jon's father who had instigated the great changes. Only two small outhouses remained from Lydia's day: a storage room and a small barn they used now as a kind of joinery workshop. Tree had expected to see faces like Etta's and Nemony's and their mother's, the Weber face, the chestnut eyes and straight smiles and also the thin, sharp-kneed Weber legs, the long back and straight posture. She had expected to find chickens pecking at dust, men and women in headscarves tilling the land.

When she left Jon's office, standing on the porch looking out over the yard, she was confronted with something altogether less familiar and more ordinary than she had expected. Her aunts and uncles had gone, they weren't there. Her mother wasn't there.

Sammy came to find her, then.

'You want to come help out in the kitchen?' she asked, and Tree nodded and followed her through the main doors, under a garland of kids' paintings, the paper curled at the edges. The kitchen exhaled when Sammy opened the door. Steam, and noise, and women.

As the afternoon passed there, Tree played with the children and spoke to the women, helped them chop vegetables and grind herbs for the barbecue. She listened to their stories. She started to feel absorbed into their warmth. Sammy gave her someone's baby to hold, a nine-week-old girl with copper eyelashes. Tree sat at a long table and the baby fell asleep in her arms and so she just sat there amid the calm of their chatter, stunned by exhaustion after the long journey, the long hard months of sobriety in London and the messy years before that she felt had curled into nothing, like smoke.

When the barbecue was ready they sat around white plastic tables in the yard and ate, a large extended family. Tree was invited to sit with the young people and teenagers, the ones she'd callowly written off as nerds but who she found now to be smart and animated. They spoke not about popular culture or their love lives but instead about the fundraising and volunteering work they did, which was the Fabelhof's over-riding mission as a community.

It was impressive, she thought, something to be respected and admired, the passion with which these teenagers talked about their charity work. Without piety or self-congratulation they spent their free time helping old and sick and injured people at Williamson Memorial Hospital, or in the town's many clinics and outreach programmes for people in need – addicts, principally. There was a drugs crisis emerging, they told her, the scale of which no one outside Appalachia seemed to grasp. The overdoses weekly, sometimes daily. The clinics doling out prescriptions without assessment, the pills making their way into children's hands, passing between them in school corridors. And yet even when they spoke about the addicts they spoke plainly, with neither criticism nor glamourisation, as if addiction were a virus contracted and exchanged by cows or swine or poultry.

Tree wondered if any of them ever stopped to wonder why people took drugs in the first place. Or what it was like to take them, what escape it might offer. She wondered what they would think if they knew all the things she'd taken and done – all the amazing times, when she was grasping the very borders of life in her hands and bending them, but all the bleak times too, the sordid and lonely ones – and she felt envious. Yes, she envied their innocence. There were no secret vices for them to withhold from their family, no disconnect between their impulses and their parents' expectations. If the community had changed dramatically since Lydia's day, Lydia and her siblings could only have been even more naive and innocent than these teenagers, and in that context Tree could see just how jarring her own behaviour, her clothes and late nights and unhinged friends and boyfriends and topless sun-bathing and cigarettes and drinking – all her teenage actions, of which that final summer in Frantoio was the sickening acme – must have been to her mother.

When the food had been eaten and a few of the adults were singing along to a guitar, Jon came to sit with Tree and the young adults. They liked him, she could tell; he teased them, they teased him a little back. He was friendlier with Tree than he had been earlier. He asked her questions about her life in London, and her family. After a while, he took an envelope from his shirt pocket and unfolded several papers to show her. On them were photos, printed in black and white on office paper.

'Here's your ma,' he said. 'I found them in our archive this afternoon. I can't give you the originals, but you can have these and I'll email the files for you to keep.'

Tree felt her stomach contract. There was her mother aged fourteen or fifteen, looking exactly like Etta and Nemony. There again as a younger girl with a squiffy brush of hair, squinting solemnly against the light.

'She was a good woman, I'm sure,' said Jon. 'I regret that I never knew her.'

'Yes. She was a very good woman.'

'I asked my parents about her a few times, actually. I was interested in the story of her leaving. But I could never find anyone who ever wanted to talk about her.'

Tree swallowed.

'I don't begrudge them. It was hard for the Hof, that she left, but we came to understand. She was suited to a wider world.'

Tree looked back at the photo, the child squinting back at her.

'Maybe.'

'She was clearly a good mother, too,' he said.

'Yes, she was.'

'It's testament to that, that you've come all this way to learn about her.'

He gazed at her steadily, his eyes very blue.

'But you don't belong here, Teresza.'

She took a breath.

'You know that as well as I do. Why are you here?'

'I wanted to—' she started. 'My mother—'

'You want to know what I see?' he interrupted, and she sensed an impatience now, an eagerness to dispatch a job. 'I see a young woman who's lost. You haven't come here to learn more about Lydia, really. You'll find that none of this is really about her. You've come to learn more about yourself.' He sighed. 'But you won't find it here, Teresza.'

He took the papers from her, folding them back up, and slid them neatly into the envelope.

'No, you won't find anything here. It's not our job, Teresza. That's not to say I don't feel for you, that you're lost. I'm sure I speak for our whole family when I say I sincerely hope you find your way.' He took a biro from his pocket, wrote something on the envelope and handed it to her. 'That's Dora's address,' he said. 'Your mom's youngest sister. She and her boy live in town. She'll be glad to see you.' Then he stood, gripping her shoulder in a fraternal sort of way. 'The bus comes down the Tug Creek Road,' he said, gesturing towards the main gate to the Hof. He looked at his watch. 'There'll only be one left tonight, so you don't want to wait.'

His hand fell from her shoulder, and he walked away.

Darkness was already falling. She stood at the gate under the weight of her backpack and looked back at the Hof, the strip lights of the kitchen spilling out onto the grass, the children and young people playing a game of chase now, back and forth across the dusky yard. Jon stood in a group of adults. He held his hands in his pockets, his stance wide. Impregnably confident. And though he was addressing them, she thought he was aware she was watching. She felt the blood under her cheeks, the prickling burn of humiliation. She turned, made her way up the track the hitched car had rattled down this morning.

She didn't know what time the bus would come. It wasn't even clear to her which was the bus stop. There were two possibilities, one a small rickety wooden shelter on the roadside, the other a tall post a hundred feet further down, with a sign that looked like an old bus timetable but was so age-worn and sun-bleached that it was illegible. She squatted down halfway between them, dropping her backpack onto the scrub of the roadside, and rolled and lit a cigarette. It tasted bitter. The barbecued meat turned itself over in her stomach. She took the printed photos of her mother out of the envelope, but she could barely make them out in the fading light.

It was getting cold. She took a blanket out of her backpack, wrapped it around her shoulders, sat on the grass and leaned back, using the bag for a bolster. She heard Jon's words again in her mind. *You're lost*. She swallowed and looked up at the sky, two or three stars already winking.

Her mother looked at those stars. Her mother walked along this road. Her feet might have stepped over the very patch of earth under Tree's palm. She told herself these things, tried to feel them, tried to see through her mother's eyes, pressed her palm down into the earth, but it didn't work. She couldn't connect to the reality of it. She could only watch the thoughts form. And then there it was: the familiar dragging in her stomach, the dreadful downward pull. She closed her eyes and clenched her jaw. It was coming.

*

351

The evening grew colder, darker. She moved to the wooden shelter to get some protection but it was no warmer there in the structure's splintery darkness. Every ten or fifteen minutes a vehicle would approach and pass in a swooping rush of light, none of them the bus. Then, when finally it came, it drove straight past the shelter and past the tall post with the faded timetable and onwards into the black of the horizon. She shouted after it and heard the shout as if it were far away. Her voice was repulsive to her.

It was half past ten when she climbed into the first car that stopped for her, her limbs stiff with cold and sitting. She felt physically sickened by then, gripped in the dread of what was coming. She showed the address to the pair in the front, a corpulent middle-aged couple, and as the car pulled away she leaned into the darkness of the back of the car with her arms wrapped around herself and answered the woman's bright questions with as much normalcy as she could muster. Yes, the accent was British, yes, from London, yes, she only arrived here this morning. No, she'd not been here before. Yes, she had family here, she'd not met them yet, yes, it would be wonderful, yes, she couldn't wait to see, and on and on. Sicker and sicker she felt with each mile and each question, the darkness outside quite black now, as if they were driving through a tunnel.

It was midnight by the time she made it to Dora's house. The pain was so vast that she could barely walk. She staggered up the path, watched her arm as it lifted up to ring the bell. She waited. A light flickered on, then another. The door opened. It took the very last of her energy to let Dora look at her, to meet the woman's eyes and find the words, just, to explain who she was and that she was sick, could she have somewhere to sleep.

She barely noticed the room she was directed to, the sofa she sat on while she waited for the woman to make up a bed. Everything was odious to her. The pattern of the sofa fabric beneath her was like worms coiling and uncoiling. Each breath hurt. She exhaled with a pant of pain when she was shown into the bedroom, and lay face down on the coverlet. Behind her, the door clicked as it closed.

She shut her eyes and she saw worms again, a writhing mass of them. Naked and mortal, like the dreadful flesh of human bodies. *I' th' last night's storm I such a fellow saw, which made me think a man a worm*, she thought. *I' th' last night's storm*, she started to hear, over and over, on repeat, as the seconds or minutes or hours passed. The voice was upbeat, bright as a children's television presenter, male, a Midlands accent. *I' th' last night's storm I such a fellow saw. I' th' last night's storm. A fellow. Such a fellow. A worm!* She groaned, curling herself into the tightest shape she could make.

She needed Malachy, that was all she could think. She needed Malachy, but she had flown away from him. Brazen, foolishly emboldened because she hadn't had an episode for almost a year now, she had willingly put four thousand miles between them. And yet there had been warning signs, she saw it now, the emboldenment one of them. Too much energy, too much wakefulness. A mounting invincibility. These things were kindling, waiting for a spark like Jon.

She pictured Malachy asleep in his London home. Soft breaths, one arm around Lucy, his infinitely well and measured and stable girlfriend. Her pretty sleeping face on his chest. The warmth of their apartment, the calm, the safety of it. They were safe and Tree couldn't be.

I' th' last night's storm, she heard again, and somehow she pulled herself up from the bed and opened the door and crept down the black corridor until she found a kitchen. How long, that journey to the kitchen. It was as if countless fingers and hands snatched in the darkness at her neck, at her back. *A man a worm.* She felt her way into the room with her hands. *A man! A worm!* Blindly, she opened the fridge and cupboards until she found a bottle of vodka, because maintaining sobriety paled in significance to the imperative, now, to stop it all: the words, the revulsion, the madness.

Because that was what it was, she realised afresh every time it came. It wasn't depression, it was madness.

She filled a mug with vodka and returned the bottle to the cupboard and took the mug back to the bedroom. Sitting on the bed, she drank half of the mug's contents in one go. She grimaced at the taste, squeezed her eyes closed, waited.

Jon's face appeared to her, his watery blue eyes. The rolled-up shirtsleeves and dry hairless forearms, the mouth framed by the dark beard, moist lips opening to speak. *I' th' last night's storm*, he started, and she opened her eyes and, wincing, drained the rest of the drink. Then flinching she went back out down the corridor, and into the kitchen, and filled her mug again and drank it.

In that way, eventually, the wound was staunched and she could sleep.

Dora kept her fed, as the days passed. She didn't ask many questions. Her kindness was the silent kind, like Lydia's. She offered to call someone, but when Tree refused she didn't insist. She brought Tree food, basic things like sandwiches and bowls of tinned soup; she switched the television on for her when Tree could make it out of bed and into the sitting room. Sometimes there was a young man there, who Tree came to understand was her cousin, Dora's son. He didn't hang around. He came and went, he was restless, he had a restless energy she recognised. It made her feel both at home and afraid. Dora had some friends who visited, portly drab women who looked at her in a way she didn't like. They scared her. When they were there she made her halting way back to the bedroom Dora had given her and held pillows either side of her head to muffle their voices.

In two nights she had finished the vodka. It was the only way she could sleep, coupled with some pills she had found in the bathroom cabinet. To her relief, the vodka bottle was replaced with a new one, and nothing was asked.

It was only on the fifth or sixth day – though in fact it could have been many more – that she thought to question the presence of alcohol in a home she would have presumed to be as puritan as its Fabelhof origins. She was sitting in the little sitting room when she had that thought, and simultaneously she noticed certain things in the room around her: the walls were cream like the rug, a wasp was flying through the air, the framed photograph on the wall had been knocked, so that it hung at an angle. Dora walked in with a cup of coffee and Tree looked at her face, took in its shape and lines and the dark roots against blonde, and when she saw these things she thought that the worst of it might have passed. She met Dora's eyes, saw for the first time that they were brown.

'You look a little better, honey.'

'Yes,' said Tree. She reached for the cup and leaned back carefully into the sofa, pulling her legs up in front of her. The skin of her knees was yellowish against the white of the frayed denim. She needed to wash her jeans, she thought, and that she might in a few days' time be able to sort some clothes into a pile and open a washing machine door and turn a dial and press a button seemed, just then, like a possibility.

She dozed off there, on the sofa, even after the large mug of black coffee. Through her sleep the voices of the television filtered occasionally, nudging her dreams so that the life she knew – her ex-boyfriend Tony and the girl he left Tree for, Malachy and Lucy, Nemony and Etta – became entwined with this other place. The best automobile repairs in Mingo County. Jonny Johnson, the Real Estate Guru. The friendly staff at the Williamson Wellness Center. Finally she dreamt that she stood with her backpack in Dora's derelict front yard, being shown around by Tuva Brøvig. Just look at the house, Tuva said; Tree would be crazy not to snap it up. This was the best neighbourhood in the county. The shadow of a swinging road sign see-sawed across Tuva's face.

That was when she found a hook to pull herself back into the world. Dora was sitting in the armchair in front of her, a large book and a pencil in her hand. She was wearing glasses, the plastic kind sold on pharmacy counters, her face small behind them.

'I've been marking some passages for you,' she said, looking up and then back down at the page, scoring it carefully. Tree looked at the bare wall behind Dora's head, its textured paint. Despair ballooned inside her. It pushed outwards; it felt as if it would burst out of her frame.

'The righteous cry out, and the Lord hears them,' Dora started in a monotone, and Tree wrapped her arms around herself and closed her eyes. 'He delivers them from all their troubles. The Lord is close to the broken-hearted and saves those who are crushed in spirit. That's Psalms 34.'

There was the flutter of pages, the clearing of her throat.

'But they who wait for the Lord shall renew their strength; they shall mount up with wings like eagles; they shall run and not be weary; they shall walk and not faint. Isaiah, 40:31.'

The pages fluttered and rustled again. *I' the last night's storm*, Tree heard, and squeezed her eyes tighter.

'I sigh when food is put before me, and my groans pour out like water. *For the things* – sorry, *for the thing which I greatly feared is come upon me*, and that which I was afraid of is come unto me. I was not in safety, neither had I rest, neither was I quiet; yet trouble came. And wait, hold on, there's more just down … Ah, yes, here. *Terrors are turned loose against me; they drive away my dignity as by the wind, and my prosperity has passed like a cloud.*'

Tree saw terrors like darting winged creatures, flying into her face.

'For destruction from God was a terror to me, and by reason of his highness *I could not endure.*'

'You think she wants to hear that?' asked a voice, and Tree opened her eyes. There was the young man, her cousin, skinny arms folded over his chest. There was the cream wall behind him, the framed photograph that hung at an angle.

'I was thinking what Lydia would've wanted me to do,' said Dora.

'Well, not that,' he said, turning to Tree. 'Am I right? What is it you've been coming off of, anyway?'

It was the first time anyone had asked her a direct question for some time.

'Nothing,' she said.

'What do you mean, nothing?' he asked, and Dora tutted.

'Leave her be, Marcus.'

'Nothing,' she repeated. 'I'm not coming off anything, I've been sober for eleven months,' but no one was listening.

'Lord knows I'm not judging.'

'No, I'd think not,' said Dora, and sighed. 'You'd hardly have a leg to stand on.'

'I know.'

'Not a leg.'

'All right, Mom. Not a leg.'

Tree turned to the window. Outside Dora's house, sunshine bloomed from behind a cloud and retreated.

'Hey,' Marcus said, and when she turned to him, he nodded to the door. 'Lazybones. Want to take a walk?'

They set off in silence. She held herself as she walked, her hands gripping her arms, and she walked stiffly, with minimal motion, as if she were carrying a jug full of water.

She hadn't noticed the street when she'd arrived, she'd barely been able to see. Now, she looked carefully around. Everything was low: low houses and bungalows, low gates, low sparse trees. A low, grey October sky. Marcus walked ahead and then waited, moved ahead and then waited, and he scuffed his trainers on the road as he did. He wanted to walk quickly, like she usually did. He lit a cigarette.

'You want one?'

She took one from his pack.

'You don't have to tell me anything,' he said. 'I can see you don't want to talk. I'll just tell you some stuff instead. I'll give you a tour of the town.' He handed her his lighter and then opened his arms wide. 'Welcome to Williamson, the biggest shithole in Mingo County, against some stiff competition. In this direction you will find some shitty old houses. In this direction, you will find some more shitty old houses. Everyone who's worth anything has left, but you've chosen to arrive. We hope you enjoy your stay!'

She tried to give him something like a smile, but her cheeks were stiff and shaky.

'OK ...' he said, and they walked a little further and then he stopped again to wait. 'I did know I had some British cousins. There's a few of you, right?'

She nodded, swallowed.

'Four.'

'Oh wait, I said I wouldn't get you to talk. Your voice is kind of weird, you know that? You sound like a bicycle tyre that's had all the air pumped out. No offence. What was I saying? Four of you, OK. That's cool. Not too many, not too few. I'm an only child and even with as many cousins as I have, it's still – it was like a graveyard growing up in our house, once she got us out of the Hof. I think my mom had me and just couldn't deal with going through that hell all over again ... I was a shitty kid. Were you?'

She dragged on her cigarette.

'I bet you had your moments. But my problem was – well, I've got a ton of problems actually, everything that could be wrong with me was wrong with me growing up, no wonder my mom was put off the whole business.'

He took a long drag of his cigarette – five, six seconds, eyes narrowed as if he was sucking the last bit of air from the world – and then he held his hand up to wave at an old woman sitting on a plastic chair outside her house.

''Sup, Rita.' The woman scowled. 'And a good day to you too. Glad life's treating you well.' He turned back to Tree. 'Your mom died, right? A few years back, was it? But you don't want to talk about that, I bet. Personally, I always wanted to meet her – the family rebel, man!' He swung his arms. 'The one that got away! The one that left the fabled Fabelhof! So long, fuckers!'

He saluted, and Tree felt something like a smile spreading through her, even if her face didn't move.

'She wrote letters to my mom, every month of the year. Did you know that? Yeah, Mom was pretty low when Lydia passed, even if she hadn't seen her in like twenty years. She always called herself your mom's little baby. Still does.'

Letters, she thought. Letters to her baby sister, back in West Virginia, all that time. It was unimaginable – Tree found that she couldn't find the energy to believe him. Her mother had never written letters.

Instead she thought of the photos they'd had at home growing up and which had occasionally done the rounds, much to her and her siblings' fascination: Lydia's family, this unthinkable family, a whole clan of brothers and sisters, one of them – it must have been Dora – a baby in Lydia's arms. Just as Tree once cradled her own sisters.

When she returned to London she would find those photos again, if they still existed, and she'd put them together with the pictures Jon had given her. She saw him again, folding the printouts, sliding them back in the envelope, handing the envelope back to her.

You won't find it here, Teresza.

*

She took to walking with Marcus whenever she felt able to, usually after lunch. They circled the town, watched over always by the brown wooded hills that surrounded it. Marcus paced ahead and waited impatiently, Tree moved with difficulty. They skirted the car park of the Williamson Memorial Hospital and she wondered if Jon was inside, washing his hands in a sink, casting his calm unknowable gaze over the troubled folk of Williamson.

They stalked the sparse storefronts of W 3rd Avenue. They passed one of the clinics the Fabelhof teens had told her about, even worse than they had conveyed with its snaking queue of shaking addicts. They stopped and stood on the Pete Dillon Bridge, a green cage-like structure rising up over the Tug Fork river, separating West Virginia from Kentucky. Marcus threw a rock and the jade water swallowed it, with a gulp.

Sometimes he was elated and full of energy; sometimes his energy was scratchy and he was agitated, jumpy, irritable. Always he talked, almost without stopping. He could be very funny, but his chatter could also be spiteful and full of loathing: for Williamson, for the big pharma companies dangling the town's inhabitants from giant paws, for Dora's neighbours, for the black-lunged and depressive miners as much as the fat cats responsible for closing the mines. The mechanisation of the coal industry, he ranted, was the nation's ultimate crime against the poor, and then almost without breath he was upbraiding the miners for their great and collective ecological crime against the planet. He railed against his old high school friends, the upstarts who'd left as soon as they could as much as the no-hopers who'd stayed. The latter he referred to universally as dopeheads. He wasn't sleeping well, he explained one day; he'd kicked a bad habit recently and moved back in with his mother, and it was hard work. She didn't ask what he'd been taking but didn't feel convinced, learning the volatile rhythms of his behaviour, that he would stay off it for long.

She was mortified to learn that he also wasn't sleeping well because she had taken his bedroom.

'What, you didn't know?' he asked, grinning. 'Don't you notice anything? Where did you think my bedroom was?'

'I—'

'You came banging on the door in the middle of the night like a crazy lady and my mom came in and kicked me out of my bed. I've been sleeping on a mattress on her floor since you came.'

'No,' she said.

'Yes.'

'You haven't.'

'I have.'

'I'm so sorry,' she said, and he smiled.

'Queen Teresza. Sleeping on my mom's floor is the very least I'd do to keep you around.'

She put off calling Malachy. He would recognise instantly from her voice alone that she was ill and then it would be like it had always been, just another time when he felt he must come to her rescue again. She didn't think he or their relationship could take it, another rescue.

And so, lying in the darkened bedroom Marcus had given over to her, she switched on her phone and answered Malachy's messages in a bright and hands-off tone that sometimes took hours, and all her energy, to compose.

Are you there? What's it like?? Are you one of
the clan now??

Haha, nah. All good here.

But what's it like??? Are you making curds and
whey and tilling the land ...?

Hmmm ... things have modernised. They're nice
though. V. welcoming. Bad reception so can
only message when I get into town.

Glad it's good and they're nice. When are you
getting back? I'm desperate to hear about it.
Don't get converted, OK??

Haha, OK! Spk soon.

You sure you're OK ...?

I'm great! Just busy. Spk soon.

The days bled into each other, so that when she emerged sufficiently from her depression to work out what day it was she learned that she'd been in West Virginia for just under a month.

'I haven't,' she told Marcus, who had folded his arms and was laughing.

'You're really out of it, aren't you?'

'But I haven't been here for four weeks. I can't have.'

'Honest to God.'

She sat back. They were sitting beside each other on the patterned sofa she'd thought of that first night as worms, the television churning in front of them at a low volume. This was it, her great trip to Appalachia, her quest. A month in the half-dark of a bedroom, a kitchen, a sitting room. She turned from Marcus and stared ahead of her, watched a helicopter shudder across the screen. The camera panned out to a wide view of deserts; beneath the helicopter a car, racing its way across yellow earth. If a whole month could evaporate like that, she thought – if time could pass with so little meaning and so little to remember – it was surely impossible to maintain that anything mattered at all. It came to nothing.

'No,' she said then, loudly, and Marcus turned to her. His bright black eyes, keen nose, cheekbones sharp as whiskers.

'Come again?'

She wouldn't believe it, that it all came to nothing. Nothing will come of nothing, she thought, and slapped her palms onto her lap.

'This film is the absolute pits,' she said. 'Where's the remote?'

She spent less time in bed. On her walks with Marcus she began to move at a normal speed, and make conversation. She felt her lethargy lift. The horror – the fingers catching at her – that had gone, for now.

In the evenings, the three of them ate and then played cards, sitting at Dora's round kitchen table.

'So how long are you going to stay with us?' asked Marcus one night, and Dora tutted.

'That's no way to make a guest feel welcome,' she said. 'Questions like that'll make her leave.'

'She'd better not,' said Marcus, and Tree looked at them and then back at her cards.

'Rummy,' said Dora, fanning her cards out on the table, and Marcus threw his down and reached for a cigarette. He offered one to Tree, and she took it.

'But you'd better start buying your own cigarettes,' he said, and Tree smiled.

'OK.'

'But seriously,' said Marcus. 'How long? Do you have a plan?'

Tree sat back.

'I came here to find out about my mum,' she said. 'About our roots, I guess. I didn't really make a plan, any further than the Fabelhof. I wanted to stay there, pitch in – I wanted to picture her childhood.'

'But then they chucked you out,' said Marcus, and Dora tutted again.

'Can you imagine,' she said, shaking her head. 'It goes against everything it's supposed to stand for.'

'It's all right,' said Tree, but she could see Jon's face again before her, the watery eyes, the glint of feline pleasure in his words. *You won't find it here.*

'Well, I was only little when Lydia left. I can't tell you much about her as a young woman. I don't even remember that man who she went with, the British man, though there used to be a photo somewhere, from some local gazette. She wrote me, though.'

She caught Tree's gaze and held it, nodding, as if she might not be believed.

'Oh yes. She never stopped writing. Every month, just about. She was – oh, she took good care of her little baby. Her baby sister. She never forgot about me, even with everything she had going on. She never let me feel forgotten.'

'That sounds like her,' said Tree.

There were boxes and boxes of letters, Marcus had told her. Tree watched Dora now, shuffling the cards in her small dry hands, lips pinched in concentration. Lydia had loved this weird little woman enough to write boxes of letters to her, over the years.

'I never knew she wrote,' she said, thinking that this might be Dora's opportunity to offer the letters up for Tree to read, but she just nodded.

'Oh yes,' she said again. She tapped the pack of cards on the table to straighten them up, and started to deal. 'Marcus, will you take the ice cream out to soften?'

Tree began to start walking on her own sometimes too, climbing the hills around the town. Some days it was hard going and bleak and she didn't go for long, but on others – particularly when the sky was high, which wasn't often – she felt really quite well. She'd open her mouth wide and pull the air in, feel it harsh and full on her tongue, and in the back of her throat, and down into her lungs.

As she walked she started to form her plan. She would make peace with not seeing more of the Fabelhof. Hardly anything remained from her mother's day, in any case. Instead, she would make contact with Lydia's other siblings. She'd speak to them, get stories of her mother, her grandparents. She'd meet the rest of her cousins. Once she'd done all that she'd hire a car or a van and leave this place. She'd drive out of town, past the Fabelhof in its corn-yellow fields to all the weird, enchanting places she'd seen on the map: Seneca Rocks, New River Gorge, Elakala Falls.

And then she'd go home. That bit worried her, still; it was so full of uncertainty, and the menace of old habits. But she'd be strong enough by then, she thought. She might even move back to Greenwich for a while and spend some time looking after Etta and Nemony, since their father wasn't going to. She'd get a new job and after work she'd cook dinner for the girls and make sure their school uniforms were washed, their homework done, revision. Etta's A-levels were coming up; she would need to knuckle down now, spend more time at home. Tree would make sure she did.

They'd watch films together; they'd go to bed early. She'd give Malachy nothing to worry about. Looking after the girls and taking care of herself – setting her career on track, and her health, and her finances – she'd give him things to feel grateful for and proud of, instead.

But the first step of her plan was more difficult than she'd anticipated.

'I'd love to meet the rest of the family,' she told Dora, several times, and Dora would nod, with a faint and undirected smile.

'Yes,' she'd say, vaguely.

Tree had never met someone so capable of vagueness as Dora. She began to suspect that it was the woman's great tool, perhaps had been essential in bringing up a child as relentlessly demanding as she imagined Marcus to have been. He was still demanding. His needs and desires were erratic, they flickered from one thing to another along with his attention.

'You need to strip the floor in here, Ma,' he'd say. 'It's disgusting, look at that, it's like it's – eugh, it's like it's *mouldy* or something, what's that – eugh, Mom?'

'Yes.'

'What even *is* that stuff round the edge there. Mom?'

'Mh.'

'It's like – ugh, it's like, almost red, it's like some rats have come and like, shat blood and then it's kind of rotted and gone like *mouldy* or, I don't know, *rusted* or some shit.'

Bent over, bare bony feet and torso, loose jeans. Peering at the point where the linoleum met the skirting.

'Mom, I'm telling you, you need to strip this stuff up, like, today. I'm going to do it now, I'm just going to strip it all up, where do you keep the wrench these days?'

And 'yes', Dora would say in that soft-focused way, entirely non-committal, a word that floated like a dove's coo along the top of things, almost as if she were talking to herself. Reminding herself of something to add to the shopping list, say, or an ingredient. 'Half a cup of flour,' she'd say in the same tone, under her breath, looking from recipe to measuring cups. 'Half a cup of flour, stir till smooth. Half … a cup …'

'What even *is* this stuff? *Gross*, Mom,' he'd repeat, peering and puffing, and in this way they'd continue, Dora never committing, Marcus obsessing about some random and pointless thing until the bubble of his focus burst and he forgot all about it. On to the next thing.

Tree didn't want to forget all about her thing, though, because it wasn't random or pointless. She'd come all this way, and all she had to show for it was Dora and Marcus in their bungalow, speaking at crossed purposes, co-existing in their particular, opposed, complementary way, like Laurel and Hardy or something. Fond as Tree had already grown of them. She hadn't learned a thing about Lydia, or the closed world that had formed her. Only that she'd written letters, boxes of them, which Tree would apparently never get to see.

'Dora,' she said one evening, and this time she was determined. She had the woman. 'I'd really like to meet some of the rest of the family.'

'Oh yes,' said Dora, spooning fish pie onto Marcus's plate, which he held up before him like a child. 'Of course.'

It was inimitable, actually. But Tree persisted.

'Can I have a number, maybe? Who's the best person to get in touch with, do you think?'

'Oh, I'm not sure.'

'Do any of them live close by?'

'Not too close, no,' said Dora, starting to eat, and Tree turned to Marcus, but he was looking down at his plate, head bowed, already shovelling food.

And so she waited until later, when Dora left them to go to bed.

'Your mum doesn't want me seeing your family,' she told Marcus. He stood, opened the fridge.

'That's because she doesn't like them,' he said, handing her a beer.

'What do you mean? She's got, what, eight siblings left?'

'Yeah. She doesn't like any of them.'

'So what happened?'

'Huh?'

'Come on. Eight siblings, and she doesn't keep in touch with a single one?'

He sighed, but said nothing.

'You don't keep in touch with your cousins?'

'Not really, no.'

'Don't they still live around Williamson?'

'Sure. Some of them.'

'And so – you don't see them, out and about?'

'Sure I do, some days.'

'Um, OK,' she said, in a voice that made it clear that it wasn't OK, but even then she got nothing. 'So there was a falling-out, of some kind.'

'Teresza—' he started, lifting his hands up, but then he let them drop. 'Forget it.'

'No, come on. Talk to me.'

'Just—'

He looked away, screwed his mouth up.

'Come on, Marcus. I know I'm being annoying, but you've got to see this from my perspective. I've come all the way here to meet my mum's huge family, and then – And, you know, I mean it's unusual to have eight living siblings and not want to see any of them. I mean, they grew up in a *commune*, cut off from the world. They must have been close in the past, at least?'

He leaned across the table, his voice very low.

'OK. Come on. Use your imagination. Why do you think Mom wouldn't want anything to do with anyone from her childhood?'

He blinked, twice.

'In a commune, as you say. Cut off from the world.'

She looked into his eyes as they blinked again, rapidly, like Morse code. Oh God, she thought. Oh God.

'Yeah,' he said.

'Something bad happened. In the commune.'

'Not *something*,' he said, nodding. '*Lots* of things. Bad things. For many, many years.'

'Fuck.'

'Yeah.'

'Fuck,' she said again.

'Yeah.'

They sat there in silence, and she held her hands up to her face, let it rest in her palms. Bad things. For many, many years.

The darkness of her palms was nice, very soft, a great relief. She realised now that the light in the kitchen had been too harsh, neon and white like in a hospital, or a school.

'Did my mum know?' she asked eventually, letting her hands drop. He lifted a cigarette and lit it, took a long drag.

'You serious?'

'Yes.'

'I mean—' He let out a little sardonic huff, not quite laughter. 'I'd say so. I'd guess she knew it only too fucking well. Wouldn't you?'

Fish pie and cigarette smoke in a small, closed room. She stood up and opened a window, and then she sat back down and held her hands again over her eyes, pressing her finger-tips into the sides of her nose, by the tear ducts. She shook her head to herself. Sometimes, with her eyes closed like this, she could see fish, lovely fish in bright iridescent colours, shoals of them darting through limpid water.

'I'd *guess*,' he said, in a low voice that was gentler than she'd heard before, 'that was why she left the damn place.'

Tree thought of her mother's face in the photo Jon had shown her. Just a little girl. And her adult, knowing eyes, beneath the scruffy hair.

It couldn't be true. She couldn't endure knowing that this was true. She opened her eyes again, into the glare.

'That's what I'd guess,' said Marcus.

He blinked, took a drag, blinked.

'Wouldn't you?'

She woke in the darkness that night and knew she wouldn't get back to sleep. She wanted to go and shake Marcus awake, get him up off the mattress on the floor and take him into the corridor and say, What do you mean, bad things? How bad? For how long? At the hands of how many men?

And: How do you know?

Other questions, too, which arranged themselves on top of one another as she sat there on the bed in the quiet night. Does Jon know? Is that why the Fabelhof was reformed? Or do they continue there now, the bad things? She thought of the nine-week-old baby, asleep in her arms in the Fabelhof kitchen as the afternoon passed. The infant's eighteen-year-old mother, with gappy teeth and small plump breasts.

And then another question formed, most pressing of all, though she could barely bring herself to ask it.

Did my mother just leave Dora to it?

When she heard Dora leave for work at daybreak – her main cleaning job in the high school, shining linoleum to squeak beneath children's feet – Tree got out of bed and pulled apart the stiff curtains. Her room overlooked the tiny yard at the back of the house and it was as depressing, really, as a back-yard could be, desultory weeds emerging from concrete as if heaving themselves out, as if with great effort. A rotary wash-ing line stood in the middle, one of the Y-shaped ones, a suburban scarecrow. A few of its green cords snapped, obso-lete. It swung slightly as she watched, hinging in the dawn air. Then there was total flat stillness, not a bird, even.

She undressed and showered quickly, holding the attach-ment over her head in the small cramped bath, with its old curtain and yellowed tiles like old teeth, the grout blackening between them. Then she dried herself, shivering, and dressed, and made a coffee to take to the blank, ticking stillness of Dora's sitting room. She took out the envelope that Jon had given her, unfolded the grainy photocopies of photos. She imagined her own baby sister there in her mother's arms, not Dora. For the shortest moment it was Nemony to whom the bad things had been done, bad things for many years, and Tree had to put the photos down then, squeeze her eyes shut.

She would kill people, if she found that that had happened. Easily, she would kill them.

Nemony had sent a text message a few days ago, and Tree had never replied. *I really miss you.* She took a breath, opened her eyes. She had left her sisters behind, just as Lydia had left Dora. Hers was, in fact, no great protectorate, nothing to feel so proud of.

Sitting down at the little telephone table, finally, she called home.

Nemony answered. It was a Saturday; it was raining in London and she had a piano lesson to go to, and couldn't find an umbrella. It was her birthday in four days, a Wednesday, and Wednesdays were the worst day of the week because they started with double maths with Mr Henderson. Tree spoke to her for a few minutes, trying to picture her looking out of a rain-flecked window, her eyebrows raised in mild despair, and then she was passed on to Etta. She told Etta that she spent most of her days in the Fabelhof, helping out in the big steamy kitchen.

So easily she found that she lied to her little sisters, with their Weber frames and faces, who had been motherless for much more of their lives, proportionally speaking, than she had. How would she ever tell them what she'd learned from Marcus, she thought as blithely she lied, and she thought that surely she never could.

'Is Dad around?' she asked Etta towards the end of the call, and Etta laughed.

'Who knows?'

'Ha. Are you girls feeding yourselves properly?'

'Yeah, of course. Were you surprised about Malachy?'

She paused.

'What about Malachy?'

'Didn't he tell you?'

'I haven't managed to speak to him yet,' she said, and she could sense Etta's confusion, the halt of it.

'What? Oh. OK. Well, he'll tell you when you next speak. He got a tattoo.'

Tree swallowed.

'Where?'

'On his arm. In the, like, crease of the elbow, the soft bit. You didn't know? Lucy got one too. Not matching, but – complementary, I guess?'

'Cool.'

She didn't ask any more. Her brother's skin was like her own.

'I've got to go now, Etta,' she said. 'I've only paid for ten minutes.'

Another lie, and Tree hated lies. She loathed them.

'OK.'

'Are you sure Nem's OK? She sounded quiet.'

'She'll be fine,' said Etta.

'So she's not fine now?'

'Oh, she's … fine. She's fine. You go have fun at prayers, OK?'

'Ha,' said Tree, and she wanted to ask for Nemony back on the line – and could have – but the truth was, she realised, sitting there in Dora's sitting room, that she couldn't take it. She couldn't take the weight of anyone else's sadness, not now. Her mother's, least of all.

She could glean nothing more from the photos. The longer she looked, the less meaning the face had, like a word repeated too many times, repeated into inanity. Because Lydia's past was gone, she thought. It had expired. Siblings scattered, the Fabelhof all changed. The bad things unreported.

Only these pieces of cheap office paper remained, scored in the centre where Jon had folded them, and four children who didn't tell each other the truth anymore.

And the letters she wrote to Dora.

When Marcus emerged Tree followed him into the kitchen. She watched him pour his coffee and shake cereal into a bowl, open a carton of milk and pour it, take a spoon from a drawer, inspect it, dunk it. Finally he looked up.

'You're creeping me out,' he said, grinning, but she didn't smile back.

'I need to read my mum's letters,' she said, and he nodded, spoke through a sodden mouthful of Cheerios.

'I know.'

He'd been right. There were boxes and boxes of them, stacked on top of Dora's wardrobe. Plain brown A4 box files, whispering with the hushed movement of paper within.

Marcus scratched his chaotic, greasy black hair, looked at her, grimaced.

'My mom never hears about this,' he said.

'I promise.'

'As far as I know she's never shown a single one of them to anyone.'

'I promise, Marcus.'

He eyed her, nodding.

'I'm … uncomfortable,' he said.

'I know. But Marcus – you're not showing them to a stranger.'

'Right.'

'You're showing them to her fucking daughter.'

'OK,' he said, grinning nervously, 'OK,' and then he stood on tiptoes, reaching up with his skinny veined arms that were like a junkie's arms, and one by one he hauled them down.

'I don't need to tell you how grateful I am,' she said, and he shook his head.

'No, Queen Teresza. No, you don't.'

Tree smiled at this odd and stray and somehow valiant young man and then she carried the boxes, four at a time, to her room and closed the door behind her.

She started from the beginning. She intended to read them systematically, in sequence. Curiously, her mother had only started to write at the very start of 1994, when Tree and Malachy were fourteen and thirteen, the girls just five and seven. And it was the younger two who dominated those early letters, but not as the wild, funny creatures that Tree remembered, enchanting and irritating her in equal measure. No, these were a mother's children, whose immunisations needed to be booked and fringes trimmed and feet measured.

Henrietta started her music class at the school on Friday, she plays very well with the other boys and girls, they have tambourines and drums –

Nemony has had chicken pox, there is a scab above her eyebrow I fear it will scar –

Henrietta fusses about food, at mealtimes she –

Tree shifted her weight on the bed. Her muscles began to itch and jump along her legs as they did when she craved movement. She got up to read the letters walking around the room, but became distracted by her mess: pieces of discarded clothing on the floor, the lazy scattering of her few belongings. She sat on the bed again. She thought that perhaps she might skip a few years, and re-ordering the boxes, which were sorted by year, she saw it, in an instant: January 1994 was when Lydia started writing to Dora. January 1994, when she had just come home from three months at the Priory.

Not that anyone would think, reading those early, almost laboriously neutral letters, that their author was a woman who'd just been through months of psychiatric treatment. The terrible truth, Tree thought, crossing her legs and stretching her neck, was that the letters were dull to her, and removed. She couldn't feel their reality. She couldn't hear within the words her mother's reality, her real attributes. Privacy and integrity and her own peculiar brand of authority.

Because there had been an authority there, a lack of porousness.

And yet she had emerged from her treatment resolving to make contact with Dora. That, at least, told Tree something. She thought that she could start to penetrate those forbidden autumn months of 1993 when their mother was away, out of sight, in treatment. The rough and furiously buried silt that must have risen to the surface there in the Priory, taking shape in that resolution.

She kept going, and as she did she realised she had to re-read whole sections. Unkindly she cringed at certain turns of phrase. *Teresza and Malachy are really, peas in a pod. Soon Henrietta will be right as rain.* Cliché, she'd think, before she could stop herself. Unimaginative.

When she was five and Malachy four her mother started to read stories to them at night, before bed. It was a new thing, mandated by Don, who had never been present at bedtime and so had not realised – until somehow or other it arose in conversation with another set of parents, or a nursery teacher – that reading was not part of their bedtime routine. No books, at bedtime, for the children of Don Travers! His fury was immense; even at five Tree knew that it was immense. Their mother had failed them in a fundamental and irreversible way. That lost early exposure to literacy could never be regained. All that could be done to right such a grave wrong was for a great library of books to be chosen and acquired, and for Lydia to cut bathtime short and with zeal to go at it – five, six, seven books a night.

She didn't like story time, their mother. She dreaded it. That, too, was clear enough to a five-year-old Tree. It was there in the grim set of Lydia's features as bedtime approached: determination combined with something else that only now, with hindsight and pain, Tree thought she recognised as an intimidated unease. Humiliation, even. As if Lydia had been forced to stand in front of a crowd and perform a delicate and complicated dance.

At school, Tree loved stories. She adored them. But at bedtime, sitting beside Malachy on the bottom bunk of their bed, clean in pyjamas with her hair wet and combed and plaited, she watched her mother work her way through sentences that, in her flat and faltering narration, were stripped of their magic. Tree was humiliated, on Lydia's behalf. She felt exasperated too. She even – which was most painful, now, to contemplate – felt something like contempt.

Sitting on the bed in Williamson, examining the bare fruits of her mother's letters, she was that daughter again. Ashamed of her mother, ashamed in turn for that shame. She was fiercely, passionately indignant against the irrepressible stirrings of her own contempt. *Odious*, she thought, *I am odious, I am the odious daughter of Don Travers*. The mean, ungenerous places where she and her father overlapped.

But something changed as she skimmed the letters, skipping ahead through the years. A different mood gathered behind the words, darkening clouds pushing up against the page. Her mother's voice became older. She became ill. *I have a cancer ...*

Even through the prosaic prose, Tree thought that she began to hear a voice. The words remained inoffensive, but increasingly the sentences were laced with something that was, Tree thought, alive and quivering. Anger, she thought suddenly, with a sort of triumph. There was anger there in the letters, unmissable. It was a subtle sheen atop the words, it gave them the sharp tang of metal.

I've had to have them removed, those things that kept all my babies alive, they've gone forever. The babies and the breasts.

I hope your hair never falls out, Dora, God forbid. What happens, when your hair falls out, is you look in the mirror and, something really horrifying happens. You find that your father stares back out at you.

The hospital I go for my appointments, it's a pleasant walk there, across the heath. And the treatments, have made my nose very sharp. Every time I cross that heath I catch a smell on the air, that reminds me of home. I mean our home. Yours and mine. The one they broke apart.

By the time Tree came to the final months of her mother's life, the light in the room was cold and low and slanted. It had started to rain, an insistent flicker against the window. She rubbed her eyes, and when she did she saw shapes dance like fish beneath her eyelids. Her head felt full with the effort of it all. She had seen a koi carp once in a pond in a museum garden, somewhere in Spain. It was twice, three times the size of the others. Bloated and huge, the skin stretched to translucent along its bulging flanks. She imagined her head like that now, gravid, her temples swollen.

This was what she'd been dreading, for all her eagerness to read the letters. The final year. The final summer at Frantoio, when her mother was so ill and Tree was so young and vain and stupid, and the bleak and silent winter that followed.

I'm sorry I didn't write, all the time we were in Sicily. It's been a long long summer. I suppose you could say, I'm tired. Hold on and hold up though, isn't that right Dora? That's what we were taught.

I saw Sister Ruth today for coffee, she's the nun who resides in the Catholic retreat house the next street along. And we were talking, I didn't tell her any particulars, but she could plainly see that my heart is broken for Teresza. My heart is broken and broken again for that beautiful girl. And, later she posted a little note through our door, with a poem she'd found by a poet Rilke, it said:

It's here in all the pieces of my shame that now I find myself again.

For a moment, you know, that made me feel better about Teresza. Dora, I believe she will find herself.

The Unwilding

Don is back. He took a longer vacation after Sicily. I thought he'd find me changed, I'm afraid I have lost 3kg somehow, but I am not truly sure he has looked at me yet.

It's hard to walk at the moment, there's much swelling in my ankles Dora but today I did manage. I enjoyed the low late autumn sun, which is the colour of straw here and just beautiful. While I was walking I thought about how children change. How can it be, that when they're tiny there's nothing, not one thing, you can't make better for them. And Dora, I also thought, I used to try to make things better for you, really I did. You were always so good. I'm so sorry, Dora, my Dora.

This thing with my ankles, it's my whole legs now. The doctor says I'm to rest them, but you know me Dora, I can't do that. I'll go mad.

I saw Sister Ruth again today, she gave me more poems to read now I'm in bed a lot. She gave me this book, and I turned to the section about death, this is what I read:

Now you must go out into your heart
As onto a vast plain. Now
The immense loneliness begins.

And Dora, now I'm afraid to open up a new page, in case I find something else makes me feel that way.

Today I dreamed of when I gave birth to a life, how I was told to get up onto the table, but I couldn't do it. They lifted me onto it but I kicked away, I shouted, the shouts seemed they weren't mine. They tried to silence me, oh they tried. But that table, it was a plank, there was no way to lay my body down. For months after every time I closed my eyes I saw that table and the sounds coming from my body like they were being torn out. Like my baby Dora, torn out too.

All I can think now is, I hope we don't leave the world the same way we come into it.

Sister Ruth wants a priest to come give me a blessing. Well I don't know about that. She says I should ask Teresza and Malachy to come home from university, well I know what that means, Dora.

When Tree came to the final letter, she supposed she should feel regret – there would be nothing more of her mother's voice, after this – but it was only a kind of bitter, grim relief. She blinked slowly. Those little fish again, darting across her vision.

She unfolded the paper to find just two lines, lonely and bare.

Don says he will accompany me to Dr Brisbane's tomorrow. I do not want that.

Dora, I'll write you soon.

She laid the letter down on the pile. The window rattled, rain quickened against the glass and quietened. The gathering gloom of another October afternoon. She had spent hours with these letters, these years and years of letters.

She bent down, then, and kissed the top of the pile. She rested her lips on the paper, felt the soft fibre of it against her flesh.

But then: *broken and broken*, she heard. She groaned as she straightened herself up. Her neck cracked as she stretched it.

Broken and broken, she heard, *my heart is broken and broken again for that beautiful girl.* She shook her head, stood up. *For that beautiful girl broken and broken, all the pieces of my shame, a man a worm an immense loneliness. You won't find it here, Teresza!*

Wildly she crossed the room, opened the door.

'Marcus?'

He emerged in the corridor, dwarfed by his hoodie.

'Thank God you're here,' she said.

'You need a beer?'

She nodded, following as he crossed into the kitchen. The ceiling light buzzed and came to life, blinking its too-white light into the room.

She leaned against the worktop. Marcus took two beers from the fridge and handed one to her.

'I read them all.'

'Was it OK?' he asked. 'I mean, not OK, obviously sad, but—'

'It was terrible, it was fucking terrible,' she said, and she drank the beer in great gulps, the bubbles prickling in her throat. As she drank, Marcus bowed his head respectfully, like a man at a funeral. Her mother's immense loneliness yawned inside her. She saw a vast plain, the horizon blackening in the start of a storm.

She couldn't abide the horror again. She wouldn't survive going back into it.

She slammed the empty bottle on the worktop, and his head snapped up.

'Marcus, I'm going to need something a lot stronger than this.'

'Yes, ma'am.'

She watched as he took a bottle from the cabinet, poured large measures of whisky into two glasses.

'Water? Ice?'

'Just give it to me,' she said, reaching out, and then she clenched her eyes shut and drank the entire measure, held the glass out again.

'You don't fuck around,' he said.

'No, I don't.'

He poured another measure, handed it to her, and she sipped it and shuddered and held it up before her, watched the rim of the glass tilt against the liquid level.

'OK then,' he said. 'If I must.'

He threw his head back and drank his whisky in two gulps.

'I need to move,' she said. 'Bring the bottle. Come on.'

*

Outside, the sun was almost setting, the day's thick clouds dissipating above. *The low late autumn sun, which is the colour of straw here and just beautiful.* She'd never heard her mother say a thing like that, she couldn't imagine it.

'I guess I thought it would be sad in a sweet way, a poignant way,' she said. 'Like, her letters would bring her back to me a little bit.'

'But they didn't?'

'No. They just reminded me what a … cunt I am. And what a miserable, terrible time I gave her. Me and my father, both.'

'Tell me about him.'

She drank again.

'You really want to know?'

'Duh.'

'He—' Then she shook her head again. 'No, sorry. I hate talking about him. The amount of time I've wasted in my life answering people's questions about him. And hearing other people talk about him.'

'Fair enough.'

'All you need to know about my dad is that no one really exists, for him.'

'How do you mean?'

'Or maybe: certain people exist for him much, much more than others.'

'What kind of people?'

'What kind of people,' she repeated, considering. 'Confident people.'

Marcus said something more that she didn't hear, she was too busy thinking about this as she walked. Was it as simple as that, she thought – it couldn't be, surely – but she watched as a catalogue of her father's favourites ran through her mind. The few he esteemed were the few who wouldn't shatter easily. And then all the others: the ones he passed over, the ones he tired of, the ones he continued to like well enough but who were, fundamentally, no longer meaningful to him. She pictured Etta, who existed for him, and then with pain she pictured Nemony. She saw them side by side in her mind, almost identical but wholly opposite. The strange alchemy of confidence, she thought.

'I said, you're confident,' he said.

'Me?'

He laughed drily, hunched his shoulders up.

'Marcus!' he cried in a bad English accent, slapping his thigh. 'Bring me another drink, right now! Hurry the bloody fuck up!'

She found she could smile, then.

'Ah, but external confidence is one thing.'

'And yours is skin-deep. Sure. I can see that. You and me both.'

He smiled grimly and nodded, his posture sinking. He kicked the scree at the edge of the tarmac, and she passed him the bottle and he stopped, took a long drink.

'Then I'm sorry,' she said. 'You wouldn't exist for him either. Not for long.'

There was no one else walking anywhere. The tarmac was

slick and wet from the afternoon's rain, the cars kicking up a small spray as they passed.

'The Appalachian Mountains.' She looked up at the watchful brown hills around them. 'They always sounded so romantic to me.'

He snorted.

'Reality's a bit different, huh?'

She nodded.

'Our moms' reality was pretty different, to be fair,' he said, and she wanted, then, to hurl the bottle so that it smashed.

'The Fabelhof,' she said. 'Give it to me straight. What was it, a total – hotbed of abuse?'

He shrugged, nodding.

'What the *fuck*,' she said.

'I know.'

'So you and I – we come from … all of that?'

He said nothing.

'And how old was your mum, Marcus? When she had you?'

'She was fourteen, Teresza,' he said, his expression bleak now. 'Happy?'

'How can you stay here? How can you guys keep living here?'

'Dude,' he said, a warning in his voice, and she realised then that it might all be old news for him, but that didn't make it any easier.

'Sorry.'

They walked on, passing the bottle between them, and in the silence her mother's words came rushing. *My heart is broken and broken again for that beautiful girl. Dora, I believe she will find herself again.* Those words, she thought, were no less physically painful than if a meat cleaver were to strike her chest, splitting the skin, chipping the bone beneath. She would rather that pain to this, would even relish it. *My heart is broken and broken again …*

She stopped and clenched her eyes shut so that she could drink a proper amount of the whisky, which was hard when she was walking.

'That bad?' he asked.

'I have this thing with words,' she said. 'It's like a photographic memory, kind of: I see and hear these exact phrases, word for word.'

'Like – earworms?'

A man, an earworm!

'Exactly. It's at its worst when I'm in an episode. I did a thesis at uni, on *King Lear* – I had a bad episode at that time, and I still remember every single word of the fucking thing. It's all I could hear for about two months straight.'

'Jesus.'

'Yeah. That was maybe my worst episode ever. I quit my degree, actually.'

'Because of the words?'

'No, because I was suicidal.'

She felt him look at her quickly, and then back at the road again.

'That'll do it.'

'I thought I was OK today, but … I shouldn't have read those letters.' She swirled her hand around by her head. 'I've got all these sentences now, packed in there. They're not going to go anywhere unless I can blot them out. They're just going to go round and round and round and round.'

'Would it help to say some of them aloud?'

'No, Marcus,' she said. 'It would make it literally a hundred times worse.'

He laughed.

'Well, what would help?'

'This,' she said, holding the whisky up. 'And company. And I'll need something to help me sleep.'

'I can provide all those things.'

He pointed up at the sky, then.

'A bald eagle.'

She looked up. It was beautiful and eerie, its wingspan improbably dark and wide, the length of a small car. That she didn't find it ominous, she realised, meant that the whisky was doing its job. She took a deep breath, smelled the rain drying on the road.

'And now?' asked Marcus.

'Now, what?'

'Well – you know, I'm worried now.'

'That I'm suicidal?' She shook her head. 'I'm not suicidal.'

'But the letters—'

'No, Marcus. I promise. That was very different, back at uni. My mum had just died, there was other stuff … I was in a very bad place. Now it's different. Anyway, I've got people I need to live for.'

'A man?' he asked, inflecting his voice with intrigue.

'My brother,' she said, handing him the bottle. 'My sisters.'

They drank as the evening blackened into night. Furiously, they drank.

They stood on the Pete Dillon Bridge in the dark like delinquents, threw stones and rocks and bottles into the rushing water. They ran through the town, they sprinted through the empty clapboard streets, they yipped like dogs. They went to the basement flat of some old friends of his, drank some more. She met a pale, mournful girl who told Tree she was beautiful. She met a boy with terrible skin and an exquisite body, wide shoulders and a triangular torso and a jawline she would have liked to run her finger along. They smoked, didn't talk much, played music that was nostalgic and bittersweet. They danced.

The opening chords of something started. A song she knew well, an unwinding guitar sequence that was like fingertips rippling across her skin. She was filled with warmth, the boy's hands were on her waist as they danced, his hips against hers. His shirt fell open over a vest, tanned clavicles and the dip at the base of his throat where she could have rested a marble, or the cushioned pad of a thumb. The jugular notch, it was called. An ex-boyfriend who'd studied Fine Art had taught her that. He'd laid her down on his bed and taught her all the names of the parts of the body she'd never quite thought about: *manubrium*, the square bone on her sternum that protruded more than other people's, *popliteal fossa*, the yawning diamond at the back of the knees, the shell-like *pinna* at the top of her ears, the Dimples of Venus at the base of her back. Countless others she couldn't now remember, that he had run his hands over, or his lips or tongue.

Hey little girl, is your daddy home

The boy took a swig from his beer and she watched his Adam's apple slide and shift as he swallowed. She felt his sternum buzz against her palm as he sang the words of the song, quiet and low so that she couldn't actually hear him.

Mm-hm, I've got a bad desire

She had never got the sex thing right. She always lost control of the thing. Men smelled it on her; they knew how to remove her agency. Other girls she knew could be in charge of their sex lives but Tree had only ever ended up serving, as if she was built simply to do the things the men wanted. Their bad desire. It blurred her own. It made it dissolve. No, she'd never got it right.

But that was all right. It wasn't surprising, with her mother for a model. Her poor, tough, wretched mother. A woman who eschewed sexuality, who was a procreator and little more. Knowing what she knew now, Tree was starting to understand all of that.

And Tree did the same thing, after all – after Sicily, after Krishna. Eschewed it all. Shaved her head, robed her fluid body in hard clothes that were supposed to look fierce and uninviting, a hand held up. She retracted the old invitations she used to send out: words and glances and touches, flashes of skin. But it takes a lot, to stop wanting to be looked at. Desired. It can't be eradicated with a buzz cut and a wardrobe change. It is a voice that is very hard to silence.

They tried to silence me, oh they tried. But that table, it was a plank … The sounds coming from my body like they were being torn out. Like my baby Dora, torn out too …

The thing was, though, that her mother didn't give birth to Tree on a table. She had her on the bathroom floor, alone. Labour came on so quickly that she didn't have time to get to a hospital. Not with any of them; they all four of them came fast and hurtling into this world.

Tree looked over the boy's shoulder at Marcus, who was sitting, small, in the middle of a large maroon sofa just like a baby in a womb, and the thought came to her fully formed, a neat, smooth pebble plucked from the mess of a riverbed:

He's my nephew, not my cousin.

My mother's only grandchild.

The son of my half-sister.

My half-sister, Dora.

Dora, my mother's first-born.

Of course.

In those photos at home of Lydia, young and afraid and obstinate and unblinking, barely a teenager, strong short arms clutching a baby Dora against her hip, it was her baby she was holding, not her little sister. The first baby she had, the one who was forced into her and torn out of her, whom she left in that place, in the Fabelhof. Whom she felt she had no option but to leave. *I'm so sorry, Dora, my Dora.*

Lydia's first child Dora, who went on to have a child of her own when she, too, was not yet a woman: the man-child sitting now so dwarfed by that sofa, so small and angry and afraid in his world, no doubt forced into her too.

That woman was deserted by her mother, Tree's mother. She was left to fend for herself, unsafe among the bad things, where kindness was nowhere to be found. Let alone King.

But it mustn't matter, any of that. Not now. She shook her head, felt the violence of it all move away like ink in water. It mustn't matter. Here she was, the song's sleazy cadence vibrating through her, that guitar rift rippling and looping, a stranger's body against her own, good desire and bad desire spreading branches through her blood, unfolding, exploring, unfolding. She would have sex with this boy and it didn't matter what he took from her, because she understood in this moment that there was nothing, actually, to take. There was nothing there.

She would go back to the Fabelhof tomorrow. She would find Jon and tell him, *You were right not to let me into your fucked-up kingdom. I don't belong there. I don't want to belong there. But I'm not lost, you were wrong about that. I have my brother, I have my sisters. My tribe.*

She laughed aloud, and the boy turned his face towards her and they kissed.

When finally she and Marcus left that basement and made their way back to Dora's bungalow the daylight was creeping. He took her hand and uncurled the fingers and laid three small blue pills in her palm.

'For the best, most blissed-out sleep you can get,' he said, focusing on her with effort. 'But these are high dose, I mean high high. I mean it, OK? Jen said just one at a time.'

'OK.'

'She said they're the real deal, OK, don't fuck with them. One. At. A time.' His pupils wide and black. 'OK?'

'OK.'

'Night, cuz.'

She watched her nephew wade into the house with all the elaborate, faltering grace of someone truly out of it, and then she turned back to the street and smoked a final cigarette on the doorstep. Not lonely, not now. No immense loneliness; none.

Tree was back. Her energy and power, her vast power. It would take her with it. She watched the sky as it whitened, the birds as they drifted up and explored. She felt the pills Marcus had given her – not one of them but two, because she could manage it – she could manage anything – unfurl their wings inside her body.

Inside, floating down onto the bed, the mattress like air beneath her back, she turned on her phone and texted her sisters.

I love you girls so much. More than anything in
the world. Look after yourselves. I'm coming
back.

Then she texted Malachy, too.

All amazing here. I feel different. I'm strong,
stronger all the time. Closer to Mum. You never
need to worry about me again.

Finally, she started a message to the Fabelhof.

FAO: Jon.

I know why my mother left.

She set her phone aside, and then swallowed the third pill
with its beautiful wings and took the phone back up in her
hands and wrote another. Her face was light, it was almost
air. Her fingers weightless, dancing across the keys. She could
no longer see the words on the screen but she could hear
them, could even taste their shape.

FAO: Jon.

I want to tell you the story of a koi carp. A great
big swollen one with teeth and big round eyes
and a fat tail that flicked like a whip. It swam in a

pond with other fish, little tiny fish. And the carp opened its mouth and gulp, the little fish were sucked right in. Only the sad thing was, those little fish all had dreams. They had hearts and heads and souls of their own, and thoughts, too, real thoughts, only no one ever heard about those thoughts. Because *gulp*, the big bulging carp slunk through the murky waters and sucked them right in.

There's a fable, for your Fabelhof.

She felt the phone drop from her hand. There were no more fables. No more stories.

There were no words now, just shape, no delineation. No borders, no distances, no doors. No membranes, even, between things.

She let herself swell into the immensity of everything, of nothing, of it all.

SICILY

The cool of the Fort is hushed like a church, or cloisters. I stand just inside and inhale, and for a moment I am back in that summer twenty years earlier. For a moment I could look down and see not the outline of my adult feet in espadrilles, but tanned little toes emerging from sandals. The uneven, incoherent toenails of a child. I would not be surprised.

I step further into the vast, white space of it and the birds in the rafters rustle and bleat. A waiting silence. The same pigeons, the same chalky splatter of their shit on the weed-strewn floor. The things that have changed are that there is blue graffiti on the far wall and an accumulation of rubbish along one side and, more impressively, half a tractor. It has been abandoned, and is I imagine long out of use, and yet its presence is jarring, I find it hard to ignore, it seems to insist on my attention. So I walk to the centre of the Fort and turn my back to the tractor and sit down cross-legged in front of that great, broken old olive press, which has not changed one bit. Our ancient altar. An ancient monument, now, to the

Travers children who used to sit before it and worship and play around and climb it, and who no longer exist. They're ghosts in this space.

I close my eyes and imagine opening my arms, wide, and having each of those four children climb onto my lap, one by one, and lay their heads against my chest. I imagine my heartbeat calming them, like the sound of the sea in a shell against their ears. A young Tree, crude and unrefined like raw honey. Malachy, who had to work too hard for us all. Etta, magnificent Etta, who always had to make herself too strong.

And me. Who somehow got stuck here in Frantoio that last summer and needs to make decisions, now.

I open my eyes and let the backpack drop from my shoulders, and I take from it a pad of blank paper and a pen, and I start.

Don Travers, you are a tyrant.
You dictated each one of our characters and livelihoods and perhaps even Tree's death by your treatment of us, by the different degrees to which you could stand and tolerate us, by your differing degrees of belief in us.

Your tyranny has driven my siblings and me apart. It has scattered and divided us.

Even those who disavow you – Zoe, Liam – are consumed by thoughts of you, and cannot remain indifferent.

I have always worshipped you. It has been a terrible, daily, hourly source of shame that you haven't appeared to find anything to admire in me in return.

You're a letch. I think.

I love you.

I don't want you to be humiliated by Zoe's novel.

I do want you to be humiliated by Zoe's novel.

You humiliated my mother, over and over and over again.

You write great novels with a breadth and brilliance of insight. But: you're limited. In yourself, you're gravely limited.

For example, you thought that Tree was trivial, but she wasn't.

You thought you could write Zoe off, but you can't.

You think that I'm weak, but you're wrong.

Don Travers – Dad – I can be ruthless, too.

I read it back. I fold the paper neatly and make to tear it, but then I pause. My hands holding the paper lower, come to rest on my knees. A bright shout, my son's, from far off; Zoe's distant laughter. The purring murmur of a pigeon. I fold the paper again, and once more still, and I slide the thickened square into my pocket.

I go back into the house through the main French doors, which are unchanged, so that I can walk down that dark and cooling corridor towards the kitchen. I stop outside what used to be the games room. It is a gym now, filled with all the bossy black and grey equipment of movement, of improvement. I stop there in that doorway where I once stood, watching my mother stroke the hair of my genuflected sister, in all the pieces of her shame. 'Kindness,' she'd said. 'Kindness, and never revenge.'

I close the door to that room that is now a gym and as I do I think, what happened here? What killed these two women? Because in a sense it wasn't the cancer. It wasn't depression, or opioids.

I take the folded letter out of my pocket, turn it in my hands. I could unfold it and tear it into tiny, irreparable pieces that float to the floor. Because I have been thinking, standing outside that games room, that perhaps I won't have anything to do with it all: revenge, or Zoe's novel, or the smallness of hatred, but particularly revenge. Even for Jon, whom I have been thinking I would like to kill, if I could. Whose throat I could in fact tear, like paper.

But I like the letter, that's the thing. I like the way it feels in my hand, the cloud-light heft of the folded square, its precise and thick and lethal corners. The words inside that might be read and might have an effect, that might perhaps break something I've never tried breaking before.

I don't tear it. My paper grenade.

I turn and step down into the kitchen, where the estate agent in her neat suit is cooing at my son in Zoe's arms.

'Come here,' I say.

Reaching my hands towards George, I take him from Zoe. He is happy as can be. I think if he were old enough to kiss me with joy, he would.

'All finished?' the estate agent asks brightly, and I nod.

'Yes, I'm finished.'

'I'm finished,' says Zoe.

'So we go.'

She gestures towards the open door to the garden, where Tree's outline once stood, a quiver of energy, before tumbling down into the room, half-leopard, half-gazelle. It is filled now with the white space of sunshine.

George sleeps on the plane, claiming my arms and chest as his bed, his eyelashes fanning out blanket-like over his cheeks. I cannot reach for music, or a snack, or my book. And so I surrender. For a while I watch Zoe, sitting across the aisle from me, looking strict and serious in her reading glasses, a schoolmarm, and then I close my eyes.

I imagine that I am Tree. I am sitting at the kitchen table in our childhood home, and the room is empty except for our mother, whom I can't see but who stands behind me. I have the sense of her solidity, her low gravity. On the table beside my hands, which are Tree's hands: the old, dark blue hairbrush with its fine, fine bristles like pony hair, the brush itself curved and smooth, a raised white floral pattern running the length of the handle and all around the paddle, like brocade.

First our mother parts my hair. Down the middle, with total precision. A line as straight as a table's edge, pulled tight so that if you stand behind me you can see the scalp between the two sections of hair, paper-white between black. One of the sections is clipped aside. I hear the little creak as the clip yawns open and then a snap, clicking into place behind my ear.

And then our mother's fingers – always smooth with cold, whatever the weather, even in the African sun of those

Sicilian summers – begin their ancient weaving. Pulling the hair tight each time it is crossed over, tugging, pulling, tightening, so that the skin of my forehead and temples is stretched and I feel alert and ready and immaculate and exact.

And then I move away from Tree, I become myself. I become the version of myself that I once was, a young girl standing in a doorway. I am watching them, these women.

Our mother runs a palm down the length of each Dutch braid. She does it not with the ownership of a mother but almost secretly, a stolen luxury. A subject, kissing her sovereign's hem. That is how she always treated Tree's hair and her height and physique and, well, her face too – her beauty, in fact. As if it was a hallowed thing, that our mother did not deserve and had nothing to do with. Something within whose proximity she was lucky to have found herself.

I would like, now, to run forward with a shout and take our mother by the wrists – to grab them tight, almost viciously tight – and say: *Touch her hair. Touch mine. Stroke the plaits, claim their knotted surface as your own. It's your hair, it's yours, you made it, touch it as much as you like. Take it, even.*

Someone bumps my elbow as they pass down the aisle, and I am back in my woman's body, in the stale hum of the aeroplane. I look down at the boy I am holding. One of his full cheeks is pushed flat against his nose as he sleeps there in the crook of my arm, his mouth agape, utterly oblivious and vulnerable and commanding. I lean right down so that the back of my neck hurts and I kiss it, his hair.

ACKNOWLEDGEMENTS

Thank you:

Clare Alexander, for your sage advice, delicate understanding and formidable energy. I'm so lucky to have you as my agent.

Kishani Widyaratna, for your vision and belief, and Michelle Kane, Liv Marsden, Jo Thomson, Alex Gingell, Eliza Plowden, Nicole Jashapara, and all at 4th Estate.

The book's earliest readers, Miriam Robinson and Antonia Thomas.

Lalu and Claudia, for your unending patience and generosity and also your truly (painstakingly!) granular attention whenever asked. Will, Miles, and our own never-disparate formation.

Petra, Skye and Carmen, glorious triad.

And James – for your immense, multifaceted support and particularly kind and stalwart brand of optimism, without which this book wouldn't exist.